THE TROPHY CHILD

www.penguin.co.uk

The Trophy Child

Paula Daly

BANTAM PRESS

LONDON · NEW YORK · TORONTO · SYDNEY · AUCKLAND

TRANSWORLD PUBLISHERS
61–63 Uxbridge Road, London W5 5SA
www.penguin.co.uk

Transworld is part of the Penguin Random House group of companies
whose addresses can be found at global.penguinrandomhouse.com

First published in Great Britain in 2017 by Bantam Press
an imprint of Transworld Publishers

A CIP catalogue record for this book
is available from the British Library.

ISBNs 9780593075210 (hb)
9780593075227 (tpb)

Typeset in 11.75/15 pt Minion by Jouve (UK), Milton Keynes
Printed and bound by Clays Ltd, Bungay, Suffolk.

Penguin Random House is committed to a sustainable
future for our business, our readers and our planet. This book
is made from Forest Stewardship Council® certified paper.

1 3 5 7 9 10 8 6 4 2

For Harvey

Part One

1

Monday, 21 September

The girls' changing room smelled heavily of sweat, mud and a sickly-sweet deodorant that was beginning to irritate the back of her throat. She didn't have a lot of enthusiasm for hockey. Not a lot of enthusiasm for school, full stop, now that she was on a probationary period. It was to be a period of indeterminate length, during which her behaviour would be monitored by a variety of well-meaning professionals.

Verity Bloom: not quite a lost cause.

Not yet.

Everyone was doing their utmost to prevent a deterioration in her performance – not least the staff of Reid's Grammar, because, up until recently, she had always been such a promising student.

'We have so much invested in her,' the head teacher had told her father. 'We want her to realize her full potential, and it would be a travesty if a girl such as Verity was not given the proper support at what is clearly a very difficult time. A difficult time for all of you, in fact.'

They had left that meeting with her father stooped, a man beaten down by life, a man who was just so tired of it all. 'You'll do as they say?' he'd asked, and Verity had shrugged her response in the way only a teenager can. 'It's this, or you're out of here,' he said.

'Would that be such a bad thing? Maybe this isn't such a great place after all.'

Her father had sighed hard.

'It costs eighteen thousand pounds a year. In total, I've spent over seventy-five thousand pounds on your education here, just so you can come out with nothing . . . Christ, Verity.'

'I wouldn't come out with *nothing*,' she'd argued. 'I could do my GCSEs elsewhere.'

And he had held her gaze for such a long time, a deep, deep sadness forming in his eyes, that, finally, she'd said, 'Okay.'

She'd said, 'Okay. I'll do it.'

Three weeks into the autumn term and the long summer break was fast becoming a distant memory. She removed her boots, her shin pads, her underwear, and made her way to the showers. She let the water run over her shoulders, the skin of her back; the temperature was kept just below optimal heat to prevent the girls from dawdling, to make certain they would be in time for the next lesson. Pointless, really. Sixteen-year-old girls were never so comfortable with their new bodies that they lingered in the communal showers. A few would try to get out of showering altogether. It had been that way since they had started secondary school, back in Year 7. But the PE staff had got wise to their excuses early on and now they documented them on a spreadsheet. Exemption from showering was not permitted two weeks in a row.

The head of girls' PE put her head around the tiled wall and scanned the assorted faces before her until she found Verity. 'Where do you need to be next period?' she asked.

'IT.'

'You can be a few minutes late. Get out now and get dry. Come and see me when you're dressed. I'll be in my room.'

Verity nodded, exiting the showers to a flurry of whispers and stifled giggles.

Alison Decker was a serious-looking woman. Verity supposed you had to be to run a PE department. Every day, she wore black Ronhill running pants and a school-issue sweatshirt with her name emblazoned across the back, as though she were on a netball tour. (She did use to play for Cumbria.)

Verity liked her. She was straightforward; you knew where you were with her. Not like the vague, flaky dance teacher, whom the girls approached when they had a problem. Or the blond-bobbed, overstyled woman they hired to coach tennis during the summer term. That woman had a sneaky way about her, and the students always felt as though she was listening in on their conversations. Alison Decker was too busy to eavesdrop. And, frankly, she couldn't care less what the girls were saying. They were students. They were meant to be organized, disciplined and exercised. She did not want to know about their personal lives.

Which made her the perfect choice to administer the test.

Verity dressed quickly, keeping her head low. She was well aware that she was being watched by the others. They were pretending to talk among themselves, pretending they weren't looking her way. An affected girl she shared a lab bench with in physics was showing pictures of baby sloths on her iPhone; her friends cooed excessively, made long, loud *awwwwww* sounds, as though they were infants once again and a puppy had been led into class.

Verity packed up her things and headed out to the main corridor. The bell was yet to sound, so it was empty save for a teacher at the far end. He was attaching a sheet of A4 to the music notice board. Once it was in place, he stood back, hands behind his head, to survey the rest of the announcements.

Reid's Grammar was no longer a grammar school but had kept the title when it switched to independent status in 1977. It was positioned on the eastern shore of Windermere, at Countiesmeet, where the old counties of Lancashire over the sands and Westmorland used to join.

Reid's was a good school. That's what everyone said: 'Reid's Grammar is a very good school,' and Verity was privileged to attend such an institution. She knew she was. And it *was* pretty idyllic. It occupied some of the most expensive land in the country. It had lake access, three jetties (belonging to the sailing school), two croquet lawns and a state-of-the-art livery where students could board their horses.

At Reid's the students wore exactly the kind of uniform you would expect them to: the prefects black, billowing gowns; Years 7 to 11 brightly coloured striped blazers, the girls long, pleated skirts. They used to wear straw boaters in the summer months but these were jettisoned after a series of stealth attacks from the kids at the local comprehensive school in which the hats ended up in a variety of places – once, on the head of a boarding mistress's horse, its long ears sticking out through holes that had been cut in the top.

For the most part, the pupils of Reid's stayed out of trouble and the school was able to maintain its untarnished reputation.

For the most part.

The bell sounded and the corridor was immediately flooded with bodies.

'*You*, boy!' came a shout from behind Verity. 'No running!'

Verity was swept along with the throng. Two boys from the year below, heading in the opposite direction, caught sight of her and immediately began pretending to strangle each other, their eyes crossing, tongues lolling out. Both shot her wicked grins as they passed. Verity stared right through them, taking a right down a side corridor and pausing before knocking on the frosted glass of Miss Decker's door.

Decker must have seen her shadow through the glass because she threw the door open, telling her to come in. She did not invite her to sit down, instead gesturing that Verity should stand to the side of her desk until she had finished filling out the under-fourteens hockey team sheet for the match against Stony-hurst on Saturday.

Verity chewed on her lip and moved her weight to her other foot.

'How are things at home?' Decker said, without looking up. This caught Verity off guard, because Alison Decker *never* pried.

'Okay,' she said.

'Okay good, or okay bad?'

'About the same,' said Verity.

Decker gave a curt nod. 'Very well. We'll wait for the start of the next lesson and then we'll get on with it.'

Verity was aware that Decker didn't have to extend her this courtesy. In fact, it was probably interfering with her schedule and would make her late for the next PE class.

'You thinking of running cross-country again this year?' Decker asked.

'Haven't made up my mind.'

'It'd be a shame not to.'

Verity shrugged.

'All right,' Decker said. 'I won't hassle you. Let's get this over with and get you on your way.'

She followed Decker to the girls' toilets. The corridor was empty again. She hung back a little as she watched Decker walk in, pretty sure of what she'd find in there.

A moment later and Decker stopped dead in the doorway, her trainers squeaking to a halt.

It was really quite theatrical.

'Do you three mind telling me what you're doing?' she demanded loudly.

'Nothing, miss . . .'

'Sorry, miss.'

'We just needed to . . .' came the voices from within.

Verity watched as three Year 11 girls exited in a cloud of

perfume. They were heavily caked in fresh make-up and scowled upon seeing Verity, as the real reason for Decker's presence registered.

'If I catch you in here again when you're supposed to be in lessons, I'll wash that muck off your faces myself!' Decker shouted to their backs, and they hurried away.

Once inside, Decker withdrew a container from her pocket and said, 'Quick as you can now, Verity,' and Verity took it from her silently, without meeting her eye.

Urinating into a beaker, aged sixteen, when your PE teacher is on the other side of the cubicle door, had to be one of life's low points. It was mortifying for Verity, handing over the still-warm sample. Alison Decker took it from her, her face a perfect mask of indifference, when Verity knew she must be repulsed, and wondering how this weekly task had landed at her feet.

'Let's go,' Decker said.

Verity followed her back to her office, neither of them speaking, and waited as she unlocked the ancient grey filing cabinet and took out the drug-testing kit from the middle drawer. Surprisingly, you could buy them on Amazon now. They were not expensive and were easy to do. This was part of the deal Verity's father had struck with the head. They would allow her to continue her studies, remain part of the school, if she agreed to weekly on-site drug tests and attended biweekly counselling sessions.

Verity *did* try telling them that she wasn't into drugs – that she had *never* been into drugs, so all of this was rather unnecessary. But it didn't seem to matter.

A minute passed. 'You're clean,' Decker said. 'Keep up the good work, Verity.'

'You betcha.'

Then Decker hesitated, as if what she was about to say was painful in some way.

'I'm here, Verity,' she said eventually. 'If you need to talk . . . anything like that.'

Decker had been told to say this. The woman did not want to be Verity's sounding board, any more than Verity wanted her to be.

'I'm okay,' Verity said, offering a benign smile.

'As you wish, Verity. Probably for the best.'

2

DETECTIVE SERGEANT JOANNE Aspinall scanned the hotel bar for signs of her date. She wondered, not for the first time, if people really did enjoy eating out and long walks in the countryside or if that was something they wrote on their profiles when they were too embarrassed to write the truth. Would anyone reply if Joanne were to write: 'Overworked copper, generally too tired to socialize, recently dumped by colleague, lives with aunt, not very good with kids.'

Probably.

She'd most likely get some weirdo who had a fetish for slightly sad, exhausted women.

A colleague from work, an officer in the mounted police, had recently been out with a guy from a dating site. He'd asked her to post her dirty underwear to a sales conference he was attending in Devizes. *To remind him of her while he was working.*

Joanne hadn't told the truth on her profile page. She'd ended up plumping for the standard 'long walks' and 'eating out' in an attempt to lure someone relatively normal. And it had taken weeks to arrange a date. One date. It should have been simple. But it had become evident to Joanne almost immediately upon joining secondchance.com that most people were not looking for love. They were looking for no-strings sex. She had spent far too many hours sifting through profiles, answering questions about herself from prospective suitors, when she could have been sleeping:

If you could change one thing about your appearance, what would it be?

Joanne did think of responding with the truth. Saying that she'd already changed the thing that needed changing – by way of breast-reduction surgery. But she got the impression that when a man asked that type of question he was hoping for an answer more along the lines of: 'I'd change my bee-stung, porn-star lips and tendency to be promiscuous when drunk.'

So Joanne had played it safe and moved on to the next candidate.

Which is how she ended up chatting online to Graham Rimmer.

Graham Rimmer, who was now quite late.

Joanne hadn't told him she was in the police. It wasn't something to volunteer on a first meeting, as she would most likely be pressed for information, and she certainly didn't want to talk shop all evening. Also, when people found out she was a detective they were in the habit of becoming rather jumpy and restless. As though she could see straight into their souls, and discover all manner of dirty secrets. Like a psychiatrist. Or a pub landlord.

Joanne signalled to the waiter. The hotel bar was busy, but he'd been glancing her way every few minutes. He knew she had a booking in the restaurant for two, and Joanne suspected that her body language was giving her away, making it obvious that she was on a first date. A first date with someone she couldn't guarantee looked anything like his profile picture.

Graham Rimmer had told her he worked for the National Trust, managing a large area of land close to Ullswater in the North Lakes, and Joanne had thought that sounded rather sexy, in a Lady Chatterley/Mellors kind of way.

That's if he'd told her the truth. And since she had listed her occupation as 'bookkeeper', she could hardly complain if it turned out to be nonsense.

'What can I get you?' the waiter asked.

'Small Cabernet Merlot, please.'

'Sure I can't get you a large?'

'I'm driving.'

Joanne checked her watch. It was 8.23, and a few couples were making their way from the bar area through to the restaurant to dine. She fiddled with her phone, checking it once more, hoping to see: 'Be there in five minutes!' Except that would be a miracle, since she'd not given Graham Rimmer her number.

'Here you are,' the waiter said, placing the glass down in front of Joanne. 'Can I get you anything else while you wait? Some olives, perhaps? Some—'

'I'm fine as I am.'

A lone guy at the bar turned around on hearing their exchange and then quickly away when Joanne shot him a look. He'd had two glasses of whisky since Joanne had arrived and she wondered if he was planning to drive tonight. He didn't seem like a guest. He wore a shirt and tie – the tie pulled loose – and he looked as though he'd been in the same clothes since morning. If Joanne had to hazard a guess, she would say he'd called in here to delay going home. He was easy on the eye, she noticed.

Then Graham Rimmer arrived.

And Joanne's heart sank. He was a bloated-fish version of his profile picture and, as he approached the table, he was out of breath, wheezing a little. He did not appear to be the type of person who was used to rebuilding dry-stone walls and untangling Rough Fell sheep from thorny hedgerows.

He thrust out his hand. 'Joanne – Graham. Pleased to meet you. Sorry I'm late.'

No explanation as to why.

He removed his leather jacket, a heavy, ancient, biker thing, and slung it around the back of the chair. The weight of it made the chair start to topple, but Graham caught it in a way that made Joanne think it happened often. 'Just get myself a drink. Back in a sec,' he said.

He made his way to the bar and ordered a pint of Guinness. As he waited for it to pour he thrust his hands in his pockets and rocked to and fro from the balls of his feet to his heels.

Joanne willed herself not to make a hasty judgement, but this was all wrong. The man on the dating site had seemed mild-mannered, gentle. This guy was boorish: the total opposite to what she had expected. He was also substantially older than his photograph had suggested, and around four stone heavier.

Graham took two large swallows of his pint before heading back towards Joanne.

Wiping the froth from his lipless mouth on the back of his forearm, he seated himself noisily, saying, 'So, bookkeeping, then. Bet you're glad to get out and about if you're stuck in front of a computer all day. Wouldn't suit me. I like the outdoors. Not that I get out as much as I used to. When you're in management, you tend to lose touch and end up in too many meetings. But hey-ho – it could be worse. You got any kids, Joanne, love?'

'No, I—'

'I've four. Two big, two small. Two ex-wives as well, who bleed me dry, but I won't go into that. It's not polite talk for a first date. Not that we need to be polite. Best to show who we are up front. I'm always the same with everyone. No airs and graces. What you see is what you get. Have you been here before? The beer's pricey.'

'My first time.'

'Mine, too. Might be the last. You say you're from Kendal?'

'Not far from—'

'I was born in Penrith. Never travelled far. Never saw the need. People are the same wherever you go. What do you do when you're not working? I don't do a lot. Don't get a chance, really. I should. I know what you're thinking. How am I going to meet someone if I don't get myself *out there?*' He made a wide, sweeping gesture, as if the world beyond the bar held all the answers to his single status. 'I didn't cheat on my wife.' He coughed. 'Sorry, *wives* . . . if that's what you're thinking. Though, God knows, I had more than enough opportunity. The first one said she didn't cheat on me but, well, she waited the standard six weeks, and hey presto, she's shacked up with someone else. Brian. Delivers cooked meats. Thought he was a mate. I don't hold a grudge. No point. Life's too short. Anyway, what was I saying? The second one, well she was a proper dragon. Married her on the rebound. I won't do that again – marry in a hurry. No offence.'

'None taken.'

'To be honest, I think she was a bit deranged. She'd not exactly been abused as a kid, but her mother used to hit her with a wooden spoon and lock her in the airing cupboard. Sometimes overnight. I think it left its mark. I tried with her. I really did. No one could say otherwise. When I think what I went through to make that woman happy. Anyway, you don't want to hear all this. As long as we stay off politics, eh? What? No, I think Cameron's a tosser. You can't have a bunch of rich bastards running the country, can you? It's not right. Farmers get a raw deal every time. I don't know why more don't stick a shotgun in their gob and end it.' He stopped momentarily to drain the rest of his pint, before telling Joanne that this dating business was thirsty work and, 'I'll just go and get myself another.'

Joanne thought about leaving. She could get in her car and go. Leave Graham Rimmer to talk to himself for the rest of the night. Or she could disappear to the ladies' and hide. The thought of a whole evening spent with him was beginning to fill her with a sickening kind of dread, but how does one get out of a situation such as this? If she'd been straight from the start and told him she was a detective she could have invented an excuse. An emergency at work. A *murder*. She could have left, him thinking no worse of her, or of himself for that matter. But, as it was, she couldn't come up with a suitable emergency that might arise from the world of bookkeeping.

A fine sweat sprung up on Joanne's lip and, as she reached inside her handbag to find a tissue, she saw the small Phillips screwdriver and the mace. Items she'd packed tonight in case her date turned out to be a demented woman killer. Funny, but that prospect had seemed a lot more likely than the need to escape a boring, overweight guy who was more likely to talk Joanne to death.

She glanced towards the bar. In the time it had taken for the Guinness to pour, Graham Rimmer had struck up a conversation with the whisky drinker in the loosened tie one seat along. He was explaining that he was on a first date and he seemed to have landed lucky, as he hadn't expected much from someone he'd found on the internet. 'Thought it'd be just the dregs,' he said.

Graham Rimmer made his way back to Joanne's table, this time neglecting to wipe the foam from his upper lip and giving Joanne a broad grin as he seated himself, telling her she had a smashing shape for a woman of forty.

All at once, Joanne felt not forty but very, very old.

Was this what her life had come to? A succession of dates like this? With men like this?

She could imagine being in bed with Graham Rimmer, him farting loudly, saying, 'Did you like that?', impersonating steeplejack Fred Dibnah on felling a chimney, finding himself utterly hilarious.

'You don't say much,' Graham Rimmer said.

Joanne tried to smile. 'Maybe I'm a little nervous.'

And he reached out and put his hand on hers. Covered it with his big, meaty fingers.

Giving her hand a firm squeeze, he said, 'No need to be

nervous of me, love. I won't bite . . . Not unless you want me to, anyway.'

Joanne removed her hand.

'I had something of a dalliance in between my marriages,' he said, dropping his voice a level. 'With a kennel maid from Wigton. Too young for me, really, but she was keen enough so I went with it. Sometimes she liked me to bite her on the—' He paused here, looking furtive, before motioning over his shoulder with his thumb.

'On the back?' asked Joanne.

'On the bottom,' he said. Then he frowned, blowing out his breath. 'I thought it was strange, and I've got to say I wasn't proper comfortable with it, but you know what they say. Takes all sorts.'

Indeed it does.

Joanne shifted in her seat and straightened her spine. 'Graham,' she said, again trying to smile a little, 'you know you listed your age as forty-seven on your profile? Well, if you don't mind my saying, you do look a *bit* older than that. How old are you, exactly?'

Graham put down his pint.

'Sixty-one.'

He arched an eyebrow and looked at Joanne expectantly. It occurred to Joanne that he was waiting to be complimented on his appearance. In another situation, she might have gone along with it, just to be polite.

Instead she said, 'You didn't think it might be unfair to lie?'

'Doesn't everyone lie about their age?'

'No, Graham,' Joanne said. 'No. They don't.'

For a moment Graham looked abashed, staring silently at his beer. Then he said, 'I think you'll find I'm a very youthful sixty-one.'

And Joanne replied, 'I'm sure you are. But, Graham, I've got to be straight with you. I'm in the market for someone a bit younger.'

He lifted his head.

'Oh, you are, are you?' he said, indignation clear in his voice.

'Yes. I am.'

Graham was put out. He ran his eyes over her disdainfully, as though to say, *Don't hold your breath*. Then he cleared his throat and stood.

'Well, if that's the way it is,' he said. 'If that's the way it's going to be, then I don't suppose it's worth buying you dinner, is it?'

'Probably not.'

Graham grabbed his jacket and departed without saying goodbye, and Joanne was left feeling quite embarrassed, but relieved nonetheless. She would not be doing this again. It had taken too much time and energy to arrange this date, only to get to the point where it was clear there was a lot more to be said for spotting someone across a crowded room, someone who stirred your interest for no logical reason that you could fathom.

Commenting on profiles, waiting days for emails to be returned, exchanging cagey details about yourself, was not how Joanne wanted to conduct her romantic life. And if Detective Inspector McAleese hadn't got cancer she wouldn't have had to, but he had promptly brought their relationship to a close upon receiving his diagnosis. Joanne had thought this was overkill at the time, as he'd been given great odds. His doctors had removed a short section of bowel and were doing chemo only as a precautionary measure. He was expected to make a complete recovery.

But McAleese had been insistent. 'It's over, Joanne,' he had told her solemnly. She hadn't been heartbroken. Just sad. Pete McAleese said his intention had been to *save* her from heartbreak. He didn't want Joanne putting her life on hold while he fought a battle, a battle of indeterminate length, and Joanne had protested, saying that she wouldn't be putting her life on hold at all. Her life was with him now.

But he wouldn't have it. And Joanne had felt like she'd fallen straight into a movie from the fifties: tearful kid on a wrap-around porch instructing the stray dog to 'Go! Just get away from here. Y'hear me?'

Joanne was the dog.

The waiter appeared at Joanne's side like an apparition. As if from nowhere. She must have been lost in thought.

'The gentleman over at the bar sent you this,' he said, his eyes dancing as he proffered Joanne a glass tumbler.

Joanne was taken aback.

'What is it?' she whispered.

'Whisky. Glenlivet. He said he thought you could use it.'

Joanne felt heat rise in her cheeks. 'Oh, I shouldn't, really,' she blustered. 'I'm not really supposed to be . . .'

She tried to gather herself.

'Please tell him thank you,' she said firmly.

'Why don't you tell him yourself,' he said, nodding his head towards the empty stool at the bar. Then he added in her ear, 'He seems like a nice guy.'

Joanne stole a glance across. The man had his back to them, and he did not turn around like some leering idiot, tipping the rim of his glass her way. Instead, he was slouched forward, elbows resting on the bar. She had known instantly he wasn't Graham Rimmer when she entered the room earlier, as his manner suggested he was killing time rather than waiting for someone.

Unlike Joanne, that is, who had sat erect in her seat, watchful, hopeful, eagerly examining everyone who entered.

She still had almost a full glass of wine in front of her. But she left it there on the table and picked up the whisky, carrying it, along with her jacket and handbag, over to the empty seat next to the man.

When she reached the bar, he turned his head her way and offered her a lazy smile. 'Rough date?' he asked, and she nodded.

'Mind if I sit?' she said.

'Go ahead.'

She arranged her jacket on the stool and dropped her handbag against the foot of the bar. Lifting the glass to her lips, she said, 'Thanks for this, by the way,' and he tilted his head as though to say, *It's nothing.*

They sat in silence. Joanne felt herself relax for the first time all day. She was working on a particularly frustrating drugs case. Their suspect, a slippery bastard who had a number of aliases but was known to Joanne mostly by his street name, Sonny, was moving heroin and assorted pills through Joanne's area. He used a variety of women to hold on to his supply, but they didn't know who or where these women were.

Joanne took another mouthful and let the tension ease from her shoulders.

Her drinking partner drained his glass and motioned to the barman for another. If he drove away from here tonight, Joanne would have to arrest him.

He turned to her. 'Was it a blind date?' he asked.

'Kind of. I'd seen a photograph of him, but it wasn't exactly what you'd call a true likeness.'

'A dating website?'

She nodded.

She took a surreptitious peek at his left hand and saw it was devoid of a ring. The skin between each of his fingers was bleached. There were also patches of white skin on each knuckle and fingertip. 'Have you ever tried it?' Joanne asked. 'Internet dating, I mean.'

'Can't say I have.'

'That's a shame. You could have given me some tips.'

He seemed amused.

'You don't need any tips,' he said. 'Just stick to people you like the look of.' And then he held her gaze for one, two . . . three seconds.

Was he coming on to her? Joanne was so out of practice she really couldn't tell. And yes, sticking to people you liked the look of was all very well, but when you didn't actually come across many people you *liked the look of* in your daily life, then you resorted to sifting through online profiles in your dressing gown, your aunt watching over your shoulder, tutting and sighing at the slim pickings on offer.

'I'm Seamus,' he said.

'Joanne.'

'It's good to meet you, Joanne.'

He didn't offer his hand, just smiled again, and Joanne could feel the pulse in her neck begin to throb. She put her fingers there to cover it.

'Are you a guest here?' she asked.

'Just stopped by on my way home. It's been a long day.'

'What do you do?' she asked.

'Accounting.'

Great. Bookkeeping was now a no-go.

'Do you live far?' she asked.

'Half an hour or so.'

'You probably shouldn't have that whisky if you're driving.'

'You're right,' he said. 'I probably shouldn't . . . but I will.'

A moment passed, and Joanne thought she'd made a mistake. He wasn't coming on to her; he was just a decent guy who felt sorry for her. Plenty of those around.

'Perhaps you'll have to stay here a while longer,' he said. 'Keep me company until the alcohol's worked its way out of my system.'

'Oh?' she said.

'Or we could have dinner, if you haven't eaten.'

'I haven't eaten.'

Seamus had accountant's hands. Smooth skin with long, fine fingers. Hands that hadn't done a lot of manual labour. Joanne put him at around forty-eight, and you could tell he was the kind of man who had been attractive in his youth, but there was a pull of worry around his mouth, as if life had taken its toll.

Did she fancy him?

Sure she did.

She took another mouthful of whisky. Again, they were silent.

Very few people Joanne came across were content to sit in total quiet. Apart from, that is, the occasional guilty, reprobate teenager she had to question. Always your typical unhappy customers. They hated the police and had no problem showing it. They didn't even say 'No comment,' taking their right to silence to its fullest extreme.

'Have you been on your own long?' Seamus asked her.

'You mean single? Not too long. I was in a relationship with a colleague, but it came to an end because . . . well, it just ended. How about you? Are you single?'

'Yes.'

'How long alone?' she asked.

'A long time,' he said. 'Too long.'

'Too long without a relationship, or too long without a woman?' she said, and Seamus shot her a mischievous, guilty look, as if to say, *Ah, you got me.*

Then he told her he'd not been in a relationship for several years.

'Any particular reason?' she asked.

He smiled. 'Didn't find anyone I liked the look of. Anyway,' he said, pushing his glass away, rising from the bar stool, 'shall we eat?'

3

The morning session was almost over. Noel Bloom took a minute for himself before the emergency appointments began to filter in, one after another, each patient a disagreeable blend of anxiety about their ailment and resentment at having to wait for up to an hour to be seen.

Two days out of each week, at 12 p.m., it fell to Noel to deal with the emergencies, while his colleagues covered the domiciliaries – the home visits. Noel preferred the house calls now, but he hadn't always. In his younger years as a GP, he'd found the amount of time they ate up frustrating. He could get through six patients in the clinic to one in the field, and almost all of them could have made it in – if only they'd tried a little harder. But patients still expected to be seen in their own homes.

These days Noel liked to take his time travelling around his catchment area, this small corner of South Lakeland. Had that happened with age? he wondered. This peculiar need to see his environment, to stop and take in the scenery? Or was it simply that he knew that, no matter how much work he got through in one day, there would always be more patients to see the next, and the day after that. Trying to get ahead in general practice was futile. He accepted that now.

On first qualifying, Noel had sometimes found his vocation

overwhelming: the hours, the responsibility, the pressure to get things right. But at forty-seven, his work was his refuge. It was where he hid from the world, knowing it was the one place he was in control, the one place where everything fitted together as it should.

His place of work was where he was needed.

He checked his watch and decided he had enough time for a coffee. He'd treated himself to an espresso maker for his birthday last year (the type with small pods in metallic colours), and it had made such a difference to his working life. It wasn't that he was antisocial, but he didn't always want to make small talk with the practice nurses, the receptionists, the phlebotomist, every time he wanted a drink from the kitchen, so the espresso maker had turned out to be an ideal solution. He drank his coffee without milk and sugar, so all that was needed was a clean cup and he was good to go. Astonishing, really, the lift it gave him. And it had the added advantage of making his small room smell like an Italian café, an effect that was not lost on the patients who entered; they inhaled deeply, enjoying the aroma, a welcome change from the smell of the Hibiscrub he washed his hands with and the lingering odours of the previous patients.

As the machine thundered to life, Noel took a moment to do a few stretches. He lunged forward, extending his left calf behind him for a count of ten, and was just in the process of switching legs when there was a sharp knock at the door. The knock was followed by a voice, saying, 'You free in there, Bloom?'

John Ravenscroft. Wearer of tweed, three-piece suits and handmade Oxford brogues. Ravenscroft spoke twenty decibels louder than everyone else and, at sixty-eight, he was the only partner remaining from the original line-up, back when the practice was first formed, in 1980.

'Come on in, John,' Noel said.

Usually, Ravenscroft spoke to Noel with the door ajar, keeping it open with the toe of his shoe while he imparted the information he needed, quick and staccato, as though to give the impression that time is money. *And, surely, we've all got better things to do than stand around discussing patients all day?*

Today, he opted to come right into Noel's room, and closed the door firmly behind him before speaking, which made Noel pause, mid-stretch. Noel stood up and gave Ravenscroft his full attention.

'Your day for emergencies, is it?' Ravenscroft asked, and Noel told him it was. 'Listen, I've just passed Polly Footit out there. Don't let her talk you into more osteopathy for her back. She keeps undressing to stockings and suspenders – full battle gear, actually – in front of young Stefan, and his nerves are totally shot. Tell her she'll have to go to Westmorland General if she requires more treatment. Tell her our budget's exhausted.'

'Will do,' replied Noel.

He watched Ravenscroft carefully, sensing that Polly Footit was not the real reason for his visit.

Ravenscroft cleared his throat.

'I notice you've been staying late,' he said.

'You notice because you've been staying late yourself, John.'

'Ah, well, that's because the bloody job keeps me alive. Whereas you . . .'

He let the words hang. Raised an eyebrow, in expectation of Noel giving him a reason for his change in habit.

But Noel couldn't give one. It was just a further indication of how shambolic everything had become.

'I've been meaning to ask about Verity,' Ravenscroft went on. 'Did the evaluation shed any light on things?'

Noel shook his head. 'According to them, it was an isolated incident. They found nothing that would make them think there would be a recurrence.'

'And how did Karen greet that piece of news?'

'As you would expect. With scepticism. She's been reading a lot about the link between cannabis and the onset of psychosis in teenagers. She's convinced that's what's at the root of all of this.'

'And what are your thoughts?'

Noel shrugged. 'I'm not sure that's what's going on with her.'

'Today's stuff is a damn sight stronger than the grass we smoked in the seventies,' Ravenscroft said. 'How is the school handling it?'

'Discreetly, but covering their arses. They don't want to lose her as a pupil—'

'She *is* an excellent student.'

'Was. Her grades are down,' Noel said. 'She's gone from "A"s to "D"s almost overnight. They think they can get her back on track, but we've had to sign up to drug tests and some counselling sessions – I assume, so that if anything happens, they've been seen to be doing everything by the book.'

'The head there is a buffoon, you know.'

'I know,' replied Noel.

'Is there anything I can do?'

'We'll be fine. But I do appreciate the concern, John.'

More lies. They wouldn't be fine. It was already too late for 'fine'. That's why he was hiding out here; he'd rather be any-where than go home and face it.

Ravenscroft put his hands together. 'Good, good,' he said. 'Right you are, then. Probably all that's needed here is some common sense and a little time for things to settle.'

'My sentiments exactly,' replied Noel.

Ravenscroft reached for the door handle. But, at the last moment, he paused.

Standing with his back to Noel, his thin frame somewhat lost in his old-fashioned suit, he appeared to be weighing up whether to turn around or not.

'Far be it for me to interfere, Noel,' he said, as he spun slowly, a peculiar look of discomfort on his face. 'A man's family is no one's business but his own – but if I may offer you one piece of advice?'

He waited for Noel to give him a sign to go on before continuing, such was his sense of propriety.

Noel nodded.

'I know little of how your family operates, and I wouldn't want to poke my nose into all of that. But I can say this: when I've been faced with challenges within my own set-up – when things have come a little unstuck, shall we say? – I found the answer never arose by avoiding going home at night.'

Noel looked at him with mild embarrassment. 'I hear you,' he said.

'Good man,' replied Ravenscroft.

Then he added, 'And you won't find any answers at the bottom of a whisky glass either, my friend.'

So Noel went home.

At six fifteen he parked his Volvo on the right-hand side of the garage.

Getting out, he could hear heavy bass coming from above and a series of footsteps moving across the floor. Ewan was Karen's son from her previous relationship, and he had been living above the garage since he had moved out of the house when he turned seventeen: an arrangement which seemed to suit everyone, particularly Karen.

Noel paused by the recycling boxes, taking a minute to squeeze the air out of a couple of plastic bottles before stamping down hard on some cardboard. He'd take the recycling tomorrow on his way to work, maybe leave a little earlier than usual and stop by the jet-wash on his way in. The wheel arches of the Volvo were caked in mud after a house call to Kentmere at the end of last week, and he really should make more of an effort.

He was dawdling. It was a familiar sensation. He found he was doing it more and more these days – giving himself a series of small, arbitrary tasks, tasks that required a modicum of concentration so that all the stuff hovering at the periphery of his brain could be kept there: nicely at bay.

They had been happy once. Hadn't they?

'All right, Dr Bloom?'

Noel turned to see Dale Brokenshire standing in his driveway, a four-pack of Stella in each hand.

'Good to see you, Dale. How's your mother doing?'

Dale coloured red and went bashful at being asked a direct question. It wasn't what people did with Dale. Usually, they politely ignored him, unsure of what to say, unsure if he could understand basic English.

'She's better,' Dale said.

'You tell her hello from me, won't you?' Noel said, and Dale shot him a toothy grin, his eyes widening and shining, as though he'd discovered something magical in front of him, right there on the garage's concrete floor.

Dale had what they referred to in infants as 'global delay'; what in adults they called a 'learning disability'. Which Noel thought wasn't really an accurate description, but it was as good as any they'd come up with, nonetheless.

Noel looked away as Dale remained rooted to the spot, eyes fixed, as was his tendency, until someone gave him permission to do otherwise.

'You here to see Ewan?' Noel asked, finding another bottle to squeeze the air from.

'Yep.'

'Why don't you go on up, then . . . if he's expecting you?'

Dale thrust both his hands forward. 'I got him these,' he said proudly, meaning the beer, and Noel mimed shock.

'Now, Dale, you are over eighteen, aren't you?' he asked, and Dale nodded his head seriously.

'Fifteenth of May, 1996,' he shot back automatically, as if Noel had pressed a button on the top of his head.

Noel lifted his eyes to the ceiling. Then he made a great show of pretending to count up on his fingers, working out if Dale's date of birth made him above drinking age. 'Yeah, you'll do,' he said finally, and he smiled as Dale's worried expression started to fade. 'You two make sure you eat something to go along with that,' he said, and Dale replied, 'I'll make sure, Dr Bloom. I'll make sure of it, don't worry.'

Noel heard Dale's heavy tread on the wooden staircase that ran up the side of the garage to the flat above. A second later, there was a pause in the music, then the sound of a door slamming, before the music started up again.

'Poor kid,' said Noel to himself.

Karen looked up from her diary, phone in hand, and said sharply, 'You're back?'

Noel shrugged, didn't answer the question and asked Karen what was for dinner.

'Dinner?' she said, and gave a small laugh. 'There is no dinner. Open the fridge and see what you can find. There's bound to be a ready-meal lying around.'

She was in her uniform of black, slim-legged trousers, a crisp, white shirt, with spiked heels and heavy gold jewellery. She wore this black-and-white ensemble so she didn't have to think too much. So: 'I don't waste time putting outfits together when I could be doing something more constructive.'

'Aren't you eating?' Noel asked.

'It's Tuesday,' she said, as if that explained things.

Noel looked at her blankly. 'Brontë and I eat on the wing, remember?' she said. 'Double harp lesson on Tuesdays. I need to be in Lancaster for seven and I'm late after seeing the consultant for Brontë's hand. Do me a favour, shout up to Brontë and tell her to get her shoes on. Oh, and tell her she needs the sheet music in the *pink* folder. Not the black one. Got it?'

'Pink, not black,' he repeated. 'What did the neurologist say?'

'What?' Karen said, momentarily thrown, it seemed, by Noel's question. 'Oh,' she said, 'he was next to useless. Says he can't find anything physically wrong with her fingers.'

'Did he speculate as to why the sudden loss of grip strength?'

'He said he thought it was psychological. Which, of course, I said was nonsense. He's referred her for carpal-tunnel tests, but only because I demanded it. Anyway, I need to get hold of this silly woman before I leave. Tell her Brontë won't be able to make the dance recital on Sunday because she's doing extra piano with Clive Lishman.'

At this, Karen raised her eyebrows at Noel. He wasn't sure why until she did it again, saying, 'Clive *Lishman*.'

Noel realized he was supposed to know who Clive Lishman was.

'Verity home?' he said vaguely, but Karen's call had connected, and she was lifting a finger to silence him. 'Samantha? Karen Bloom. Glad you're back. *Finally*. Yes, we'll need to give Sunday a miss on account of Brontë securing some time with . . .'

Noel left her to it and wandered through to the lounge, expecting to see Verity supine on the sofa, school socks around her ankles, an assortment of snacks, apple cores and empty cups by her side. But the room was empty. It was neat and untouched.

He took the stairs two at a time and, seeing Verity's room also empty, he crossed the hallway to Brontë's.

His younger daughter was kneeling on the floor, her back to him, surrounded by maths worksheets. Karen ordered them online. 'Hey, kiddo,' he said, and she turned.

'Hi, Daddy.'

'I have a message from Mum. Get your shoes on, and remember to take the pink folder. Not the black. Or was it the other way around?'

Brontë tidied away her papers. 'The pink. She already told me.'

'I think you should hurry,' he said, as Brontë dragged herself to her feet obediently. At ten, none of the recalcitrance of the typical teenager was yet manifesting. Brontë was an easy child. A sweet girl who did exactly as her mother asked of her. Sometimes, Noel watched and marvelled at her malleability. Verity was nothing like that. Verity was headstrong, like her mother; neither could be forced into doing something they did not want to do. It was probably the thing that had attracted him to his ex-wife in the first place. Jennifer had never been the type to follow orders blindly.

Brontë reached for the folder and smiled at him politely as she passed by.

She looked pale.

He would have to talk to Karen about it, because Brontë had been this way since returning to school after the summer break. She needed to spend more time outside. She needed more downtime. Karen pushed her hard and, though he tried not to interfere with her parenting methods, he could see that the child was beginning to tire.

As she got to the small landing halfway down the stairs, Noel called out, 'You feeling okay, Brontë?'

She looked at him and blinked. 'Course, Daddy,' she replied. 'My fingers are still a bit numb, but I think they're definitely getting better.'

It was her right hand that was affected. Her dominant hand. And it had started a few months ago. At first, they had thought nothing of it. Anyone who practised an instrument every day was bound to get muscle fatigue at some point, and Brontë studied two. But then she began to drop things. And she wasn't able to fasten the buttons of her school shirt. And could no longer grip a pencil properly. Noel told Karen to let her have some rest and, reluctantly, she'd agreed, but there was no real improvement.

So Karen took it upon herself to 'strengthen' Brontë's hands herself – something which led to an unfortunate incident with Verity; they were still dealing with the aftermath.

'Have a good lesson, sweetheart,' Noel said.

'I will,' she replied, just as Karen's voice rose from below.

'Hurry!' Karen shouted. 'You've not even got your shoes on. You know how I hate to be late. Being late is not who I am. Not who *you* are, Brontë Bloom. Late people are not only disorganized, they are disrespectful of other people's time. Is that how you want to be regarded? As disrespectful?'

Noel exhaled, closing his eyes briefly before crossing over to Verity's room once more.

He hadn't noticed before, but at the foot of her bed was a pile of clothes – her uniform. He opened her wardrobe and realized that her trainers were missing. She'd gone for a run. They used to run together. When did that stop exactly?

He returned downstairs to catch Karen flying out the door, arms filled with folders, bottles of water, a bag of satsumas and three sticks of Peperami. 'Did you speak to Verity this evening?' he said hurriedly.

'About what?'

'Just, you know, did you talk to her at all?'

'Why should I, Noel?' and she frowned at him, as though he were asking something impossible of her in her role as stepmother to his elder daughter. 'I'm late, I really need to—'

He reached out and caught hold of her arm.

'Try. Please, Karen. Try. Do it for me.'

And she shook him off, staring at him hard. 'Trying is all I do around here, Noel. In case you hadn't noticed.'

4

Wednesday, 23 September

Verity disembarked from the bus one stop later than usual and pulled out the business card from her pocket to remind herself of the exact address. Psychotherapists don't tend to advertise their services too brazenly, so, as she stood in front of the small brass plaque with the name Jeremy Gleeson on it, she double-checked it against the card before pressing the bell next to it.

Verity had asked if she could see a woman instead when her dad had suggested Jeremy Gleeson.

'I think it would be easier to talk to a woman,' she said, and her dad had agreed, but unfortunately, there wasn't any choice.

At first, they'd gone down the NHS route. It didn't look good, after all, for the daughter of an NHS GP to seek treatment in the private sector. But even if Noel had managed to fast-track Verity, it would still be over six weeks before they were offered an appointment – which Verity's stepmother said was 'Outrageous.'

Verity got the impression her father would have been willing to wait. But ultimately, the decision was made for them, because Verity's head teacher had demanded to see evidence of her treatment programme within the next fortnight. And so, in a hurry, her father had done a Google search of local therapists and, after a brief phone chat with Jeremy Gleeson, declared him 'fit to do the job as well as anyone'.

'It's a formality, Verity,' her father had told her as he left for work that morning. 'Don't get too het up about it. We just need to be seen to be doing *something*.' Which Verity knew he would never have said if her stepmother was in the room. Karen thought she was unhinged. If it was up to Karen, Verity would be sectioned.

The door was opened by a woman with crêpey skin and tight, platinum curls. Verity recognized her from the vet's. And then, later, the post office. People commonly switched jobs around here when they got fed up. 'Come in, dear,' she said, and ushered Verity into a small side room containing three chairs and a water cooler. The walls were covered with a number of landscapes badly executed by a local artist, and for sale. Verity wondered if Jeremy Gleeson dabbled in watercolour when he wasn't fixing damaged minds.

'He won't be long,' said the woman, then disappeared before Verity had time to answer.

Then a door in front of her flew open, making Verity jump, and the person she presumed must be Jeremy Gleeson walked towards her, his arm extended, saying, 'Miss Bloom. Glad you found me. Come on in.'

Verity was too shy to do anything other than mutter a quiet hello. She followed her therapist into his office, where he asked her to sit wherever she felt most comfortable. Verity glanced from the chair to a narrow, firm couch to what looked like some kind of gaming chair, feeling like a rabbit caught in the headlights.

'Perhaps the chair to begin with?' he suggested, and Verity said, 'Thank you. Yes, the chair.'

He gave her a moment to settle herself while he shuffled a pile of notes around, before fixing her with a smile. 'The first thing we ought to do is congratulate you for coming here, Miss Bloom.'

'*Okay*,' Verity said, unsure.

'It's a very brave thing to do.'

'It is?'

'Yes. It is. All right if I call you Verity?'

'Fine by me.'

Verity wasn't sure what to make of him. She'd seen counselling sessions on TV. Seen people confiding in their therapists on American sitcoms. But nothing about this set-up fell into the category of anything she'd seen before. She wasn't creeped out by him. He seemed a genuine enough guy. He had sandy-coloured, receding hair and freckled skin that was lightly tanned. His smile was friendly.

'Is there anything you'd like to ask me before we start?'

Verity shrugged and looked around the room, taking in the framed certificates, a photograph of Gleeson in a cap and gown standing with a nicely plump woman around his age who was wearing a pink suit.

Verity nodded towards the photograph. 'That your wife?'

He seemed pleased she'd noticed the picture. 'Yes,' he said. 'That's Heather. We're at my graduation. A proud day for both of us.'

'What did you do before you did this?' Verity asked.

'I was a blacksmith.'

'You're kidding me?'

'No. I did it for twenty years.'

'And so the natural progression was to do this, obviously,' she said.

He smiled. 'Let's just say I'd outgrown my profession. I was ready for something different.'

'My dad says everyone should have at least one career change.'

'He does?' Jeremy said enthusiastically. 'And what was his?'

'He hasn't had one. He's been a doctor all his working life. Are you a doctor?'

'No.'

'Not even a pretend one?'

He laughed. 'Not even that.'

'How do I know you won't screw with my mind, then?'

'You don't,' he said. 'This relationship is all about trust, it's all about a deepening trust developing between—'

'Whoa!' said Verity, holding up her hands. 'That's sounding a bit paedo. A bit "It'll be our little secret" kind of thing.'

Jeremy Gleeson paused. After a moment's thought, he said, 'Perhaps I ought to think about rewording that.'

He lifted a fountain pen from the desk and began rolling it between his fingers. 'Your dad told me it was your school, Reid's, who requested that you see someone.'

'That's right.'

'How do you feel about that?'

'I feel like . . . do I call you Jeremy?'

'Whatever you're comfortable with.'

'I feel – not to cause offence or anything, Jeremy, because I'm sure you're very good at what you do – but I feel like my time could be better spent getting on with work. I have a ton of coursework to do. Although I do understand why they want me to see you.'

'Why do you think they want you to see me?'

Verity looked out of the window. 'To stop me from doing what I did again.'

'Do *you* think you'll do what you did again?' he asked.

'Of course not.'

'Because . . .?'

'Because it's not like . . .' Verity sighed. Closed her eyes briefly. 'It's not as if I go around doing it every day.'

'Would you say you felt in control when you attacked your stepmother, Verity?'

'In control?' she repeated. 'I'm not sure I understand what you mean.'

'Did you feel like it was you . . . doing what you did? Or did you feel compelled to do it by, say, an outside source?'

Verity arched an eyebrow. 'An outside source?'

Jeremy Gleeson nodded.

'You want to know if I'm crazy. That's what you're asking, isn't it?'

'I wouldn't have put it quite like that,' he said.

'Strangling your stepmother "for a sustained period", as they reported it, is a crazy thing to do, whichever way you look at it. It was actually no more than a few seconds. But no. I wasn't compelled by voices in my head. Or weird visions. Or hallucinations.'

'Were you under the influence of drugs at the time?'

'No.'

'You're certain about that?'

'Jeremy,' Verity said flatly, 'it was *all* me.'

'But there *were* drugs found inside your locker?'

'That's right. There were.'

'Would you say you had a reason for doing what you did, or is that something you find hard to talk about? Maybe even hard to think about?'

'I don't find it hard at all,' Verity said, and Jeremy nodded, waiting for her to go on.

'I hated my stepmother in that moment, and I wanted her to stop what she was doing,' Verity said. 'I wanted Karen to stop and she *just wouldn't.*'

5

THE THING THAT people didn't get when they accused Karen Bloom of being a tiger mother was that she wasn't at all offended by it. Even when it wasn't said in a jokey, leg-pulling kind of way. Even when it was meant as an insult.

Karen *was* a tiger mother, and she was proud of it. Why shouldn't she be? Just because ordinary mothers had decided it was wrong to push their offspring, just because they took the easy way out, saying it wasn't a mother's place to mould a child into greatness, it didn't mean Karen had to go along with it. Because they would say that, wouldn't they? It was an easy way to justify their own lazy lives, their own acceptance of mediocrity. And Karen was very sorry, but she wasn't having that for Brontë.

It was her responsibility – her *duty*, in fact – to prepare Brontë for the life ahead of her in the best way she knew how. Life was a competition. Only the best and the brightest succeeded, and if that meant Karen had to put her own hopes and dreams on the back burner while she invested everything she had in Brontë's future, so be it.

She had tried it the other way, and Ewan was the result.

Lazy, disrespectful Ewan. She loved him, naturally. He was her son – of course she loved him. But she had failed in her parenting the first time around, and she wouldn't do it twice. Not with Brontë. Not with such a remarkable child.

'Don't you think you should ease up on her scheduled

activities?' the other mothers would say. 'A child needs to be a child, after all.' And Karen would think: *Here we go.* Envy camouflaged as concern. Jealousy dressed up as self-righteousness. Karen would smile politely, saying that Brontë could cope. That she positively thrived on hard work. When really what Karen wanted to say was: *All this input would be pointless with your child. Your child would remain ordinary – pedestrian – no matter what you did.*

But Karen didn't air those thoughts because Karen was a nice person. And nice people didn't say things like that.

It was 5.20 p.m. and Karen was where she could generally be found: behind the wheel of the car, parked, waiting for Brontë's lesson to finish; this time, it was piano. From five thirty they had half an hour to get from Grasmere to Windermere, to be in time for her tap class, and in this time Brontë also needed to eat and complete her reading homework. Which, if Karen was correct, was chapter twelve of *Holes* by Louis Sachar.

Karen had recently started to zone out when Brontë read, because Brontë could sound a little Dalek-like – something Karen had tried to work on. Karen would repeat sentences, emphasize particular words, trying to get some light and shade into her daughter's delivery, but, alas, nothing had worked, so she was taking a short break. For now, she let Brontë read however she liked, as long as it got done; though she knew it was a problem.

A friend of Karen's had enrolled her child in the Stagecoach Theatre Arts School because she felt her daughter was lacking in self-confidence, and Karen was looking into the idea for Brontë. The problem was, it clashed with her Saturday harp tutorial and Karen had promised herself that music would come first, no matter what. Music came before play dates, sleepovers, before friends' birthday parties. Music came first because it had to. There was no point giving your child these opportunities if you were going to go at them in a half-hearted way. To excel took real commitment. On all levels. Something the other mothers at school appeared to be ignoring, if their appearance was anything to go by. Those women were not *quite* doing the school run in their pyjamas, but they weren't far off.

But what if Brontë *did* grow up without adequate public-speaking experience? That was sure to hamper her chances of performing well at university interviews. So it had to be addressed. It was needling Karen more than she had realized. Perhaps she should make an allowance just this once and—

The car door opened and Brontë climbed in, telling Karen in a strained voice that she was starving and she really needed to eat something, 'Straight away, Mummy.'

'You'll have to eat and read at the same time,' Karen said, turning the ignition and checking her mirror before quickly pulling out in front of a learner driver whom she couldn't take the chance of getting stuck behind.

Brontë took three fast bites of her cream-cheese sandwich before reaching into her rucksack to retrieve *Holes*. Then, without any prompting from Karen, she methodically thumbed through the pages until she found her spot and began to read.

She read as if there was a full stop after each bloody word.

Karen had to do something. She would speak to Brontë's teacher first thing tomorrow. See if she knew of anyone who could tutor Brontë and get her out of this awful habit. It was actually quite embarrassing.

The traffic slowed. There were temporary traffic lights up ahead. Karen watched Brontë. Watched as she ran the fingers of her bad hand shakily underneath the words as she spoke them out loud.

Surely she should have stopped with that by now?

6

NOEL BLOOM HAD been supposed to be heading home when he found his car unexpectedly steering itself into the car park of the Wateredge Hotel.

One drink.

One drink wasn't going to hurt anyone.

And the great thing about this kind of hotel, as opposed to, say, a pub, was that nobody there would know him. Not the guests. Not the staff. None were local to the area – they were mostly Europeans who came for the season – so he could slope in and out in relative safety.

Sometimes Noel found his recognizability burdensome. It wasn't as if he'd signed up for it. Not like the rock stars and football players who bemoaned their inability to leave a hotel room to fetch a pint of milk. Noel had never imagined that being a small-town GP would prevent him from going wherever he pleased. But it did. He couldn't frequent popular local restaurants or bars, for fear of bumping into patients, all wanting a piece of him, all wanting to ask about the side effects of their statins or what the cause of their night-time restless legs was.

Noel sat in the hotel bar, gazing out at the lake beyond, and thought about Verity. He really should go home and talk to her about the counselling session. Find out how she had got on.

He glanced at his watch.

Seven forty.

He wondered if she'd opened up to the guy. He couldn't see it himself. Verity had been a closed book since the incident; no one could get through to her. In desperation, he'd gone to talk to Verity's mother about it. But of course, Jennifer couldn't exactly talk back, because of her condition. There was something oddly comforting about her presence, though, and he could now see why patients often came to him asking for a referral to someone 'who would sit and listen to their problems'. Someone who wouldn't judge.

Verity's therapist wasn't what Noel would class as qualified, but who was any more? You had bank clerks doing hypnotherapy in their garage conversions, beauticians injecting poison into people's foreheads. The veterinary surgeons had it right. They had long lobbied against anyone but themselves performing anything invasive on animals, and the industry was a lot safer because of it.

Verity was still on the waiting list to see an NHS psychologist, so if it turned out to be a waste of time with the Gleeson fellow, there was still that.

But had Verity talked about *him* at her appointment? Perhaps she'd said he was a shitty, absent father.

When Noel was a child every father he knew had been absent, and that's how he and his friends liked it. Noel looked at the dads of today and didn't quite know what to make of them, all wearing their sling and their nappy bag with pride. It went against his instinct to be provider, protector. He wasn't sure he had what it took to be one of those men. He was far more comfortable leaving the early-years stuff to the woman in his life – first Jennifer, and then Karen. Neither had complained that he wasn't very hands-on, that he partook little in the raising of Verity and Brontë. But now he questioned if his idea of normal dad behaviour had in fact been wrong. Could he have done more? Should he have done more?

*

'How was it?' he asked Verity when he returned home.

'How was what?'

Noel tilted his head to one side and waited for Verity to reply.

'It was fine,' she said eventually. '*He* was fine, if that's what you're asking.'

'Did he . . .?' Noel paused, searching for the right words – words that would not provoke an attack. 'Did you get into what happened that day?'

Verity shook her head. 'Not yet. But I'm sure we will at some point. Happy? Anyway, do you want some of this?'

Verity was stirring the contents of a deep stainless-steel pan. Her damp hair was pulled back into a ponytail and her skin was flushed and fresh from the shower. She wore grey yoga pants and a vest.

'What is it?' he asked.

'Pasta. What else? I've made enough for me, Ewan and Dale, but I can probably stretch to another portion. As long as you're not too hungry.'

'What about Brontë and Karen?' he asked, and Verity gave him a look as if to say, *What about them?* 'They'll have eaten by the time they get back,' she explained.

'What kind of pasta is it?'

'Penne with tomato, chilli and salami.'

'Where'd you learn to cook that?' he asked.

'I have a brain,' she said. 'I can follow a recipe.'

Verity was acting as though she did this every day, and it struck Noel, suddenly, that she might very well do just that.

After draining the pasta in the sink, she picked up her phone and handed it to Noel. 'Here,' she said, 'text Ewan and tell him it's ready while I get this into the bowls.'

She was treating him as the child. She was the mother. It was her way of acting around him, her way of connecting, and he sort of liked being bossed in this way by her. Better than her recent silences, anyway. He did as she asked – texted Ewan – and as she tipped the sauce over the pasta, stirring and adding a handful of Parmesan and some chopped parsley, he asked her how often she fed Dale.

'Whenever he's here,' she said casually. 'I don't like to eat alone, and I can hardly cook for Ewan and leave Dale out.'

'No, I don't suppose so, but—'

'His mum works evenings and he can't cook for himself.' She shrugged as if it was no big deal.

Noel set about grabbing the cutlery as Ewan and Dale filtered in, silently, woollen hats pulled low, though the temperature outside was still close to seventy degrees. An Indian summer. That's what people were saying. Didn't they say that every year? Two warm days in September and it was an Indian summer. It wouldn't last. It never did.

'Hello, lads,' Noel said, and both seemed bemused but not put out to see him.

Dale said, 'All right, Dr Bloom?' as was his way. Noel could smell the customary scent of weed hanging off their clothes. It was sweet, musty and really quite lovely, and for a split second Noel felt a rush of yearning to be seventeen again. Smoking the afternoon away, nothing in the world that needed to be done except vaguely think about A levels or how he might go about persuading a pretty girl to have sex with him at the weekend.

'You're back early,' commented Ewan, spooning penne into his mouth. And then, without waiting for Noel to respond, he looked at Verity. 'Good this, V. I think I like this one better than the chicken meatballs. What do you think?' he said, now addressing Dale.

Dale smiled at Verity. He had always been enraptured by her, and she handled him sweetly. 'I like all of them,' he said, dropping his eyes to his food.

'I tried to get away a bit earlier today,' Noel said. 'Trying not to be married to the job so much.'

'Good plan,' replied Ewan. 'Any dessert, V?'

'The freezer's bare,' she said. 'You could take a box of cereal back up with you.'

Ewan shook his head. 'Nah. We'll head out and get something later. We're going to dye Dale's hair. You want to come and give a hand?'

'What colour?'

'Black.'

Verity smiled and shook her head. 'I'll leave you to it.'

Noel tried to act nonchalantly as he ate, glancing at the three unlikely dining companions around the table and wondering how long this arrangement had been going on. Probably a good while, he now realized. Stupid, really, but it had never occurred to him that Karen left the two older children to fend for themselves. Stupid, because what had he supposed they'd been doing? Karen didn't cook during the week. She and Brontë would 'eat on the wing', as she liked to say, and he was rarely home in time for dinner. Funny, but for all Karen's *standards*, for all her constant striving to give Brontë the best possible start, she was remarkably lax about their daughter's nutrition, which Noel couldn't quite make sense of. When he raised the subject Karen would counter his questioning with 'Where exactly do you expect me to feed her this home-cooked meal you're so set upon, Noel? At the side of the M6? In between her harp lesson and her maths tutorial?'

Noel paused, his fork halfway between his bowl and his mouth, and said to Verity, 'This is good. Really good, actually. You have quite a talent, Verity.'

'One of my many,' she said.

'I don't see why that simple-minded nincompoop must spend *all* his waking moments at this house,' Karen said as she removed her shirt. 'Does he not have friends of his own type he can hang around with?'

50

Noel was on the bed in just his boxers. He had a new vitiligo patch forming to the left of his bellybutton. His patches tended to form symmetrical patterns – had done since his late teens, when he developed the condition, and he was sure to get one on the right within a few months. He flicked through the channels one way and then the other. There was nothing on. He didn't watch the news before bed any more as the images lodged themselves in Karen's brain and she had trouble sleeping. The fact that she had had trouble sleeping before they met, when she had no TV in her bedroom, was beside the point.

'His own type?' Noel repeated vaguely, and Karen stopped what she was doing and faced him.

'Retarded. Challenged. Whatever the accepted phrase is.'

'Oh,' replied Noel. 'I think Ewan likes having him around.'

Karen sniffed. 'Yes, well, and we know why that is.'

Noel paused on a programme about benefit fraud. If Karen noticed him watching, she would make him turn over. Noel's last tax bill was over forty-six thousand pounds, and Karen had been horrified. If she caught sight of the fat woman in the vest who was cheating the system, a cigarette dangling from her mouth, her husband dozing on the sofa with two English bulldogs, she'd get herself into such a state she'd need to do an hour of yoga before she could even get into bed.

Karen eyed the screen and Noel changed the channel. *Newsnight*, with the sound muted, would have to do.

'We all know he does it just to get at me,' Karen said.

'We all know who does what?'

'Ewan. It's another of his little protests. "Look at my stupid friend. See, not only is he not going anywhere, he's not even able to achieve—"'

'Karen. I think you're being a bit harsh.'

'Am I?'

'They've been friends since primary school.'

'Because he knew it irritated me. What I don't get is why, every time I come in the house, that boy is in my kitchen?'

Noel shrugged. 'I don't think it's a big deal. Dale's someone for him to hang out with. His other friends are probably . . . busy.'

As soon as the word was out of his mouth Noel regretted it.

'Busy? Of course they're *busy*. I had that awful woman Pia Nicholls lording it over me at tap class today. "Hamish has been down to Oxford, looking around, blah, blah, blah. Thinks he might want to do PPE." '

'Honey, I don't think Ewan was ever on course to get the grades to go to—'

'That's hardly the point,' she snapped. 'When Pia tells me what Hamish is doing, I'm supposed to follow it with – what exactly? "Yes, yes, I'm so proud of Ewan. I think he'll stay above the garage smoking weed for another year if I'm lucky. Don't they grow up quickly? So proud. So very proud." It's bloody humiliating is what it is. And that's exactly why he does it.'

Noel thought about the young mother who had been in the surgery that morning. She had just received a definitive diagnosis of cystic fibrosis for her baby boy. She'd cried into her hands for a full hour because she knew what it meant. Knew there was a chance she wasn't going to see her son grow up to get married, to have kids of his own. 'It's like letting go of all the dreams you have for them,' she sobbed, and Noel had said, 'Yes. That's exactly what it was, and it was cruel.'

Noel watched his wife through the doorway to the en suite bathroom. She was pulling cotton wool firmly over her eyelids then raising her brows high on her forehead as she removed the smudged mascara from beneath her lashes. She looked hard. She'd become hardened. Her skin stretched taut over her skull.

She'd left her laptop open the other day on her Facebook page, and Noel had noticed she'd updated her profile picture. In it, she was unrecognizable. And it wasn't until Noel spotted that the bedroom carpet was the backdrop that he realized Karen had taken the selfie from above, lying down. He assumed this was to make her appear younger, but instead it created a curious wind-tunnel effect. The photo looked quite unlike his wife.

Karen caught his gaze in the mirror. She scowled a little. She hadn't always been this way. *They* hadn't always been this way. Granted, with second marriages, and with stepchildren involved, there was always going to be an element of pretence, an element of fake joviality; it was necessary to keep the show on the road. But they had had their moments. Enough moments to constitute what most considered a happy existence.

When had things changed?

Perhaps Ewan starting senior school had been one of the triggers. Not that Noel was blaming him. The kid had seemed to like school well enough up to that point, but failing Reid's entrance exam had been a real blow to his confidence and, after that, he seemed to coast. Well, wilful disengagement might be more accurate. Karen took the whole thing personally, as though Ewan's lack of application and subsequent poor reports were a direct reflection on her. That's when Noel first noticed her 'step up' her mothering of Brontë to another level. It was when he began to think of his second wife as 'achievement-obsessed'. Brontë could only have been three or four at the time.

Then, of course, Verity had to move in with them and that, too, had not been without its own set of problems.

Noel softly patted the pillow beside him. 'Come to bed, love,' he said.

And Karen dropped the cotton wool in the waste basket before striding across the room.

'It's just so bloody humiliating,' she said again.

7

Sunday, 27 September

At 2.30 p.m. Verity and Brontë turned left out of their driveway and began to walk the short distance down the hill towards the recreation ground. The air was thick and hot, the sky a cloudless blue. They were sisters but were allowed precious little time together usually, but because Clive Lishman, musical genius, had cancelled Brontë's piano session at the very last moment, here they were. Together.

Karen had been apoplectic. And Verity had found Brontë at the bottom of the stairs, crying, unable to say why exactly but, reading between the lines, Verity assumed it had something to do with Karen's raised voice coming from the kitchen.

Karen had no qualms about subjecting her children to her rages, unlike a lot of Verity's friends' mothers, who would seethe quietly next to the kettle, as though they weren't sure whether to trust themselves with the hot water. Unlike them, Karen let it all out. And whoever was close by got the full force of it. Which led, naturally, to each of them escaping as best they could – with the exception of Brontë, who *couldn't* escape. Brontë was Karen's pet project. And if you asked Verity, it was tantamount to child abuse what that woman inflicted on her poor half-sister.

When Verity was hospitalized after the attack, people had kept asking her if she knew why she'd tried to strangle her stepmother.

And she'd answered them truthfully: 'To stop Karen.' But, apparently, this was not enough of an answer, as Karen had been left with purple bruises necklacing her throat, so Verity had to stay in hospital for another five days while her head was CT'd, her hormone levels measured, her responses to various stimuli tested. No conclusions were drawn except to say she was not considered a danger. Neither to herself nor to Karen. Which Karen didn't exactly agree with. She had taken to walking out of any room Verity occupied and to shielding Brontë, not allowing the sisters to be alone together in case Verity should suddenly get the urge to attack.

And since Karen also insisted on filling every moment of Brontë's time with something constructive, something productive, something life-enhancing, Verity barely got to see her sister, and she missed her.

Verity had moved in with her dad and his new wife when she was eleven years old. Not an easy age for a girl, particularly a girl like Verity, who was still mad as hell at her father for moving in with Karen and her unborn child five years before that. Verity had hated this child. Had hated Brontë with a vengeance. And, over the years, Verity's mother had fuelled that fire.

When Verity was packed off to her dad's for good, what she had not expected was that she would grow to love her little sister. Love her to the point that she would do pretty much anything for her. Because Verity understood that, on some level, if it were not for Brontë, she would not have survived life with her dad and Karen and Ewan. She was too mixed up. Too full of hate about her new situation. And Brontë had become her relief valve.

Verity would not let Karen mould her sister into some weird, unhappy little automaton. She would not stand by and watch her drain the life from Brontë. And that day, when she found Brontë crying on the stairs and Karen shouting into the phone, Verity suggested they go to the rec to take Brontë's mind off things for a bit.

She wrote Karen a note and left it on the kitchen counter: 'At the rec. Back 1 hour.'

Now, Verity intertwined her fingers with Brontë's as they came close to the road, ready to cross. When Verity had been around the same age as Brontë, soon after she'd moved in with her dad and Karen, Karen had allowed her to go to the rec on her own. She'd also allowed her to go to the library, the post office, even to Boots, where she could kill close to an hour on a Saturday afternoon, swiping lipsticks on the back of her hand and different-coloured nail polish on each fingernail. But things had changed. That's what Karen had said about keeping Brontë at home unless there was a suitable adult to go along with her: *Things have changed.*

When Verity asked her stepmother what exactly she meant by this, Karen told her that children could not go out alone any more because it wasn't safe. And when Verity asked why it wasn't safe, Karen glared at her, nodding her head towards Brontë, which is what she did if something wasn't suitable for Brontë's young ears, before mouthing: 'Kidnapping.'

But because practically everything out of Karen's mouth was a total load of shit, Verity decided to do a little investigating of her own. What she found was that kidnapping was rare. Super-rare. Brontë had more chance of growing up to become prime minister than of being kidnapped. She was twice as likely to die in a plane crash – and don't even get her started about being struck by lightning. It was a wonder Karen let her move unsupervised between the house and the car, the odds were so stacked against her.

Verity presented her findings to Karen after Brontë had complained that her friends were meeting on the rec without her, going to the corner shop on their own, some learning to be independent in preparation for catching the train to Kendal, where they were going to attend secondary school. But Karen had looked at Verity and frowned, wrinkling her nose in distaste, as if she could smell something bad.

'That's okay for everyone else, Verity. But not for me. Not for my child.'

My *child*.

Not my *children*.

Verity knew she didn't count as one of Karen's children; she was her stepdaughter, and that was okay by her. She didn't want to be Karen's child. But what about Ewan? Where did he figure in all of this?

'Never run across the road chasing after your friends,' Verity warned Brontë now, as they stood at the kerb.

It was ridiculous. Brontë should have been taught this stuff when she was six.

'Promise,' Brontë said, in her small voice.

'Never believe a boy if he tells you you're ugly,' Verity said.

And Brontë looked up at her older sister, wide-eyed and innocent. 'All right,' she said.

If Karen wasn't going to prepare Brontë for independence and teenage life, Verity would do it herself.

Somebody had to.

The girls had been at the recreation ground for almost half an hour when Verity decided there was no real reason not to pop across the street and pay her mum a swift visit. She'd left the house with the idea that she might, and had packed a small gift for her mother, just in case. The sun was warm overhead and Verity had rolled her jeans up to above the knee and pulled the straps of her vest wide to try to rid herself of the white marks she had acquired over the summer.

Minutes earlier, she'd seen Dale, with his newly dyed black hair, finishing off his duties. He was doing an apprenticeship for Lake District Landscapes – a firm that dealt with grounds maintenance and street cleansing, mostly for the local authority. Often Verity would see Dale emptying rubbish bins at the side of the road, clipping hedges, that kind of thing. This being a holiday area, Dale didn't do the usual Monday to Friday, but tended to work weekends and be off work midweek, when it wasn't so busy with tourists. Dale did what he always did when Verity was near, and that was blush and drop his head low, before lifting one hand and showing his palm, staying like that for just a second too long. It would be clear to anyone watching that he wasn't a full shilling.

Verity watched Brontë. She and her friends were on the other side of the rec, sitting in a circle, playing some sort of game where, periodically, one girl would stand and recite a few words, before dropping down to sit cross-legged again.

To the left of the girls was a young woman with two Rottweilers. She stood a fair distance from the group. The dogs were on leads, lying watchful; though they seemed well behaved, Verity's protective instinct kicked in. Just when she was thinking that perhaps nipping across to see her mother was not such a good idea, the woman received a call on her mobile and began shouting a string of abuse into it. She dragged the two dogs to their feet and marched off. A powerful breed, Verity thought, as she watched the dogs move. Yet they walked with such grace. Verity had always wanted a dog, something small that could curl up on her lap while she watched TV, nestle on her pillow at night-time. But Karen was not a dog person. Nor a cat person, come to that. She'd allowed Brontë a lop-eared rabbit, on the strict understanding that it was Brontë's sole responsibility. Brontë being so busy, though, she had forgotten to clean out the hutch regularly, and the wet bedding had caused the poor thing to die of hypothermia in the middle of winter. Verity had felt responsible. She should have attended to it. Brontë's eyes still teared up at the mention of him.

Verity got to her feet, grabbed her rucksack and made her way across the grass to where the girls were sitting.

As she drew near, they stopped their game, momentarily embarrassed by her presence. 'Will you be okay for a bit?' she asked, and Brontë looked up at her questioningly. 'I'm just going across the road to see Mum.'

'Can I go to the shop?'

'You don't have any money,' Verity said.

'I brought some.'

Verity said it would be better not to. They'd go together on the way home and buy an ice cream. Maybe a magazine. One of those pre-teen things that had lots of pictures of Taylor Swift – but not so many of Miley Cyrus, now that she had her tits and her tongue hanging out half the time. Verity warned Brontë not to leave the rec without her and said that she'd be back in ten.

Fifteen at the very most.

It was not like a normal nursing home. Verity had never been inside a normal one, so she had nothing to compare it to, but when her father had found a place for her mother here he kept emphasizing the point that it *was not like a normal nursing home.* Those, apparently, were filled with rows of wingback chairs, vacant-faced old ladies hem-rolling their skirts, and with a TV blaring out soap operas that nobody watched. That's what he had said, and Verity had no reason not to believe him.

Applemead was known locally as a Cheshire Home, but its correct title was 'Applemead – part of the Leonard Cheshire Disability (registered charity no. 218186)'. That's what it said on the plaque above the door, and Verity would study the number, thinking that there were an awful lot of charities out there.

Before her mum became ill, Verity would pass Applemead and barely notice the place. It was a large three-storey stone building with numerous turrets, and with a semi-circular lawn in front.

You could hardly miss it, but it blended in with all the other buildings of Windermere. Once her mum became a permanent resident, Verity could virtually sketch the place from memory.

Incidentally, Leonard Cheshire had been an RAF pilot. He started the charity after the war, opening a residential home for disabled ex-servicemen, and Verity's father said he was the kind of good egg this country didn't produce any more. By the 1990s, there were almost three hundred Cheshire Homes worldwide, mostly set up by groups of volunteers from the local community. Their aim was to provide support for disabled people and encourage moves towards independence. This was written on a plaque on the wall in the reception area and Verity would read it each time with a heavy heart, because that was not part of the deal for her mother. Jennifer Bloom would not become independent. She would remain here as long as she stayed alive.

Her father said that most nursing homes housed the elderly: people waiting to die – so that was the other difference. Applemead was home to people of a variety of ages. Her mother was only forty-five, and there were other, youngish 'residents' with neurological problems, like her mother. One poor woman with early-onset dementia was in her early fifties, and this was a real tragedy, so Verity understood. But not for the woman herself, who appeared perfectly happy wandering around the place, moving ornaments, smiling benignly at visitors as if this were her house and they were all welcome guests.

The door opened and care assistant Jackie Wagstaff, who had been at Applemead for a couple of years now, welcomed Verity in her usual manner. 'Afternoon, you. Come to see Mum? She's outside, being read to. Do I need to take you through or can you find her yourself?'

Verity told her she could find her on her own and wouldn't be staying long.

'How is she?' Verity asked.

'Same as. Same as. Shaking's worse than ever. We gave up trying to get her into her trousers this morning. She's in that dress you like. The one with the stripes. Madeleine Kramer's with her. Reading some historical nonsense. I told her your mum prefers thrillers, but that woman always acts like she can't hear a word I say.'

Verity's mum did like historical fiction. It was Jackie Wagstaff who preferred thrillers.

Jackie walked off in the direction of the kitchen, leaving Verity to her own devices. Verity signed in, printing her name in the leather-bound book next to the bowl of boiled sweets that the lady with early-onset dementia liked to offer to visitors. Then she made her way to the back of the building, nodding and smiling at the residents, who, for reasons Verity didn't fully understand, were always exceptionally pleased to see a young person about the place. They practically keeled over from pleasure if someone brought in a baby. Or a dog.

Outside, Verity said, 'Good afternoon,' to two residents, one of whom was accusing the other of wearing her cardigan, before spotting her mother's wheelchair, partially hidden by the rhododendron. She approached slowly. Madeleine Kramer had caught sight of her but continued to read in her melodious voice, and Verity could see that her mother had her eyes closed and was enjoying it. Verity could not make out the title of the book but she could see a sliver of white, white skin and some tightly curled red hair. So Verity assumed they were back with the Virgin Queen again.

Madeleine was one of the regular volunteers. Her mother's favourite. She was tall and elegant with bobbed silver hair and always wore a vivid shade of plum on her lips. Verity thought she was quite beautiful; she looked like Helen Mirren. As well as Applemead, she helped out at the Save the Children charity shop, delivered meals on wheels, listened to primary-school children read, walked dogs at the animal shelter and ran elderly folk to hospital appointments. 'Hey,' Verity said softly, and Madeleine paused in her reading. Her mother opened her eyelids, a smile ready in her eyes upon hearing her daughter's voice. Her mouth didn't smile too well any more, such was the cruelty of MS, and she could form a few words only after a struggle.

Madeleine closed the book and touched Jennifer's clasped, quaking hands. 'I'll come again tomorrow,' she whispered. 'We'll continue then.'

'I'm only staying a few minutes,' said Verity. Turning to her mum, she said, 'I've left Brontë over at the rec alone. I just wanted to see you. I can't stay.' Then she turned to Madeleine, who was standing, smoothing her skirt, placing the book inside her straw bag, hurriedly, as if she suddenly had somewhere she needed to be. 'Perhaps you could come back in a little while?' Verity said. 'Ten minutes?'

Madeleine shook her head. 'I was almost finished. I can't stay myself today either. And we've read this one before, haven't we, Jennifer?'

Jennifer couldn't respond, just quaked hard in her chair, her knees lifting with what Verity knew was excitement at seeing her daughter. She would have to strap them down in a moment.

Madeleine Kramer leaned over and planted a kiss on the top of Jennifer's head. 'See you soon, dear,' she said.

When she was out of sight, Verity reached over and braced her mother's legs with the Velcro strap, whispering into her ear, 'Got something for you. Come on.' She released the brake and tipped the wheelchair back a little on its rear wheels so she could spin it on the spot. Then, pushing her mother to the bottom of the garden, she headed towards their secret place.

Verity stole the joints from Ewan.

Every couple of weeks, when she knew he was out she would sneak up to his flat above the garage, using the key her father kept in the front of the cutlery drawer – along with the fuses, pen lids, old batteries, rubber washers and paperclips. Ewan liked to have his weed ready-rolled. Verity had turned up once when he was really bombed and Ewan had taken a joint from his secret stash, warning Verity not to tell anyone where he hid it. He clearly didn't remember this – damaged short-term memory, and so forth – because he didn't change his hiding place and Verity was able to help herself whenever she needed to.

Ewan had modified the three DVD cases holding the *Godfather* trilogy, and each one housed around thirty joints, packed together neatly, like in an old-fashioned cigarette case. Verity would remove one from each case and shuffle the rest around so there were no gaps left. She didn't take more than three or four joints – any more, and he would have noticed. But occasionally, when she'd stockpiled, she would sell them back to Ewan and Dale. She said she got them from a kid at school, and Ewan would pay her less than they were worth – though she could tell he felt pretty guilty about this afterwards.

Verity poked her head out from behind the large, ornamental barrel positioned towards the back of the gardens to check no one was heading their way, and asked her mother if she was ready. Jennifer closed her eyes once in response. Then, in one swift movement, because she had to be quick, Verity held the joint inside her mother's lips, keeping it steady as her mother trembled, and lit the other end, instructing her mother to 'Inhale now.'

Before Reid's had discovered drugs inside her locker and decided that weekly urine tests were the way forward, Verity would light the joint herself, because it was easier. She never really inhaled much, because she didn't care for the feeling of being stoned and the stuff played havoc with her lungs when she ran. But she couldn't take the risk now and so getting the thing to light could be tricky, sometimes taking three or four attempts.

Today, her mother managed it the first time. Verity watched

as she took a shaky inhalation, her eyes closing and the corners of her mouth lifting just a little as the drug hit her brain.

Verity withdrew the joint for a moment while her mother exhaled, before replacing it between her lips again.

Typically, it took around ninety seconds for her mother's tremors to subside, and Verity thought it was one of the most beautiful things she was likely to see in her lifetime.

Three more long drags and her mother's eyes, now a little bloodshot, would dance into life and she would be able to form words. Not many – she was pretty stoned, after all – but some.

'You're a good girl,' her mother whispered.

'Aren't I just?' said Verity, smoothing down her mother's hair. Her mother tended to sleep fixed in one position, as her limbs locked totally during the night. In the morning, her hair would stick right up on one side, even after a thorough wetting and combing (which was often accompanied by a lot of cursing) by Jackie Wagstaff.

'You know I love you,' her mother said.

'I know because you tell me. How are you feeling today?'

'Life is good,' her mother said, and she smiled.

One of the unexpected symptoms of her mother's MS was the passivity that had developed alongside the illness. After she was first diagnosed, and in the early stages, her mother had railed against it, fought with everything she had to impede the physical decline. And then, one day, she just stopped. Verity didn't think it was a conscious thing. She hadn't given up. It was as if her body had taken over and decided it knew what was best. When Verity questioned her father about this, he told her that it happened. MS patients became passive, as if they accepted their fate – perhaps it was nature's way of helping them manage the disease long-term.

Verity replaced the joint. 'Take another,' she instructed, and her mother inhaled, blinking a couple of times.

'It's strong,' she said.

'I thought it might be,' replied Verity. 'It's been stinking out my cupboard. I had to put it inside two of Karen's Tupperware containers.'

Her mother took a sideways glance. 'How is the lovely Karen?'

'Making Brontë's life hell. The usual.'

'And your life?'

'She could be worse.'

When her mother was first institutionalized, as she liked to call it, she would ask about Verity's life with her dad and Karen, following it with 'It kills me that you have to live with that woman.' Verity felt guilty about living with them, and her mother felt guilty about not being able to look after her daughter any more. Of course, Verity, being only eleven, couldn't articulate any of this to her mother for some time, and it was only when she was mean to a child in school and her father was called in, after the child's parents had accused her of emotional bullying, that her dad had taken the trouble to ask, 'What the hell is going on with you, Verity?'

'You all done?' Verity asked, and her mother nodded.

Verity spat on her fingers and extinguished the joint before hurling the evidence high over the fence at the bottom of the garden.

There must be quite the collection on the other side. Verity wondered who might live there. She'd heard once of a stoner who chucked dimps out of his attic window, only for his father (a keen horticulturist) to discover a new species of herb growing right outside his back door. Verity supposed this was probably an urban myth, but then, those Russian scientists *did* find a fir tree growing inside a man's lung a few years back. So it might be true.

As Verity turned around she saw that her mother had angled her face towards the sun and was wearing an expression of pure contentment. When Jennifer was first diagnosed, sunbathing was not recommended for MS sufferers, and this had come as a terrible blow to her mother, who positively withered in the Lake District's appalling winter weather. For the first few years she avoided it, doing as the leaflets said, doing anything she could to prevent the forward march of the disease. Now, if there was even a hint of sunshine, Verity would find her mother outside. Jennifer had always had her doubts about the sun thing anyway. Vitamin D had been proven over and over to boost the immune response and, since MS was basically a total fuck-up of the immune system, sunshine was now considered a 'good thing'. Science had eventually caught up with what her mother had known all along.

'Wheel you back?' Verity asked, and her mother shook her head.

'I'm staying out here.'

'Where's the electric chair, anyway?'

'Charging,' her mother said.

'If I leave you all the way down here, they might not find you.'

Her mother didn't bother to open her eyes. 'They'll find me,' she replied. 'It's not as if I can get very far.'

'Your bladder okay?' Verity asked.

'Near empty,' her mother said.

So Verity kissed her mother goodbye, leaving her there in the sun, face tilted towards the sky, and went back across the road to the rec to collect Brontë.

8

KAREN CHECKED HER watch.

How long had they been gone? It was definitely over an hour. Probably closer to ninety minutes, in fact.

What had she been thinking, allowing Verity to take off with her child like that? On finding the note, she should have marched down the street and insisted they return at once.

This was all Noel's doing. Before he'd left for wherever it was he was going that morning, he'd told Karen she needed to show Verity that she still had some confidence in her.

Naturally, Karen had gaped at him. *Confidence?* Had he completely lost his mind?

'You need to meet her halfway, Karen,' he'd said, reasonably, as if what Verity had done could be chalked up as normal adolescent behaviour. As if Karen should be rolling her eyes, saying, *Bloody hell, teenagers, eh?*

'You need to do your bit to rebuild the trust between the two of you,' Noel said.

And Karen had replied, 'Do I?' while Noel did what he always did when she wasn't playing ball: sighed, pulled his fingers through his hair, gave her the kind of strained, pleading look which, frankly, made her want to throw a tantrum. A great big, spectacular tantrum – as a toddler might do in the confectionery aisle of the supermarket.

When *had* she last thrown a tantrum? Karen wondered. Whenever it was, it had been far too long ago.

Karen didn't believe in keeping a lid on things, picking your battles, and all that other claptrap parents were advised to do. When did people stop being parents, exactly? Karen knew when – when they were scared to death their kids wouldn't love them any more if they scolded them, that's when. When they'd fallen out of love with their spouses and so the thought of conflict with their child, the thought of saying a simple 'no', panicked them beyond measure. For Christ's sake, people didn't even scold their dogs any more.

Karen harboured no such fears. She didn't mind playing bad cop. Didn't mind being the one to implement the rules. Children needed rules. Of course they did. They needed boundaries and routine. They needed to know that the person in charge was exactly that. *In charge.* That's where their sense of security came from. Children certainly didn't need a parent as a friend. Good God, no. Karen was Brontë's *mother.* She did not need to be her friend. And, anyway, Karen already had enough friends. Five, to be exact – and she was doing her utmost to get rid of one of those.

She checked her watch again. Should she be worried? Yes, she should be. Because Brontë was with Verity. How could she not be worried?

She dialled Verity's mobile. Straight to voicemail.

'Back in an hour,' the note said, and Karen had fought the urge to go to the rec. And she hadn't. She'd heard Noel's voice in her head, prattling on about a new start and rebuilding relationships, and had made herself a cup of redbush tea and worked at steadying her nerves. Now, she was regretting it.

She would play hell with Verity when they returned. Her anger was building steadily as the minutes passed, and she was almost looking forward to them coming through the door so she could unleash it.

Suppressing emotion was bad for you. Everyone knew that. If it didn't come out one way, it would come out another – as illness, or disease. Karen suspected (though she never actually aired this view to anyone) that this was what had happened to Noel's ex-wife. That woman had been so full of hate when Noel left her. *Ding-dong* – it didn't take a genius to work out what was going on.

'See you on the way down,' Jennifer had said to Karen the day Noel left her, and Karen had never forgotten it. What a thing to say. Jealousy. That's what that was. And look where it had got her. In a wheelchair, that's where.

Also worth mentioning was the fact that Karen's uncle had suffered from MS for thirty years now, and he seemed to manage his illness perfectly well. He did it with a combination of clean living and keeping active. He even played the occasional game of tennis.

Or did he have ME?

She could never remember. She readjusted the painting the cleaning woman left perpetually crooked. She did this to prove to Karen that she'd cleaned the thing. Rosa, a fifty-something Filipina, had a number of these quirks, which irritated Karen. But since good cleaners were thin on the ground, she ignored it. She shared Rosa with another family – the Haworths. Well, perhaps 'share' was the wrong word. She borrowed Rosa for four hours, two days a week, and paid Jeanette Haworth direct. There was probably something illegal about this arrangement – subletting your Filipina was almost certainly improper – but after losing cleaner upon cleaner Karen was prepared to go along with almost anything. Noel didn't know the intricacies of the arrangement. He never asked, so she never told him.

Karen straightened the magazines on the ottoman. She got on her hands and knees, retrieving a balled-up pair of socks which belonged to Noel from beneath the couch. She heard the back door fly open. It was done with such energy, such force, that the handle banged hard against the wall. Karen blew out her breath in annoyance. There would be a mark there now, perhaps even a hole in the plaster. Karen lifted her eyes to the ceiling – *Give me strength* – and walked through to the kitchen, ready to blow.

What greeted her there made her stop dead in her tracks.

Verity: hair wild, eyes wild, breathing hard and ragged. Verity, who ran every day. Verity, who ran like a gazelle and barely seemed out of breath, ever, because she was capable of running a half-marathon rather fast.

Verity's face was tear-streaked and she had blood seeping down her arm from a scratch that ran the full length of her right bicep. Her vest was mud-smeared, her knees grazed and she was covered in grass stains.

For perhaps the first time in Karen's life the words would not come. She stared at Verity and could feel the strength leaving her legs.

She was going down.

Karen knew it but was powerless to stop it from happening. Fleetingly, the image of the bouncy castle they'd hired for Brontë's birthday popped into her head; the thing collapsing in on itself at the end of the day as its air supply was shut off.

Verity said, 'Brontë's gone.'

And Karen was just about able to whisper, 'Gone?'

'Gone,' said Verity.

9

DS JOANNE ASPINALL stared at the computer screen in front of her. The drug dealer Sonny O'Riordan was giving her a headache, and she was starting to think that her detective skills were on the blink.

She wondered if it was possible that the neural pathways within her brain, pathways that had always been so good at forming connections – connections where there had been none – had suddenly dried up.

Or what if she had simply run out of talent?

People lost their edge often enough, so it wasn't beyond the realms of possibility that Joanne had lost hers. Sportsmen became injured and never returned to form. Surgeons lost their steady hand and had to change discipline. Marksmen lost their nerve and were retired. Why should Joanne be any different?

Except she didn't feel as if she was losing it.

She felt as if the answer was right there, just out of reach, and if she could only stretch a little further, if she could only think a little harder, then it would all fall into place.

Joanne had been scanning through various pictures of Sonny for the past hour, pictures that were on his known associates' Facebook pages. She noticed that Sonny liked his badass T-shirts and was particularly fond of one with the slogan: 'AK47 – When You Absolutely Positively Gotta Kill Every Motherfucker in the Room'.

And one that said: 'Getting You Wet Since 1991'.

Sonny was a career criminal. She'd had dealings with him back when she was a bobby on the beat and Sonny was a juvenile – going by his birth name then: Michael O'Riordan. Since then, you could bet that, if Sonny was awake, he was doing something illegal, though he and Joanne had not crossed paths since he'd upped his game and got into the supply and distribution of various class As. He'd gone off the grid, but his name kept popping up across Cumbria and Joanne was not going to stop until she found the little shit. And little he was. Five feet four and no more than eight stone with his hair wet and a gun in his pocket. A real runty-looking thing, too. Joanne thought that if he'd been born at a different time, or in a place without decent healthcare, he'd have been unlikely to survive infancy.

'Oh, Sonny,' she said to the screen now, 'where are you hiding out?'

It was Sunday afternoon and she didn't really need to be at her desk, but she had little else to do, so she might as well be there, combing through Sonny's file. Her Aunt Jackie was on a late – the two–ten shift – so she would have the house to herself but, weirdly, lately, Joanne had noticed a kind of malaise settle over her whenever she was alone. She couldn't quite motivate herself to do anything and where, once, she had relished her time away from work – taking long baths, reading crappy romance novels – none of it seemed to hold her interest of late.

She wondered if she was becoming one of those coppers who, over time, became married to the job.

Joanne shook her head as if trying to rid the thought, but then caught sight of her reflection in the now blackened screen. She looked tired. Or old. She wasn't sure which.

In the dreams of her youth Joanne had seen herself with a couple of kids by now. She thought she'd be ferrying teenagers back and forth to football practice, spending her Saturday afternoons washing dirty kits. Later on, a curry perhaps, in front of the TV, enjoying a film and a ten-pound bottle of wine with her spouse.

They weren't exactly big dreams. She hadn't been expecting glamour, long-haul holidays, expensive shoes. Just the basics afforded to most decent human beings.

Funny that Joanne had always imagined herself as the mother of teenagers, she thought. As though she could bypass the baby and early-years stages entirely. Joanne couldn't be sure, but she didn't think she'd be great with babies. They frightened her, with their all-encompassing neediness, their helplessness. And she didn't get the yearning to hold a child and sway on the spot, to kiss its head, to sing nonsense softly in its ear, the way she saw other women do. Perhaps this was part of the problem. Perhaps men sensed the lack in her and went the other way. Most of them were babies themselves, so that was probably it.

Idly, she glanced at her mobile to see if there were any new messages. There was one from Jackie telling her to record an episode of *19 Kids and Counting* at 9 p.m. Jackie watched all manner of US reality-TV programmes. She couldn't get enough of them. Joanne reckoned if they combined a couple and called the show, say, *Property-developing Dwarves*, Jackie might reach near-nirvana.

On her phone there was also a message with a photo from her old friend and colleague Ron Quigley. Ron had been pensioned off early because he had arthritis in both knees and ankles, and he seemed to be on one long holiday with his wife. He sent Joanne snaps from wherever he was (at present, standing at the entrance to the Caves of Drach, Mallorca), just like the series of photographs featuring the stolen garden gnome, working his way around the globe.

There was no message from Seamus, she noticed.

Seamus, the man with no surname from the hotel bar – and, later, the hotel *room* – earlier in the week.

Joanne hadn't meant to sleep with him.

She didn't have many rules, but that was one of them: do not sleep with a man you have just met. But she broke it willingly on Monday night, once she had a couple of whiskies inside her.

Did she regret it?

A bit.

She regretted having slept with a man – a nice man – whom she now expected would call. And, clearly, that wasn't going to happen.

That was the part she regretted. Not the actual sex. That part had been good. And really rather lovely – considering they'd only laid eyes on each other a couple of hours previously.

Seamus the accountant with the nice hands was funny and clever and sexy, and throughout their dinner Joanne had caught herself gazing at him, thinking, *If this man doesn't suggest getting a room, I might just break another rule and do it myself.*

Ultimately, she hadn't needed to. She thought he might have made booze the excuse, saying something along the lines of it being a shame they couldn't enjoy another drink, since they were both driving, and so on and so forth. But halfway through her dessert of frangipane tart he'd looked at her, seriously, and said, 'Spend the night with me?' and 'Yes' popped straight out of Joanne's mouth before she had the chance to play hard to get.

Which was all very well and good, but look at what she was doing now? Killing time, on a sunny Sunday afternoon, in a stuffy office, chasing Sonny O'Riordan, trying to take her mind off things.

Foolish woman, Joanne. Foolish, foolish woman.

This really was teenage behaviour. She should be above all this by now. Lord knows she'd had enough practice at being let down by men in the past.

But Seamus the accountant was the first man Joanne had gone to bed with without her T-shirt on for around – oh, it had to be at least eighteen years. She didn't go all the way with

Seamus – she didn't remove her bra. She wasn't quite ready for *that*. The scars beneath each breast and around each nipple were still pink and a little raised. They would fade, apparently. 'Turn to silvery threads no more than stretch marks,' the surgeon had said.

This was after he told her he was very pleased with the operation. 'I'm very pleased with the result,' he had said, but he didn't look pleased. Joanne suspected it was something he said automatically to patients on the first ward round of the day after surgery to allay any fears they might have. And she was proven right, because the following day she could hear him saying the exact same thing to a woman in the next bed along who'd had a tummy tuck.

Joanne had asked the woman how she came to get a tummy tuck on the NHS, as she had assumed that plastic surgery of this kind, without a medical reason, was something that had to be paid for privately. With no hint of shame, the woman replied, 'I told my doctor I couldn't stand the way it slapped around when I was on my hands and knees having sex. And he said he could see how that could be psychologically damaging.'

Indeed, thought Joanne.

Incidentally, Joanne didn't mind the scars. She didn't even mind if they didn't fade completely; she was just so relieved to look like a normal person instead of a cartoon version of what a woman should be. She was now a sensible 36D, and when Seamus the accountant had gone to remove her bra and Joanne had said, 'I'd rather not,' he hadn't done what she imagined he might do. He had not frowned, asked her why not, asked her if she was prudish in some way. He had simply nodded and touched her through the silk. His touch was light – the touch of a butterfly, in fact – as though he understood. And Joanne wondered if he somehow knew more than he was letting on.

In the morning, Seamus left early. At around five. And that

should have been her first clue. He's probably married, Joanne thought, lying there watching him dress. She hadn't noticed the patches of white skin covering his torso, his upper arms, because they'd had the lights off. But in the morning light Joanne thought them strangely beautiful.

He looks like a lovely tortoiseshell cat without its fur, she had thought, idly.

She'd asked Seamus if he wanted her number, and even though she suspected he was married he said yes and dutifully punched the digits into his mobile, telling her he would call her later that day.

Time to move on now, she decided, shutting down the computer and grabbing her bag. She slipped her mobile into the side pocket, purposely not checking the screen as she did so, and considered this a small victory in her effort towards ridding her thoughts of Seamus.

Pushing her chair away from the desk, she heard it ring.

'DS Aspinall,' she said.

'Joanne? You still upstairs?'

It was Rebecca Fowler, the duty sergeant at the front desk.

'I'm here,' Joanne said.

'Oh, great. Look, I've just had a call from a couple of officers out your way in Windermere. A girl's missing, and—'

'What age?'

'Ten. She's only been gone an hour or so – looks like she could have wandered off – but the mother's a stroppy sort. She's demanding a detective on the scene and I wondered if you wouldn't mind calling in, showing your face. She won't deal with the uniformed officers.'

'I'll do it,' Joanne said, and reached for a pen. 'Go ahead with the address.'

10

'WHERE THE FUCKING hell are you?'

Good question, thought Noel.

He'd headed off earlier for a drive, something he did on Sundays to escape the house (sometimes, Karen), and now he wasn't exactly sure where he was. He had the satnav of course, safely stowed in the glove compartment. He could plug it in and find his location within seconds. But there was something quite romantic in following his curiosity, driving without an agenda, driving until he found something of interest – and granted, yes, that was usually a pub.

He had headed north that morning with the vague notion of visiting Peebles, the old market town in the Scottish Borders. He hadn't been there since . . . had he ever been there? He couldn't remember. But it sounded like a nice place to spend an afternoon, so he filled up the Volvo with fuel and bought a copy of the *Sunday Times*.

But Noel hadn't made it to Peebles. Heading over Shap Fell, he'd seen a sign for Haweswater.

Haweswater is a man-made reservoir that was built by flooding the Mardale valley. It was done specifically to supply water to the people of Manchester, back in the twenties or thirties. Noel remembered learning about it in primary school: how the villages and farms had been lost; about the outcry from the local communities at the disappearance of what was supposed to be one of the prettiest valleys in the whole Lake District. So he'd pulled off the A6, thinking it was high time he took a look at Haweswater, deciding he could stop there for an hour, maybe more, and still make it to Peebles later on, if that's what he wanted to do.

Noel spent a few pleasant hours on the banks of the reservoir, longer than anticipated, his only company the occasional guest from the nearby hotel out taking a stroll. The air was still, the water a deep, deep, cobalt blue, and he sat reading happily, first the sports supplement (did every sportsman have a beard now? And they weren't even good beards. Kris Kristofferson's in *Convoy* – now *that* was a beard), then the news review and finally the culture section.

Studying the movies for the week ahead, he made a mental note to record a Spanish film which was going to be shown late on Tuesday. It had been adapted from a Ruth Rendell novel and it sounded right up his street.

Then he was heading north again, passing through a village he hadn't caught the name of, his plan being to find a cosy-looking pub and stop for a late lunch – something substantial, like game pie or lamb shanks. Something that would tide him over until night-time, if necessary. And it was at this point that he received Karen's call.

'Where the fucking hell are you?' Karen screamed at him. And as he began to stutter out his reply he realized she was crying.

'Karen?'

For a while she couldn't answer.

He could hear the sound of her breath, short and rasping, as if she had developed some sort of respiratory problem. Bronchiectasis, it sounded like, when the walls of the lungs become dilated and full of holes.

'I don't actually care where you are,' she said, quieter now, her tone more measured. 'You need to come home. Brontë has gone.'

'Gone where?' he asked.

'Just gone. We don't know *where*. Your idiot daughter lost her. She took her out and came back without her. No one knows where Brontë is. No one's seen her. I don't know what to do. I don't know what to think.'

'Have you called the police?'

'Of course I have.'

In the lounge, Noel found two police officers, as well as Karen and Verity. He recognized the officers from having attended unexpected deaths as the on-call doctor over the years, but he introduced himself all the same. He shook hands and thanked them for coming so quickly.

'Not a problem, Dr Bloom,' one of them said, and Noel had the sense that he was supposed to know the officer's name. He might be a patient he'd not seen in a while. It wasn't as if Noel could remember everybody.

The other officer – a clean-cut guy in his early forties with a deep tan and a Mr Punch chin – told Noel that they were going through the events leading up to Brontë's disappearance in an attempt to work out what might have happened. And it was at this point that Noel took a proper look at Verity.

She was wedged at one end of the sofa, as far away from the others as she could possibly get, her legs twisted beneath her. Her shoulders were somewhere up near her ears. She was covered in mud and scratches, and her eyes were red-raw and bulging.

Noel moved towards her, crouching down and laying his hand on top of her foot. She was icy cold. 'Hey,' he said, when she didn't look at him.

She dipped her head lower, her eyes focused on the arm of the sofa. 'Hey,' he said again, giving her foot a gentle squeeze, but she shook her head as though she wasn't physically able to meet his gaze. As though he should leave her be.

A couple of tears slid down her cheeks and dripped on to the skin of her chest. He took a clean handkerchief from his pocket and pressed it against the scratch running down the length of her arm; it was beginning to seep. 'How'd you do this?' he asked.

'Looking for Brontë,' she said.

He moved the handkerchief up to her cheek and tried to dry her tears. 'It's okay,' he whispered.

'Okay? *Okay?*'

Karen.

'Why don't you tell us what exactly is *okay* about this situation, Noel?'

Noel didn't have an answer and instead turned his attention back to the two police officers. 'What do we do?' he asked. 'What happens now?'

The first officer told him that Verity was about to provide them with a list of the names of Brontë's friends who were at the recreation ground with her at the time Verity left. At this, Noel did a double-take.

'That's right,' Karen snapped. 'Your daughter left her there. Alone. While she went to visit her bloody mother. She's yet to provide us with an answer as to what was so pressing. Why it was so important to see her mother that she couldn't stay and look after her sister.'

Noel turned to Verity. The tears were falling fast now.

'Verity?' Noel said.

And Verity replied, crying softly, 'She's not a baby. Brontë's not a baby, she's ten years old.'

'But she's *my* baby!' Karen yelled. 'Not yours. The decision was not yours to make. Can't you understand that?'

The tanned officer asked Verity why she hadn't taken Brontë along with her to visit her mother, and Verity hesitated.

'I think I can answer that,' said Karen. 'Verity's mother is sick. She lives at Applemead, and it is full of people with the kinds of disabilities that can be shocking for a child. I have never wanted Brontë to go there. There was never a *need* for her to go there.'

The officer looked at Verity, his expression posing the question: *That the reason?* and Verity nodded, saying, 'Pretty much. And I thought that because she was with her friends, and her friends were playing there on their own, that she was old enough to look after herself for ten minutes. It's not like I left her at a train station. Or in the middle of a city. It's the *rec.*'

The officer told Verity that he was sure Brontë's attention had been caught by something and she had just wandered off.

'Oh, *do*, please, stop saying that,' Karen said. 'Brontë did not *wander off.* And we are wasting time going over this when you should be out looking for her. And when is that detective getting here, anyway? Surely he should have been here by now. You did make the call, didn't you?'

11

J OANNE STOOD OUTSIDE the front door, warrant card in hand, straightening her spine in an attempt to appear more professional than she looked. She wasn't in her usual workwear: of tailored black trouser suit (sometimes grey). Instead she wore a powder-blue linen dress which was cut above the knee; this was partly on account of it being the weekend but mainly because of the heat. The day seemed to be getting hotter as it went on. Unusual for September. It wouldn't be long before she was packing the dress away beneath her bed, along with her sandals and shorts, ready to pull out her winter wardrobe again. She looked around at the pretty front garden, the large bay trees in pots flanking the front door, thinking that soon it would be Christmas. How depressing.

There was a squad car in the driveway – a Freelander – as well as two Volvos with private number plates which Joanne assumed belonged to the child's parents. She was here far too early, of course. The child hadn't been missing more than a couple of hours, and it wasn't protocol to have a detective involved at this stage. Kids tended to turn up. But the mother had been described as 'a stroppy sort', had demanded a detective, and Joanne wasn't exactly doing a lot else, so here she was.

Joanne thought the description was probably a little unfair. The mother would be going insane with worry and wouldn't be at her best. Who would be?

She pressed the doorbell and heard it chime. A jaunty tune

rang out. Joanne really wished people would think longer about these things before they installed them. Back when she was a PC and she was tasked with the responsibility of informing the next of kin of a dead relative, she had encountered a number of these silly-sounding doorbells. The ghastly inappropriateness of what she had to follow them with led Joanne to knock instead.

The door opened, and there stood a uniformed officer who Joanne liked well enough. 'Hello, Dave,' she said quietly, and he invited her to come in.

'Family's in the lounge,' he said.

She hadn't got through the door, hadn't even had the chance to introduce herself, when the woman before her said, 'Who the hell are you?' The violence of her reaction was startling.

'Detective Sergeant Joanne Aspinall.'

The woman was thin, elegant and well groomed. She had the demeanour of a person organizing a smart function rather than that of a desperate mother, and Joanne studied her closely.

'Apologies, apologies,' the woman said quickly. 'I was expecting a man. I didn't mean to be rude. I'm Karen Bloom, Brontë's mother. This is my husband, Noel.'

Joanne gave the stock smile she used for these occasions, murmuring, 'No harm done,' before turning around to the person behind her, who was perched on the edge of the sofa. He stood up and extended his hand, saying, 'Good of you to come, detective,' and his gaze locked on to hers.

Joanne froze.

She was face to face with Seamus. Seamus, whom she'd gone to bed with just six nights previously.

Just to check Joanne wasn't going completely insane, she shot a fast look downwards to examine his hands.

And, yes, the vitiligo was there, evident between his fingers.

Joanne lifted her head and watched as Noel Bloom swallowed

hard. There was panic in his eyes as he waited for her reaction. He was wondering what she was going to do next.

Christ! she thought.

There was an extended moment of silence, a moment of supreme awkwardness that shouldn't really have occurred under the circumstances, but she was floored by the situation in which she found herself.

'Good to meet you, Mr Bloom,' she said eventually, and watched as the fear in his eyes began to dissipate a little.

'It's *Dr* Bloom, actually,' said his wife from across the room. 'Not that it matters. But it is *Dr* Bloom,' and Joanne nodded.

Well, he's married, thought Joanne, so at least she had her answer as to why he hadn't called. So there was that. She had been teetering on the edge of that bleak territory that came with radio silence, when she examined anything and everything that could possibly be wrong with her.

But he was married. Good. No self-flagellation required tonight.

Except she'd had sex with the father of a missing child.

Not good. Not good at all, Joanne.

Noel gestured to a crumpled-looking teen at the far end of the sofa. 'This is my daughter Verity,' he said. 'She was with Brontë when she disappeared.'

The poor kid looked like she'd been the victim of a violent attack. She was scratched to hell, and what should have been a pretty face was hidden behind a mask of terror.

'What Noel means to say,' interjected Karen, 'is that Verity was not with Brontë when she disappeared. She had abandoned her. And that's why we have no clue as to what really happened.'

Okay, thought Joanne. So there was a dynamic at play here that she didn't yet understand. She would need to tread carefully.

'You've checked the surrounding streets? With friends and family?' she asked.

'No one's seen her,' Karen said. 'It's as if she's vanished into thin air.'

'Where was she last seen?'

'The recreation ground. She was by the cricket pitch with a group of girls from school.'

Joanne turned on the spot and addressed Dave, the uniform in the doorway. 'We interviewed these girls yet?'

'Not yet.'

'Let's get some names and talk to them. See if we can figure out where she's got to.'

Not exactly normal procedure, but Joanne asked for a few minutes alone.

Karen Bloom eyed her rather suspiciously, but since Karen had never been part of a missing-child investigation before she could hardly argue it was against police protocol, and showed her into the study. Joanne said she needed somewhere quiet to make a few calls, but in reality she needed to get away from Noel Bloom. Somewhere to gather herself and clear her mind. A place to ready herself to tackle the task ahead.

When he popped his head around the door and asked if she needed anything, Joanne declined. Then he mouthed, 'Sorry,' silently, and Joanne wondered just what exactly he was sorry about.

Sorry he had slipped her one and not called? Sorry he was married? Sorry his kid had gone? Sorry he was now a suspect?

Whatever it was, he *did* look sorry.

Dave had filled her in on the family dynamic – the fact that Karen Bloom was not Verity's mother – and that went some way towards explaining Karen's behaviour. Though, in Joanne's experience, it was unusual for a mother not to blame herself to *some* extent, even if she wasn't at all responsible. Joanne supposed it went with the territory. She'd heard women say that they felt entirely guilty about whatever had happened to their child. *What could I have done to prevent this? What should I have done?*

Odd, then, that Karen seemed to be placing the blame of her child's disappearance squarely on the shoulders of her stepdaughter.

Joanne surveyed the study: large rosewood desk, leather chair. The house was a new build – maybe ten years old – but the decor and furnishings made for a slice of Victoriana. There were a number of photographs on the desk, not put there by Noel Bloom, Joanne assumed, because did men really go to the trouble of sourcing photographs? Buying silver frames? If they did, she'd never met one.

There was a picture of Karen and Noel's wedding – somewhere hot. The Caribbean, most likely. Karen stood with her body angled towards Noel, her head thrown back, laughing. Noel stood square to the camera, smiling but with a slightly puzzled expression, as if he'd been told a joke he didn't quite understand.

There was also a picture of Noel, Karen and Brontë at Disney World. Brontë looked to be around five, Minnie Mouse ears on her head, and Joanne wondered if Verity had been invited on that holiday. Perhaps she was the one holding the camera.

Lastly, there was a picture of Verity alone. A generic school photograph taken recently. The pretty girl was there all right, smiling warmly for the camera, but something in her eyes told you the smile would be dropped the second she was allowed to.

Joanne wouldn't like to be in Verity's shoes right now.

'So, we have a group of officers conducting door-to-door inquiries around the recreation ground. And if Brontë hasn't been found by this evening we'll have a bulletin go out on the late slot of the regional news saying we're concerned for her safety.'

Joanne was in the Blooms' kitchen. Noel had been out searching for his daughter with his stepson, Ewan, to no avail, and he was looking increasingly haggard with every minute that passed. Karen was pacing. She had been pacing for over an hour now, and Joanne knew better than to try to talk her out of it.

Karen stopped and turned towards Joanne.

'That's it?' she said.

And Joanne said she wasn't sure she understood Karen Bloom's question.

'That's all you've managed to arrange in the time you've been here?' she said.

Noel put his arm out towards his wife and touched her shoulder. 'Karen—' he began, but she shrugged him off.

'This is no ordinary child, detective,' she said. 'I'm not sure you understand just how vulnerable Brontë is. She's not *like* other children. She's not been brought up to *be* like other children. She is remarkable in school and a gifted musician, but she does not know how to fend for herself. She absolutely would not go anywhere of her own accord. Someone has taken her. Someone has taken her, and you seem content to sit here, doing nothing at all.'

Joanne took a deep breath.

'Mrs Bloom,' she said, 'right now there is nothing to suggest that an abduction has taken place. Nothing at all.'

Karen stared at Joanne. 'You're wrong.'

'The best thing that we can do is to keep searching for Brontë, and if you can continue calling everyone you know – anyone who has had any contact with her recently, any contact at all – then that is our best—'

'I'm sorry,' Karen said, 'but I really don't think you're getting this. I know my daughter. I know my daughter better than anyone. She would not go to someone's house. She doesn't do play dates. She doesn't do sleepovers. She doesn't have time for any of that. She's a musician.'

'What does she play?' Joanne asked.

'The harp. The piano. Not that it's relevant. Why are you asking me these questions?' shouted Karen. 'Why aren't you closing roads? Searching houses? What are you doing wasting time asking me about this stuff? Do you even know what you're doing?'

'Mrs Bloom, I assure you I—'

'Noel, get me the phone.'

'Karen,' he said, 'don't be—'

'Get me the phone! I'm calling the police. I want someone else. I want someone who actually knows what they're doing. I'm sorry, Noel, but now is not the time for politeness. This is a joke. This woman is a fucking joke.'

12

WHEN SHE WAS little, Verity had been secretly excited by the idea of divorce. She had attended the prep, and everybody's parents there were married. Verity wasn't aware at the time that some of her classmates' fathers were on to their second, sometimes even their third, family; she just thought they were really, really old. Like grandad old. So when her mother first told her about the proposed split, about her father moving out to live with another woman, for a day or so Verity was rather thrilled – though she knew she should be sad. She'd seen films that showed exactly how she should behave: upset, tearful, asking the inevitable 'Is it because of me?' question – which Verity later became quite sure no child had ever uttered in the entire history of divorce.

Her mother and father had sat her down, her dad crying, her mother serious, trying to keep her anger under wraps. And they explained what was going to happen. 'It doesn't mean I don't love you,' her father had said, and Verity remembered thinking, *That never even crossed my mind*. 'It's just that, sometimes, grown-ups run into problems and find it hard to live together.'

Verity was going along with the running-into-problems story when her mother stopped her father mid-sentence. 'Noel. Enough of the crap. Tell her the truth.' And her father gave a long sigh, as if the truth was something he couldn't quite manage.

Her mother sat forward in her chair. 'What your daddy is

trying to say, honey, is that he's met someone else and he likes her more than me.'

'Actually, Jennifer,' her dad cut in, 'that's not quite right, I *don't* like her more than—'

'He likes someone else,' her mother went on, 'a woman called Karen. Who I expect you'll meet soon enough. And this woman is going to have a baby. Your daddy's baby. So I've asked him to leave and go and live with her.'

Verity knew one thing: only married people had babies. So how was her daddy having one with someone else? Someone he wasn't married to?

This paradox continued to confuse Verity. Right up until she learned about sex from a rather gauche girl in school named Clover whose father worked away on the rigs. Clover's mother was very forthcoming about sex. And Clover took great delight in educating her classmates accordingly, adding colourful details here and there. And even after all of her school education, Verity still couldn't say for sure whether the details she'd learned from Clover were true or not.

If the bed is wet, the sperm can swim across the sheets.

If you have sex while you're on your period, then your baby will be born left-handed.

What Verity now understood, though, was that her dad had been having sex with Karen while he was still married to her mother. And as she became older, this did nothing to improve her relationship with Karen. Of course, all things being equal, she should have been just as pissed off with her father, if not more so. Perhaps she was emulating her mother, who, for years, seemed to have reserved a special kind of hatred for Karen but had managed to drop her anger towards Noel fairly early on. Verity still didn't fully understand her own feelings about all of this, and as she sat at the kitchen table, her face in her hands, opposite the detective who Karen had just declared unfit for the job,

Verity decided she would tell her therapist, Jeremy Gleeson, about it at their next session . . . If Brontë came home, that is.

If Brontë didn't come home, then—

'Here's what I need you to do, Verity,' the detective said. 'I need you to start from the moment you left the house. Then tell me everything that happened, up until you realized Brontë was missing.'

'She's already done that,' said Karen.

'Not with me, she hasn't, Mrs Bloom. Verity, go on, what time did you set out?'

'Two thirtyish.'

'And how was Brontë?'

'What's that got to do with anything?' asked Karen.

'Mrs Bloom, please. If you can't let Verity answer for herself, I'm going to have to ask you to leave the room.'

'This is my house, detective. It's my child who's missing. I'm sorry but I'm not going anywhere.'

The detective stared levelly at Karen before turning her attention back to Verity. 'Please go on.'

'Brontë *was* a little upset,' Verity said. 'She was supposed to be having a piano lesson with some guy, but he cancelled. And Karen was annoyed. So Brontë got a bit tearful about the whole thing.'

'This was why you offered to take her to the rec?'

'I wanted to get her out for a while.'

Verity stole a glance at Karen, worried she was going to blow up for making Karen appear partly responsible. Verity watched as Karen opened her mouth to speak, before closing it again.

'What did you talk about?' the detective asked.

'Not a lot. I was teaching her about road safety. Brontë doesn't go out much on her own, and so she's pretty crap at crossing the road.'

'Was she still upset by the time you got to the rec?'

'No,' Verity said. 'She was fine by then. She was happy.'

'Why are you focusing so much on my daughter's state of mind?' Karen demanded. 'What are you suggesting?' She turned to Verity's father. 'For Christ's sake, Noel, can't you do something? Or are you going to stand there, as per usual, and—'

'Mrs Bloom,' the detective said, perhaps a little wearily now, 'I don't know your daughter. And I need to know as much about her as I can. That's it. I don't have any other agenda except finding Brontë. Let me do that, and I'm sure you'll soon have your daughter back.' She didn't wait for Karen to respond, instead turning to Verity.

Verity was impressed. The detective had the patience of a saint, as far as she could see. Karen made a habit of getting people's backs up. In fact, Karen positively enjoyed getting people's backs up – often to the point that they couldn't bear it and had to leave. This woman seemed unaffected, and without Verity really meaning to, because it was very inappropriate, given the circumstances of their conversation, she found herself warming to the detective across the table.

The detective smiled at Verity, giving her a conspiratorial *I'm on your side here* look.

'Has Brontë ever mentioned running away to you?' she asked.

Karen released a bark of nasty laughter. 'Good God,' she said to herself.

Verity said no, Brontë hadn't mentioned running away.

'Ever said she was unhappy at school?' the detective asked.

'She got pretty tired sometimes. She didn't always want to go. But she wasn't unhappy—'

'Brontë does very well at school,' Karen said. 'She has no problems with the work and has always been remarkably popular.'

'What about friends?' the detective asked, again ignoring Karen. 'Are there any in particular? Any that she's close to?'

'Eleanor O'Connor.'

'Was she at the rec?'

Verity shook her head. 'I don't think so. No. I didn't see her there.'

'Okay,' and the detective paused, glancing at Karen before asking this, 'if Brontë *was* to run away – and I'm not suggesting for one moment that she has – where do you suppose she might go?'

But Verity was at a complete loss.

13

Monday, 28 September

Noel was watching his wife sleep. The lights had been left on in the hallway outside their bedroom and he watched as her chest rose, gave a slight judder, then fell again. Her face was tense and twitching. Noel didn't want to imagine what sorts of dreams she was having.

Karen had finally, at around 4 a.m., succumbed to a sleep she neither wanted, nor thought she needed, a sleep she'd been fighting off valiantly up until then. Noel had managed half an hour's slumber at around two, and that would be enough to keep him going throughout the day without feeling like he was one of the walking dead.

Appallingly, Brontë was still not home.

When the police had left the previous evening, Noel hadn't allowed himself to consider the possibility that Brontë would be away for the night. The four of them – Noel, Karen, Verity and Ewan – had sat in front of the TV, watching the presenter on Border News inform them that police were becoming increasingly worried about a missing ten-year-old from Windermere. Anyone with information was encouraged to get in touch. The presenter then adjusted her concerned, mournful expression before moving on to one of the many human-interest stories Border News was so fond of: a charity bike ride to raise funds to renovate a kids' playground; a dog who'd run over a cliff edge on the way up Great Gable found unharmed but dehydrated by a park warden. Nobody spoke as they watched the rest of the bulletin, each one of them thinking: *That's it? That's all you have to say on the matter?*

Ewan and Verity had taken themselves off to bed when they realized that there was nothing now to do except wait around for morning to come, and this had left Karen and Noel in what felt like an eerily empty house. Neither one of them wanted to speculate on where their daughter might be.

Noel had thought things would move faster than they did. He had expected that the detective would coordinate a search of some kind, but she'd said no, that would be done in the morning. *She* would be coordinating it. Karen was made to understand that DS Aspinall would be leading this case, whatever Karen might feel about it. And so Noel had gone out again. He had woken Ewan and taken him with him as Ewan insisted he accompany Noel when he searched. This time, they followed the beck, the stream that ran alongside the recreation ground, which in winter swelled so much it was dangerous for kids to play near but which now, after the spell of dry weather they'd had, was no more than a gentle trickle.

They walked alongside the beck all the way through Sheriff's Wood until it flowed into the lake, casting the beams of their torches along the banks, across the water. Noel's heart stuttered inside his chest whenever he came across a plastic bag, a McDonald's shake container, anything that could be mistaken for his daughter's pale, pale skin.

On their way home, they took a different route. They picked their way through the woodland, shining their torches across the bracken, through the saplings, up high to the branches of the oaks and the ancient elms. Noel felt guilty if he missed even a patch, guilty that he wasn't covering the whole damned area. But mostly he felt guilty that he'd been unable to keep his younger daughter safe.

One of the few roles he felt he had as a father was protector. And he'd not even managed to do that.

After checking the rec one last time, they returned home, beaten. Noel knew the sensible thing to do would be to get some rest so he could do a better job tomorrow, but he hated himself all the same for coming home having found nothing.

Helpless. That's the word parents used when their children were gravely ill. *We feel so helpless*, they'd say, and up until that moment Noel thought he'd understood what it meant to feel that way. Now, he realized he'd been way off. *Helpless* felt like a chasm had opened up inside him and all the usual buoyant feelings had been sucked out, replaced by a great big shitload of nothingness.

*Hope*less was a more apt description.

He reached out and touched his wife's head; the dream seemed to have passed and she looked more peaceful. He wondered how long she'd stay like this. Karen didn't sleep well at the best of times. And he was uncertain whether it would be better to remain here, next to her, ready to try to soothe her when she woke, or if he should go downstairs and straighten up the house for the invasion of people that was scheduled for a few hours' time.

The detective would be back and, not for the first time in his life, Noel hated himself for allowing his dick to get him into trouble. (It hadn't happened often – two or three times at the most, but the repercussions of sleeping with Karen, in particular, seemed considerable.) Consummate professional that DS Aspinall was, though, she had not shown a flicker of recognition in front of Karen. And Noel had found himself a little in awe of how she conducted herself, putting together the beginnings of an investigation. Particularly when Karen was – well, particularly when Karen was being Karen.

Karen's parents would be arriving from Macclesfield. Bruce and Mary Rigby. Bruce was ex-army. He was discharged when he was in his mid-forties and had the idea of using the skills he'd acquired managing soldiers to managing civilians. Within a few years, he'd started and then bankrupted a number of businesses: buying and selling used cars, manufacturing and selling low-fat ice cream. And yet he still saw fit to advise Noel on the financial side of the GP practice he worked in, something that Noel tolerated because, if he didn't, Karen became defensive, accusing him of mocking her father. Which, in a way, he supposed he would be.

Noel didn't enjoy their visits. Bruce was a doer, a man who couldn't sit still, a man who stripped down to his vest to work in their garden and would give Noel chores to do if he caught him standing still. He cut his own hair – number six all over, and would bring his clippers with him and threaten to cut Ewan's, sometimes even Noel's. Noel thought he spoke like a football pundit: *At the end of the day . . . You must give it one hundred and ten per cent . . . In no way, shape or form . . .*

Mary was easier. She was a passive, quiet woman with rolls of soft flesh which her husband would poke as he passed, and legs marbled with blue veins – like Stilton. Mary doted on her grandchildren, and Noel often thought that if he could only pack Brontë off to Mary's for a week, where she could make jam, crochet and watch kids' TV while stuffing her face with marshmallows and chocolate fingers, she would be all the better for it. But that couldn't happen. One, because Bruce would be there, being constructive, repeating the mantra he'd passed down to Karen: *We do the things we have to do so we can do the things we want to do.* Two, because Brontë was gone.

Karen's eyelids flickered, and she scratched the tip of her nose without waking up. Asleep, she was so different. She looked like the type of woman he could have fallen in love with.

At around five years into their relationship, that was a lie he used to tell himself: *She's the woman I fell in love with.*

As though this was a *greater* love than he'd had the first time around, with Jennifer. As though, with Jennifer, he'd sleepwalked into the relationship but, this time, it was *real*. Other men fell prey to this same self-deception, Noel had noticed, when they'd been caught playing away from home. Once they were in a new relationship, they professed to experiencing a deeper, never-felt-before connection, as if to prove to the world that they hadn't made a mistake, they'd not made a total fuck-up but instead it had all unfolded exactly the way it had been supposed to.

Noel worried that, on some level, he was just repeating the failings of his father, a likable, womanizing drunk who was great fun at a party but dead by fifty-five.

Karen murmured in her sleep. He would never leave her. He knew that. In the past few years, they'd reached the stage of leading emotionally separate lives, and the unfortunate strangling episode by Verity had pushed them apart further still, but he had seen the effects of a broken marriage on Verity, and had vowed he would never inflict that sort of pain on another child. And Brontë wasn't as tough as Verity. Or as tough as Verity pretended to be, anyway.

Karen murmured again, her eyelids half lifting, and there was a moment, a tragic moment, when she looked at Noel lazily, almost sexily, when he knew she had forgotten. He tried to smile, to prolong the illusion of normality for a few more seconds, but failed. Her eyes rounded with fear and she sat bolt upright, saying, 'She's not back? She's still not back?' and Noel shook his head, sadly.

'No, love, she's not. I'm sorry.'

Karen was out of bed in an instant, flitting around the room, tidying up as she went. 'I can't believe I slept. I can't believe I slept,' she said, before disappearing into the en suite to shower and clean her teeth. She emerged minutes later, telling Noel that he should have his shower now. 'It's going to be a long day,' she said, and he did as instructed, knowing that to disagree at this point would be counterproductive, if not actually cruel.

As they dressed, Karen didn't mention Verity. But he knew she wanted to. She wanted to unpick the circumstances of Brontë's disappearance, blaming his daughter, as she had yesterday, and he could see it was taking all her restraint not to. She kept taking sharp breaths before letting the words die in her chest. She cast Noel a black look, rolling the words around inside her head, he imagined.

Noel considered telling Karen just to come out with it. To say what she had to say. But he didn't. He took the coward's way out and pretended he couldn't read his wife's thoughts because, in the end, what good would it do, letting her have her say?

A few hours later, when he and Mary arrived, Bruce showed no such restraint, asking Karen immediately, with Noel well within earshot, 'What were you doing, letting that unstable girl be in charge of Brontë?' He'd been in the house for less than thirty seconds, and he'd cut right to the chase. Noel had been on his way to his home office. He'd greeted his in-laws but had drifted out of the kitchen, unnoticed, as soon as he was able. Noel paused in the doorway, craning his ear to catch Karen's response to Bruce's question, but heard nothing. Karen would be mouthing her words, knowing he was listening.

'I hate to say it, Karen,' Bruce went on, his booming, drill-sergeant voice echoing along the hallway, 'but has anyone actually asked the girl if she hurt Brontë? No? Well, why the hell not? She wasn't shy about putting her hands around *your* neck, was she? So why has nobody interrogated her?'

Noel sat down at his desk and rubbed his face with his hands. He could make out the sound of someone trying to shush Bruce. Probably Mary.

'Shut up, woman,' he snapped. 'A child's life is at stake. I will not pander to people's feelings. That girl needs to be questioned. Did you tell the police about her history of mental illness? Did you? Bloody hell, Karen, what's the matter with you?'

Noel's eyes rested on the photograph of Verity. Her eyes seemed sad. How long had she been sad? Probably the whole time she'd lived with Noel and Karen. A girl shouldn't be without her mother, he thought. Fucking MS.

He heard footsteps coming from the room above. Verity's room. She was up. Noel thought he'd better head back to the kitchen and face Bruce himself rather than letting him interrogate Verity alone. That would be carnage. She had not hurt Brontë. You only needed to take one look at her to know that. But Bruce, with his black-and-bloody-white view of the world, would not see it that way. He dealt in facts, as he would proudly declare. *I'm a facts man myself.* It was Bruce's way of dismissing anything anyone had to say that he didn't agree with.

Noel entered the kitchen. Karen and Bruce stood next to one another and Mary was over by the toaster, buttering a plate of crumpets. Mary cast Noel a guilty glance when he came in, but the other two flat-out ignored him, as if he were inconsequential, not part of the discussion.

'Bruce,' Noel said, 'you need to lower your voice. Verity's on her way downstairs.'

Bruce shot Noel an incredulous look.

'She did not hurt Brontë and you know it,' Noel said.

'At the end of the day, I'm afraid I know no such thing,' replied Bruce. 'What I know for certain is that daughter of yours tried to kill *my* daughter. My only daughter. And in my eyes, that makes her more of a suspect than anyone. Now if you want to bury your head in the sand, that's your business, but this is my family, too, Noel. And I won't have you sabotaging—'

'Dad,' Karen said, and she nodded her head towards the doorway where Noel was standing.

Noel turned around and there was Verity, looking worse, if that was possible, than she had the night before. The shadows beneath her eyes were blue bruises and the skin around her cheeks and temples had a greenish hue. She looked ill.

'Morning,' Verity said quietly, and she moved past Noel towards the fridge. 'Hi, Bruce. Hi, Mary.'

Mary smiled. 'Hot crumpets here, if you're hungry, sweetheart,' she said, but Verity shook her head, saying, 'Maybe later, thank you.' She poured herself a glass of milk and drank it standing up, looking out of the window.

Nobody spoke. Noel glared at Bruce, warning him not to start. And Bruce glared back, harder, letting Noel know who had the upper hand here.

'There's no news?' Verity asked, turning to address the room.

Still there was silence.

Fear crept into Verity's dead eyes. 'Has something happened?' she whispered. 'Have you heard something bad?'

'No,' replied Noel.

Bruce cleared his throat.

'Actually, Verity, we were just discussing something.' And he let the words hang momentarily.

'Oh,' she said, looking uneasy. Then, as if something had dawned on her, she said, 'Do you need some privacy? I can leave, if you all need to—'

Bruce held up his palm to silence her. 'It's not that. Stay as you are . . . After some consultation between the four of us, we've decided it might be wise to let the police question you again, Verity.'

'Hang on, Bruce, that's not what we decided,' said Noel.

Verity looked at Noel. 'Dad?' she said weakly.

'In view of what happened,' Bruce went on, 'in view of what happened between Karen and yourself, and since you *were* hospitalized, we think it would be prudent to let the police dig a little deeper into your relationship with Brontë. We really must leave no stone unturn—'

'You think I hurt her?' Verity asked, mouth gaping.

'We're not saying that,' Bruce said.

'You think I could *hurt* Brontë?'

'It doesn't matter what I think,' he said. 'It's getting to the bottom of what actually happened between the two of you that I'm interested in.'

Verity looked at Noel. 'Is he serious?'

Noel sighed, tried to find the right words, but Karen jumped in before he could answer.

'Verity, you need to understand that we're just thinking of all the possibilities. Everything and anything to help the police. I think my dad has a point. We need to be fully transparent so the police have every possible chance of finding her.'

Verity swallowed. Not meeting Karen's eye, she asked, 'What do you think happened to her?'

But Karen wouldn't answer.

14

JOANNE MADE HER way into work. There was a meeting scheduled for six thirty with the acting DI – Detective Inspector Patricia Gilmore – to discuss the Brontë Bloom case. And Joanne was to meet Ron Quigley's replacement – her new partner. She'd been working the Sonny O'Riordan case alone, as there was a period of four weeks between Ron's enforced retirement and when his replacement could start. Joanne assumed she would be pulled from the Sonny case this morning and moved to work on the Brontë Bloom one instead. She'd implied as much to the Bloom family last night, after losing patience with Karen. The woman's persistent questioning of Joanne's abilities and her demand for someone else to be in charge of the case had eventually got the better of Joanne.

Joanne knew she was being unfair in thinking it, given the circumstances, but watching that woman in action she could totally understand why Noel Bloom might need to seek solace elsewhere.

'Joanne, this is DS Oliver Black. Oliver, meet DS Joanne Aspinall.'

DI Gilmore informed Oliver Black that Joanne had experience with missing children and that she would be heading the investigation. Then she told Joanne that Oliver was from Glasgow and had experience in *just about everything*, and left them to get acquainted.

'Fancied a change of pace?' Joanne asked Oliver, and he smiled, mildly, saying, 'No. The wife's from around here,' he explained. 'We have a baby, and she wanted to be near her mother.'

'Oh, okay. Welcome, then. It's good to have you here.'

Oliver Black was around six foot six, thin as a whippet, with dark hair, dark eyes and thick, Parker-from-*Thunderbirds* eyebrows. If she had to guess, she'd say he was an Italian Scot – not simply from his build and features but from the cut of his suit and the way his tie fitted snugly up against the collar of his shirt. Joanne's Aunt Jackie maintained that *all* Italian men knew how to wear a collar and tie (as did Prince Charles, incidentally).

Joanne took a seat, waiting for the meeting to start, and decided then and there that she liked Oliver Black. She'd felt some trepidation about having a new partner, as she and Ron had rubbed along together nicely for years, but then he had announced that his knees were beyond shot and that he felt he was becoming a liability. But as she glanced across to Oliver, watching as he smiled pleasantly at his fellow professionals – no swinging his dick about, trying to compensate because he'd transferred to a position with less prestige than his previous one – she knew they'd get along.

'So, you're aware we have a missing ten-year-old,' DI Gilmore began. 'Joanne was at the house last night. Anything jump out at you straight away, Joanne?'

She shook her head.

DI Pat Gilmore was mid-fifties, with auburn, frizzy curls that she kept secured at the nape of her neck with a large, tortoiseshell clip. It was the type of wild, untamable hair that Joanne reckoned the average girl would have done a fair amount of crying over back in her youth.

'Nothing as yet, ma'am,' Joanne said. 'The girls who were with Brontë Bloom just before she disappeared have been questioned. They all said the same thing. Brontë left the group without saying where she was going and made her way across the recreation ground to the gate on Park Road. After that, they didn't see her.'

'She give a reason for leaving?'

'Just said she was off.'

'Can you see anything beyond this gate from the recreation ground?' DI Gilmore asked.

'No. There's a privet hedge that runs the length of the rec. Once you go through the gate, the road is out of sight.'

'So she could have gone through the gate and got into a car?'

'That's my best guess. No one saw her after she left the rec. If we do a press conference today, then we may get someone coming forward who might have seen her on foot. But as yet, no sightings.'

'CCTV?'

Joanne shook her head. 'It's residential. There are a couple of cameras in Windermere village, by the shops, but that's it.'

'Okay. Get the council cameras checked and see if there's any private footage. Then let's get banging on the doors of all known sex offenders, say within a four-mile – no, make that a six-mile – radius. I'll arrange a press conference for this afternoon. You okay to prep the mother, Joanne?'

'I was going to head over to Brontë's school. But I'll pay a quick visit to the family first, let them know the score.'

DI Gilmore dismissed Joanne and Oliver Black, telling them to press on, while she delegated other tasks to the officers remaining. Patricia Gilmore was on loan from North Cumbria CID until McAleese was fit enough to return to work after his chemo. And though perfectly competent (she had slotted in rather well, in fact), her scant knowledge of the geography of South Cumbria, and her ignorance of day-to-day workings of the area, meant things always took a little longer to get underway than they usually would. Joanne noticed that Pat Gilmore had taken to getting a couple of detectives out on the road, asap, to try to counterbalance this delay. Today those detectives were Joanne and Oliver.

Joanne drove. She didn't give Oliver the option and, if he was at all perturbed by this, he didn't say. He climbed into the unmarked Ford Focus, pushing the seat back as far as it would go to accommodate his rangy frame and his long, long legs, and Joanne shot him a look, and said, 'How do you cope with air travel?'

'I don't. Scared of flying.'

'Really? Why?'

'I think it's the "no escape" part,' he said. 'Anything happens on that plane, you're pretty much screwed.'

'You know it's the safest way to travel,' Joanne said.

'So they say.'

'Doesn't your wife mind?'

'She goes away with her mother.'

'And you stay home alone?'

'Aye.'

'Don't *you* mind?' Joanne was thinking that *she* would very much mind missing out on a foreign holiday. Surely they could do a cruise or something. But Oliver Black cast Joanne a sideways grin and said, 'I don't. Not since the baby arrived, anyhow,' and it struck Joanne that a fear of flying might come in rather useful if you didn't fancy the idea of seven days without a minute's peace.

'How old?' she asked.

'Twenty-two months. Candice is potty training.'

'Candice the baby or your wife?'

'The wife. Esme's the baby.'

'Esme,' Joanne repeated. 'Nice.'

They wound their way past Staveley, through Ings, and were driving along Windermere High Street when Joanne said, 'I should probably prep you about the mother.'

'Okay,' Oliver said.

'She doesn't have a great deal of faith in me. Maybe she'll do better with you around but, yesterday, she wanted me off the job. Of course, she's stressed out to hell, but she's pretty combative, so be on your guard.'

'Noted,' Oliver said. 'And what about the husband?'

'Oh, he's . . .' Joanne paused.

She was about to say – actually, she didn't know what she was about to say, which was rather worrying. So she settled on pretending to adjust her rear-view mirror, before continuing with: 'He's a GP. Seems like a nice enough guy.'

'She's what you'd call unstable,' Bruce Rigby was saying, and Karen was nodding along in agreement. 'Yes, "unstable" is the word I would use. And we think it would be wise to press her a little. Lean on the girl and see what she has to say for herself.'

Karen Bloom's father looked as if he was dressed to go for a run. Kind of. He wore a white vest and cargo shorts, along with a pair of cross-terrain shoes. As soon as Joanne and Oliver arrived he took charge, instructing them on what the best course of action would be, and the interrogation of Verity was right at the top of his list. He didn't trust her, he said. 'Attacked Karen and nearly strangled her to death,' he added. And Joanne wondered why this had not been mentioned yesterday. Not that she thought the girl had killed her sister or anything. Joanne had been doing the job long enough now to know that she got a feeling for people, and she didn't think Verity Bloom had anything to do with the disappearance of Brontë. It just didn't work for her. The girl's guilt and fear were genuine. She had answered everything Joanne put to her sensibly and immediately. No vague answers. No answering a question with a question. No looking down, looking left, looking up. The girl was sincere. She was openly upset at the disappearance of her sister, and Joanne didn't think for a second that she'd harmed her.

But strangling your stepmother?

Interesting.

Joanne assured Bruce Rigby that they would question Verity again later that morning when they returned to do a dry run of the press conference with Karen and Noel. But, for now, she was on her way to Brontë's school.

'School?' Bruce and Karen repeated in unison.

'I need to talk to her teachers. Anyone who's in contact with her day to day. We need to check her locker. See if we can find anything.'

'Oh,' said Karen.

Noel Bloom had remained quiet during all of this, but Joanne was aware of his presence. When Bruce was putting forward his case against Verity, Joanne had glanced towards Noel and seen his jaw working overtime. Can't be easy listening to your father-in-law accuse your daughter of something sinister. But Noel didn't rise to it. He caught up with them when Joanne and Oliver were on their way out of the door. Joanne paused where she was, waiting for him to speak, but Noel shook his head. A silent *no*. Instead, he gestured towards her car: *We'll talk there.*

Once at the car, though, he seemed reluctant to say what it was he wanted to say. Joanne, feeling he might need some help, eased him along by asking, 'You get any sleep at all, Dr Bloom?'

'A little.'

'A tough time for you all,' she said.

Oliver took a step back from them, perhaps sensing that Noel needed some space. And Noel pulled his fingers through his hair and took a breath. Eventually, he said, 'I'm frightened. I'm frightened for Verity. Bruce seems intent on trying to pin something on her and I'm worried you'll waste time looking in the wrong places. Brontë's been gone for over seventeen hours now and—'

'Verity's not my priority,' Joanne said. 'I *will* question her

108

again, later, because I need to. But I don't have her in mind as a suspect.'

Noel blew out his breath, relieved.

And then he did something very silly.

He reached out and, just briefly, touched Joanne's elbow. She found herself staring at her arm at the point of contact.

'Thank you,' he said. 'Thank you, Joanne,'

Once they were inside the Focus, Oliver Black looked over at Joanne quizzically, arching an eyebrow.

'Jo*anne*?' he said, his tone oddly mocking.

'What?'

'He called you Joanne. Not DS Aspinall. You two know each other?'

Joanne shrugged. 'No.'

She turned to Oliver and saw that his eyes were alive with mischief.

'He was quite tactile. Wouldn't you say?'

And Joanne said, 'I really don't know what you mean.'

15

JOANNE INDICATED RIGHT and pulled into the gateway of Reid's Grammar.

'Jesus Christ,' Oliver Black said. And then he was silent in awe, surveying the grounds, as Joanne drove slowly, gravel pinging up inside the wheel arches of the car.

The sweeping driveway bisected a huge front lawn flanked by a low, neatly trimmed box hedge. Over to the left stood a hexagonal bandstand of wrought iron, painted white, with a steeply sloping roof. Next to that was a flagpole on which a huge Union Jack hung limply, unmoving in the still air.

Oliver let out a long, low whistle between his teeth. 'How much?' he said.

'To come here?' replied Joanne. 'Twenty grand a year, or thereabouts.'

Dotted around the grounds were sets of tables and chairs, wooden benches and picnic tables, as if pupils were encouraged to enjoy the grounds, perhaps take tea, as if they were elderly guests at a country-house hotel.

A monkey-puzzle tree stood tall and alone on the right-hand side of the lawn, its trunk surrounded by a circular seat. Upon the seat sat two girls, aged around twelve, and they were reading.

Joanne had telephoned ahead and was told she would be met by the deputy-head teacher of the senior school: Miss Montgomery. And whatever Joanne had been expecting, Miss Montgomery was not it. The name had evoked a wiry woman in a kilt. A Miss Jean Brodie type. But the Miss Montgomery who met them on the front steps was in her early thirties, a clod of adobe foundation covered her skin, and she wore a pair of eighties-style tortoiseshell glasses which took up a large portion of her face.

Miss Montgomery's heels tapped on the parquet floor as she, Joanne and Oliver Black made their way along a lengthy corridor where huge portraits of previous head teachers hung. Each wore a black gown and a stern, formidable expression, as if teaching was not a role to be enjoyed, but endured.

Miss Montgomery said, 'Here we are, then,' and stopped. She gestured to an alcove on the left, a space of around fifteen feet square, with four ladder-back chairs set against one wall. 'Please wait,' she said, and off she went to get the head.

This was all taking too long for Joanne's liking. She needed to talk to Brontë Bloom's teacher, have a quick search through Brontë's things, and then be on her way. But when she'd explained about the missing child on the telephone, she was told she would be escorted around the prep school by the headmaster. *He'll want to be kept fully informed.*

The alcove was panelled in dark oak and the air felt heavy and still. All around her, Joanne could hear the muffled sounds of lessons in progress: the voices of teachers gently rising and falling, the faraway shouts and sounds of a sports lesson.

Then the bell rang and, suddenly, the corridor was filled with students.

A blast of noise hit her as classrooms emptied into the corridor. Pupils moved quickly, talking fast, in accents very different from Joanne's, girls with their long, brown legs, boys with traditional barber haircuts from the forties: short back and sides, but with thick, floppy fringes to be flicked repeatedly.

Oliver caught Joanne's eye and shook his head in amusement.

'Good morning, sir!' came a voice from further along the

hallway, then another, and another. The greeting was said with such respect, such vigour, Joanne found the formality of the thing almost moving. These teachers were actually treated with respect. It was like going back in time.

The corridor began to empty and a tall gentleman appeared wearing a gown over his suit. He carried with him a diary of sorts, or perhaps a hymn book, and held out his hand, firstly, to Oliver, saying, 'I'm Edward Cope. I'm the head here. Terrible business, this thing with . . .'

He paused and Joanne realized he didn't know the child's name.

'Brontë,' she supplied, and he said, 'Yes, yes, of course.'

He gestured towards the far end of the corridor. 'Shall we?'

Joanne and Oliver followed as he marched along, toddling behind like students.

'The prep is attached to the rear of the senior school,' he explained. 'You *can* reach it from our second entrance, but I felt it was important to take you through there myself. What more can you tell me about what's happened?'

'Very little,' answered Joanne.

He slowed, frowning at Joanne, then he began examining her as though trying to work out if she was being purposefully evasive. If she was, he wasn't at all happy about it.

'We have very little to go on,' she explained.

'Ah,' he said, picking up the pace again.

At the end of the corridor they turned right. 'I'm afraid I can't tell you anything either,' said the head. 'I have very little interaction with the pupils of the prep. But I have had some dealings with her older sister.'

'Verity,' said Joanne.

'Yes. She's had a few problems of late, but we've been supporting her through her difficulties. A bright girl.'

'Yes,' agreed Joanne.

'But troubled.'

They passed closed door after closed door. Each contained a small square of fireproof glass, and Joanne stole a quick look through them and was surprised at how well behaved the children were. Each child sat tall in their seat, eyes to the front of the class.

They passed another classroom and then they came to some double doors. The head punched in a code and after walking through they found themselves in a pretty courtyard.

Rosemary and thyme grew in elegant beech planters. 'Made by our students in wood tech,' the head informed them. A mosaic of the monkey-puzzle tree found in the front grounds covered part of the wall. 'Ex-pupil. Very talented. At St Martin's now.' They crossed the courtyard to the prep, which had the same formal feel to it as the senior school, but now the sounds of children were audible. Some were singing, some reciting poetry. A piano was being played somewhere and the air smelled of buttery biscuits.

The head signalled for them once again to follow him, before stopping outside the second classroom on the left. 'We don't want the children upset by your presence here,' he said sternly. 'That's the most important thing. We don't want them thinking that a child-snatcher is on the loose and have them frightened in their beds. Is that clear?'

'And if there is a child-snatcher on the loose?' Joanne asked.

'Well, he didn't take her from *this* school. As I understand it, she was taken from near her own home. So there is no need for these children, or their parents, to become hysterical.'

She nodded. She got it. *Do not tarnish the reputation of Reid's Grammar in the course your investigation.*

Joanne took out her notepad. 'Where were you between two and three o'clock yesterday afternoon, Mr Cope?' she asked him.

Edward Cope stuck around for a short while, overseeing Joanne's interaction with Brontë's class teacher, standing over the shoulders of the young students, commenting on their work, offering gentle encouragement, as though it were something he did all the time. From the kids' reactions, though, it was clear that he did *not* do it all the time. They were anxious. They weren't sure how to behave with him in such close proximity.

Brontë's teacher was young. Miss Lucy Gilbert looked to be around twenty-one and Joanne suspected this was her first gig after graduating. She was a bundle of nervous energy, answering each of Joanne's questions with round eyes while breathing in short, sharp gasps, as if she'd been plunged into freezing water.

Joanne touched Miss Gilbert's shoulder briefly, whispering that she had nothing to worry about, and might she want to settle herself, otherwise her pupils would sense her unease? Grateful for the advice, Miss Gilbert took a couple of breaths to steady herself before leading Joanne and Oliver to Brontë Bloom's tray, pulling it out for them so they could examine the contents.

'I'll take this out there if that's okay,' said Joanne, motioning to the corridor beyond the classroom, 'and let you get on with your lesson. If you could just point us in the direction of her locker? And perhaps you could join us in ten minutes or so and answer a few questions about Brontë?'

Miss Gilbert nodded repeatedly, and checked her watch, before leading them into the corridor. She scanned the lockers, looking for Brontë's name. 'Here,' she said.

When she'd left, Joanne removed the contents: three empty water bottles, a pair of soft plimsolls, a scrunched-up white polo shirt with the school's logo on the breast and a pair of navy gym shorts.

'Anything?' Oliver asked.

'Nothing.'

She moved on to the tray. It was stuffed full of photocopied activity sheets, along with scrap paper used for drawing. Joanne examined each of the drawings for anything out of the ordinary, but all she saw were the efforts of a not particularly skilled ten-year-old who liked to sketch rabbits. Some stood upright and wore outfits.

Joanne sifted through the detritus – a few sweet wrappers, pencil shavings, a sock, until her eyes landed on three pieces of A4 at the bottom of the tray. They had been folded in half, fashioned into makeshift greeting cards. The front of each was decorated with hearts – again, badly drawn. Brontë had not yet got the hang of the shape and the hearts were elongated, stretched, each one out of proportion and kind of sad-looking. But they had been done lovingly, each in a different shade, and with adornments of dots or trailing ribbons.

Joanne opened the first one. Inside were the words: 'You are the best person I know.' No signature. So Joanne would need to check if this was Brontë's handwriting, or if she was the recipient of the card. In the second was written: 'Thank you for being kind.' And in the third: 'You make my heart happy.'

Oliver read the cards and said, 'What d'you reckon?'

'If she made these they were done recently. They're clean compared to the rest of the junk in here. She must have hidden them at the bottom of the tray so they wouldn't be found. She clearly likes *somebody*, that's for sure.'

Oliver nodded.

'And . . . I may be way off here,' Joanne said, 'but I'm guessing these cards were not made for her mother.'

Joanne presented the cards to Miss Gilbert, and they compared the writing in Brontë's project exercise book (currently, the Second World War; before that, the Amazon rainforest), and there was no doubt they were written by Brontë. 'For any reason in particular? An art project?' Joanne asked, and Miss Gilbert said no.

'She's made these in her spare time. Sometimes, at the end of the day, I allow free drawing time – she must have made them then.'

'Any idea who they're for?'

Miss Gilbert screwed up her face as she tried to think. 'I can't imagine they're for a boy. Brontë seems very innocent to me, and not interested in boys. But I've only taught her for a few weeks, so I couldn't say for certain.'

'Bright, though,' Joanne said. 'Her mother says she's a very gifted student.'

'Bright?' repeated Miss Gilbert.

'Yes. Bright,' said Joanne.

Miss Gilbert looked uneasy at this, turning around to check over her shoulder as the classroom door was open.

She shook her head.

'Not so bright, then?' asked Joanne, surprised.

'I'm afraid not,' Miss Gilbert said, rather guiltily. 'But she *is* a lovely, pleasant girl. Very quiet. And she has a problem with her hand at present, which I think has affected her confidence. I understand from her previous teacher that Brontë *used* to be more outgoing, more chatty. But she became a little withdrawn around the time Mrs Bloom clashed with her teacher over some issues, mostly to do with Brontë's education. Mrs Bloom also abused the support staff on a number of occasions – to the point that she is now allowed to speak to a teacher or a classroom assistant only if there is a third party present.'

'Can I speak to this teacher?'

'She accepted a post in Germany.'

'Have you had any run-ins with Karen Bloom yourself?'

'Not yet, thank goodness. But she did make it clear at the start of term that Brontë's education was a priority to her. She wants very much for her daughter to succeed and to do well at Reid's. She told me she was prepared to do anything to ensure this and said she was happy to do extra work at home with Brontë. If I could provide her with some.'

'And did you?'

'I didn't get around to it straight away, and so I believe Mrs Bloom employed a tutor for Brontë instead.' Miss Gilbert closed her eyes briefly before exhaling. 'Listen,' she said, 'Karen Bloom is particularly motivated. Far and above any of the other Reid's parents, I'd say. But to be honest, they all ask for extra work for their children.'

'Who? The parents?' asked Joanne.

Miss Gilbert nodded. 'The poor kids really don't get a minute to themselves.'

16

KAREN BLOOM GLARED at the two detectives. Joanne could feel her thinking: *Idiots. Both of you.*

'How the hell should I know?' Karen said. 'Love letters and hearts? Isn't that what all little girls do? Scribble boys' names and draw love hearts?'

'Brontë's never mentioned a crush?' Joanne asked.

'No, Brontë never mentioned a crush, because there *was* no crush. She's ten years old. She doesn't talk about boys. She's not interested in boys.'

Joanne took the home-made cards from Karen's hand and slipped them inside a plastic wallet. Then she told Karen that, rather than hold a full press conference, DI Gilmore now wanted to have Noel and Karen interviewed in their own home. She wanted to record an appeal with only a couple of journalists, to get the message out straight away. 'How do you feel about doing it this way?' Joanne asked.

'Fine,' replied Karen.

'We'll need to run through it first, go over what would be best to say to—'

'I've seen these things on television, detective. I'm not stupid.'

'I know that, Mrs Bloom. But we do have a particular way we like these appeals to go, so if you wouldn't mind—'

Karen waved Joanne's comments away with her hand. 'Whatever you want me to do, I'll do it. Just arrange it.'

Two of Joanne's contemporaries were coordinating a search party which would begin at the recreation ground. She understood that there had been a good turnout – word had spread fast within the community, neighbours had turned up to volunteer, and both Noel and Karen wanted to be part of it. But Joanne had told them not to join the search party just yet. She needed them nearby for two reasons, firstly to record their statements so they could be circulated to the press, and secondly so she could observe their behaviour.

Karen was not conforming to type. She was not acting in the way you would expect the mother of a missing child to act.

Did this make her guilty of something?

Absolutely not.

But it did stir Joanne's interest because, as yet, Karen Bloom had not lost control. Sure, the woman was frayed and frightened, barking out commands at anyone within hearing range, but she'd not yet openly cried for her child.

Perhaps it would happen when she was on camera. Because, with the exception of one, maybe two, Joanne had never witnessed a parent of a missing child make it through to the end of an appeal without breaking down. Not that Joanne *wanted* to break this woman. She just thought her behaviour odd. And of course, if *she* thought it odd, so might the general public.

Which is what made these appeals risky.

Ultimately, though, what choice did they have? A child was missing. The appeal would have to go ahead whether Joanne deemed Karen Bloom suitable for the job or not.

The telephone rang and Karen shot out of the kitchen to answer it.

'Wait,' said Joanne, and Karen looked at her, appalled.

'*Wait?*' Karen said. 'I won't wait. What if it's Brontë?'

'You can answer, Mrs Bloom, but put it on speakerphone.'

Karen nodded and picked up. Before saying hello she switched on the speakerphone and held the handset out in front of her, practically brandishing it at Joanne.

'Hello?' she said shakily.

And the caller could be heard: a throat clearing.

'I'd like to speak to Mr or Mrs Bloom, please.'

A woman. A woman with a low, gravelly voice and an accent Joanne couldn't immediately place. Norfolk, perhaps? Joanne wasn't sure.

'Who is this?' Karen asked.

'Am I speaking to Mrs Bloom?'

Karen looked to Joanne for direction and Joanne nodded her assent.

'This is Mrs Bloom,' Karen said, holding the handset nearer to her mouth now, to make certain the caller could hear her clearly.

'I have important information for you regarding your daughter, Mrs Bloom.' At this, Karen started to shake. Her hand vibrated so violently that Joanne stepped forward, ready to take the phone from her if necessary.

'Go on,' managed Karen.

'My name is Deena Morgan, and let me say how sorry I am that you and your family are suffering in this way.'

The caller paused, and there was a moment of silence. 'Thank you . . .?' Karen said cautiously.

'I have received information about the whereabouts of Brontë, and—'

'Where is she?'

'Mrs Bloom, I—'

'Where is she? If you know where she is, don't make me wait. Please,' she said, her voice cracking. 'We really can't wait any longer.'

'I understand how terrified you must feel, and that's why I felt compelled to speak with you.'

Joanne took out her mobile phone and pressed record. She made a circling action with her left index finger, instructing Karen to keep going, to keep the caller on the line.

The caller said, 'First, I must tell you, Brontë is alive.'

And Karen's eyes spontaneously filled. 'Thank God!'

'She's alive, but she is very scared, Mrs Bloom. And it's important that you get her home quickly.'

'I want to. I need to. But where is she? We don't know where she is.'

'She is surrounded by trees.'

'Okay.'

'She is alone and surrounded by trees and she is very scared, Mrs Bloom.'

'Help me find her, please! That could be anywhere. I don't know where to start. I don't know where to look. If you know where she is, then you must—'

Karen stopped. Then she frowned.

'There's water nearby,' said the caller hurriedly. 'A small body of water in which I can see Brontë's reflection. She's calling out to you, Mrs Bloom.'

Joanne let her arm fall to her side just as Karen's face hardened.

She brought the phone closer to her mouth and spat out the words: 'Who is this?'

'Mrs Bloom,' the caller stammered, 'I'm here to help. I can locate your daughter, I'm certain of it. But I need something of hers – clothing, a hairbrush, a favourite toy—'

'Drop dead.'

'Mrs Bloom, please, I—'

'Get. Off. The. Fucking. Line.'

'I know I can find her.'

'Get off the line, you stupid, crazy bitch. Get off the line before I find out where *you* live and shove your crystal ball down your throat!'

Karen replaced the handset with a trembling hand and turned to Joanne.

'What the hell happened there?' she asked, and Joanne said, 'I should have answered. I'm sorry.'

'But how did she know how to reach us?'

'You need to expect more of these,' Joanne said. 'It's normal.'

'Normal? How can that be normal?'

'These kinds of cases attract all sorts of oddities. She won't be the last.'

'But how did she get my number?'

Joanne shrugged helplessly. 'I assume they comb the regional news agencies looking for stories and track people down via the BT website. Like I said, there'll be more. The best you can do, Mrs Bloom, is ignore them. Treat them like telesales callers – which is essentially what they are. That woman will be calling someone else by now, someone who's lost a dog . . . or a wedding ring.'

Joanne thought about forewarning Karen Bloom about the religious zealots who'd be busy copying out passages from the King James Bible, ready to send along for her to read. But, for now, she decided against it.

Almost twenty hours since Brontë had disappeared, and Joanne was preparing Noel and Karen Bloom for the broadcast. 'Firstly, you appeal for your daughter's return,' Joanne began, 'and this is better if it comes from you, Mrs Bloom.'

Karen nodded.

'You want to keep it open. You want to look into the camera and ask Brontë to come home, as if you are speaking directly to her.'

'But she hasn't run away.'

'Even so, tell her she's not in any trouble and you just want her back safe with her family.'

'But—'

'Mrs Bloom, this is how we need you to do it. Once you've asked Brontë to come home, then you appeal to the public, say that if anyone knows where she is, please could they contact the police. Say whatever comes naturally to you at this point. Say you're desperate to have her home, but in your own words. Then DI Gilmore will make a short statement assuring anyone with information that they need not give their name to the police.'

'Okay,' replied Karen. 'I can do that. But what if I become too upset to speak?'

'Dr Bloom can take over. To be frank, though, Mrs Bloom, if you become tearful you'll attract the attention of viewers, and that's really what we want right now. We need people to stop what they're doing and watch. Keep it simple. Tell Brontë you love her and you need her home.'

Which is exactly what Karen did.

Joanne had harboured doubts about Karen Bloom's ability to appear like an average mother, desperate for her child's return. She'd thought her aggressiveness might surface and that she might very well lose it. But she remained calm, tearfully requesting the general public's assistance in the safe return of Brontë, doing exactly as she had been instructed. It went more smoothly than expected, and the segment would be aired on the one o'clock news. It was all going according to plan, all going so well, until Oliver Black found Joanne and gave her the news. She was on the phone in Noel Bloom's home office, on a call about a potential witness.

'Joanne, we have a problem.'

Joanne raised her finger, signalling to Oliver to wait a moment, while she copied down the details being given to her.

House-to-house had turned up a woman, an elderly woman, a resident of Applemead Cheshire Home, who had information on the disappearance of Brontë.

Oliver stood in the doorway, his head dipped slightly, his face grave.

'What kind of problem?' Joanne asked, putting down the phone.

Oliver beckoned her to follow him.

Joanne caught sight of Karen. 'Bloody hell,' she said to Oliver, and rushed across the lawn. Oliver told her he'd tried to pull Karen away, but to no avail.

Karen Bloom was surrounded by TV people. Someone held a microphone beneath her chin, and Karen's face was flushed and contorted as she spoke. There were three cameras on her and Joanne did not want to be in the shot, so she tried to catch Karen's attention, gesturing from behind the camera people. It was fruitless. It was a one-woman show. Karen was staring down the lens of a camera, the merest hint of madness in her eyes. She was speaking directly to the viewers, just as Joanne had instructed her to when pleading for the safe return of Brontë.

'I know what you're thinking,' she was saying. 'You're thinking we're one of those impoverished families you see on the news. Appealing for help when, all the while, they've hidden their child's battered body in the shed. Or the attic. Well, we are *not* one of those families. We love our child. This is not some council-estate case. This is a cherished child who's gone missing.'

'Do the police have any leads at this stage?' a female reporter asked.

'None,' she said. 'As of yet, they have no idea what happened to my daughter, and I can only assume Cumbria police are woefully unprepared for this type of incident. It's a shambles. An absolute shambles.'

Joanne thought she could feel rain.

17

NOEL KNOCKED TWICE and waited.

When there was no reply, he called out her name, softly, so as not to spook her. Verity had gone back to bed. She had not gone to school today.

Still no answer, so he knocked again before trying the handle. The door gave way and Noel stepped inside, into the darkness. He couldn't yet make out the shape of the bed, the desk whose sharp corner was in the habit of attacking the side of your leg if you strayed too close.

Noel stood glued to the spot, hesitant to advance further.

'Verity, love,' he whispered. 'You still in here?'

Verity's room caught the morning sun. This hadn't bothered her until she turned fourteen and then she had declared it impossible to sleep in. He'd had blackout blinds fitted, expertly, evidently, as he could barely make out the bed as he made his way towards it.

'Verity,' he whispered again, reaching out and patting the covers, finding what felt like his daughter's leg.

Now there was movement. And a second later, light, the room suddenly illuminated as Verity switched on the bedside lamp.

Earbuds in, Verity looked at him, her expression wary, frightened. He gave her a reassuring smile, mouthing, 'It's okay,' as she cut the sound from her iPod. Her cheeks were flushed a baby pink and he suspected she'd been lying with her duvet pulled right up, covering her face, in an attempt to shut out the world.

'You're hiding up here, then?' he asked, and she nodded. 'Okay if I sit down?'

Verity wriggled herself into a sitting position. She was still in her pyjamas, her hair in a tatty knot. She looked just like her mother. Jennifer used to fashion her hair in a similar way: piled high on top of her head, sometimes secured with a pencil.

'Have you eaten?' asked Noel.

'No.'

'You should, you know. You should really try to—'

'Have *you* eaten?' she asked accusingly.

'No,' he admitted. ' . . . Can't face anything right now.'

Verity hung her head. 'Me neither.'

There was so much he wanted to say. His daughter was in pain, and he wanted to fix it, take it all away. He wanted to say, 'Don't worry. It'll turn out okay,' like he usually did when she was distressed. 'In a week or two you won't remember what you were worrying about,' he would say, and this would bring her comfort. Because, usually, it was true.

'They blame me,' Verity said.

'No,' replied Noel. 'It's not that. Karen and Bruce are not blaming anyone. They're scared.'

'They blame *me*,' she said again, crying now.

What could he say? They did blame her.

'They're right to blame me,' she went on. 'I shouldn't have left her. I should have stayed with her. What if Brontë never comes home? What if—'

Noel put his arm around his daughter. 'Shhhhh,' he whispered. 'Stop this.'

'She'll be so scared, Dad. She's not used to being without one of us. She's going to be so frightened . . . I read about a girl and this freak took her and locked her in a cellar and made her do—'

'When did you read this?'

'This morning. I searched "kidnapping", and don't tell me I

shouldn't have, because I know I shouldn't have, but I just needed to know *something*. I needed to know what could have happened to her.'

'No. No, you don't need to know that.'

'I feel so bad. I feel like I've got this huge stone in my stomach. But I feel like if I know what she might be going through, then maybe it won't be quite so bad for her. Like I'll be able to under-stand . . . and, maybe, if she *does* come home, I might be able to help her.'

Noel held Verity a little away from him. 'Promise me you'll stay away from that stuff. You have to, Verity. Promise me.'

'But what if she's already dead?' she cried. 'What if she's dead and we don't know it?'

'She's not.'

'But she's so small, Dad.'

'I know.'

'She'll be so frightened.'

'I know.'

'What if they don't find her?'

'They will.'

He held on to his daughter again, as she wept in his arms.

18

'THERE'LL BE REPERCUSSIONS, of course,' Joanne said to Oliver Black as she swung the Focus out of the Blooms' gateway and drove down the hill towards Applemead.

They could have walked. It was only a few hundred yards.

And Joanne *should* walk more. It was one of the few things she disliked about her job – the fact that it was almost completely sedentary. She had thought she covered quite a few miles in a day. In and out of the car, never standing still for long. She'd felt quite complacent when she had uploaded the step-counter app on to her phone, thinking she'd easily be covering more than the advised ten thousand paces.

In fact, she achieved less than two thousand, which was a total disgrace. If she stayed at home watching daytime TV she'd clock up more than that hunting for the remote control.

'What do you suppose made Karen Bloom go and say a thing like that?' Oliver asked.

'You mean, "This is not some council-estate case"?'

Oliver nodded.

'She *is* a bit bonkers. But I can see her way of thinking. She hopes that by pointing that out to the general public they won't be dismissive about Brontë's disappearance, they'll take it seriously. Which they probably will now. Trouble is, they'll hate her for it. Nothing worse than saying, "My child is more important than your child because we've got money." '

'Do you think you should warn her of the repercussions?'

Joanne shrugged. 'Probably.'

Joanne hadn't been inside Applemead before. Her aunt had been employed there for a couple of years now, after becoming tired of working in community care. Actually, that wasn't quite right. Jackie had loved community care, but the younger members of staff had become woefully unreliable, and Jackie would find herself covering for those who'd failed to turn up, often doing back-to-back shifts.

And she wasn't getting any younger.

Jackie also had a crap pension, no savings and a large debt she didn't like to talk about. So, short of a miracle, Jackie would be staying put in Joanne's spare bedroom until well into her retirement.

Not that Joanne minded.

Well, sometimes she minded.

Oliver pressed the bell, and the door was opened by an immaculately dressed gentleman of around eighty, carrying an ivory-handled walking cane. Joanne presented her warrant card, and the man told her he was a volunteer. 'Would you like to follow me through to the office?' Joanne cast about for any signs of Jackie but she didn't see her.

They waited outside the office, where a rather shrill-sounding lady was speaking on the telephone. 'I appreciate it's not an ideal situation, but it's proving very difficult to keep the two of them apart. They say they're quite in love . . . No, we're not allowed to lock service users inside their bedrooms . . . Yes, I know it's dreadfully upsetting, especially with your mother so recently deceased, Mrs Biddle . . . I do understand, honestly I do, but . . .'

The speaker tried to placate Mrs Biddle with more words of apology before ending the call. Joanne heard her sigh weightily before presenting herself to the detectives.

Smoothing down her pleated, Black Watch tartan kilt, she

said, 'So sorry to have kept you, but this is turning out to be one of those days.' She introduced herself as Esther George. She had a nervous smile, and said it was she who had made the call to South Cumbria CID about the witness, Winnie van Breeda.

'Winnie's fairly lucid today,' she told them, 'but she has good days and bad days.'

'Dementia?' asked Joanne, and Esther nodded.

'She's quite the character,' she said.

They followed Esther George along a prettily decorated corridor: antique occasional tables, tasteful prints on the walls – not at all institution-like – and made their way into a lounge at the back of the building. It was full of plants and books. There was no television. Winnie van Breeda sat alone in the bay window, gripping her handbag to her, as if there might be a thief on the loose.

There had been no mention of dementia when Joanne received the call about this witness, but she tried to remain positive. Most witnesses got things wrong anyway. White men became black. Beards became sunglasses.

People didn't set out to deceive, but their memories were unreliable, especially when there was high emotion involved. So Joanne had learned to take descriptions with a pinch of salt, and it wasn't until a set of features had been corroborated by two or three witnesses that she would take it seriously.

'Winnie, here are the detectives I told you about,' Esther George said loudly.

No reply. Winnie eyed them with distrust, pulling her handbag in a little tighter.

Winnie's fine hair had been fashioned into a bun on the top of her head, but there wasn't enough hair to hold it there. Joanne could see her scalp. It was covered in age spots and there was a dark, raised, circular mole above her right ear, the size of a five-pence piece. The kind the BBC website tells you to have checked by your GP but not to get unduly worried about.

'How are you today, Mrs van Breeda?' Joanne asked, thinking she may as well try to get the woman to talk, since she was here.

'Dying,' Winnie replied dryly.

Esther George huffed in mock-annoyance and bent at the waist, squeezing Winnie's elbow with her hand. 'You are most definitely not dying, Winifred van Breeda. You are in the best of health. Now shush with all that nonsense.'

Winnie threw Joanne and Oliver a pained look as if to say, *See what I have to put up with?* Esther babbled on, saying, 'Now, Winnie, you need to tell the police officers exactly what it was you saw when the little girl went missing yesterday.'

Winnie shook her head.

'Please, Winnie,' pressed Esther. 'They really need to find her. They need your help.'

But Winnie stood firm; she was not going to talk.

'How about *you* tell us what Mrs van Breeda said?' Joanne suggested to Esther.

'She didn't tell me anything. That's the problem. After one of your officers showed her a photo of the child, she later told a member of staff that she saw who took the girl. But when I questioned Winnie about it, she refused to talk.'

'Did she tell the member of staff what, exactly, she saw?'

'No.'

'Okay,' said Joanne. 'Then we have a problem.'

Joanne glanced around the room, hoping that an answer to their dilemma might present itself. When her eyes drifted back towards Winnie van Breeda, Joanne saw that the woman was staring right at her. Staring intently, as if trying to will some information across the space between them.

Joanne smiled. She tried to make Winnie feel more at ease with her presence and, in return, Winnie angled her head towards Esther, narrowing her eyes and thinning her lips.

She wanted Esther out of the room.

'Would it be possible to get some tea?' Joanne said to Esther. 'If it wouldn't be too much trouble. It might just settle Mrs van Breeda enough to talk.'

'Tea? Of course. I'll need to find another body to replace me, though. We don't allow our vulnerable service users to be alone for longer than a moment with people they don't know.'

Esther left the room, and Joanne took out her notepad. When she looked at Winnie, she saw that she was smiling triumphantly.

'Are you ready?' Joanne asked, and Winnie said, 'I am.'

Winnie shifted in her seat, straightening her spine as if readying herself for a job interview, then uncrossed her ankles, before asking Oliver if he would mind placing the footstool beneath her feet. Oliver obliged, and Joanne got the sense that Winnie was enjoying the attention.

'You're a handsome man,' she said to Oliver as he squatted by her knees. 'A very handsome man, indeed. Are you married?'

'I'm afraid I am.'

'And is she good to you?'

'Very,' he said.

Joanne heard footsteps in the hallway and turned to see Jackie enter the room. Her aunt looked harried. Her face was slick with sweat and she had a tea towel slung over her forearm. 'Will this take long?' she asked, and Joanne was about to tell her she wasn't sure how long it would take, was about to introduce her new colleague, when Winnie said to Jackie, 'Oh, it's *you*. I don't want *you*.'

Jackie remained impassive, as if she'd heard all this before.

'Why don't you want me, Winnie?' she asked, goading.

'Because I don't like your face.'

'Well, that's not very nice. It's the only face I've got. It's not like I can change it, can I?'

'Well you should, because it's appalling,' said Winnie, folding her arms.

Jackie shook her head and sank down heavily on the sofa

opposite. She used the tea towel to dab at her forehead. 'You need to be firm with her,' she warned Joanne. 'Be firm with her, or she'll run rings round you. Used to be a schoolmistress. Didn't you, Winnie?'

Winnie scowled in the direction of the window.

'Bet you were a real tyrant with those poor kids, weren't you?' Jackie said.

'I shan't speak to you, you vulgar woman,' said Winnie.

'Good,' replied Jackie.

Joanne raised her eyebrows at Oliver. 'Meet my aunt,' she said, and Oliver smiled in Jackie's direction. They were getting nowhere fast. Perhaps Oliver should try questioning Winnie, since she seemed so charmed by him.

Joanne gave Oliver a look to indicate: *Your witness?* and he nodded his assent, taking a seat in the high-backed chair next to Winnie.

'Mind if I ask you a couple of things, Mrs van Breeda?' he said, and, of course, she was all smiles.

'Not in the least,' she answered.

Joanne could hear Jackie tutting from across the room.

'Yesterday, when Brontë disappeared, you say that you saw—'

'*Who?*'

'Brontë Bloom,' replied Oliver. 'The missing girl.'

'They called her *Brontë*?' Winnie asked incredulously. 'After Charlotte Brontë?'

'Or Emily,' supplied Joanne.

Winnie snapped her head around and gave Joanne a glare. 'I always preferred *Jane Eyre*. Cathy Earnshaw was a silly fool, and I had little time for her.' Then she said, 'They *really* called her Brontë?'

'Yes,' replied Oliver patiently. 'They really did.'

'Fools themselves, then,' she said.

'So can you tell us what you saw yesterday afternoon?' asked Oliver again.

'Certainly. I was in the drawing room at the front of the building, sitting at the window, watching the world go by, as I often do after my afternoon cup of tea. The child you're talking about came out of the park gates and stopped to talk to someone.'

'How do you know the child was Brontë?' Joanne interrupted.

'Because I saw her photograph. How else do you suppose I knew it was her?' She rolled her eyes at Joanne's idiocy before continuing. 'They talked for some time, and I was quite taken aback, because they seemed to be on familiar terms, and I thought this unusual. So you could say my interest was piqued, and I watched the two of them intently for as long as they remained there.'

'And would you know this person if you were to see them again?' asked Oliver.

'I would. I'd recognize her anywhere.'

Joanne felt the first stirrings of excitement.

'Do you know this person's name, Mrs van Breeda?' Joanne asked, thinking that, if they had a name, they were home and dry. She could have Brontë Bloom home within the hour.

Winnie van Breeda sat up a little taller in her seat.

'I most certainly do know her name,' she answered proudly.

Joanne held pen to paper in readiness.

'She is the Queen of England,' said Winnie.

19

FLEETINGLY, NOEL THOUGHT about his patients. He had called his partner, John Ravenscroft, just before six that morning, to tell him of Brontë's disappearance and that he wouldn't be at work. John typically rose sometime around 5 a.m., so Noel knew he'd be awake. John had remained uncharacteristically silent after Noel had imparted the news, and for a moment Noel wondered if he'd passed out from the shock.

'John? You there?' he'd asked, and John had answered solemnly, 'I'm here. Just haven't got any words for you, I'm afraid.'

'There are no words.'

There was a locum they used in case of absences, Leonie Merritt. She was a plump, pleasant, horsey type from Keswick who smelled of hoof oil and wore old fleeces covered with animal hair. She'd given up full-time general practice when her fifth child was born, but she was happy to cover for absentees, as long as it wasn't for more than a few days a month. The patients complained about her, though. Not because she was lacking but because they still stubbornly clung to the notion of a family doctor being available twenty-four/seven, all year round.

Noel wondered which patient she was treating now.

There was a knock at his home-office door. 'Come in,' he said, and Joanne Aspinall appeared. He'd been told she had gone to interview a potential witness.

'Any joy?' he said.

'An unreliable witness, as it turned out.'

Noel's heart sank further. He wanted to thank her for trying, but it seemed superfluous.

Joanne took a step forward before closing the door behind her. 'I wondered if I might have a word about something.'

'Let me,' he said, realizing that this was overdue. And it really wasn't good form to let this go unsaid any longer, regardless of the god-awful crisis he had on his hands. 'I owe you an apology. I shouldn't have lied about my identity and I certainly shouldn't have spent the night with you. Obviously, you can see that I'm married, and I'm very sorry. And I'm sorry you find yourself here in the midst of all this after what happened between us.'

Joanne raised her eyebrows. 'I was going to say that we need to re-interview Verity.'

'Ah.'

'But thanks for the apology. Though it really wasn't necessary.'

'I think it was.'

'I wasn't completely truthful myself,' she said.

'Wait. What? Are you married, too?'

Joanne smiled and shook her head, 'No. I'm not married.' And there was a moment. An odd, awkward moment. A flicker of something in which Noel sensed they were both thinking the same thing: perhaps if this had happened at another time, another place . . .

Joanne dipped her head. Noel saw the way she threaded her hair behind her ear when she thought she was being watched. The way she instinctively pulled her jacket close around her body to preserve her modesty.

'Well, I appreciate your discretion,' he stammered on. 'I know it can't have been easy being faced with me when you arrived yesterday, and I'm grateful for the way you've handled the investigation, considering.'

Joanne shrugged, as if to suggest it was all in a day's work, before asking Noel if he'd heard about what Karen had done in front of the press, and on camera.

'She gave me the general gist.'

'You might want to talk to her.'

'I did. I told her she could very well find herself a hate figure if she went on like this.'

'What was her response?'

'Let's just say she didn't exactly appreciate the advice.'

'Well, we really don't need the public turning on her at this point,' Joanne said. 'Maybe I could give her a few tips.'

Noel smiled bleakly. 'Good luck.'

Noel thought Joanne might leave then, but she didn't. She stayed where she was, looking around the room, examining the bits and pieces he'd accumulated over time. He watched her face, wondering what she might say next. She hadn't yet made him feel like a suspect in the disappearance of his daughter, but he knew she must be considering the possibility.

'So, then. Verity?' he said, breaking the silence.

'Verity.'

'Mind if I ask why?'

'No particular reason. We have so few leads to go on that we need to go back to the source. The house-to-house has turned up nothing, and neither have our other points of inquiry. When we come to a dead end, we go back to the start to see what we might have missed.'

'Would it be okay if I explained this to Verity before you begin? She's pretty shaken after Bruce's allegations this morning, and I think she'd answer more clearly if she knew you weren't accusing her of harming her sister.'

'Sure. But I'm happy to talk her through it.' Joanne paused. And then, after a moment's thought, she said, 'Bruce is kind of tough on her, isn't he?'

'Bruce is kind of tough on everyone.'

*

They assembled in the kitchen: the two detectives, Karen, Noel and Verity. Bruce and Mary weren't there, thankfully. Mary had been visibly shocked by the total lack of food in the house, so Bruce had taken her to Booths to buy provisions. 'Just to tide us over,' Mary said, but Noel fully expected her to return with a carful of groceries. She didn't drive any more. Not since she'd clipped her wing mirror reversing out of their driveway and Bruce had declared her to be *a menace on the roads*.

Joanne Aspinall and Oliver Black asked Verity once again to take them through the events of the previous day, step by step, leading up to Brontë's disappearance. Verity was calmer today, less skittish, and Noel was proud of the way his daughter was handling herself with the two officers. Karen stayed quiet, over by the Aga, biting her lip, eyes darting back and forth across the width of the room as if she were watching a tennis match.

'So you arrive at the rec and you position yourself a little way from Brontë and the group of girls,' Joanne Aspinall was saying to Verity. 'Can you recall anyone strange nearby, anyone doing anything you might think of as weird?'

Verity closed her eyes, as if she were replaying the scene inside her head.

'Nothing I would call weird,' she said. 'There was a woman with two Rottweilers. She was shouting into her phone. She was angry. But she left before I did.'

'Which direction did she go?'

'Towards Droomer. Away from Brontë's friends.'

'What else?'

'There were other small groups. People I recognize, but I don't know their names. There were some kids on the skate park, a few playing cricket, lots of children on the playground. Too many to remember, really.'

'No one struck you as strange?'

Verity gave a nervous kind of laugh. 'No one except Dale.'

'Dale?' said Joanne.

'I was joking. Dale's not strange. But most people think he is.'

'Who's Dale?'

'Dale's just a kid. He's over here a lot. He's friends with Ewan. He works for the council, removing litter, cutting hedges and stuff. That's what he was doing yesterday . . . at the rec.'

Noel watched Karen. She was staring at Verity, processing what she was hearing.

Noel felt he should say something. Give some sort of explanation about Dale's learning disability but—

'Dale Brokenshire was there?' Karen cut in. 'Dale was at the rec, yesterday, and you're only telling us this *now*? Why didn't you tell us before?'

Verity was perplexed. 'Why would I?' she said. 'It's only Dale.'

Karen looked to Noel. 'Jesus,' she said, and at the same time she lurched to one side, losing her balance. She grabbed the work surface, trying to steady herself. 'Jesus,' she said again. 'What has he done to her?'

Noel got to his feet. 'Karen, wait, we can't go jumping to—'

'Where is he?' Karen yelled. 'Is he here? I bet he's here. He's always here. Christ. Isn't that what they say? Someone known to the family. Someone under our own bloody roof?' She put her hands to her face. 'Noel, go and get him,' she said. 'Go and find Ewan and get them both in here, now.'

Noel took the wooden steps two at a time to the flat above the garage and looked through the window. He could see the two boys asleep on the sofas. He rapped on the door before turning the handle and entering. The television was on. A film was playing: *Donnie Darko*. Something to do with a giant rabbit?

Gently rousing first Ewan and then Dale, he told them, 'You need to come to the house right away. The police are there.'

He neglected to say it was Dale, specifically, they wanted to talk to, worried the kid might bolt, and instead played it down. Everyone else had been interviewed, and now it was just their turn to be questioned.

'I still feel kind of stoned,' Ewan murmured, trying and failing to pull on his right trainer.

Noel took the shoe from him and loosened the laces, widening the top, as he would have done back when Ewan was ten years old. Ewan's father had taken off when Karen was pregnant with him. She had always been sketchy about the details, not wanting to return, she said, to a time when she was at her lowest. 'What's important is what's ahead,' she would say, and Noel supposed it suited him not to know the details.

Perhaps if Karen had been his first wife he would have needed her to fill in the blanks. Perhaps he would have wanted to know more about the man who came before him. The man who'd cruelly left his lover high, dry and pregnant. As it was, he had enough of his own shit to deal with – what with leaving Jennifer – and he didn't feel the desire for any more drama.

Ewan had gone through a stage when he was fifteen, a stage when he wanted to trace his real father. But Karen had given him nothing. She told him if he wanted to go there, that was his choice, but she would have nothing to do with Ewan, should he make that decision. Ultimately, he didn't. Noel suspected it was probably laziness on Ewan's part that prevented him from taking further steps to find his dad, rather than any loyalty he felt towards Karen. Though, who knew? The lad had never been very forthcoming about his feelings.

Quietly, Noel suspected that he'd not been the best substitute father. He had always got along with Ewan, but they didn't talk much. Did that really matter, though? When Noel was a teenager, he had had a friend, Alan, who lived around the corner. It was Alan's dad who ran them to rugby practice, Alan's dad who ran them to football in the summer, Alan's dad who stood silently on the sidelines. There had been a kind of comfort in Alan's dad's steady silence, and Noel wondered if he'd modelled his relationship with Ewan on it: staying on the periphery, letting someone else do the talking.

Noel handed the trainer back to Ewan.

'Thanks. Will they . . . you know . . . the police, I mean, will they . . .?'

'Arrest you for smoking weed? Least of their worries, I should think. You might want to wash your face, though. For your mother's sake.'

'They figured out what happened to Brontë?'

Noel shook his head.

'Shit,' said Ewan. 'I really thought she'd be back.'

'They're drawing a blank. That's why they need to talk to you two. Make sure they've not missed any of the small details.'

Dale had still not spoken, and it was only now that Noel noticed he didn't look too good. The skin of his face and neck was a bloodless white and he was staring down at his knees.

'Dale?' Noel said, upbeat. 'You ready to roll, my friend?'

And Dale rose to his feet. His expression was one of undisguised sorrow.

20

JOANNE RECOGNIZED THE boy as soon as he walked in.

Dale. The name had triggered a memory of something – she wasn't sure what – but when she saw him it came back to her in a rush.

He trudged in, following Ewan. Both their heads down, both smelling of teenager: sweaty hair, trainers riddled with athlete's foot. Joanne once had a boyfriend who had had a perpetual case of that particular fungus. The smell had never quite left her.

Joanne tried to remain impassive as Dale Brokenshire raised his hand to her by way of a greeting.

'Dale,' she said. 'How are you?'

'Very well, Mrs Aspinall. Very well, indeed, thank you for asking.'

Joanne didn't dare look at what was going on with Karen Bloom after this exchange. Instead, she kept her eyes focused straight ahead, requesting both boys to sit at the kitchen table, asking them if they were happy to answer her questions.

'We are, Mrs Aspinall. We will answer, won't we, Ewan?' Dale said eagerly, and Ewan nodded his head at his friend in a kind way.

Oh, Dale, Joanne thought. *Please don't be involved in this.*

Rarely did she actively will a person to be innocent, but today was one of those days. Looking at Dale's face – his open, trusting, face – she felt her stomach fold in on itself, because Dale didn't look good on paper.

Should she take him away with her now and continue with this at the station?

'I want you to know I didn't do anything wrong, Mrs Aspinall,' he said, and Joanne smiled.

'Good, Dale. I'm pleased to hear you say that.'

'Not like last time. That *was* wrong,' he said, and he sat back in his chair and shook his head from side to side as if to emphasize the point.

Ewan gave him a quick dig with his elbow and told him to shut up. But Dale, baffled by this, nudged him back and said, 'I always tell the truth. Don't I, Mrs Aspinall?' and Joanne said, 'Yes, Dale, you're very good at telling the truth.'

Karen was no longer able to hold it together, and there was the sound of a cup slamming down hard on to the draining board, and Karen advanced towards the table. 'Would someone mind telling me what the hell is going on?'

Dale flinched.

Ewan said, 'Say nothing, Dale. Not. One. Word.'

And, for a moment, nobody spoke.

Joanne had met Dale around a year ago, when he was eighteen. He'd had underage sex with a girl of thirteen, whom he had believed to be sixteen. To the rest of the world, Chloe Swift looked like a girl of thirteen trying to appear sixteen. But to Dale she absolutely *was* sixteen— because, as Joanne found out, Dale took everyone at their word and didn't always have the ability to distinguish fact from fiction. Dale slept with her a number of times, over a two-month period.

Then Chloe Swift's mother became aware of the situation and called the police.

Trying to wade through the considerable number of texts and messages that passed between the two of them in an attempt to figure out the truth, Joanne had wondered how the girl had time to attend school at all. There were literally thousands. And the sexts – though not as pornographic as they might have been (mostly, young breasts thrust high and proud in a selection of push-up bras, naked selfies taken from above; a lot of Chloe's bare bottom, which flummoxed Joanne, as she couldn't work out how she'd got such a good shot) – were also too numerous to count.

Dale's mother had accompanied him to the station. She was a slow-witted, smelly lump of a woman who thought that bossing Dale about, loudly, in the presence of an officer, would give the impression that she was a good mother. It didn't. She kept telling Dale to own up to what he'd done and take the punishment he deserved, which really didn't help Joanne, because all Dale could do was cry into his tea, unable to get the words out.

Eventually, after picking through the evidence, Joanne found many instances of Chloe purporting to be older than she was. And after informing Chloe's mother of this, she decided to drop the charges. Dale did not get a criminal record and, judging by Karen's expression now, the situation had not become public knowledge in Windermere.

Now it seemed as though that might be about to change.

'How does he know you?' Karen asked, and Joanne said she wasn't at liberty to say.

'Dale,' Karen said, 'tell me how you know this detective. What did you do that was wrong? You said you did something wrong. What was it?'

Dale looked to Ewan for guidance. And Ewan was staring back at him, mouthing, 'Say nothing,' when suddenly Karen slapped her son hard across the back of the head, shouting, 'Stay out of this!'

Then she slapped Dale, too.

Not *quite* as hard. But shocked by her actions, Joanne, Oliver and Noel jumped forwards, each making towards Karen.

Dale waved them off. 'I'm okay, I'm okay,' he said quietly.

'Dale,' Karen said again, 'if you don't tell me right now what you did, you will never set foot in this house again. Is that what you want?'

'No, Mrs Bloom.'

'So speak.'

Dale shifted uncomfortably in his seat before taking a breath. 'I don't want to say it in front of her.'

'What do you mean?' asked Karen.

He gestured towards Verity. 'I don't want Verity to hear, if that's okay, Mrs Bloom.'

'Why ever not? What's Verity got to do with this?'

Dale dropped his head.

'Dale, speak or I'll . . .'

He cast a quick glance at Verity before looking down again, examining his hands.

'Dale, I mean it,' Karen said.

At this, Verity spoke up. 'Dale,' she said gently, 'I already know.'

He lifted his head.

'It's okay,' Verity said. 'I know about it. Go ahead, tell her.'

And so he did. In his own words, he relayed what had happened for Karen's benefit, and it wasn't easy for any of them to hear. Clumsily, he explained how he'd come to have sex with a thirteen-year-old girl, and how he was very sorry for doing something so wrong.

'What the hell have you done with Brontë?' Karen yelled when he had finished. 'Where is she, you backward fucking pervert?'

'I promise, Mrs Bloom,' he answered, 'I haven't done anything with her.'

'Get him away from me. Somebody – Jesus! – somebody get him out of here!' she screamed.

And Joanne probably would have gone ahead and removed Dale from the Blooms' kitchen, just to get the kid away from Karen, when in walked Brontë.

In walked Brontë Bloom. Not a scratch on her and, it turned out, unwilling to tell anyone where she'd been.

Part Two

21

Monday, 5 October

Verity could hear classical music playing in a faraway room. She had no idea who the composer was but she recognized the piece from a car-insurance commercial. After gawping at Jeremy Gleeson's set of watercolours for what felt like the hundredth time, she decided he must be running late and so she pulled out *Educating Rita* from her rucksack. She may as well do something useful. And the play needed to be read by the end of the week. She was up to the part where Rita returns from poetry summer camp and Frank's not sure if he likes her any more. Verity wasn't sure if she liked the new Rita either.

Jeremy Gleeson's elderly receptionist with the tight curls had been replaced by a sullen girl not much older than Verity herself. Verity wondered if she read the patients' notes when no one was looking. She would, if she were left alone with them.

She flicked through the pages of the play until she found her spot, then she sensed movement from within Jeremy Gleeson's room. Previously, he staggered his clients. Verity assumed he did this to protect client confidentiality, so she felt a small stir of nervousness as she heard the sound of a chair being scraped across the floor, a nose being blown, footsteps approaching.

The door opened and Verity held her book up high, not wanting to make eye contact with the person leaving. When Jeremy

Gleeson said, 'Are you coming in, Verity?' she was a little stunned to see him standing there alone, eyes red-rimmed and watery.

'Sorry to keep you so long,' he added.

He had clearly been crying, and Verity was hesitant to peer at his face. She had never seen a man cry. It was very unsettling.

Should she ask if he was okay?

She didn't have the nerve. Instead she made a bit of a fuss organizing her bag, pulling up her school socks, before settling herself on the narrow couch so she didn't have to look at him.

'Again, apologies for keeping you waiting,' Jeremy said.

'It's no bother.'

'I believe you've had quite the week.'

Verity turned her head towards him briefly. 'You could say that.'

'How's Brontë doing?'

'Brontë seems to be A-okay,' she said. 'It's everyone else that's having difficulty. No one knows how to act around each other.'

'I imagine your stepmother is rather upset.'

' "Uptight" would be more accurate.'

'How are you two communicating?'

'We're kind of not.'

'Why is that, do you think?'

Verity shrugged. 'I don't know. It's just easier, I guess.'

Jeremy Gleeson paused long enough for Verity to know there was something big coming. She stole a quick look his way and saw that he was making notes with his big, fat, fountain pen. She wondered if she should get up from the couch. She did feel a bit exposed, lying there, her school skirt riding up.

Jeremy placed his pen by the side of his notes and sat back in his chair. He made a tent with his fingers, something her English teacher did when he wanted to appear more intelligent than he actually was, and said, 'Do you ever have feelings of rage towards Karen?'

Verity tried not to laugh. Only *every single day.*

Brontë had returned home perfectly fine, as far as anyone could tell. She was examined by a police doctor who pronounced her to be fit and well and said there were no signs of assault or trauma. Which seemed to Verity like a very positive result. It *was* a positive result, wasn't it?

Karen appeared to think otherwise. She bombarded Brontë with questions. She wouldn't accept her story of wandering off and hiding out in her friend's father's shed for the night (more of a garden room than a shed, apparently. 'It had a TV, a PS4, a fridge and everything.') Karen just couldn't comprehend why Brontë would want to be alone for a day.

'Alone?' Karen yelled at her. 'You're ten years old. Ten-year-olds don't seek solitude!'

But if there was more to Brontë's story, she wasn't telling. Not even when Verity got her on her own and said she would *never* divulge anything her stepsister told her. Not even when Verity said she could confide in her, and she would never tell Karen where she had been and with whom.

Brontë stuck to her story and remained tight-lipped. Even when the kind detective sat her down and said how important it was that she tell the truth about her whereabouts. If someone had helped her, if someone had hidden her on purpose, then the police absolutely needed to know. It wasn't a game, the detective said, running away like this. It was incredibly serious.

Still Brontë wouldn't tell. Still she stuck to her version of events.

Of course, this sent Karen totally out of her mind. Because if no one had taken her daughter by force, then what did that mean?

That she had left of her own accord? That she had left on *purpose*?

Karen couldn't accept this, and so she spent every spare second grilling Brontë, bargaining with her, promising all manner of treats if she'd only reveal the truth.

So yes, you could say that Verity felt rage towards Karen. Because it was pretty clear to everyone that Brontë had run away precisely *because* of Karen.

But since these counselling sessions were in place because Reid's Grammar had requested them to cure Verity of the rage she felt towards her stepmother, she said to Jeremy Gleeson, pretend-innocently, 'I just feel really sorry for her.'

'Sorry for her? Why?'

'Because she's had her feelings hurt. She can't understand why Brontë would leave. She's humiliated and can't face the fact that it might've had something to do with her.'

'Do *you* think it had something to do with her?'

'Yes.'

'Has Brontë confided as much to you?'

'She's staying quiet on the subject.'

'Why do you think that might be?'

'She's not an idiot. She knows the repercussions would be massive if she admitted she ran off because of Karen's punishing regime.'

'Does your father have an opinion?'

'If he has, he doesn't share it.'

'Hmm,' he said. 'Perhaps you could talk to him about it.'

'Isn't the point that I talk to you?'

'Well, yes. But what we want is for you to work towards a feeling of ease when you're around your stepmother. Mutual respect, so to speak. So we don't have a repeat of the situation where your feelings get out of control, to the point that you attack her again. We haven't really worked through the details of the attack. Perhaps now would be a good time.'

'If we must.'

'Do you find it hard to relive those feelings?'

'I feel like I talked a lot about the thing when it happened. And there wasn't actually that much to say. Besides, we have already discussed it, haven't we?'

'Not to the extent I would like.'

'You asked if I attacked Karen because I was told to by voices inside my head. And I said no. You asked if I was under the influence of drugs. And I said—'

'Ah, yes,' he said. 'Why *were* you using drugs?'

'I wasn't.'

'But they were found in your locker?' Jeremy Gleeson tilted his head. Gave Verity a look like, *C'mon. You're not really going to say they were for someone else, are you?*

Verity exhaled. Closed her eyes.

All at once she felt silly lying down on his silly couch. She realized she'd been lying there with her arms crossed protectively over her chest, in an attempt to prevent her small breasts pointing skywards. Verity sat upright. Then she asked Jeremy Gleeson if it was okay if she moved to the chair instead. He told her it was and, once she was settled in it, he asked if she now felt comfortable to answer his question.

'The joints are for my mother,' said Verity.

No response, so she continued: 'You've probably already heard she has MS. She's pretty ill. The weed helps. That's it. No big drama. I don't get stoned. I don't like the feeling, to be honest. It makes my stomach swim.'

'Thank you for your honesty.'

Verity shrugged. 'What's next?'

'Back to the attack on your stepmother.'

Verity rolled her eyes. 'I've already told you—'

'You've told me what the attack *wasn't*, Verity,' he said, 'but you've yet to tell me what it *was*.'

'I don't understand.'

153

'What made you go from doing whatever it was you were doing to putting your hands around Karen's neck?'

'She was hurting Brontë,' Verity said simply.

'Hurting her how?'

'Brontë has some kind of weird problem with her hand. She plays the harp and the piano, *a lot*, like, she has lessons *all* the time. And suddenly she couldn't hold things any more. She could barely hold on to a glass, and kept dropping things.'

'Go on.'

'Well, at first my dad thought it was something like repetitive strain injury and told Karen to cut down on both music lessons and practice . . . which maybe she did, maybe she didn't. I can't remember. But Brontë's hand was getting really bad and she was getting really distressed. She couldn't do her homework or even brush her teeth. My dad said he thought it was . . . what's the thing golfers get when their hands spasm and they can't take a putt?'

'The yips.'

'Yeah. He said darts players get it, too, and can't let go of the dart. Well, he thought it was that. He thought it was linked to performance anxiety and that Brontë needed complete rest. Except, one day, I heard shouting and crying. And when I went into the kitchen, Karen had a set of weights on the table—'

'Weights?'

'Yeah, dumbbells. Pink. She was screaming at Brontë to hold them in her hand to build the strength back up. And Brontë was crying and shaking with the effort, and I don't know, a switch kind of flicked in my head and the next thing I knew we were on the floor . . . and, well, you know the rest.'

'A switch flicked? That's what it felt like?'

'That's the best way I can describe it.'

'And did you lose your awareness of what was happening for a time?'

'I'm not sure. Maybe.'

'What happened when you realized you were hurting her?'

She paused.

'Verity?' Jeremy Gleeson prompted.

Eyes down, brushing the fluff from the hem of her school skirt, Verity asked, 'Who gets to know about what I tell you in here? Because they said in the hospital it was confidential. But I was there to be assessed, so I'm pretty sure everything goes back to my dad and Karen and whoever else wants to know.'

'This is entirely between you and me. I don't have to turn my records over to anyone . . . Verity, did you know you were hurting Karen?'

She nodded.

'And how did you feel about that?' he asked.

'I knew I had to stop,' she said. 'Of course I knew that. The thing is, I really didn't want to. I'm pretty sure I *wanted* Karen to stop breathing.'

22

Thursday, 15 October

Antidepressants.

That's what Bernadette Mercer said.

Noel had been in this situation before, with Bernadette's daughter, and it hadn't been an easy conversation to have then either. Ultimately, he'd given in to Bernadette Mercer's demands and written a script for a course of beta blockers. But he hadn't done it gladly.

'Are you sleeping okay, Stephen?' he'd asked the teenager in front of him.

Stephen Mercer was the kind of awkward, twitchy kid who would cut off his right hand rather than make eye contact. The kind who'd be in charge of the lighting at school productions. Stephen stared fixedly at a spot behind Noel's shoulder, as if Noel were addressing him from behind the potted palm over in the corner of the room.

'He wakes up in the night. Don't you, Stephen?' his mother said.

'How often?' he asked Stephen.

'Three or four times a night,' his mother said.

'Do you use your computer before bedtime?'

'He has to,' replied his mother. 'He won't get through his work unless he puts in the hours, Dr Bloom. You, of all people, should know that.'

Noel would like to say that this was a rare occurrence, but it wasn't. He would now see five or six teenagers a week with anxiety-related conditions. Most, though not all, stemmed from exam fear and an increase in the academic workload. Things had changed. In Noel's day, a few kids from each class were bright – bright enough to go on to university. No one was expected to get straight 'A's. The few that did were considered freaks, kids to be avoided because they had no social skills and did odd things like keeping dead squirrels inside their lockers, or studied instead of, say, showering. These days, everyone was expected to get straight 'A's. British parents, though they wouldn't admit it, were sneakily adopting the Chinese model of parenting, whereby anything less than an 'A' was considered a failure. 'Yes, yes,' they would say, '*of course* there's more to childhood than endless studying,' but they still wanted the 'A's. They meant that a balanced childhood was okay for someone else's child. Not theirs.

Their offspring were buckling under the pressure and Noel now regularly saw what were once classed as adult stress-related disorders appearing in children as young as thirteen. He had heard of one case, a girl who'd had a nervous breakdown, sitting her A levels *inside* a psychiatric unit, after having been sectioned under the Mental Health Act. Noel despaired. It was not what he wanted for his own children, not what he wanted for the young people of Windermere either. There had to be more to life, surely?

Of course, he'd cautioned Karen about it, a few days after Brontë's return, when he could see Karen picking up right where she left off: the reinstatement of the maths and science tutor, the music lessons, some new woman she'd found to sort out Brontë's reading; and she'd made inquiries about a Saturday drama club. He'd said to Karen, 'I thought you'd want to tone down all of this nonsense, now that we've got Brontë back safe and sound.' Be grateful for what we have, and so forth.

Karen hadn't replied.

So he had lost his temper. 'Why can't you just be content with her the way she is?' he yelled. 'Why the need for all this constant . . . *improvement*? You carry on, Karen, and you will *break* this child. Do you understand that?' And Karen had looked at him with such a strange mixture of confusion, pity and disgust. As if she'd stumbled upon him masturbating joylessly in the shed or something.

'Apart from the palpitations and the acid reflux, Stephen, which I know we've treated in the past, what other symptoms are you experiencing?'

This time, unexpectedly, Stephen spoke up.

'I'm just really, really tired all the time. I don't have the energy to do anything.'

Noel used to hear this phrase only from new mothers. TATT would be written in the notes of practically every mother of a newborn; it was natural they were tired all the time – they had a baby to look after. Unless you have a live-in nanny, there's really no escaping it.

But now he was typing TATT for every other teenager who walked through the door, and he wondered if the UK was on the brink of an epidemic.

'Have you ever self-harmed or felt suicidal?' Noel asked.

'No.'

'Well, with that in mind, I think, rather than going straight ahead with medication, it would be better for you to have a break from things in general. We all need time to recharge, reboot, and you're no exception, Stephen. You're suffering from overload, and I fear that medication is not the answer here. Ultimately, what you need to do is less. Less of everything.'

Stephen looked at his mother.

'Dr Bloom,' she said. 'We went through this with my daughter.'

'I remember.'

'And I recall you giving out the same advice then.'

'It's the best advice I have.'

'That's as may be,' she said, 'but Stephen can't afford to take time off from school. If he misses one lesson he'll fall behind. The teachers are hardly going to teach him individually upon his return. What he needs is something to get him through this difficult patch *right now*. We're not asking that he stay on the pills for ever.'

'Mrs Mercer, my point is that it's *always* difficult. The workload doesn't let up, that's the problem. And where the medication might help with his anxiety, it may also make him feel even more tired. And I wonder if that's the best thing for Stephen, when he's already struggling with his energy levels.' He turned to Stephen. 'What commitments, other than school, do you have at the moment?'

Stephen sighed desolately, as if simply listing his activities was too much. 'I'm doing Duke of Edinburgh Gold—'

'Which requires you to do volunteer work and the like, yes?'

'I help out with swimming lessons after school and on Saturday mornings.'

'What time on Saturday mornings?' Noel asked.

'I have to be at the pool by seven thirty.'

Noel looked briefly at Stephen's mother to prove his point, but she had her head angled towards her son.

'Anything else?' Noel asked.

'I have a job in a café on Sunday afternoons.'

'Because he needs to learn the value of money,' supplied his mother.

'Anything else?' Noel asked Stephen.

'I'm doing Grade Eight French horn.'

'How much practice does that require?'

'Supposed to be ninety minutes a night, but I do around thirty.'

'And which A levels are you doing?'

'Biology, physics, chemistry and maths.'

'Because you want to study . . .?'

'Dentistry,' his mother answered proudly.

Noel failed to see how plodding up and down the fells in the pouring rain to gain a Duke of Edinburgh Gold award would enhance a career in dentistry, but he knew better than to ask. These days, it was all about showcasing your abilities to get that elusive university place. Problem was, instead of making these kids stand out as individuals, as leaders, in Noel's view all it showed was that they could bear more drudgery than the average child.

Come to think of it, though, that might be quite valuable for a career in dentistry.

'Mrs Mercer,' Noel said patiently, 'it would be very easy for me to do as you ask and write a prescription for Stephen for—'

'Lovely, that would—'

'Much easier,' Noel continued. 'But we need to address the *cause* of this problem rather than merely treat the symptoms. I can see that you're concerned about Stephen's future and I applaud that, it's the mark of a responsible parent. But this is Stephen's life, too, and I wonder if he really wants to go down this road? . . . Stephen?' Noel prompted.

Stephen hesitated. 'I'm not really sure what I want to do.'

'Understandable,' said Noel. 'Well, here's what I suggest. I think you should take a break from the French horn, for a starter. And reduce your volunteering to one session per week or else stop altogether. Focus on your A levels and make sure you don't use your computer after eight thirty in the evening. That should improve your sleep pattern. Take a thirty-minute walk four or five times a week, and if you can, cut out caffeinated drinks. How does that sound? Can we try it for a fortnight? Does that sound doable?'

'Doable?' Mrs Mercer said, her voice laced with sarcasm. 'It sounds positively utopian . . . On top of that, Stephen will be filling out his UCAS form shortly – so what do you suggest, Dr Bloom? That we simply lie about his extracurricular activities? Pretend he's still involved in the things he's not?'

Noel gave her a look like, *It's your call.*

He'd probably have lied if it were him. Shown initiative and so forth.

'Come on, Stephen, get your coat,' his mother said, standing.

'I'll see you both in a fortnight, and then you can report back on how you got on?' Noel said hopefully. And Mrs Mercer answered, 'Yes, yes,' while sweeping her son out of his office without bidding Noel goodbye.

She would be back tomorrow, requesting to see John Ravenscroft instead, Noel presumed. She'd try her luck with him.

John gave out amitriptyline more readily – his reasoning being that the stuff was, at least, pretty benign.

Noel watched Bernadette Mercer exit the room, the sight of her skinny arse saddening him. Because he knew that, if he didn't do something, it would only be a matter of time before he'd be having this same conversation with Karen.

Before Brontë, too, would need antidepressants, just to get through the working week.

23

NOEL GOT HOME at around seven, to the sound of the phone
ringing. He dropped his laptop case in the hallway before
answering it.

'Hello,' he said.

Nothing.

'Hello,' he said again.

He was just about to hang up when he heard the caller's breath,
thick and heavy, down the line. 'Now, look here—' Noel began,
irritated.

'Can you put me on to Karen?'

It was a man's voice. Sounded rather abrupt. Sounded, from
his turn of phrase, like he knew Karen.

'Who should I say is calling?' Noel said, his interest piqued.

'Tell her it's Russell Wallbank. Again.'

Noel carried the phone through to the kitchen, where,
unusually, Karen was preparing a meal. Karen liked to say she
didn't cook; she 'arranged food'. And that's what she was doing
right now: sliding cold, roasted chicken thighs on to plates, along
with a sad-looking salad, and some cheese and onion crisps.

'For you,' Noel said.

And Karen mouthed, 'Who is it?'

Noel covered the microphone with his thumb. 'Russell,' he
said, the guy's surname having been immediately erased from
his memory. 'Says he's called before?'

Karen snatched the receiver from Noel and cut the call off without speaking.

This might have surprised Noel under ordinary circumstances, but they'd had a glut of these unsolicited calls of late.

'Any more trouble today?' Noel asked, washing his hands at the sink. He'd seen four sets of parents that day with children suspected of having intestinal worms. He scrubbed the skin beneath his nails with a nail brush, as if he were readying himself for surgery (for as long as it takes to sing 'Happy Birthday' twice, he remembered from his student days).

'Just a few nutters,' Karen replied. 'All suggesting I hand Brontë over to the authorities. That it's tantamount to child abuse, what I put her through. Blah blah blah. Nothing new.'

'Did you respond?'

Karen stopped what she was doing and looked straight at him. 'Of course I responded. You can't just let the trolls get away with it. They'll go on to attack someone else. Someone weaker. Someone vulnerable.'

Noel poured himself a beer. He could only have the one, as they were going out and he'd said he'd drive. A friend of Karen's was opening a new restaurant-cum-wine bar in Bowness, and they'd been sent an invitation. Noel had tried to get out of it. Twice.

'Still,' he said, 'the police did say that the best response to these people is no response.'

'That's right, Noel,' she said flatly. 'They did.'

Somehow, after Brontë had returned home, there was an implication in the press that Karen was pretty much responsible for her daughter running away. One headline read: PUSHY TIGER MOTHER DRIVES DAUGHTER TO RUN AWAY and there was an article about the effects of what they called 'extreme parenting' and the damage it could do to a child's wellbeing. Experts were quoted, saying how important it was for a child to have unstructured and unsupervised play. How taking part in too many organized after-school activities could actually be detrimental to a child's brain development. Then it went on to print a full list of Brontë's out-of-school activities. 'I know exactly who it was who sold me down the river,' Karen said when she read the article. 'It was that fat woman who sits behind me in church, snivelling into her tissues. She's never looked me in the eye.'

Noel wasn't sure how that particular woman could know so much about Brontë's timetable and suspected it was someone closer to home.

He *did* notice, however, that they'd listed only around two thirds of Brontë's extracurricular activities. But he decided, wisely, to keep this observation to himself.

The publication of the article had prompted the construction of a website in honour of Karen entitled 'Bitch Mother'. It featured Karen's moment of madness, when she declared in front of the cameras that the Blooms' was not 'a council-estate case', they had not hidden away their own child, as well as a number of pieces relating to crazy mothers throughout the years (both factual and taken from fiction). Visitors to the site were encouraged to comment, which they did in droves. Many shared their own horror stories of being brought up by an unstable parent – though a lot of these cases, it had to be said, were clearly psychiatric ones, and not just a question of overzealous parenting.

Noel counselled Karen to stay away from the internet and ignore the sea of abuse as much as possible, thinking that to interact would only encourage the haters. But she was adamant that she needed to stand up to the bullies. To the extent that she'd already had one poor woman claim she was seeking legal representation after Karen went after her.

The woman – Pauline Something-or-other from Swansea – had sent Karen messages along the lines of her needing locking up for incompetent mothering. And Karen had managed to track

Pauline down on Facebook, and then made an elaborate arrangement from the photographs of Pauline's five kids. The photographs came complete with captions: Terminally Unemployed, Morbidly Obese, Drain on the NHS.

It was a bloody awful thing to do. Terrible, really. But, secretly, in a small part of him, Noel did rather admire Karen's spirit.

What *was* proving harder to deal with were the death threats.

They had started off pretty generalized: This woman should be shot. Strung up. A hand-delivered envelope was pushed through their letterbox with a note inside – DIE KAREN BLUME – which the police took away promptly for forensic testing.

But they had since escalated to include snippets of personal information. And this worried Noel. They knew, for instance, that Karen had become pregnant with Brontë while Noel was still married to Jennifer. It didn't seem to bother Karen particularly. She said it was customary for someone in the public eye to be targeted. And Noel wondered if, for a second, Karen had confused herself with some minor celebrity or other. As if she, too, fully expected the paparazzi, with their telephoto lenses, to start shooting pictures of her in her Ugg boots and dressing gown as she was putting out the rubbish.

Noel was worried about Brontë, too. It crossed his mind – more than once, he had to admit – that some wild fanatic might steal her away for real this time. That they might take her to their home and allow her unstructured play and unlimited TV time.

But Karen said he was being ridiculous about that as well.

'Should I do some microwave rice, or are you okay with the crisps?' she asked him.

'What?' Noel said, miles away.

'Rice?' she said, waving the bag in front of his face. 'Takes two minutes.'

'I thought we were eating out,' he said.

'Just nibbles, apparently.'

Noel sat down at the table and picked up the day's paper. Kate, the Duchess of Cambridge, now had a fringe. Excellent, he thought. Now he could sleep easy at night. He folded the newspaper in half and placed it on the chair next to him.

'Shout for Brontë?' Karen said.

'Verity, too?' he asked, but Karen said she thought Verity had already eaten. 'I'll go check just in case,' he said.

Verity *had* eaten. A mushroom-and-Parmesan omelette, when she had come in from her run. She was on the phone to her friend when Noel entered her room. 'No, I told you,' she was saying, 'I only like Coldplay's "Fix You" in an *ironic* way. Like when some tragic teacher uses it to accompany a PowerPoint presentation. Or it's played over footage of starving people in Sudan.'

Once she'd ended the call, she told Noel she wasn't hungry, and he said, 'Come and join us for dinner anyway?' And Verity frowned, looking at him as if to say, *Why would I want to do that?*

'Because I never see you,' he explained. 'Because, by the time I come home, you're already up here for the night.' He paused. 'And because I miss you,' he added.

'You miss me,' she said, deadpan, but half smiling all the same.

'Yeah. I miss you. Go on. Indulge me. I won't make you do it every night.'

Verity pulled her legs out from under her. She did her homework in the middle of her double bed, music on, folders scattered; the duvet was littered with pens, scraps of paper, a calculator, a hole punch. 'I've got quite a lot of work to do,' she said, but it was a lax attempt at an excuse. She was already climbing off the bed.

They descended the stairs with Brontë in tow, Noel asking Verity how her session with Jeremy Gleeson had gone.

'He'd been crying,' she said.

'Crying? How d'you know?'

'It was kind of obvious.'

They went into the kitchen, and Karen must have got wind of their conversation because she said, matter-of-factly, 'Gleeson? Oh, that's because his wife left him.'

'Not exactly very professional of him, all the same,' said Noel.

'I didn't mind,' said Verity.

'You don't want me to look around for another counsellor?'

'No. We're building a relationship.' And Noel wasn't sure if she was being sarcastic or not.

Karen put a plate down heavily in front of Noel and stopped, surveying Verity sceptically. 'What do you talk about when you're with him?' she asked.

Verity shrugged. 'This and that.'

'And by "that", I suppose you mean me?'

'Not really. You do come up, but mostly we talk about how I'm feeling.'

Karen went to the fridge to get Brontë some apple juice. Noel kept telling her that it was just liquid sugar, but she was insistent she had to get vitamin C into Brontë somehow.

Karen handed the glass to her daughter, instructing her to 'Drink!' before turning her attention back to Verity. 'But when I do come up in conversation,' she continued, 'what advice does Jeremy Gleeson give?'

She said his name with derision, following it with 'You do know he used to be a blacksmith?'

'Yeah, he told me,' said Verity. 'But Karen?'

'What?'

'You know you really can't ask me this stuff.'

'The Thirsty Lizard,' Noel said, pulling into a space opposite the wine bar. 'What sort of a wanker name is that?'

Karen was applying her lipstick. She didn't reply, just shot him a look before saying, 'You're not going to be like this all night, are you?'

Noel sighed. 'To be honest, I don't really want to be here, Karen.'

'You've said. But here is where we are. It's been almost three weeks since . . . *Brontë*, and we need to show a united front, that it's business as usual. People talk, Noel. You know they do.'

This was how Karen referred to what had happened. A pause. A short intake of breath, and then: *Brontë*. Not *Brontë's disappearance*. Or: *The night Brontë didn't come home*.

They climbed out of the car and crossed the road. Karen wore a tightly fitted, classically cut jade dress, and she'd straightened her blond hair and let it fall loose around her shoulders. She had heavy, smoky eye make-up and nude lips. She looked a lot like one of those Sky Sports News presenters with the toned upper arms – the ones that you're supposed to find appealing but don't for some reason. Or maybe that was just Noel.

Karen said, 'Try to enjoy it. You never know, you might just surprise yourself.'

'But you don't even like this woman . . . Heather . . . Helen . . . whatever her name is.'

'Fiona. And we're here because, if we didn't come out soon, it would look like we're avoiding everybody. Which we're not. Now, for Christ's sake, Noel, get a grip and stop being so fucking . . . Fiona! Hi! Crikey, it looks sensational. I can't believe what you've done with the place. Stunning. Absolutely stunning. You remember Noel?'

Fiona was one of Karen's gym ladies. She'd renovated the old Thai restaurant and turned it into this – brasserie? bistro? – because she felt she needed a project. 'Felt like her brain was turning to mush,' Karen had told him.

Noel held out his hand. He was about to say, 'Very pleased to meet you, Fiona,' and tell her what a wonderful job she'd done on the building.

'Noel is my GP,' she said, laughing merrily at Karen's mistake.

And Noel smiled, weakly. 'That's right. Of course I am.'

'Not that I ever go,' she went on. 'I'm *never* ill. In fact, I can't remember the last time I even caught a cold. I'm like my mother in that way . . . strong constitution. She never succumbed to illness the way others seem to . . .'

Noel's eyes glazed over, and he let Fiona's words float by him like passing soap bubbles. He could do this quite readily – zone out, while still giving the general appearance of alertness. Someone had put a champagne flute in his hand, and he downed half the contents, nodding, smiling, saying the odd 'Quite' and 'Oh dear', as Fiona became animated, telling Karen about the details of the renovation, which (based on Fiona's frequent use of the phrases 'over budget' and 'bastard tradesman') Noel grasped had not been so straightforward. Still, she was smiling as she moved her eyes around the room, looking very pleased with herself.

'Noel!' Karen snapped, and he flinched.

'What? No need to shout, Karen. I'm standing right here.'

Karen rolled her eyes at Fiona in exasperation. 'He does this,' Karen said. 'Earth to Noel! Fiona was asking if Verity might like to do a few hours a week waiting tables.'

'What? Here?' he said.

'Yes. Here,' said Karen, and regarded him levelly.

'Oh, I'm not sure it's a good time for her right now.'

Karen frowned. 'Why isn't it a good time?'

'Well, she has school. I mean, it's an important year for her.'

Noel glanced at Fiona and saw that the smile she'd fixed there earlier was beginning to cave in slightly. 'It was just an idea,' Fiona said quickly. 'Thought she could do with a little extra money. Teenagers can be so expensive, can't they?'

Karen ignored her. 'I think it would be good for Verity, Noel. I think her getting out of her own head for a bit would be good for all of us. And it would teach her that money doesn't just grow on trees, that if you want something you have to work for it. I think that's a valuable lesson.'

Noel didn't really have an issue with Karen's argument; what she was saying did make sense. But he didn't want Karen deciding what was best for Verity. And besides, Verity's grades were beginning to recover after the blip she'd had, and wouldn't it make more sense to concentrate on that for the time being? He aired these thoughts to Karen in what he thought was a reasonable manner but then realized he must have been saying the words through his teeth, as Fiona began murmuring appeasements such as, 'Just a thought . . . Not to worry.'

Fiona grabbed a champagne bottle from a passing waitress and topped up their glasses as Noel and Karen stared at each other.

'And more to the point,' Fiona babbled on, 'she'll want to spend as much time as she can with you, I'm sure, before she heads off after Christmas.'

'Heads off where?' asked Noel.

And Fiona gave a loud honk of laughter.

Then she turned to Karen and all the blood seemed to drain from her face.

Noel regarded her steadily. 'Goes where, Fiona?' he repeated.

She swallowed. 'To school?' she said in a small voice. Then she looked at Karen and mouthed, 'I'm *so*, so sorry,' before dipping her head and slinking away.

Noel waited a moment.

'What does she mean, Karen?'

'Nothing,' Karen said, rattled, glancing around to make sure no one was listening. 'Fiona's getting mixed up.'

'*What* school?'

'It's nothing. It doesn't matter. It was an idea I had. It's really not important.'

Noel put down his drink on a nearby table. Folded his arms.

'Cut the shit, Karen. You tell me what's going on or I'll make a scene. Do you want me to embarrass you in front of all these people?'

Karen moved in closer to him, angling herself alongside Noel so she could speak into his ear rather than face him.

'I found a school,' she said.

'Why? Where?'

'It's in Inverness, but listen—'

'No way.'

'Just listen. Please. It's got amazing facilities, and they're doing some really wonderful work with kids who've got . . . issues. Most of the kids there are super-bright, kids like Verity, who need a little extra pastoral help, kids who should be performing but need a different approach.'

'Inverness is nearly six hours' drive away. In good weather.'

'I know. That's the downside. But honestly, Noel, you really need to take a look at the literature before you go slamming me for this. It's not only about achieving academic success, they do yoga and meditation and guided imagery, and it's all integrated into the school day. They get these kids right, Noel. Do you understand what I'm saying? They get proper help, and instead of struggling with their feelings, they explore them. And they've found, when they do this, the academic stuff tends to sort itself out. Their results are phenomenal.'

'Verity's had enough upheaval.'

'I agree. And I think this would be a stabilizing force.'

'I won't take her away from Jennifer.'

'I know.'

'Besides, Jennifer would never agree.'

Karen paused. After a moment, she said, 'She thinks it might be a good idea.'

Noel pulled back. 'You talked to her? You talked to her before you talked to me about this?'

'I knew you wouldn't want to take Verity away from her mother. That's a natural reaction. Which I can totally understand. But when I thought about it I realized you'd be doing her a disservice. Letting your emotions get in the way of what could be something fantastic for Verity. She's a gifted girl, Noel. She has a brilliant mind, we know that. And yet she's not performing in school, she's miserable at home, she has very few friends, and she's just not *happy.*'

'And Jennifer said *what* exactly when you presented her with this?'

'Well, we didn't exactly have a full-blown conversation, as you can imagine. But I showed her the prospectus and I explained that I thought Verity needed more than we could give her right now. She was a little saddened, but she seemed to agree. And she did that, Noel, because she's willing to put her daughter's happiness above her own.'

Noel sighed out long and hard.

'Verity knows nothing about this?' he asked.

'No. At least, I don't think so. I wouldn't dream of speaking to her about it until you've made your decision. I was thinking it would probably need to come from you anyway. Perhaps we can all get together, Jennifer, too, and talk it through to see if . . .'

'I need a drink,' Noel said. 'A proper drink.' And he moved off towards the bar.

24

Tuesday, 20 October

Karen pushed the trolley along the aisle for the third time. It wasn't as if Booths was a large supermarket; it had – what? – five or six aisles? She should be able to find nutmeg. Perhaps she was looking in the wrong place. Perhaps it was with the muesli. Why did Noel need nutmeg anyway? Thoughts of her mother's egg-custard tart came back to her and Karen was filled with a sudden sense of longing. Her mother was useless at most things, but she was an extraordinary cook. Until her mid-twenties, Karen had never had to think about a meal, let alone make one. That's when she discovered she had no real interest in the preparation of food, or even that much interest in eating it either. Karen would order the first thing on the list from any fast-food menu and eat whatever showed up.

But now she had this list. Noel's list.

As yet, he was refusing to talk about Verity moving schools, told her he'd think about it at the end of the school year. Maybe now would be the time to leave him? Christ knows, she'd thought about it often enough. Logistically, though, she couldn't seem to make it work. She wasn't sure Noel *earned* enough to run two homes, pay two sets of school fees and provide for his invalid ex-wife. Presently, he was pursuing some silly new notion which irritated her beyond measure. He kept saying that families who ate together were somehow happier – 'They're happier, the children are brighter, more intelligent' – and so Noel 'wanted to get back in the kitchen'.

Karen tried arguing that this was just nonsense printed in the Saturday *Telegraph*'s Weekend section. Crap written by journalists to make mothers feel worse than they did already. But he wouldn't have it.

It's scientifically proven, he said.

And she'd said, 'Yes, yes, just as parents who read to their children have more intelligent offspring.' That was nonsense as well. *Of course*, people who bothered to read to their children had cleverer kids, because those parents had a higher than average intelligence to start with. Just as a woman who bothers to make a full roast dinner midweek to justify her existence is more likely to have brighter children than someone who feeds their kids on Asda's value pizzas.

It was hardly rocket science, but Noel had given her a withering look, saying, 'Please, just get the ingredients.'

He was making ragù. Which was essentially spaghetti bolognese, but Noel said that title was incorrect because no one in Bologna called it that. They called it ragù. And Karen thought, *really, Noel, I don't give a shit. I'd rather just nip to Marks & Spencer on my way home from Brontë's harp lesson and buy a stack of spaghetti-bolognese ready meals. Sorry, ragù.*

But, he *wanted to get back in the kitchen.*

Karen suspected this was to curb his drinking as much as anything else. She'd noticed he'd been putting more away than usual. But she didn't say anything, because she could see he wanted to delude himself with the idea of the kitchen being the heart of the home. So she let it go.

And all the shitty stuff in the media of late *had* taken its toll on him. She knew some patients had been asking him about the real reasons behind Brontë's running away, but when she asked him about it he brushed it off, as if it were a minor issue. As if he was dealing with it. But this whole thing had aged him. *And* he'd started smoking again. He came home smelling like Russell used to when he'd had a row with someone at work: stale smoke, alcohol, mints and whatever floral soap he'd managed to scrub his hands and face with in the gents.

She hadn't told Noel about Russell.

She'd toyed with the idea, just in case Russell took it upon himself to turn up at their door, but in the end she had decided she would face that particular problem if it arose. It was unlikely anyway. Unlikely he'd make the three-hundred-and-fifty-mile journey north, because if Russell was anything like the Russell Wallbank of old, he would have trouble scraping together enough money for a fish supper, never mind enough to make it all the way to Windermere from Brighton.

He had contacted her a couple of days after that clip had been shown on TV. Karen had dropped Brontë at school and, on returning home, had begun a thorough, systematic search of her daughter's bedroom in an attempt to find something – *anything*. Anything to shed light on who could have taken her daughter and held her hostage for over twenty-four hours. Karen was hoping to find a gift of some kind, maybe a present that Karen had never seen, and then she would have what she needed to prove that she was right. Right in thinking that Brontë had not left of her own accord.

When she was half underneath Brontë's bed, her skin itching from all the dust that Rosa had neglected to deal with, she heard the phone ring.

She wriggled out, answered it, and heard a voice say, 'Guess who?'

It was a voice she recognized instantly as belonging to Russell Wallbank.

'I don't know,' she said tentatively.

'Sure you do, Karen,' he said, and she felt a chill run through her. 'Long time no see.' And then he laughed in the way he used to do when something wasn't funny.

'I saw you on the news,' he said. 'Looking good, Karen. Looking very good. I see life's been kind to you.'

Karen didn't speak. She was trying to work out if Russell could know her address and, with a sickening dread, she realized that, yes, if he'd found her phone number with her name and postal town, then her address would be listed on the British Telecom website as well.

'What do you want?' she whispered.

'Just to chat.'

Karen could hear the sound of a faraway siren. Did he still live in Brighton?

'How long has it been?' he said.

She didn't answer.

'It must be – what? – getting on around nineteen years now?'

'Around that.'

'And you're married to a doctor,' he said. 'How did that happen?'

'The usual. We fell in love.'

'There was a time when you loved me.'

'Yes, well, all good things come to an end eventually, Russell.'

'You left without saying goodbye,' he said. 'That was kind of shitty.'

'Sorry.'

'I looked for you. I left messages for you. Did you get them?'

'I was ready to move on.'

'With *my* baby?' he hissed.

Karen closed her eyes. 'What is it that you want, Russell?'

'Just to talk.'

'So, we've talked. I'm going to go. I have things to do and I don't think it's a good idea for you to call here. I have a life. I have—'

'I'll be in touch,' he said. And before Karen could say, 'No, please don't,' he hung up, leaving her standing in the hallway, wondering if the back door was locked.

Karen left the cereal aisle now and headed over to the fresh counter for some pancetta and five hundred grammes of minced steak.

Chatting to the butcher was Pia Nicholls, someone Karen had hoped to avoid for at least a couple of months, until this nonsense in the press had been wiped from everyone's minds and they all got back to thinking just about themselves again.

Karen paused, deciding whether to change direction, but she dallied for a moment too long and, before she knew it, Pia was telling the butcher in that overloud voice of hers that she had all manner of tasks to do and really must get this pork tenderloin into its marinade. Then she swung her trolley around, almost crashing into Karen.

'Karen! It's you! How are you?'

Usually, Pia Nicholls was elegantly dressed, even if she always looked rather old-fashioned (her favourite song was 'Africa' by Toto). Today, though, she wore a pair of black skinny jeans which she really didn't have the legs for, and a weird woollen cape which Karen knew would turn into a rag the minute it was washed.

'Lovely to see you, Pia,' Karen said to her, inching away. 'How are the family? Good, I hope? Anyway, so sorry, but I have to run, I'm actually late for—'

Pia reached out and clutched Karen's arm.

'Karen,' she said, her face grave with concern, 'this is me you're talking to. Your friend. Don't feel you need to dash. We should talk. How about coffee?'

'I really—'

'Great. Meet you in the café in five minutes. Do you have much left to buy?'

Karen reluctantly shook her head. 'I'm almost done.'

'Excellent,' Pia said. 'My treat.'

Karen thought about bolting through the front doors of Booths, leaving Pia Nicholls waiting for her in the adjoining café, bewildered and alone. As a teenager, Karen had often fantasized about breaking her right arm during exam season so that she could be excused. And once, she actually went through with it, persuading her big-boned friend to jump up and down on her wrist during lunch hour. The pain *had* been worth it. Right up until she was informed that she would be dictating her answers to a member of staff instead of taking the exams with the rest of her year. Then it had absolutely *not* been worth it. And Karen wondered if bolting from Pia Nicholls might also have its own unique set of repercussions.

She told the cashier, wearily, that yes, she had forgotten her Bag for Life, so yes, she would require carrier bags, and yes, she had her Booths card, and no, she didn't want any cash back, before paying and heading towards the café, her mouth set in a grim line of resignation.

Pia was her friend, she'd said. They should talk, she'd said. But this would not be friends talking.

This would be Pia dressing up her interrogative questions as those of an anxious ally while Karen sidestepped her queries, answering like a politician and sticking to the script she used whenever anyone began to probe too deeply.

The thing was, Karen did like Pia Nicholls. She was one of the few mothers she knew who actually had some backbone, who stood up for things she believed in, rather than scurrying around like a frightened mouse, which was more typical of the majority of the mothers at Reid's. Karen said no to those mothers when they invited her to attend scented-candle parties, or school fund-raisers, giving Brontë's tight schedule as an excuse. But really, it was because she couldn't bear to spend an evening listening to their apologetic small talk, their petty worries and fears about their offsprings' futures.

Pia, though slightly on the stupid side, knew who she was and didn't mind offending you if she thought something needed saying. Which Karen had always admired in a person.

Karen removed her shopping from the trolley, leaving it alongside the potting compost and cheap bunches of flowers. Not allowed, but sod it. Then she went into the café. Pia was sitting at a table by the window. Good. Hopefully, she might get distracted and start to bitch about the people who passed by.

Karen sat down while Pia pushed a coffee her way, once again plastering a look of deep sorrow on her face, until Karen said, 'Oh, do stop it, Pia. It's not that bad.'

'But the website is so ghastly!' she exclaimed. 'I sent you a text. Did you get it?'

Karen had received lots of texts of support from her 'friends'. People were outraged. Anything at all they could do to help, just ask, they said. But Karen knew very well that if she did call on them for help, there would be excuses made, her calls would go unanswered.

People, she'd learned, had a tendency to scatter when the press was involved.

'Is there any way you can put a stop to the maliciousness?' Pia asked. 'Can you take legal action?'

Karen shook her head. 'Freedom of speech. People can say what they like.'

'But how is Brontë coping?'

'Fine. Absolutely fine. Back into the swing of things. Busy, busy.'

'Did she give you any indication where she might have been when—'

'No.'

'Nothing at all that—'

'No.'

Karen took a sip of her coffee and smiled sweetly at Pia. She could push all she liked, but Karen wasn't about to give her anything.

'I like your cape,' said Karen, and Pia looked at her in surprise.

'You do?' she replied, pleased, fingering the neckline. 'I wasn't sure at first.'

'It really suits you. Goes nicely with those jeans.'

Pia preened a little at the compliment, saying something flattering about Karen's choice of handbag in return, in that way women feel they must do when praised. It was a silly dance they did, and Karen wondered how many of these exchanges were genuine. Probably about one in ten. She often found herself commenting positively on the things she liked least about a particular woman.

Why was that? she wondered. She really couldn't say.

'So, I've not seen much of Ewan,' Pia said casually, as if by way of an afterthought. 'He and Hamish don't seem to be as close as they once were.'

'Different interests, I suppose.'

'Did I tell you we employed a woman to help with Hamish's personal statement? A total whizz. Eight hundred pounds, and worth every penny. She seems confident that Oxford will be impressed.'

'That's good,' Karen said.

'Hamish can't wait to leave home. That's a positive sign, isn't it? I'm trying to take it as a good sign, and not as an insult. I'm not sure how I'll cope when he *does* leave. Roger says so little nowadays it'll be like living on my own.'

'You'll adapt.'

'Yes, yes, I know. Have to throw myself into something. Keep occupied, that's the key.'

'Absolutely.'

Pia drained her coffee cup and took a look around the café,

waving to a couple of Reid's mothers she'd noticed over by the entrance. They waved back enthusiastically, happy to have been noticed by Pia, as she carried a lot of clout at the school.

'Useless, those two,' Pia said under her breath. 'I had them baking cookies in the school kitchen for the summer fair, and would you believe it, they could only seem to put one batch in the oven at a time? When I asked why they didn't use the *other shelves*, they looked at me as if I was speaking a foreign language.' She shook her head, something Pia often did, since she considered herself to be one of the few competent people on the planet.

Karen was wondering how much longer she would have to stay, and sifting through excuses, when she noticed that Pia's face had suddenly taken on a high colour. She was building up to something.

Pia took a steadying breath and leaned in towards Karen. 'I heard some news the other day. Well, not news as such – a rumour maybe.'

'And . . .'

'And I wondered if you could tell me if there's any truth to it.'

'I'll try my best.'

'It is rather delicate,' Pia said.

Karen waited. 'Well, you certainly have my interest.'

'It's about Ewan,' Pia said, and Karen thought, *Oh*:

Now she knew what was coming.

'People are saying he's been *arrested*,' Pia said, scandalized. 'Is it true?'

'Absolutely not true,' Karen said.

'Then why . . .?' She paused. 'They're saying it's to do with drugs, Karen.'

'He hasn't been arrested. He was cautioned.'

And Pia's hand flew to her mouth. 'Oh, so it *is* true! You must be going out of your mind.'

'Not really,' explained Karen levelly. 'I was the one who called the police. I needed to put a stop to it, and it seemed as good a way as any.'

Pia stared at her, shocked.

Karen had called the police about her own son.

If you asked her, Ewan needed a sharp shock to get him back to the land of the living. She would not watch him screw up his life any more than he already had. And yes, he'd hate her for it. But so what? This is what parenting involved. Hard decisions. She was his mother, she reminded herself. He didn't have to like her.

Pia was blinking rapidly, as if grit had blown into her eyes. 'Did Ewan ever mention whether Hamish—' And she halted, biting down on her lower lip. 'Did he ever say if Hamish had dabbled in—' but Pia couldn't bring herself to say the word 'drugs', and Karen suddenly understood the true reason for this impromptu powwow.

Nothing to do with friendship. All to do with finding out if her son smoked weed.

Well, as far as Karen knew, Hamish was too much of a goody-goody to smoke even tobacco, but she went right ahead and said, 'I'm sure it was only once or twice, Pia. I really wouldn't make a fuss about it if I were you.'

Pia started to stammer some sort of reply, while gathering up her shopping and making a hasty exit.

Poor Hamish, thought Karen. The kid could deny it for the rest of his days and Pia still wouldn't believe him.

Never mind. Life was unfair that way.

She finished her coffee and wended her way through the tables before going out to the car park. There was a biting chill to the air and she found herself suddenly looking forward to winter. After half-term, the last of the tourists would be gone. She'd be able to find a parking space in Windermere instead of driving around twice, often three times. The air would smell of wood-smoke and the view from her upstairs windows wouldn't be occluded by leaves. Brontë would be on her way to finishing Grade Six piano, and there would be less pressure. Yes, she thought to herself, winter was going to be good.

She opened the boot of the Volvo and took a minute to arrange the bags so the contents wouldn't tip out if she should take a corner too quickly, and then she climbed into the driver's seat.

Turning the key in the ignition, she became aware of a sound that shouldn't be there. It was an unfamiliar rustling of cheap fabric, nylon on nylon. She flicked off the radio, which had come on automatically, to work out what it was.

She felt something sharp against her neck. A point pressing in, just below her right earlobe.

Then, a trickle of warmth running down to her clavicle.

'Don't speak,' a voice said.

25

WHEN NOEL GOT the call that Karen hadn't collected Brontë from school, he had no other alternative than to bring Brontë to work with him for evening surgery.

He'd found a spare desk among the receptionists and set Brontë up with a stack of printer paper, a red and a black ball-point and some Post-its. It was the best he could do under the circumstances.

Each afternoon, Verity would catch the bus home from school – she finished forty minutes later than Brontë – and Noel had assumed she would be around to babysit while he got on with patients. The trouble was, when he called Verity's mobile, there was no answer. Which Brontë told him meant she must be doing cross-country, as that was the only time Verity would be without her phone.

He did think about roping Ewan in, but Ewan was always stoned. And though Noel was desperate, he could see it wasn't good form to leave ten-year-old Brontë with someone incapable of forming proper sentences. So into the car she went. Happily, he thought, even though she was missing her dance lessons.

After surgery, he took her for pizza and ice cream. Verity had been in touch, saying she was fine to look after herself until they came home. She didn't want to join them at the restaurant, as she had a ton of prep to do for her geography coursework. 'Rivers and shit.'

Noel checked his watch. It was seven fifteen. He wondered

where on earth Karen could have got to and when it would be an appropriate time to contact the police. He knew that twenty-four hours had to pass before a person was considered missing, but didn't it look a little odd if you actually did wait the full twenty-four hours? He wasn't sure.

Brontë made a grand attempt on her pizza, leaving only two slices, which Noel polished off with a large glass of Barbaresco, then ordered a Scotch. It occurred to him, the Scotch warming his belly through, that he rarely had his younger daughter all to himself. No one's fault but his, he supposed, but something that certainly needed remedying.

Methodically spooning strawberry ice cream into her mouth, Brontë looked just about as happy as he'd ever seen her.

'It's really good, Daddy,' she said.

'That, I can see,' he replied.

He passed her a napkin so she could wipe her chin, and his thoughts unexpectedly turned to Jennifer. She had seemed to know how to make kids happy.

His ex-wife had run a rather haphazard household and you had never quite known what you were going to get when you walked through the door. Often Verity would be in front of the TV, a bowl of cereal in her lap, while Jennifer was in the kitchen with a glass of wine and a cigarette, nattering to one of her family members who happened to have called in.

There were a lot of them. They were like a clan. Jennifer had three brothers: all good-looking, good-hearted, but each one a bit of a scally. Noel would find a stolen portable TV on the kitchen worktop, a new camcorder without a box, a set of steak knives, and once, a young Japanese maple, its roots held in a carrier bag. It had clearly been stolen from someone's garden, but Jennifer's youngest brother, Dominic, had thought it would look good in their rockery. He was happy to plant it himself if Noel didn't have the time, he said.

If it wasn't one of the brothers, Noel would find a crying spouse in his kitchen, Jennifer shaking her head and dishing out cigarettes to the wounded party, saying that her brothers were always the same – *terrible Casanovas* – and she wished she could promise they would be better behaved in the future, but it was unlikely.

Noel hadn't set out to marry into a Catholic family. He had been brought up a Catholic, his mother dutifully attending Mass each week, but he had the sense that church was something that gave their weekends some structure rather than giving them anything spiritual. By the time he was a teenager and playing rugby most Sundays, his mother had stopped going altogether, and it wasn't until he began dating Jennifer that he found himself back inside a church.

It was hard to explain what it gave him, since he was a firm non-believer, but the sense of family, the sense of belonging he felt there among Jennifer's many brothers and cousins and uncles and nieces, was something that drew him to Jennifer in a way he'd not felt with other women. Well, that and the fact that he wanted her. Wanted her badly. She was wild and funny and warm and unpredictable. She was fiercely loyal and terribly irrational. He'd never met anyone like her. After all the affected, wishy-washy girls he'd dated, Jennifer was a force of nature. He had to marry her. He simply had no choice.

Shame he fucked it up.

Sometimes he wondered how it had happened. How he went from being married to one perfectly decent woman to being married to someone else. It all seemed to happen so fast, as if it had its own special kind of momentum. As if once Karen had given him that look, lying on the treatment couch in the surgery that day, a sultry look that said *I'm game if you are*, he was thrust on to a moving walkway. A walkway which, even when he tried to get off it, even when he tried to put a halt to things, he moved ever closer towards Karen and Ewan and further away from Jennifer and Verity and the happy life he'd once had.

He should have got off. If he'd had the guts, he would have got off.

Sleeping with Karen was supposed to be a one-time thing. He wasn't making excuses – it was, he knew, a disastrous moment of weakness, one which he regretted the second it was over. What he hadn't expected was that Karen would become pregnant as a result of this one encounter. Stupid, but had he even asked if she was on the pill? He couldn't remember. And so, when she had presented herself at the surgery a few weeks later and said that she intended to keep the baby and that she wanted *him*, Noel panicked.

He called Jennifer immediately, thinking: *Damage limitation, face the thing head on, admit the mistake.* And of course Jennifer did the only thing *she* could do, which was to throw him out.

He set up home with Karen almost immediately, everything a kind of blur, and it was only later, after Brontë was born, that he thought to question his decision. He would find himself daydreaming, fantasizing about a little flat, a place he'd rented instead of shacking up with Karen, a place from which, if he resided there long enough, and said sorry enough times, Jennifer might allow him to return home.

But men like Noel didn't do that. They didn't turn their backs on their illegitimate children and fund them from afar. Not like the men of old. Modern men like Noel left their wives, and they started again. They forged ahead and tried not to think too much about the past.

And to be fair, he'd made the best of it. It hadn't been awful. In the beginning, it was actually pretty good. He grew to love Karen and Ewan. Brontë, naturally, he loved at first sight. They'd not made a bad stab at a new family, he thought, all things considered.

Noel drained his glass.

'Time to go, kiddo?' he said to Brontë, and she pleaded for more ice cream. What the hell, he thought. 'Vanilla this time?' he asked.

'Vanilla,' she said assuredly.

Ordering the ice cream and another Scotch, Noel decided they could walk home. The night was clear, he could leave the car, it was only a twenty-minute walk at the most, and with Karen not about, there was no real reason to hurry back straight away.

Karen.

She'd tried to befriend Verity back at the beginning. Verity was like a pet project of hers, and he'd catch Karen looking at him as if to say, *Look! Look at me bond!* He tried telling her to ease up a little, as it could be painful to watch. Verity would be scowling, mortified. But Karen seemed to think it was the one thing she could do that would make Noel feel good about the situation. So she'd set to with gusto, always asking Verity about her day, her friends, occasionally even about her mother. And Verity, being so conflicted and not wanting to betray Jennifer in any way, would respond with things like 'Fine'. Or 'Okay'. Or sometimes with nothing at all.

Once Brontë was born, Karen had given up pretending to be interested in his daughter, and she, Noel, Ewan, Verity and Brontë began to function a little better as a unit when they were together. Karen complained about Verity's weekend visits. Verity complained about the weekend visits. And every fortnight they would fumble along, Noel suspected, as many a fractured family does: with lots of underlying tension and many things left unsaid.

From around the age of twelve Ewan hadn't been around much. He would leave the house early, carrying either a skateboard or a football, and return home as it went dark. This relationship seemed to suit both Noel and Ewan, as neither wanted anything more from the other than for things to be as easy as they could be, and Noel was keen not to mess up the arrangement.

'When will Mummy be back?' Brontë asked now, as they made their way up the hill, hand in hand, Noel staggering a little.

'Soon,' he said mildly.

'But when?'

'In the morning, I guess.'

'Oh,' said Brontë. And she seemed immediately deflated by the thought of Karen returning.

Noel gave her small hand a squeeze.

He'd never asked her where she had gone when she went missing. Everyone else had, of course. Over and over. No one really bought the falling-asleep-in-the-shed story, least of all Karen. Karen had gone so far as to view the said shed and was having none of it. But Noel thought that it *could* be possible, so he'd decided he wouldn't ask Brontë about it. Not until enough time had passed that it wasn't a big deal any more. Not until he found the moment. The right moment, in which she might tell him the truth.

A moment such as this, perhaps?

He stopped walking and turned to face her. Taking both her hands in his, he said, 'You know, Brontë, there's been something I've been meaning to ask.'

Her face was open and trusting, and he felt himself sway slightly to one side. Really, this ought to be done when he was sober.

'That day that you left us,' he went on. 'Well, we were really worried, and I wondered if—'

'Daddy?'

'What is it, love?'

And gently, she removed her small hands from his before looking over her shoulder. 'Can I tell you at home instead?' she whispered. And he said, 'Okay.' Okay, that was fine by him. Then she linked her elbow into his and they set off at a faster pace than before.

'Daddy,' she said as they reached the brow of the hill, Noel panting a little from the exertion, 'do you think, if Mummy *doesn't* come home, that we could go to that restaurant again tomorrow?'

26

'MY WIFE IS missing.'
DS Joanne Aspinall was at the hairdresser's when she got the call. It was 7.45 p.m. and she had the last appointment with Marc 'with a "c"' Finch. Marc stayed late one night a week, on Tuesdays, to allow his clients who worked full-time the chance of an appointment. He'd quit working Saturdays when he'd turned fifty; 'I've given my life for this bloody job,' he liked to say, rather dramatically. Marc Finch's salon used to be called Mark David's, back when it was fashionable for every male hairdresser to have two Christian names above the door, and he had cut Joanne's hair for ever. Not that she came in regularly. She didn't have the time. Sometimes she could go a year without a haircut, and she'd sit, sheepish and apologetic, as Marc huffed and sighed, holding up the ends of her hair between his fingers, shaking his head, telling her what a disaster it all was.

Today he'd persuaded her to have a fringe.

'So you don't have to Botox your forehead,' he said.

Joanne was unoffended and let him chop away, Marc telling her that she was going to have to let him colour it sooner or later, or else people would realize just how old she really was.

'My wife is missing,' Noel Bloom said again. The call had come through with 'unknown number' on the display, and when Joanne learned it was Noel, she was momentarily thrown. She was taken back to the morning after they'd had sex, watching as

191

Noel punched her number into his phone. Later, when he hadn't called, she assumed he'd deleted it. Or else never really put it in there to begin with.

'Missing how long?' she asked.

'Since around three this afternoon.'

Joanne checked her watch. Almost five hours. No big deal.

'She didn't pick up Brontë after school and I don't know where she is. I'm not sure what to do.'

Joanne mouthed to Marc to give her a moment, and he put two fingers to his lips, signalling that he was off for a smoke. 'You've tried calling her?' she asked Noel.

'Repeatedly. And I've tried locating her iPhone but I can't seem to for whatever reason. I'm worried.'

Joanne thought that Noel sounded a little drunk. 'Did you argue?' she asked.

'Not really.'

'Not really?' she mirrored. Then she paused. 'It's just that, sometimes, we get women taking off after an argument to teach their spouse a lesson. It's not uncommon. They often stay away for the night. Usually, they go to their mother.'

Joanne could hear Noel tapping something against his desk, a pen maybe. 'I really don't think she'd do that,' he said. 'She'd know Brontë would be distressed at not being collected, and Brontë had dance lessons booked for this evening. Karen's not the type to let people down; it goes against her nature.'

Joanne thought about the aftermath of Brontë's return. She hadn't been able to get the girl to talk to her. Brontë was adamant that she'd fallen asleep in her friend's dad's shed and pretty much slept the day away. If it had been another child, Joanne would have dismissed it as complete nonsense and interrogated her until she caved in. Problem was, Brontë did look absolutely exhausted. In fact, Joanne was hard pressed to imagine a more wan-looking creature. And so, after another couple of attempts, she gave up and let Brontë go to her bedroom while she returned to the station to deal with the paperwork.

'You've called Karen's parents?' she asked.

'I didn't want to worry them.'

'Her friends?'

Noel sighed. 'Not really sure where to start there, to be honest.'

'You don't know their numbers?'

'I don't know their names.'

'Ah. I see. Well, I would certainly give her parents a call in the first instance, and see if she's turned up there. Aside from that, there's not a lot we can do, since she's only been missing for a few hours. See if you can find out where she was today, see if anyone saw her this afternoon.'

'Okay. Will do.'

'Anything I can help with, just call. And if she doesn't come home tonight, call me first thing.'

'Okay, but . . . Joanne?'

'Yes?'

'You don't think anything's happened . . . I mean, you heard about the trouble she was having with the death threats and so on?'

'I'd say it's unlikely.'

'Right.' He sounded unconvinced.

'People make a lot of noise on the internet, but they very rarely follow up on it in the real world.'

'Right,' he said again. 'Yes, that's what I thought. It's just . . . it really isn't like her not to come home. And Karen is . . . well, Karen's a lot of things, but she doesn't tend to behave irrationally.'

Joanne wasn't quite sure what she was supposed to say to that.

'I'm thinking maybe there could have been an accident,' he said.

'A car accident?'

'That's what I was thinking,' he said. 'Yes.'

'You'd have heard something.'

'But what if I was on the line? What if the police couldn't get through?'

'They don't use the telephone for that, Noel. They come to your door.'

'Ah, yes, of course.'

'Listen, do what I said: call around. See if you can find out where she is. If she doesn't turn up, get back in touch. I'm sure there's a perfectly good explanation. Sometimes people just want to be alone for a while and they drop off the radar.'

'But—'

'Happens more often than you'd think,' she said.

She ended the call and stared at herself in the mirror. Marc had cut half a fringe and the rest of her hair hung long over her left eye. A cheesecloth scarf and some eyeliner, and she could join the New Romantics.

Curious that Karen had done a bunk, she thought.

Noel Bloom was right when he said that she didn't fit the usual criteria. Pushy mothers tended to pick up their kids at the school gates, whatever was happening; she wouldn't abandon that responsibility just to prove a point. Pushy mothers didn't get hysterical and move back in with their mother. They needed to show the world their family was watertight. Unshakable.

So where was she?

Where *was* Karen Bloom?

27

Wednesday, 21 October

Joanne reached across to her bedside cabinet and checked her mobile phone. She set it to silent each night, as her mother, who lived in Tenerife, was in the habit of sending sentimental texts and photographs of Laddy, her aged, wire-haired Jack Russell. Last week her mother had sent a video of the dog scampering about at Playa de las Américas; she feared he might not make it through to Christmas. She wanted Joanne to have a record of him still enjoying life.

As far as Joanne could tell, the dog looked fine, and she was more interested in the beach itself, which was a lovely creamy-white colour, and no longer had the black volcanic sand that was there when Joanne last visited. Winter sun was all very well but there was something not quite right about returning to the hotel room with black grit wedged between your toes, loaded inside your bikini bottoms.

She hadn't missed any calls. Joanne switched on her lamp. The room was still in complete darkness, even though it was getting close to 7 a.m. The clocks would go back on Sunday, it was the end of British Summer Time, and though Joanne didn't much care for the dark evenings, she cared for the dark mornings even less. Going to work in the pitch black depressed her.

She swung her legs out of bed. Downstairs, she could hear

Jackie moving around the kitchen. She opened her bedroom door and could instantly smell sausages. Jackie, after giving up on Weightwatchers, Slimfast, Herbalife, Slimming World and the 5:2, was back on the Atkins Diet. And she'd lost nearly a stone. Joanne had also lost weight – eight pounds, without even trying – which she was quietly pleased about, though the lack of carbs in the house was beginning to get to her. She'd returned home with a poppy-seed loaf the other day and when she'd gone to make some toast and marmalade before bedtime, she had found it gone. Confiscated by Jackie.

'You want a sausage? Cumberland or Lincolnshire?' said Jackie, as Joanne flicked on the kettle. 'And you'll need to put some more water in that.'

'Cumberland,' Joanne answered. She could find the sage over-powering in the Lincolnshires.

'You'll tell me if my breath's disgusting, won't you? What with all this meat,' Jackie said.

'Sure.'

'I flossed last night, and it smelled like roadkill.'

Joanne dropped a teabag into an oversized mug. 'What shift are you on?'

'Two–ten,' replied Jackie.

'Then why are you up at this time?'

'Couldn't sleep. And I thought I might nip to Kendal and have a breeze round the shops. You need anything?'

Joanne shook her head.

'I could do with some new shoes for work,' Jackie went on. 'Maybe treat myself to a handbag.' She rattled the frying pan backwards and forwards so the sausages span around, mostly settling brown side up.

'Do you ever see Dr Bloom around your place?' she asked Jackie.

'At Applemead?' Jackie replied. Joanne nodded. 'Yeah, every

week or so,' she said. 'About half the inmates are his patients. Why d'you ask?'

'No particular reason.'

Jackie put the lid on the frying pan and turned to Joanne, hands on hips.

'Don't tell me he's caught your eye.'

'What? No. Nothing like that.'

'You're sure? Because he has most of the staff falling over themselves to be in the same room as him when he visits. Good-looking fella.'

Jackie was off men. After suffering a major heartbreak the previous year, she now declared she was on the lookout only for 'a rich old man with a heart condition and a limp penis'.

Joanne said, 'Noel Bloom called me last night.'

'Called you for what?'

'His wife hadn't come home.'

'Well, what's that got to do with you?' Jackie asked.

'I worked on the case when his daughter went missing.'

'So, can't he keep track of anyone round his house now?'

Joanne steeped her teabag until the water was a dark mahogany. Then she added the milk. Jackie always added the milk first, which drove Joanne to distraction. George Orwell had written an entire essay on the proper way to make tea, and he maintained that if you added the milk first you were liable to put too much in. Which is exactly what Jackie did. Every time. They could argue for days over the point so had come to this agreement: neither would make the other a cup. From then on, they would make their own. Unless they had company, that is, and then the argument would continue once again where they'd left off.

'What do you think of Dr Bloom?' Joanne asked carefully.

'What do I think of him with regards to what?' Jackie replied.

'Just, you know, generally.'

Jackie shrugged. 'Seems all right. Not like that pompous bastard Ravenscroft.'

'Ravenscroft's not pompous, he's just old-school. He's been my doctor my whole life and I've never had a problem with him.'

'He thinks the whole of Applemead should bow to greet him when he turns up. I hear him bellowing along the hallway and I head in the other direction. Bloom's much better. Doesn't speak to me like I'm an idiot. Doesn't speak to the inmates like they're idiots either . . . He still thinks a lot of his wife.'

'His wife?'

'Not his *wife* wife. His ex-wife. The one with MS.'

'Oh,' Joanne said, remembering now. The one Verity Bloom had been visiting the day her sister disappeared.

'He comes to talk to her now and then. Jennifer can't say much back, but sometimes he sits with her for hours. Sometimes he isn't even talking. I take him a cuppa and he'll be in a kind of trance.'

'Do you think he still loves her?'

Jackie shrugged as if to say, *How would I know.* 'He just seems really sad,' she said.

Joanne drank some tea and looked out of the kitchen window to the small enclosed back yard beyond. 'Interesting,' she said.

And Jackie raised an eyebrow. 'Is it?'

Joanne was behind the wheel, heading towards Kendal via Ings, driving directly into the rising sun. She rummaged around in the glove compartment, trying to locate her sunglasses, to no avail, and had to make do without. The trees were a riot of colour. All that sunshine in late summer had brewed some dazzling shades, and the leaves were just beginning to fall, peppering her windscreen.

She passed a 'For Sale' sign, and another, and then another. You could be forgiven for thinking everyone wanted to move away from the Lake District, but they didn't. People still wanted to live here, to retire here. The area never lost its pull. But the sharp rise in house prices that had started around thirteen years ago – with some properties doubling, some tripling, in price – meant that a lot of older people were sitting on properties with an overinflated value. And with the tightening of the restrictions by mortgage lenders in the last few years, younger buyers couldn't borrow the money to buy them. The Lakes was now full of big houses becoming more dilapidated by the month, belonging to people who wouldn't slash the asking prices to something reasonable because they were so pissed off at having their pension funds robbed by the banks.

Joanne wondered how long it would go on for. Till they died, she supposed. The elderly could be stubborn like that.

Her phone was ringing, so she pulled off the road at the petrol station at Plantation Bridge. 'Joanne? It's Pat Gilmore. Are you on your way in?'

'I am,' Joanne said.

'Listen, you'll need to double back. A car's been set on fire on the Newby Bridge road, next to the lake, a little past Storrs Hall. It's a botched job, but there's blood on the front seat.'

'Okay.'

'And, Joanne?'

'Yes?'

'The car belongs to Karen Bloom.'

A number of things went through Joanne's head when she received information about a potential crime scene. And she tried to ignore all of them as promptly as she could.

Of course – because this wasn't just any crime scene – her brain was making leaps, her thoughts heading off at all sorts of crazy tangents. Joanne had done a meditation class once – with Jackie. Well, it was half yoga, half meditation, and Jackie had dragged her along because she thought it might help her achieve a full night's sleep. The instructor (a woman in her fifties whom Joanne had picked up once for peeing drunkenly next to the Baddeley Clock) told them not to try to empty their brain of all thoughts completely but to watch them pass through as though you were just a casual observer. Joanne was asleep within five minutes, dog-tired as she was from a fifteen-hour shift the day before. But Jackie, wrestling with her overactive mind for a full hour, declared meditation to be next to useless, because all she did was lie there thinking of all the things she had to do and didn't have the time.

Joanne indicated right and cut through on Ratherheath Lane, past the pond where lads and dads liked to fish, past the static caravan park and on to the Crook Road. Here, she put her foot down, knowing the bends and curves of the road better than any other, and she tried to think about anything but the crime scene. Her aim was to process the facts as they were presented to her without her judgement being coloured.

When she arrived, there was a knot of people next to the road. There were no CSIs yet – it would take them over an hour to arrive from their base – and the area was being taped off. Joanne was briefed by a couple of uniforms and told that Pat Gilmore had said that Joanne's first priority should be to interview the witness who had found the car.

The Volvo wasn't visible from the road – a laurel hedge had been allowed to grow as tall and wide as a gypsy caravan – so she needed to know what would bring a person to this spot. Very few were brave enough to walk along the Newby Bridge road. Banked by dry-stone walls, with no pavement, this popular thoroughfare was not for the faint-hearted. Cars travelled along it fast. Much faster than they ought to.

Without getting too close, Joanne looked at the Volvo. The back door on the driver's side had been left open slightly and, according to DS Jason Weaver, the fire had been started on the rear seat. It hadn't spread far, though. Absence of a combustible, Joanne assumed.

Kids, perhaps? Maybe.

Underfoot, the ground was hard and covered with dried leaves. It was unlikely they would find any footprints or drag marks.

Joanne headed towards the lake. This morning the water was blue-black. It would be the obvious place to dump a body if Karen Bloom was, in fact, dead.

Many bodies had been found in the lake over the years. Most tended to resurface within four to seven days. A dead human body is heavier than water and so sinks immediately upon submersion. Those poor witches. All innocent, as it turns out.

Without obstruction, a body will continue to sink all the way down to the lake bed. It's only after the bacteria inside the gut have worked through the process of decay (the body fills with carbon dioxide and sulphur dioxide) that a body floats back up. Freezing temperatures slow this process, but the lake had had all summer to heat up so the water was not especially cold. At a rough estimate, if Karen Bloom's body was in there, and the divers didn't find her, Joanne thought they could expect to see her bobbing about on Monday. Tuesday at the latest.

Unless she'd been weighed down, of course.

Two bodies had been found in the lake since Joanne had joined the CID. Both young men. Both the result of drunken nights out gone horribly wrong. If Joanne had a teenager at home, she would have two rules: no motorbikes (Joanne wondered how on earth the Organ Donor Register would function without the constant offerings of body parts from dead motorcyclists); and no drinking alcohol next to water.

Other than that, she reckoned she'd be pretty laid back.

Both of the drowned men had been found face down, which

was another quirk of the drowning process. Men would resurface from the depths face down, whereas most women would be found face up, the gases collecting inside their fatty breast tissue. Joanne hoped she wouldn't be the one to find Karen Bloom floating face up in Windermere.

Joanne checked the bank for footprints, but as she had suspected, with the ground dry and hard, there was nothing.

Really, what she needed to do now was establish whether Karen Bloom was still missing. But that would mean calling Noel. And if his wife *hadn't* come home, then this news of the dumped Volvo should really be delivered face to face.

Ideally, delivered by her. Since you really wanted to gauge the reaction of a person when there was evidence of foul play.

For now, though, that would have to wait. She had a witness to interview.

28

NOEL AWOKE AND looked at the empty bed beside him.
He should have called Karen's parents. He should have
called them last night. Why hadn't he? Because he'd carried on
drinking, that's why.

'Shit,' he muttered, seeing the time. He'd slept later than he'd
meant to. He'd slept through his radio alarm. He could just
about hear Rod Stewart singing 'In a Broken Dream' through his
hangover. Shit.

The song ended with the DJ thanking the listener for sending
in their favourite movie track. Noel tried to place what film the
song was in. '*Breaking the Waves*,' he said to the ceiling, thinking,
Not a happy watch. Not exactly a date movie.

He turned his head from side to side and his brain seemed to
slosh around inside his skull. How much had he drunk? No point
in thinking about it. It didn't make it any better. Noel had learned
over time that the best way to cure a hangover was to drink a pint
of milk and do some vigorous exercise, all the while ignoring the
voice inside his head lambasting him for his excesses. Guilt and
hangovers were such unhappy bedfellows.

He got up. Last night, stumbling up the stairs to bed, his plan
had been to rise at six thirty and jog to Bowness to collect his car –
two birds, and so forth. Now, he wouldn't have time for that, as he
needed to get Brontë and Verity off to school and himself to work.

He also needed to report his wife *officially* missing. A quick call to Joanne Aspinall probably wouldn't suffice, and he was guessing that was going to take a little longer than a couple of minutes. *And* he needed to call Bruce. Tell him he didn't know where his daughter was.

He showered fast, and shaved, cursing when he nicked the tender skin just below his left ear.

'She's still not back?'

Noel turned around to find Verity. She was dressed in her school uniform and wore a curious expression. Mischievous, perhaps, but trying not to be.

'She's not back,' he said.

'Where d'you think she is?'

'I really couldn't say.'

'But she *will* come back?'

'I expect so.'

Noel splashed cold water on his face, rinsing away the shaving foam.

'Do you want some crumpets?' Verity asked.

'That'd be lovely. Feed your sister, too, while you're at it. I'm running a little late.'

'Already have.'

The three of them could walk down to get the car together. That would be the best thing to do. He cleaned his teeth, taking extra care to brush the back of his tongue – something he never found easy – gagging loudly, dry-heaving dramatically, like a cat being sick, before rubbing a little more toothpaste on to his teeth to mask the smell of booze. Mouthwash was no use in these circumstances. The high alcohol content made you stink even worse. He took out a clean shirt.

Staring at his collection of ties, he wondered which one to wear. Black was too funereal, and might give the wrong impression when one's wife hadn't come home, but he couldn't very well wear one of his jaunty ones either. He settled on the maroon with the thin blue stripes. Not his favourite, by any stretch, but appropriate, he decided. Then he made his way downstairs, making a mental note to call Ewan when he got to work. He didn't have time to go up there now.

Noel had called in to the flat above the garage last night to tell Ewan his mother hadn't come home, and Ewan had looked like he'd not moved for three days. 'Your mum hasn't come home,' Noel had said, and Ewan, barely looking up, said simply, 'Oh.'

Ewan wasn't speaking to Karen, on account of her arranging for the police to pop in the week before and have a quiet word about the quantity of weed being smoked on the premises. Noel had told her it wasn't a great idea, but she'd gone ahead all the same, telling him to keep his nose out. Ewan was her son, she said. She wasn't going to sit around and watch him waste his life any longer. It was high time he contributed.

Contributed to what, Noel wasn't sure. The household expenses? The conversation? The economy?

Verity had prepared the crumpets just the way he liked them: browned to the point of being almost burnt, laden with enough butter so that it dripped down the side of his wrist. She'd also made him an extra-large milky coffee, which he gulped down gratefully. And she made a face as if to say, *Thought you might need that.*

She was now brushing Brontë's hair, and Brontë wore a peaceful, noble expression, not unlike a horse enjoying a good groom.

'We'll need to head off early,' he told them. 'I left the car in Bowness, so we'll walk to collect it. I'll drop you both at school from there.'

Verity glanced his way. 'Fine by me,' she said. 'What time do we need to go?'

'If we leave here in the next five minutes, we should make it in plenty of time and—'

There was a knock at the front door.

Odd, he thought, that the caller hadn't used the bell. Though he did hate that bell. Hated the silly tune it played. He wiped his buttery hands on a piece of kitchen towel and dabbed at his chin before answering.

'Can I come in, Noel?'

It was DS Joanne Aspinall. She looked grave.

'The girls are in the kitchen,' he said, glancing behind him briefly to check if one or other of them had followed him to the door.

'I need to talk to you. Is there somewhere we could go?'

Noel saw the solemn determination in her eyes and opened the door wide to allow her in. 'The office,' he said.

He walked after her along the hallway, feeling his heart begin to pound faster. Once inside the office, door closed, she asked him to sit down, and then asked if Karen had returned home.

Noel shook his head. 'No,' he said. 'She hasn't.'

'Then, I'm really sorry to inform you of this,' she said, not taking her eyes off his for a moment, 'but we've found her car.'

'Where?'

'At the side of the lake.'

'And Karen?'

'She's not in it.'

'Oh,' he said. 'So you've not found a body, then?'

'No.'

'So she could have just left it there,' he said.

'Maybe.'

'Maybe?' he repeated.

'There are traces of blood on the front seat.'

'Oh,' he said.

'And there had been an attempt to set the car on fire.'

'Oh,' again.

'Which leads us to think that she didn't just abandon it.'

'No,' he said. 'Of course.'

'Noel, I need to ask you when it was that you last saw your wife?'

'Yesterday morning.'

'Did you speak to her after that?'

'I didn't, I'm afraid.'

'And besides the problems she was having with the internet trolls and so forth, can you think of anyone that may have wanted to harm her?'

Suddenly, Noel felt like he was watching a movie. *Can you think of anyone who would want to harm your wife?* the detective asked, and the respondent would say, *No!* Horrified. *She was liked by everyone.*

Noel looked at Joanne sadly, and said, 'Yes, I would think there are a few people capable of hurting Karen.'

'What about ex-boyfriends? Any problems in her past that you can think of?'

'Not that she mentioned.'

'What about Ewan's father? Is he around?'

Noel shook his head. 'Do you think she's in the lake?' he asked.

'It's too early to speculate.'

'But if you *had* to speculate?'

'Then I would say she could be in the lake.'

Noel weighed up this information. He studied his fingers. The vitiligo was spreading again. It happened in times of stress. He didn't like to admit it, but it was true. When Ewan was small, his friends had been fascinated by the disease. *Why is your skin patchy like that, Dr Bloom?* And he would tell them his flesh had been burnt to a crisp when he was rescuing a baby from a burning building.

Dale was the only one who still believed that story.

'Mind if I look around?' Joanne said.

'Here?' replied Noel.

'Yes, here.'

'Help yourself,' he said.

Then he looked at Joanne. 'You've changed your hair,' he said.

29

*Y*OU'VE CHANGED *your hair.*

Joanne couldn't imagine someone saying such a thing after being told that their wife may be rotting at the bottom of the lake.

She drove back to the crime scene, where Oliver Black would be working by now. Her witness had not given her anything interesting. He was an unemployed tree surgeon, which Joanne thought was interesting in itself, since there was nothing *but* trees around here. He must have been pretty terrible at his job, or else downright dangerous, not to be employed. He wore a camouflage fleece, and a red neckerchief on his head. The neckerchief was knotted at the nape of his neck in much the same way Joanne's mother used to wear one, back in the seventies when she worked in the garden, or had the stepladder out for something.

When Joanne questioned her witness about his work situation he became hostile and defensive, telling her that his last boss was an absolute twat, and that if he went around accusing his best workers of stealing the machinery, then he could shove his job. All this to say that he was temporarily employed to dog-sit for an elderly couple who owned the land on which the Volvo was parked and who were currently holidaying in Santorini. He had been walking their four dogs when he found the car.

'Did you touch it?' she asked, and he shot back, 'No.' Fast. A little too fast for Joanne's liking.

'Are you sure you didn't touch the car?' she said. 'Because we'll be taking prints and we'll need to eliminate you from our inquiries.'

Kicking the ground with the toe of his paratrooper boot, he admitted to 'having a little poke around'.

'Did you remove anything from the scene?' she asked.

'No.'

'You're certain about that?'

'Certain.'

A pause.

'Well, nothing except for a couple of Booths carrier bags from the boot,' he said.

Joanne rolled her eyes. 'Carrier bags containing?'

'Some minced beef, carrots, onions . . . nothing major. I thought I could knock up a shepherd's pie.'

Joanne wondered if anything was sacred any more.

'We think a woman may have died in that car,' she said, annoyed, and he shrugged, giving her a look as if to say, *Well, I wasn't to know that.*

She took his details, handed him a card and told him that he could leave. They'd be in touch, she said, and she could see him regretting ever getting involved. He'd given her his mobile number, stalling on one of the digits, and Joanne suspected he'd switched the 3 from a 4 or else a 2. She did it herself sometimes, with acquaintances she had no interest in forging a friendship with, or when she was caught by someone on Kendal High Street conducting a survey. 'My mobile number?' she'd say innocently, before reeling off a jumble of figures that was totally unworkable. Anyway, she thought, watching the witness skulk off through the trees, she could catch up with him whatever his number was. She knew where he was staying.

You've changed your hair.

Surprisingly, after Noel Bloom had made this comment, she

found herself giving him and his two daughters a lift to Bowness to collect his car. He told her he'd left it outside the Italian restaurant last night after drinking a little more than he'd planned, which was evident from the stench of alcohol on his breath. His girls chatted away pleasantly in the back seat. They did not seem remotely distressed by Karen's absence, Brontë, particularly, peppering Joanne with questions about her work as a detective.

'Have you ever seen a dead body?' she asked.

'A couple,' replied Joanne.

'Do the police have to call you ma'am, like they do on TV?'

'No. They call me Joanne.'

'What about your boss?' she asked. 'Do you have to call *her* ma'am?'

'No. We call each other by our first names.'

'Do you have your own gun?'

And so on.

When she'd taken a look around the house she'd found only one thing of interest. She'd been on the hunt for bloodied clothing, so the first place she headed to was the utility room, where she checked the laundry basket, the washer and the dryer. In the dryer, she found one lone white polo shirt. It had a Reid's emblem on the breast and, by the size of it, Joanne assumed it belonged to Verity. Strange to dry only one item of clothing, Joanne thought, so she questioned Verity about it.

'It was dirty after cross-country,' she explained. 'I needed it again for today.'

'You have only one?'

'Yes.'

'And you didn't think to wash any other clothes while you were at it? Strange to wash one thing, don't you think?'

'Not really.'

'Where did you run?'

'Near school. We have a fixed route.'

Near school was where Karen's car had been found.

Joanne made a note of it.

Noel didn't want to tell the girls about Karen's car having been found, telling Joanne he would 'deal with it later'. And when she had questioned him about Karen's parents, asking if they'd heard anything from their daughter and could they shed any light on her whereabouts, Noel's eyes had flicked sideways, evasively, before he mumbled, 'They weren't in.'

'How about you try them again?' she'd pressed.

And he'd said, 'Leave it with me.'

In the rear-view mirror, Joanne watched the girls climb into Noel's Volvo.

For a strange second, when they'd got out of her car, she had thought Noel was going to lean over and kiss her goodbye.

Not that she wanted him to or anything.

'How *much* blood?' Joanne asked Oliver Black.

'A lot, apparently.'

'Like a *lot* lot?'

'Yes. And there's spatter on the dashboard,' he said. 'Of course, we can't know yet if it's Karen Bloom's blood, but it doesn't look good. They're saying it'd been cleaned up. Not well – it's smeared all over the front seats – but there's been an attempt at a clean-up, that's for certain.'

Joanne asked if they'd located blood anywhere else, and Oliver told her they'd found a couple of spots towards the lake. Trouble was, there had been high winds in the night, which had blown the leaves around to heaven knows where, so it was unlikely they'd find more. They were hoping to discover something in the soil samples taken from the shoreline.

DI Pat Gilmore was near the boot of the Volvo, wagging her finger at one of the CSIs. This was a habit of Pat's which Joanne didn't much care for. Joanne felt as if she was being lectured and, from the pissed-off look on the face of the CSI, so did he.

Pat called her over. 'Joanne, what do you know?'

'Husband hasn't heard from her since yesterday morning. He called me last night to report her missing and—'

'He called *you*?'

'Yes.'

'Why you?'

'I suppose he didn't know what else to do. Too early to report her gone.'

The CSI cleared his throat. He'd pushed his mask up and was wearing it across his forehead rather than covering his nose and mouth. 'Or,' he said, 'the husband was making it *look* like he was doing the right thing. Who better to call than the person who'd be investigating?'

Pat Gilmore rolled her eyes dismissively at the officer, saying, 'Yes, yes, thank you, Miss Marple. We'll all stick to our own jobs, if that's okay with you.'

She turned back to Joanne. 'Where was he last night?'

'Took his youngest out for dinner and then stayed at home with his kids.'

'And this morning, how did he seem to you? Nervous? Edgy? Frightened?'

'Hungover.'

'What did he say when you told him we'd found the car?'

'Not a lot. He looked surprised. It seemed genuine.'

'Upset?'

'Not really.'

'Don't suppose he knows of anyone who'd want to hurt her?'

'She's had a few threats.'

'Okay, well, let's leave this in the hands of Jason here and head back. I'll call North West Marine. We're going to need divers, and we're going to need dogs. Whoever left this car here scarpered on foot, so let's see if we can trace them. And we'll get the husband interviewed this afternoon, see if we have a wife killer on our hands.'

Was Noel Bloom capable of killing his wife?

Absolutely. Didn't mean he did it, though.

As much as Joanne liked to concentrate on the hard facts in front of her, she tended to get a feeling for who was telling the truth and who wasn't. Sometimes she got it wrong. Not often. And at the moment she couldn't see Noel Bloom taking a knife to his wife and dumping her body. Granted, he was not as fretful as perhaps you might expect, but shock was a funny thing. Joanne had delivered enough bad news to enough people to know they didn't do what they did on TV. Most didn't cry. Most did everything they could *not* to cry in front of a police officer. As if bravery was the one thing the situation warranted above all else. Some laughed. That was the trickiest to deal with, since Joanne would have to wait it out, wait it out until it dawned on them that this was not a joke and they would now spend the rest of their lives reliving the moment, the moment when they got it so absurdly wrong. She'd never had anyone collapse or faint. But it didn't mean she wasn't ready just in case they did. What she hated most was silence. Silence was the worst.

They drove back to the station in convoy, DI Pat Gilmore in front of Joanne, Oliver Black behind. Pat Gilmore was on her mobile phone the whole way, and she wasn't a great driver. She was doing less than twenty around some of the bends of the Crook Road and Joanne looked in her rear-view mirror to see Oliver Black miming putting a gun to his head, losing the will.

A lot of blood.

A lot of blood was indicative of repeated stabbing. And though Joanne had never dealt with a stabbing before, she knew about slippage.

Slippage occurred when the perpetrator's hand, slick with the

213

victim's blood, slipped down the knife, causing wounds to their own palm. It was almost impossible to stab a victim more than a couple of times without incurring some slippage. So, with any luck, they'd find traces of the killer's blood in the front of Karen's car as well.

As Joanne drove, she cursed out loud.

Why the hell hadn't she thought to check Noel Bloom's palms?

30

Noel dropped a pod into the espresso maker. He pulled down the lever, pressed the button on the top for a large cup, and bent down to inhale the aroma. He alternated now between decaf and the real deal, but found he was enjoying the decaf more and more. He might switch altogether. Particularly with his blood pressure the way it was. He'd been borderline high and noticed an immediate drop when he'd cut his caffeine intake, so perhaps he should go for it. Hard to give up his first one of the day, though. Particularly on a day like this.

He needed to call Bruce and tell him about Karen. He should do it right now. Now would be the time to do it, before he started work.

He drained his cup. Then he rifled about in the bottom drawer of his desk until he found his stash of TicTacs, and poured a few from the box directly into his mouth. He knew his breath still stank of booze, but he'd just have to keep some space between his patients and himself.

His first of the day was a post-partum check-up. He always enjoyed these. He liked babies and, at six weeks after the birth, the mothers tended to be upbeat and optimistic. The real exhaustion didn't tend to kick in until around weeks eight to nine. That's when the babies who'd been peaceful and easy up to that point – 'good babies' – suddenly seemed to find their lungs, causing merry hell in the household.

He stood at his open door, waiting to greet the patient, knowing she'd have her hands full with baby, nappy bag, and so on, and watched as she waddled towards him, still with the distinctive duck-like gait of the heavily pregnant.

As she approached he said, 'Your hips sore, Hazel?' and she replied, 'Killing me.'

He took the baby from her arms and she handed him over gratefully. This was Hazel's third son. Each had been over ten pounds. Noel cradled the child in the crook of his right arm and asked Hazel how the baby was doing.

'Him? Oh, he's right as rain.'

Hazel was correct; he was. You only needed to look at the child to see he was thriving. That was the thing with babies – generally, if they looked all right, they *were* all right, regardless of what their parents had to say.

'And you?' Noel asked. 'How are you?'

'Tired. Sick of being fat. Sick of not having a second to myself.'

'I can refer you to the physiotherapist for your hips if you like?' but Hazel waved away his suggestion, as if that would be more hassle than it was worth.

'I'll cope.'

When Noel had first become a GP, he would examine a woman physically at her post-partum check-up. Make sure her abdominals had knitted together, ask if she'd resumed intercourse. Now he did very little, just had a general chit-chat. Mostly, he was there to reassure them that whatever they were feeling and going through was entirely normal. It was okay *not* to be completely besotted with this new life they'd created. It was okay to hate their husbands a little.

Karen had struggled in post-partum with Brontë. She'd had a tricky birth, a seventy-two-hour slog that had ended with forceps and then Brontë being pulled from Karen with a ventouse.

Her strange, conical head had remained that shape for far longer than Karen could really cope with.

Noel hadn't had a lot of experience of bad births. During his training he'd been attached to a midwife-led centre in North Wales, and the staff there did such a fine job of preparing women (lots of walking, lots of squatting, lots of talking through their fears about the birth process) that his boss was rarely called upon to assist. And then of course Verity's birth had been such a breeze. Two big pushes from Jennifer and Verity had shot out like a salmon. And Jennifer had such an array of relatives on hand to help out afterwards – everything from cooking, to her siblings taking turns to push the pram around Windermere so Jennifer could get some sleep – that his home took on an almost party-like atmosphere for a while.

Very different to his experience with Karen.

'It's normal to feel like this,' Noel would tell her when he found her crying on the bathroom floor at two in the morning. And she'd scream back at him, '*Normal?* How do you know what's fucking normal?' and he'd look at his ravaged wife and have no clue how to help her. Of course, it might have helped if he'd known her a little better before she became pregnant. If they'd been more of a couple. She later told Noel that she'd struggled in the weeks following Ewan's birth, too, and perhaps if Noel had known this he could have supported her more.

Once, at his wits' end, he'd almost found himself saying, *It wasn't like this with Jennifer,* but managed to stop the words from escaping just in time. One of life's great taboos: comparing one's current wife to one's last. But Karen must have seen it in his face nonetheless and she went for him with the baby monitor, hitting him over the head with it repeatedly until he promised he would never measure Karen against his 'inbred bog-trotter of an ex-wife' again.

In the end, it passed, as these things tend to. But the first thing

Karen did was to get herself sterilized, even though Noel pleaded with her against it. 'You're too young,' he said. 'You might want more children,' he said. 'Let me have the snip. It's so much safer . . . statistically.'

'I won't go through that again,' she told him.

'So don't. Let me. I really don't mind and—'

'Noel. I won't go through that again.'

And the matter was closed.

He wondered, over the years, if having more children would have been better for Karen. Perhaps, if she were saddled with another one, she would have had to lower her standards and Brontë would have been given an easier ride.

Now they'd never know.

In his arms, baby Jonathon gurgled and smiled. Noel pulled a surprised face, touching the side of Jonathon's mouth to get him to do it again.

'You're using birth control?' he asked Hazel, not moving his gaze away from her bonny baby.

Hazel made a snorting sound. 'What do you think? Course I am.'

'Great. Any worries? Any concerns?'

'When can I start exercising?'

'With the pain in your hips the way it is, I wouldn't do anything right now.' Strictly speaking, it wasn't her hips that were troubling her, it was her sacroiliac joint. 'Anyway, what's the rush?'

Hazel lifted her shirt and took two great handfuls of belly. 'This,' she said.

'Give yourself a chance, Hazel. You've only just given birth.'

'It's disgusting.'

'It's what happens.'

'Not to the celebs, it doesn't.'

'Yes, well, they have an army of people helping out. And besides, I heard that some celebrities are paying for surrogates now so they can keep their bodies exactly the way they are.'

Hazel sat back in her chair and gaped at him.

'*Really?*' she said. 'They're *pretending* to be pregnant?'

'So I've heard.'

Noel had no idea if there was any truth to this rumour, but he'd brought it up a couple of times recently, and his post-partum ladies certainly left a lot happier than when they'd walked in.

The office phone was ringing.

'Excuse me a moment,' he said to Hazel, and picked up.

'There's a DS Aspinall on the line for you, Dr Bloom,' said the receptionist. 'Sorry to disturb, but she says it's important.'

'Put her through, Mandy.'

Noel handed the baby back to Hazel, just in case he needed to make a note of something, and said, 'Joanne. Hello again.'

'We're going to need to talk to you, Noel. At the station. Any chance you could come in around lunch?'

'Sure.'

'Do you want me to send a car or can you make your own way?'

'I can drive myself.'

'Great. See you later, then.'

'Joanne?'

'Yes?'

'Do I need a lawyer?'

31

DI PAT GILMORE was standing by the whiteboard. On it she'd written Karen Bloom's name, and drawn a big circle around it, and yesterday's date. The day she went missing.

That was it.

'So we're working on the assumption that the blood in the car is from our missing woman,' she began. Pointing her marker pen at DC Gidley, the young officer sitting next to Joanne, she said, 'Hannah, you find out where Karen Bloom was yesterday, where she went, who she spoke to. She had around six hours to fill, between dropping her child at school and when she was expected back there. Find out who her friends are, where she shops, if she goes to zumba, anything.'

Jackie went to zumba at the Ladyholme Centre twice a week. Joanne had joined her once for moral support. Never again. Too noisy. Too sweaty. She couldn't imagine the likes of Karen Bloom jumping up and down next to Jackie in her leotard, bits jiggling, but you never knew. People could be surprising.

'Joanne,' Pat Gilmore said, 'I want you and Oliver to compile a list of potential suspects. Who doesn't like this woman? Who's had run-ins with her in the past? Her handbag and wallet were still in the car, so that rules out a robbery gone wrong. From the amount of blood, I'd say we're looking at multiple stab wounds. In my view, this has personal vendetta written all over it. Start

with those close to her and work outwards. You've got the husband coming in?'

'He'll be here at lunch.'

'Happy to assist?'

'Asked if he needed a lawyer.'

Pat Gilmore raised her eyebrows. 'Did he now?'

'So, personal vendetta?' Oliver Black said to Joanne. They'd gone
into a side room to 'brainstorm'.

'Pat's right,' Joanne said. 'This doesn't look like a random act
to me. Trouble is, Karen's upset quite a lot of people she didn't
actually know. And they all took her comments personally.'

Joanne sat back in her chair and exhaled. List of suspects?

Try *everyone*.

Oliver had a sheet of A4 and at the top he'd written 'Noel Bloom'.

'His daughter tried to strangle Karen Bloom in the summer,'
Joanne said. 'Verity Bloom. Remember?'

Oliver added Verity's name below Noel's.

'And we need to get hold of Karen's computer and find out
who was sending the hate messages,' she said.

Oliver wrote 'trolls'.

'And look into any ex-boyfriends,' she said.

'What about that kid she slapped in her kitchen?' Oliver asked.

'Dale? I don't think he's one to hold grudges, but go ahead,
add him anyway. And I want to interview Brontë again. The girl
went *somewhere* for twenty-four hours, and I doubt it was
that shed.'

'But the guy who owned the shed *did* say it was possible someone had been in there overnight.'

'He also said it was possible someone hadn't. Have we still got
someone working on that?' she asked, and Oliver nodded. Told
her nothing new had come up. 'I just can't help thinking this is

linked,' she said. 'I mean, a kid disappears for a day, then her mother disappears a few weeks later? What are the chances?'

'We could do with a body,' Oliver said.

'Yes,' replied Joanne. 'A body would be good.'

'Do you mind showing me your hands?'

Joanne sat opposite Noel in the interview room with Oliver Black alongside her. They'd had the decorators in last week and the room smelled pleasantly of fresh paint. Joanne had always liked that smell – the newness it evoked, as if the room she was entering was spotlessly clean. As a general rule, though, the interview rooms were *not* clean. For no other reason than the cleaner was crap. Crap and old. But no one had the heart to get rid of her, as she'd been here for thirty years, demoted to cleaner when funds no longer stretched to a perky lady with a tea trolley delivering Battenberg and fig rolls twice a day.

Probably just as well. They all carried a lot more weight than they used to. Most of Joanne's colleagues today couldn't run; they were short of breath after climbing the station stairs. And for a time this had concerned Joanne. How on earth would they catch anyone? That was until she realized that most criminals were also too fat to run away from the police. She'd watched some footage recently of the miners' riots in the eighties. Men as old as fifty hightailing it across fields, vaulting over fences. That would never happen today.

'Am I under arrest?' Noel asked.

'Not at all. You're free to leave whenever you like. Though we do need help finding your wife, Noel. And I'm sure you can appreciate you're the obvious place to start.'

Noel held out his hands for inspection. He had about him a faint smell of cigarettes. She hadn't known he smoked. Joanne watched as Oliver noticed Noel's vitiligo for the first time, grimacing slightly, and Joanne almost said, 'It's not contagious, Oliver,' but she didn't.

Noel turned his hands over to reveal his palms, and Joanne found unexpectedly she was holding her breath.

They were clean. No cuts.

'Good,' she said. 'Now, if you could talk me through when you last saw Karen again, so my colleague here can take a few notes.'

'Yesterday morning. I left as normal for work. Usually, I leave the house just before Karen, at around eight fifteen.'

'And what were Karen's plans for the day?'

Noel paused, lifting his eyes to the ceiling, trying to remember. 'The same as always, as far as I'm aware.'

'What does she do when Brontë is at school? Where does she go?'

Noel looked at Joanne straight. 'You know what? I have no idea.'

'What, you don't talk? You don't discuss your days with each other?'

'Not really.'

'Why is that?'

Noel gave a laugh. 'I don't know. You tell me.'

'You don't seem too upset by the news this morning, if you don't mind my saying.'

'What reaction were you hoping for?'

Joanne paused. She glanced at Oliver, who was looking back at her with a curious expression.

'Did you do it?' she asked Noel.

'Did I do what?'

'Did you hurt your wife?'

'Of course not, Joanne. You know I didn't.'

At Oliver's request, they took a short break. Outside the interview room, Oliver looked at Joanne with what she thought was weary resignation and said, 'I'm not sure this is exactly professional, Joanne.'

'What? You think I'm being too blunt?'

'I think, by the way you're talking to him, that you two know each other personally in some capacity and you're failing to disclose it.'

Joanne folded her arms and sighed out a long whoosh of breath. 'How did you come to that assumption?' she asked crossly.

'Because I'm a detective?'

Joanne stayed silent. Then she closed her eyes and whispered, 'Fuck.'

'What happened?' he asked.

'You're going to actually make me *say* it?'

'I'm not going to make you say it, but if we're going to interview the guy with the idea that he may have murdered his wife, I could do with knowing what's going on . . . And he likes you, by the way. Not sure if you're aware of that, but he does.'

Joanne shook her head. 'He doesn't.'

'Suit yourself,' said Oliver.

Joanne paused. Took a breath. 'So, it was just one night,' she said. 'And I didn't know he was married.'

'Was this before Brontë Bloom disappeared?'

'God, yes.'

'And then what happened?'

'In the morning we went our separate ways. He told me he was an accountant. The next time I saw him was the day Brontë went missing.'

'And you've not liaised since?'

'By "liaise", you mean . . . sex?'

'Yes,' he said.

'No.'

'But you'd like to?' he said.

'I'm not answering that.'

'Okay, let's forget about it for now. But if it comes up, I knew nothing about it.'

If it looked like Noel was guilty, Joanne would be pulled from the case. She would most likely be pulled from the case anyhow and would receive a dressing-down from Pat Gilmore for not mentioning the fact that Noel Bloom had *had sexual relations with that woman*. And that woman . . . was her.

Joanne wondered if it was possible to jeopardize an entire police career by sleeping with the wrong person. Probably.

Noel had removed his suit jacket and loosened his tie. He looked as if he hadn't slept. But then Joanne realized that he always looked that way. Even after the night they'd spent together – after he had fallen asleep, spooning her from behind, his breath warm on the skin of her shoulder – he'd woken up looking like he needed another six hours.

'I have to ask where you were yesterday, Noel,' Joanne said, and he nodded.

'At the surgery from around 8.25 a.m. until 1 p.m., and then it was my afternoon to do the home visits.'

'Where did you get to?' she asked.

'Firstly, to Cleabarrow, near the golf club. Then another at Applemead. And, lastly, I visited a woman at Storrs.'

'Storrs?'

'That's right.'

Storrs Park was pretty close to where Karen's car was found. And to where Verity had been running.

'What time were you there?'

'Must have been around three,' he said.

'And you can prove this?'

'I wrote up my notes on the desktop at work later on. I suppose if you want absolute proof I was with those patients you'll have to ask the patients themselves. I'd be happy to send through their names and numbers when I get back to Windermere.'

Joanne nodded. 'We're going to need to look at Karen's computer as well, if that's okay with you. Follow up on some of those threats.'

'Fine. Call in for it whenever.'

'How's Verity these days?'

Noel went to answer and then stopped himself. After a brief moment, he said, 'She's fine, Joanne. Why do you ask?'

'Just interested. She still seeing that counsellor?'

'She told you about that?'

'Your father-in-law did. He said she was seeing someone to help with her violent urges towards Karen. Are the sessions still going on?'

Noel shifted uncomfortably in his seat. 'Look,' he said. 'Reid's Grammar requested those sessions. In my view, they aren't necessary. Verity lost her temper with Karen and struck out. It was a one-off incident.'

'Struck out? I was told she performed a sustained attack in which she tried to strangle her stepmother.'

Noel gave Joanne a withering look. He seemed to have an array of withering looks. 'You know she didn't do this, Joanne.'

'I don't know that, Noel,' she said. 'And neither do you.'

32

KAREN'S PARENTS WERE on their way.

'Christ,' Bruce had said to Noel when he phoned earlier, 'why didn't you call yesterday? Why are we finding this out now?'

Noel could hear Mary whimpering like a whipped dog in the background.

If Karen was gone for good Mary wouldn't get over it. Noel knew that. Bruce would. He'd soldier on, Noel suspected, as his military training had taught him to, and he would not be broken.

Mary would be torn apart.

'We'd had a few cross words yesterday,' Noel lied. 'I thought she had gone off on her own to prove a point. I really didn't want to trouble you with it. I suppose I was embarrassed, Bruce.'

'So why not call us this morning, when she wasn't back?'

'The police came . . . and I needed to go into the station to give a statement. I'm really sorry, but time just got away from me. Before I knew it half the day had gone.'

'What else did they say? Have the police found anything to suggest what happened?'

'Not as yet,' Noel said.

He did not tell him about the blood.

'They told me to keep an open mind,' he added. 'Said to remain optimistic.'

Another lie.

Noel wasn't a natural liar, but something about Bruce made

the lies tumble out of him at an alarming rate. Ordinarily, it was harmless stuff. *Yes, the gutters were cleared out at the end of November, Bruce. No, sadly my finances won't stretch to any more investments right now . . . Yes, I realize it is a missed opportunity.*

He'd tried to talk them out of coming to Windermere. 'There's really nothing you can do. There's nothing any of us can do,' he said to Bruce. 'You may as well sit tight until we have some more news.' He didn't want them there. The last thing he needed was Bruce in his home, bossing him about, scrutinizing his every move. Which was why he'd delayed telling them in the first place, he supposed. Because he knew Bruce would say, 'We'll be on the road in an hour.' Which he had. And so now they were.

Noel wondered idly if perhaps Mary would bring a fruit cake. She seemed to have a production line going from late September through to Christmas, each one progressively more booze-laden than the previous, and they would all coo over it during the grand unveiling on Boxing Day. (Though not Bruce. *Too rich. Marzipan repeats on me something terrible.*)

Would Noel still have to spend Christmas with them this year? He really hoped not.

Noel put the idea out of his head for the moment and opened the fridge. They were almost out of milk. Then he checked his watch. He should have been back at the surgery for three thirty, but of course he'd had to call and ask for someone to cover his appointments. Not that he wanted to. He'd far rather have been at work than dealing with Bruce and Mary, but he could see it wouldn't look good. He could imagine Joanne Aspinall assessing him suspiciously in that way of hers: *You went to work?* Frowning at the same time, the skin between her eyes puckering a little, but still quite pretty all the same.

He wondered if she'd ever been married. She gave off an air of independence, but that didn't mean anything. The divorcees he saw at work were fiercely independent. Suddenly, women who had been Tired All the Time would be out jogging at six in the morning, taking college courses in nursing and accountancy, and generally making the world go round.

He'd never been with a truly independent woman. Once Jennifer became pregnant, she gave up being on a career path, as her mother had, and as her mother had before her. In Jennifer's grandmother's day, in Ireland, it was not considered decent for a heavily pregnant woman to be seen at work, and Noel had questioned Jennifer about it, saying that surely she didn't think this was still the case?

'Absolutely not,' she replied. 'I hate my job. Always have. It's boring as hell and I can't wait to give it up.'

He didn't mind. Why would he?

Karen, meanwhile, didn't have a job when they met, and she gave the vague excuse of 'It's not quite the right time' as the reason for this.

And then she found out she was pregnant, so that was that.

He wondered what it would be like to be with a woman such as Joanne. She was looking for love, he knew that. But a woman like her wouldn't want his baggage. They never did. They wanted the dream, the fairy-tale. They didn't want a twice-married heavy drinker who was responsible for three kids and an ex-wife with MS. (And there was also the small matter of her thinking he might have murdered his wife. Or else his daughter had.) Still, he reflected on that night they'd had together, and he couldn't shake off the thought of her. Joanne was a woman starved of touch and he was a man starved of warmth, and the two of them had found each other in the most unlikely of places.

Would it happen again?

Doubtful.

From the way Joanne had questioned him earlier, he got the impression they thought Karen was dead. He assumed they'd found more evidence than they were willing to share. So he knew he had to tell Ewan and the girls of the possibility of Karen never coming home. They'd want to know what Bruce and Mary were doing there. And once news that Karen's car had been found abandoned got round, the whole village would be talking about it.

How should he go about wording it? he wondered. He didn't want to alarm Brontë unnecessarily, but he needed to prepare her, and it would be wrong to keep it from her. He wondered if he could drum up the emotion necessary and realized rather quickly he wasn't sure he could. This could turn out to be one of those moments. A defining moment in Brontë's life which, if played wrongly, she could use as a stick to beat him with when she was older and her life hadn't turned out the way she'd wanted it to.

You didn't even cry for her. Not one single tear.

The truth was, he wasn't particularly sad that Karen had gone. The Catholic and father in him had been prepared to stick the marriage out for the duration. He'd screwed up one child's life and he didn't plan on screwing life up for Ewan and Brontë as well. 'You can't stay together if you're not happy, just for the sake of the kids,' folk liked to say, and Noel thought, *Yes you can. You can do exactly that.*

But now life had presented him with this way out. He was going to have to *act* upset if he was going to pull it off, or else there would be suspicion. Already Joanne had queried his initial response to Karen's disappearance, so he needed to up his game. She'd actually been rather tough on him, relentless in her questioning, which should have had him panicked, but he'd found it all rather appealing. She'd become quite the school ma'am, and he expected she got results. One of those relentless detectives who never lost a case.

For a second he pictured her naked in his oval bath at the end of a hard day, her lovely hair spilling over the edge. He would bring her large glasses of red wine and small squares of cheese, and he would soap her feet while they discussed cases, and—

The doorbell was ringing.

Noel stood at the mirror in the hallway. The one that Karen would scowl into each day before leaving the house. Unusually for him, he looked quite healthy. A little too healthy, considering the circumstances.

Noel gave his eyes a hard rub with the heels of his hands. Then he unstraightened his collar, pulled his tie over to one side and ruffled his hair a little.

'Bruce, Mary,' he said solemnly when he'd opened the door, and gave a small shudder, as though a cry were trapped inside his throat. 'Thank God you've come.'

33

Joanne was back at the crime scene. A day had passed since the Volvo had been found but, as yet, they were no closer to determining the whereabouts of Karen Bloom. So Joanne returned to the start. It's what she always did when she didn't know where to go next. She went to the scene and let it speak to her.

The Volvo had been removed, taken away for further forensic testing, and so far they had found only Karen Bloom's blood inside the vehicle. The marine unit had two divers in the lake again today, as yesterday's dive had found nothing. The dogs hadn't turned anything up either. They'd followed a trail through the trees down to the lake and along the shoreline for around fifty yards or so. But then it seemed to come to a complete stop. There were a number of possible reasons for this: carrying Karen's body, the suspect had waded into the lake and swum off (quite tricky, and unlikely, in Joanne's opinion); the suspect had been picked up by an accomplice in a boat (possible); the dogs weren't very good at their job (unlikely); or the handler, Dave, wasn't very good at his job (more than possible, actually). Joanne had met Dave on a number of occasions. He was a burly guy who was into Second World War memorabilia and was considered by most to be a first-class twit. He referred to himself in the third person when talking to his dogs, which Joanne found unnerving: *Find it for Dave, boy! Dave's right here by your side, boy!* Joanne wondered if he did the same thing when speaking to his wife.

It was raining. Not ideal, as Joanne had been hoping to perform her own search now that the CSIs were mostly done with the scene. The ground was already sodden and squelchy underfoot. Joanne wore hiking boots and jeans, but really, wellies would have been the better option.

She performed a thorough fingertip search where the Volvo had stood and when she found nothing there she began to make her way towards the lake. It was eerily quiet. There was no sound from the road and all at once Joanne felt vulnerable out here on her own. She should have asked Oliver to come, too.

The lake water was a muddied green. Its surface rippled in the light wind. A few minutes later a steamer passed. It was full of passengers, its windows fogged. A few of them were braving the open top deck in their waterproofs, and they waved to Joanne, happy to see some life other than the ducks, geese and swans, so she waved back. Someone might remember seeing her if she should disappear from here.

Joanne tried to shake the thought from her head, and moved on. The rain grew heavier. She wondered if this was the start of the *real* rain. Usually, they would get another week of dry weather and would be well into November before it became what Joanne thought of as 'monsoon season'. November was meant to be lived indoors in the Lakes. It was the time for open fires, thick stews and box sets. Most complained, but Joanne quite enjoyed it. There was a certain freedom of mind that came from knowing you couldn't do anything constructive during the November rains and that you might as well surrender to the sofa for the duration.

Joanne followed the path along the shore, checking behind her every few steps, as she was now a long way from the road and totally isolated. She headed to the point at which the scent had dried up for the dogs the previous day. To the left side of the path, beneath the shelter of trees, there were batches of leaves that had remained dry. Joanne picked up a branch to poke around with. Or to poke *someone* with if necessary.

Ahead of her was a large holly, its branches filled with orange-red berries. As her boot crunched on the desiccated leaves, out of nowhere there was a loud clap of wings and three sets of wood pigeons flew in front of Joanne's face.

She spun to the left and stumbled a few paces. Her breath caught in her throat. Her heart jackhammered inside her chest. A cold sweat sprang up between her shoulder blades.

Then she saw it.

To the left of where she stood, fifteen feet or so away from the path, was a silver birch.

Joanne moved closer to examine it further. Something inside her stirred.

Pulling on her gloves, she touched the bark carefully. Put her nose to it and inhaled.

A blood smear. No prints that she could discern, but someone with a significant wound had grabbed on to this tree.

And if *this* blood didn't match the blood inside Karen's car, then Joanne could very well have a suspect. And if *that* suspect was listed on the DNA database, then Joanne could have a name.

She smiled, feeling rather pleased with herself.

34

'THREE DAYS? WHY three days?' Joanne asked, furious.
'That's how long it takes.'

She was on the phone to the lab. They'd come out to collect the sample and Joanne had called to find out how long it would be until they had the results, expecting them to say by the following morning at the latest.

'But we've had samples back in a matter of hours before now,' she said.

'Good samples,' the technician replied. 'This is dried-out blood on the bark of a tree. It's more complicated. To be honest, it's going to be three days minimum.'

Joanne cut the call and banged on the desk with her fist.

'Not what you were hoping for?' asked Oliver Black, without looking up.

'Not really.'

'See, if this was CSI Miami,' he said, flicking his pen between his fingers, 'we'd have the suspect's address, phone number *and* his mother's maiden name by now. We'd be on our way to arrest him.'

'And we'd have guns,' she said.

'We could wave them around when we entered his sleazy drug den,' he said.

'And shout, "Get on the fucking floor!"'

Joanne had never shouted 'get on the fucking floor' at a

suspect in her life. Maybe she should, just to see how it felt. She could practise on Jackie.

With the delay of the forensic evidence it meant they were back to standard detective work: knocking on doors, calling hospitals and surgeries to see if anyone had come in with a knife wound to the hand, speaking to Karen's acquaintances, picking through her life, her computer, to see if anything strange stood out, contacting ex-boyfriends, ex-partners (they could locate only one for now, a bobby living in Belfast whom she'd dated when she was seventeen and could prove his whereabouts at the time of Karen's disappearance). It was monotonous work, which would usually be covered by an officer junior to Joanne, but short of anything better to do, she and Oliver set out to try to find something of interest.

'We could do with a body,' Oliver said again.

'Yes,' replied Joanne again. 'A body would be good.'

Oliver was driving, his long thin pianist's fingers wrapped around the wheel. Joanne found herself thinking about Noel Bloom. Had she thrown herself at him that night at the bar?

A little bit. But her blood had been running hot with good whisky, and she'd not had sex in . . . well, it had been a while.

She gazed out of the window at the wet sheep, the low black cloud.

'Filthy day,' remarked Oliver.

'Prepare yourself for another thirty at least,' she said, but Oliver didn't seem particularly put out. 'Is Glasgow any better?'

'Not a lot.'

They were on their way to interview Mrs Pia Nicholls. An acquaintance of Karen Bloom's, she'd been identified as one of the last people to see Karen at around 1 p.m. on Tuesday and Joanne wanted to hear for herself what the woman had to say. Joanne wasn't expecting Pia Nicholls to shed much light on Karen's disappearance directly, but DC Hannah Gidley had reported Pia to be the kind of gossipy woman who knew everyone and anyone, and there was always a chance it would turn up something.

'What kind of woman would you say Karen Bloom is?'

'I'm not sure I know what you mean,' replied Pia Nicholls.

They were at Reid's Grammar. Pia had agreed to meet but said she absolutely had to finish dealing with the prizes for the Christmas raffle and simply needed to meet *on campus*. Joanne said, 'Bit early for that, isn't it?' and Pia had sounded horrified, saying, 'Absolutely not,' and that they were already way behind schedule.

They were an enigma to Joanne, these types of women. The ones who made themselves indispensable for good causes that Joanne reckoned were not really good causes at all, because everyone involved seemed to have a hell of a lot more money than she did already.

'It's a straightforward question, Mrs Nicholls. What kind of woman is Karen Bloom?'

'She's . . .' Pia paused, then sighed, before finally saying, 'I'd say that she's a good parent,' as though that was the sum of Karen Bloom.

Joanne waited.

'Look,' Pia said primly, 'I'm not really sure what you're asking. Do you want me to *divulge* things about Karen, because I can assure you, detective, I am not the type of woman to gossip, and—'

Joanne held up her hand. 'Gossip is exactly what I need in this instance, Mrs Nicholls. It just might save Karen Bloom's life. She is missing and we need to find her, and to do that we need to know as much about her as possible. Things that she would tell her friends. Things that even her husband might not know.'

Pia put down the book of raffle tickets and swallowed. On the table were a dozen bottles of champagne, a stack of leather-bound books and a hamper from Fortnum's containing dry goods. All this as well as a voucher for seven courses at the Samling, a week's accommodation in Corsica and a boxed Hermès scarf. Each item had a raffle ticket attached to it. It was a far cry from the Christmas raffle at the station. Last year she'd won a pair of tights.

Pia turned to Joanne, and a shadow seemed to fall across her face. 'Karen Bloom screwed my husband,' she said tartly. 'There, detective, is that gossip enough for you?'

'She did?' replied Joanne, surprised.

'Yes. She did. Four times.'

'Would you be able to tell me how you came about this information? If it's not too much of an intrusion.'

'Roger told me in a fit of guilt. That's my fool of a husband.'

'And you remained friends with Karen Bloom?' Joanne was frowning. 'That's quite unusual.'

Pia tried to shrug it off. 'She doesn't know I know.'

'You never wanted to confront her?'

'Of course I did. I hated her for it. I still hate her for it. But I had to think long and hard about what would happen. And the reality was that, if I said anything, everyone would know. The state of my marriage would become open season and I just wasn't prepared to put myself, or my son, Hamish, through that kind of hell.'

Joanne nodded.

'Hamish applied to Oxford,' Pia added, as if by way of explanation. 'Roger promised it wouldn't happen again. And I said it had *better bloody not happen again.* Then I told him that of course I would need a new kitchen. And that was the end of the matter.'

Joanne phrased the next question as tactfully as she could. 'Do you know if she slept with anyone else's husband?'

'I heard rumours. But Karen and I didn't have the type of relationship in which we confided secrets.'

'Did she have that kind of relationship with anyone?'

Pia shook her head. 'She was pretty cold. She liked to stay on the periphery.'

'How did Karen seem to you when you saw her last?' Joanne asked.

'No different to usual.'

'Worried? Harried? Anything like that?'

'If she was she didn't show it. We were talking about her son. He's on drugs, you know. It's terrible, really. Drugs tear families apart. Karen reported him to the police. So that's who I'd be looking at if I were you . . . There was always something a little off about Ewan. Even when he was small he was a strange kid. I used to say to Roger, "That child is not right." I could never relax when he was in the house . . . always thought I'd find him torturing the cat or something. Eerie, now I come to think of it, but I always got the impression he didn't like his mother.' Pia looked past Joanne towards the window. 'Or maybe it was the other way around,' she said, almost dreamily. 'Maybe it was she who didn't like him.'

Joanne knew what Pia meant about Ewan. She didn't think the kid was actually dangerous, but he had a *look* of danger about him. He reminded Joanne of a black-eyed boy who span the waltzers at the travelling fair which came to Bowness each August. He was usually shirtless, of course. And for three consecutive summers from the age of thirteen, Joanne felt the kind of keen longing that comes only from wanting a bad boy.

Back in the car, Oliver said, 'So Karen Bloom cheated on your Noel, then.'

And Joanne snapped back, 'What do you mean, *my* Noel? He's not *my* Noel.'

'Do you think he knows about it?'

'I'm not sure,' she said.

'He never mentioned it to you?'

'What, like, my wife has been fucking someone else, Joanne. That's why I'm fucking you right now. Strange, Oliver, but no. He never mentioned that.'

'Well, at least we have a motive.'

Joanne turned to him in her seat. 'You think Noel Bloom killed his wife because she was sleeping around?'

'People kill for less.'

Oliver was right. They did. Human beings were so full of emotion. That was the problem.

They could kill for a reason that to them felt like the *only* reason and to Joanne and the rest of the rational, thinking population felt like absolutely no reason at all.

35

FROM THE KITCHEN window Noel watched a cock pheasant pecking around in the soil near the hydrangea. Noel didn't like hydrangeas. But every garden seemed to require one so, naturally, they had theirs. It was the only plant left with some colour on it and, really, that should have pleased him. But the grotesque purple flowers were turning an ugly combination of taupe and violet – corpse-coloured, in fact – and Noel was filled with the urge to grab the scissors he used for trimming the fat from rib-eye steaks and start deadheading the thing.

The pheasant lived between their house and next door's. It had taken, at around five every morning, to shouting and opening its wings in the branches of the large yew between the properties, which Noel didn't really mind, and shitting on the lid of the wheelie bin, which he did mind.

Perhaps he should shoot it, he thought. But then he never had been much of a shot.

He'd heard a report on the lunchtime news that the lead shot from expended cartridges was poisoning wild birds in huge numbers – the birds ingesting the shot thought it was grit. This had darkened Noel's mood considerably. Well, that, along with the discovery of the prospectus for that school in Inverness Karen had been so keen on for Verity. It had been inside Verity's wardrobe, which meant she knew about it but had purposely said nothing. He'd been putting away some freshly washed clothes when he found it stashed beneath her sweaters on the top shelf. He didn't know what to do. Should he talk to her? Tell her he'd never considered it as an option? It all seemed a bit late in the day now.

Noel grabbed a teaspoon from the drainer and stirred the last dregs of his tea before downing it. He turned around and saw Bruce eyeing him suspiciously over the top of his reading glasses, which was nothing new. Bruce had been eyeing him suspiciously for years; at least now he had a real reason, Noel thought. Bruce seemed to feel this way, too, as where, once, he would slip in some small talk after a period of prolonged staring, now he no longer felt the need.

'Can I get you another drink, Bruce?' Noel asked, and Bruce shook his head.

'I've had enough bloody tea.'

'Something to eat, then?'

Bruce didn't answer. Instead he pushed his glasses up the bridge of his nose and resumed reading the *Westmorland Gazette*.

It would be time to collect Brontë shortly. Noel had quite enjoyed playing taxi, kissing his girls as they left him that morning, watching as Brontë ran to meet her friends, little girls that *surely* he should be familiar with but wasn't.

Noel often heard parents talk of play dates, sleepovers. Was it normal not to allow them for Brontë? Not that there were such things in Noel's day. You went outside and found someone to play with, and tried your best to avoid getting beaten up by a bigger kid from the Protestant primary. When he was with Jennifer, their home had often been filled with troops of little girls at the weekends, all in various shades of pink. Jennifer would arrange sleepovers, marching them to the Co-op in their pyjamas to buy marshmallows to toast, or else laying treasure hunts around the house which they had to follow using only a torch.

It wasn't right to boycott the company of other children for the sake of music practice. He'd said as much to Karen and she'd shut him down, saying he had no idea of the level of dedication needed, and *this wasn't some whim, Noel.* Brontë was *talented.*

Of course, with Karen gone now, he could do what the hell he liked.

These past few years, even when Karen wasn't in the house he could feel her presence. It was subtle: the slight feeling of dread in his stomach, a heaviness across his upper trapezii that never seemed to lift, regardless of how many times he rolled his shoulders or stretched out his neck. When Karen left a room, the air was charged. And Noel would find himself with the urge to leave but without any logical reason why.

Now all that had stopped. Even with Bruce and Mary here, he felt lighter, suddenly able to breathe. And he had to refrain from sucking in great lungfuls, declaring, 'Ahhh. Smell that? Fresh air at last.'

Bruce closed his newspaper. 'Why aren't you out looking for her?' he said abruptly.

Noel thought carefully before answering. 'Her car was found next to the lake, Bruce,' he said. 'You do understand that they think she might be in there?'

'That's according to you,' Bruce replied dismissively. 'I've not been told that.'

'So you think I'm making it up?'

'What I *think* is that you seem to have accepted the disappearance of my daughter rather readily. I can't accept that she's dead in that lake. Not in any way, shape or form until . . . until . . .' Bruce removed his glasses and dabbed at his right eye. 'We can't accept anything until we have evidence,' he said.

'Bruce,' he said wearily, 'I've not accepted Karen's disappearance at all. I can't bear not knowing where she is. But I have to collect the girls soon and I need to stay strong. What good would trailing around by the lake do? She could be anywhere. The police really have no idea what's happened to her.'

'What about her phone?' Bruce said. 'Why can't they trace her through that?'

'Her phone was in her handbag. Along with her wallet and keys. It was left inside the car,' Noel said gently.

'So she has nothing at all with her? Nothing she needs?'

Noel shook his head. 'I'm afraid not.'

'So she wasn't robbed, then?'

'No.'

Bruce pinched the top of his nose with his thumb and fore-finger, trying his best to push back the tears. 'But why would someone want to hurt her?' he said. 'Why hurt Karen? It just doesn't make any sense.'

Mary was lying down in the upstairs guestroom when Noel returned home with Brontë and Verity in tow. Brontë had a double piano lesson booked for that evening and had asked Noel about whether she needed to go to it or not. To which Noel had replied, 'Do you want to go?' and she said she didn't.

'But you'll still need to pay for it, Daddy,' she said earnestly, and Noel thought, *Actually, no, I don't.* Those bastards had drained enough money out of him over the years, preying on Karen's deluded view of her daughter's talent. They could sing for their money, as far as he was concerned.

He'd told the girls about the discovery of Karen's car while they were still in the school car park. Verity had enough intelli-gence not to blurt out, 'What? She's dead?' in front of her sister, but gave Noel a hard stare which he interpreted to mean the same thing, so he said, 'I just don't know, love.'

Now they were back at home and Noel wasn't sure what to do next. Mary came downstairs, smelling of air freshener, her face puffed and doughy, her skin a washed-out white. She didn't look capable of doing anything other than sitting still. But they would still need feeding in the next hour or two, so Noel suggested, 'Fish and chips?' and Bruce muttered, 'I suppose so.'

Ewan and Dale joined them. Well, Dale actually had a jumbo sausage, and Bruce a sorry-looking steak pudding, but they all congregated together at the kitchen table for the meal. With food inside Mary, her colour was returning and she was able to say the odd word. Noel had tried to ply her with Scotch, saying the situation clearly warranted it, but Mary declined. Noel had seen her drunk only once. It was at a gathering for the launch of one of Bruce's many businesses, and Mary had become unexpectedly girlish and flirtatious, lifting her dress above her knees as she sashayed around the room. Then she began dipping her index finger into her Slippery Nipple, or some dreadful cocktail containing Baileys, and popping it in her mouth suggestively. Noel didn't witness Bruce's ticking-off but he suspected it must have been pretty harsh because, notwithstanding the Christmas cakes, Mary hadn't touched a drop of alcohol since.

'You've injured your hand,' Mary said to Dale, as he sawed through his sausage.

'Secateurs,' Dale answered, and turned his palm over, showing Mary the full extent of the injury.

'How did you manage to do *that* with secateurs?' snapped Bruce, and Dale shrugged as though he had no idea, completely unoffended by Bruce's tone.

Bruce was frowning hard at Dale, trying to work out what this slow-witted boy was doing at his daughter's kitchen table, eating his way through sausage and chips, chewing with his mouth open.

'I'm accident prone,' Dale said helpfully.

And Bruce muttered, 'Is that what they're calling it nowadays.'

They ate in silence, none of them really sure what to say to one another, until Mary blurted out to nobody in particular, 'The batter is ever so light on this fish.' And since no one else saw fit to answer, Noel agreed with her that it was.

'I'm not fond of the addition of beer to fish batter,' she went on, and Noel said no, him neither.

'Nor do I like goose fat on roast potatoes,' she said. 'It's ever so expensive, and lard is just as—'

'Jesus Christ, woman!' Bruce yelled, slamming his fist down. 'Give your witterings a rest for once.'

Scolded, Mary looked down and proceeded to eat in silence, cutting each chip in two before lifting the fork to her mouth. Noel caught Verity's eye, and she mouthed, 'Poor Mary.'

Bruce and Mary had never been 'Granny and Grandad' to Verity, as they were to Brontë and Ewan. Karen had encouraged it to start with, but Jennifer went apoplectic when she found out, saying, 'What? Are you going to start calling Karen *Mother* now as well? They're not your grandparents, so you're not to call them that. They are NO RELATION.'

Noel looked at Mary. Poor Mary indeed.

Out of nowhere, Bruce said, 'You know, this never would have happened if you were a better husband,' and it took Noel a moment to realize he was referring to him. 'All Karen ever needed was your support.'

'Bruce,' Noel said, 'I—'

'For all Mary's faults and failings, I have never wavered in my support of her, because she is my wife. I've supported her one hundred and ten per cent.'

Noel, unsure of where Bruce was going with this, decided to stay quiet for the time being.

'What did you do when Karen got all that abuse on the internet?' he said. 'What did you do, Noel? Because, from where I was standing, it looked like you didn't do a bloody thing.'

'I don't know what I *could* have done.'

'She dealt with it alone! Like she's had to do everything. You didn't once step up and say, "Enough! This is my wife!" No. You did what you always do, Noel. You buried your head in the sand and hoped it would go away.'

Noel thought about arguing the case, but Bruce was now shaking badly and his right eye had begun to water again.

'She was loyal to you, and what did you give her in return? She worked tirelessly for the good of this family. She was devoted to each of you. And what did you do for her?'

Mary put down her knife and fork and placed her hand on top of Bruce's. 'Bruce, dear,' she said to him, but he shook her away.

He pointed his knife at Ewan. 'And *you*,' he said. 'My daughter did not raise you to be such a total waste of space. What is it that you actually do, anyway? Because no one ever seems to be able to answer that question.'

Ewan hung his head.

'And you,' he said, turning his attention to Brontë. 'Your mother gives you everything. Everything. She puts all she has into securing a decent future for you. And how do you repay her? By running away? Do you know how much trouble you caused by doing that? Are you even aware?'

'That's enough, Bruce,' Noel warned.

'It's not nearly enough,' Bruce said.

'Bruce, what's your point?'

'She deserved more!' he yelled. 'More from all of you!'

'But I gave her everything I could,' Noel said weakly.

'You did?' And, at this, he laughed. 'You call hiding yourself in work, barely coming home to see your family, you call that *everything*? She was left to deal with her drug-addicted son *alone*. Your violent daughter *alone*. Raise your other daughter *alone*. Where were you, Noel?'

'I—'

'Did you even ask if she needed help? Or were you too busy chasing other women again?'

'Bruce. Stop.'

'What? You think they don't know what their father is? You think this is news to them? Listen up, kids, Daddy here has a problem with women. And drink. And dealing with his responsibilities. And if he'd been here just a little bit more for Karen, then maybe she'd be here now.'

'You're saying I caused this?'

Bruce folded his arms in defiance. 'That's what I'm saying.'

Noel looked at each of the children, and they looked back at him, waiting for an explanation. Should he explain? He couldn't explain. He didn't know himself.

He exhaled. Sitting back in his chair, he ran his hand through his hair. Bruce was glaring at him hard, also waiting. Noel wasn't sure if Bruce was planning to hit him, but he decided then and there that if Bruce went for him he would take the punch. He'd not been punched in over twenty years, but he reckoned he could withstand it.

'Maybe she did deserve better from me,' Noel said quietly. 'Maybe I did let her down. You're right, Bruce, I am a long way from being the husband and father I want to be.'

Dale rose in his seat.

Scraping his chair as he reached across the table for more ketchup, he said, 'Aw, I think you're a pretty good person, Dr Bloom.' He was chewing loudly. 'Don't be too hard on yourself.'

'Yeah, Dad,' Verity agreed. 'You're a good guy.'

The kids were exchanging knowing glances with one another and Noel wondered if he was missing something. They appeared tight. Together. All on the same team.

And Noel never did find out whether Bruce was planning to throw that punch or not. Because, seconds later, DS Joanne Aspinall was back at his front door, her hair wet from the rain, her expression grim.

'I'm really sorry, Noel,' she said to him, 'but we've found her.'

36

JOANNE AND OLIVER Black had been exiting through the gates of Reid's Grammar after interviewing Pia Nicholls when they received the call about Karen. They had been embroiled in a hot debate about private schooling. Oliver thought that private schools should be abolished, that the middle classes were taking over the entire country, and so forth, but Joanne's view was: if you could afford it, why not? Not that she cared one way or the other. She didn't have children, nor was she likely ever to have children, so how people chose to educate their offspring was their business.

It was raining again. Sheets of water blasted the car from the west, and Oliver set the wipers to super-fast to be able to see through the screen. Every few seconds, though, he would flick them back to a slower speed, as though the rapid setting were somehow emasculating, before switching once more to fast mode when he couldn't make out the road in front.

They were at the water's edge when they pulled Karen out. The divers had found her around twenty feet from the shoreline, at a point around fifty yards south of where the Volvo was abandoned. They were lucky. The lake is eleven miles long. One of the divers had followed a hunch. He told Joanne he felt like he was being guided to Karen Bloom by something otherworldly.

'Karen's ghost?' Joanne suggested, faintly mocking, and he scratched his chin, replying, 'I don't know. Maybe.'

The opposite bank of the lake was hardly visible in the murk and Joanne thought, *What an unpleasant place to die.* But then she supposed when compared with, say, being dumped inside a suitcase in the Thames, as one poor woman had been recently, it was not all bad. The water was at least clean here.

Joanne held on to her hood with her hand to prevent the wind sweeping it off her head as Oliver looked at her bleakly and said, 'Stabbed.'

'How many times?'

He was squatting at the side of Karen's corpse. 'I can see one in the neck. And one . . . no, make that two, here at the top of her chest.'

Three wounds. So not the wild, frenzied attack DI Gilmore had thought it would be, after all. Maybe this wasn't a personal vendetta. Tech had examined Karen's phone and computer, and there had been nothing to suggest she was planning to meet someone she knew. No arrangements had been made. Maybe she didn't know her attacker. Karen was still fully dressed, so there was that. Joanne thought that being told your wife/daughter/mother had been murdered was one thing, but to be told she was first the victim of a sexual attack was quite another.

Of course, Karen *may* have been raped. But it was unlikely a killer would re-dress a victim afterwards, particularly if he was planning on disposing of her body in such a crude fashion as this.

'The wound to the neck is probably what caused all the blood,' Oliver said.

Forensics had found evidence of blood splatter on the Volvo's dashboard, windscreen, sun visor and the internal casing of the driver-side door.

'The carotid would do that,' Oliver added.

Joanne squatted down next to Oliver and surveyed the body.

Karen's lips and eyes were bulging madly. She was the colour of a beluga whale. Another day in the lake, and she probably would have resurfaced of her own accord.

'Oh, Karen,' said Joanne sadly. 'Who did this to you?'

'There couldn't be some mistake?' Bruce Rigby asked, and Joanne shook her head in response.

'I'm sorry,' she said, 'but no.'

'Bodies are so changed when they've been submerged in water, couldn't it be—'

'It's definitely Karen, Mr Rigby,' Joanne said.

He started to cry then. His wife said nothing, too stunned to speak. So Joanne looked at Noel. 'Sorry,' she mouthed silently.

'Where is she now?' asked Bruce.

'On her way to the mortuary.'

'At the hospital?'

Joanne shook her head. 'The public mortuary linked to the coroner's court.'

'Can we see her?' he asked.

'Not right away.'

'There'll be a post-mortem?'

'Yes.'

'How did she die?' he asked.

'Best to wait for the results of the post-mortem examination, Mr Rigby.'

'Did she suffer?'

'I'm sorry, but I can't tell you anything more than I already have.'

'That means she did?'

'No,' Joanne said. 'It means I just don't have that information.'

Bruce Rigby seemed to accept this, so Joanne told him there would be a family liaison officer contacting them within the hour. 'Jared Dockray,' she said. 'He'll be able to assist you with the facts as they come in.' And, with that, she stood. 'Mr Rigby . . . Mrs Rigby . . . Dr Bloom,' she said, addressing each of them in turn, 'I'm very sorry for your loss.'

Oliver Black handed Joanne a sherbet lemon. 'The husband didn't say a lot, did he?'

'Not much,' Joanne agreed.

'It was as if he was expecting it.'

'Maybe he was.'

'You think he did it?'

'His alibi checks out,' she said. 'He would've only had around forty minutes in which to kill her, dump her in the lake and get himself home and cleaned up. Not a lot of time.'

'Enough time, though,' Oliver said.

'Yeah,' Joanne replied. 'Enough time.'

They dropped the pool car back at the station, listened to what Pat Gilmore had to say and then headed home. The post-mortem would be done some time the following day, so while they were waiting for the forensics she advised they get home early, ready to start at seven the next morning.

The moment had long since passed for Joanne to raise the subject of her and Noel Bloom's *encounter* to Pat Gilmore. After interviewing Noel, she had thought of coming clean, owning up to what had happened.

I know I should probably have mentioned this sooner, but . . .

But the fact was she was still the best detective to investigate the case. She knew the family. She knew the victim. She knew the suspect (if, indeed, Noel became a suspect). She had a privileged insider's view into the dynamics of the Blooms and she just wasn't prepared to hand over the case to another detective simply because she'd had a one-night stand the details of which she could barely remember.

Okay, so she could remember some of it.

Most of it.

But that didn't mean she wasn't capable of doing her job, capable of doing it better than anyone else.

If she had to put Noel Bloom away for the murder of his wife, she would do it.

She would do it in an instant. Of course she would.

37

Saturday, 24 October

Verity found she couldn't drag her eyes away from the square patch of pale paint where Jeremy Gleeson's graduation picture had once hung. She assumed its removal meant it was over with his wife, as she had featured in the picture. He wasn't crying, though, so that was good.

'I didn't expect to see you today,' he said over his shoulder. He was searching through the filing cabinet beyond his desk to retrieve her notes.

Verity was perplexed. 'Have I come at the wrong time?'

'No, no. Just, what with . . .'

He let the sentence hang and Verity wasn't entirely sure what he meant.

'What with . . .?' she repeated, hoping he might continue.

He seated himself and treated Verity to what she supposed was a concerned, sympathetic look but, somehow, he didn't quite pull it off. It ended up appearing mildly scolding.

'I thought you'd be with your family,' he said. 'Because of the discovery of . . . the body.'

'*Oh*,' Verity said, it dawning on her at last. He hadn't expected her to keep her appointment because Karen was well and truly dead, dead for certain, the upshot being that Verity couldn't attempt to strangle her any more.

Their sessions might now be considered superfluous.

Thinking about it, her dad *had* seemed surprised when she'd said she was on her way over to see Jeremy Gleeson. When she was halfway out of the door, he'd said, 'You're still going?'

And Verity said, 'Yes. I think it would be useful to talk. Don't you?'

She hadn't been lying. She did want to talk. So there was that, and the fact that she needed to get out of the house. She had felt bad leaving Brontë. Brontë had asked her not to go, weeping a little when Verity said she would be out for a couple of hours. She had considered bringing her little sister with her, but in the end she had decided against it. Brontë was the main reason she was here, after all.

Jeremy Gleeson offered Verity a glass of water, something he'd not done in their previous sessions, and Verity wondered if this was a new thing. Like the folded blue waffle blanket at the foot of the couch was a *new thing*. She told him she wasn't thirsty, thank you.

'How are you, Verity?' he asked.

'Me? Oh, I'm fine.'

'Really?' he said sceptically. 'You're bearing up okay?'

She realized she'd sounded flippant, and she hadn't meant to. What she meant was, compared to everyone else, she was doing okay, because 'You do remember, Karen wasn't my real mother?'

'Certainly. But things can't be easy for you right now, at home. It's a very upsetting time for everyone, I imagine. Everyone – including you, Verity.'

Verity studied Gleeson. Was he testing her? Testing her reaction to Karen's death?

'I'm okay,' she said again. Cautiously this time.

He nodded. Gave her a look as if to say, *As you wish.*

'In fact, that's pretty much the reason I've come here,' she went on. 'I did *think* about cancelling, but I thought you might be able to help me with something. Maybe give me some advice.'

'Advice?' Jeremy Gleeson sat up taller in his seat. 'I'll certainly try my best.'

'Well, because Karen's not my mum, I'm kind of having difficulty, showing . . .' Verity paused. 'I'm finding it hard to—'

'Know how to act?'

'Exactly. Karen was Brontë's mother, so of course Brontë is properly heartbroken. And even though Karen could be a bitch, she's totally devastated. And I keep trying to comfort Brontë, but I'm just not sure if I'm doing enough. I'm trying, but it doesn't seem to be helping. I can't seem to make her feel any better.'

'Is that your job, Verity? To heal Brontë of her grief?'

Verity took a moment to consider the question. Eventually, she said, 'I think it is. I'm the only person in the house who wasn't related to Karen. I'm not feeling upset by her death the way everyone else is, so, naturally, I should try to help Brontë get through it. I thought you might be able to give me some lines or something. Something I could say that might make her feel a bit better.'

'I'm not sure grief works like that.'

'Oh,' Verity said, disappointed.

Jeremy Gleeson smiled a compassionate smile and tilted his head. 'How about you tell me a bit more about what's going on at home. Who else is there?'

'My dad, obviously.'

'And how is he?'

'Seems okay. He's holding it together for the sake of everyone else, I think. Karen's parents are pretty cut up about the whole deal. And my dad's been doing his best to talk to Ewan – that's Karen's son – but Ewan's gone kind of quiet. He stays in his flat, gaming all the time, which is not unusual, but he hardly speaks at all, which is not like him. I think my dad's getting worried. He asked me to spend some time up there with Ewan, but I get the impression he'd rather be on his own, or else with his friend Dale.'

'Has he talked about the murder?'

'Ewan? No. I asked if he wanted to talk about his mum, but he said he didn't. Do you think I should ask if he wants to come and see you?'

'You could suggest it. If you feel it might help.'

'I'll put it to my dad.'

Verity peered out the window as Jeremy Gleeson excused himself to blow his nose. There was a loud, honking noise, like a goose or a baby elephant. 'Had a mild cold,' he said. 'Apologies.'

Venetian blinds covered the large bay window, the slats angled upwards so you couldn't really see much, just make out the general shape of the odd passer-by.

Verity turned her head back to face Gleeson. 'Do you know what Brontë said to me yesterday? She said, "Nothing like this has ever happened to me before," and I didn't know what to say. She seemed . . . lost. What would you have said?'

'I don't think there *is* a good response to that, Verity.'

'But I feel so sad for her.'

'Try to think that being with your sister is enough for now. Don't think that it's up to you to fix it. It's *not* fixable, and each one of your family members will have to work through their grief at their own pace. It's not something that can be made better with words.'

'But I feel so guilty.'

At this admission, Jeremy Gleeson regarded Verity with an apprehensive gaze.

'Guilty?' he said casually. 'Why guilty?'

'I'm not sure.'

'Do you feel bad about what happened to Karen?'

'Not exactly.'

Jeremy Gleeson swallowed. Examined his fingernails momentarily before saying, 'Do you feel guilty, Verity, because . . . because you think it may have had something to do with you?'

Verity frowned. 'What? Karen's death?' she asked.

'Yes. Karen's death.'

Verity shook her head. 'No. I don't feel guilty about that at all.'

38

Monday, 26 October

Four days of constant rain had brought down a large section of the dry-stone wall at the front of Noel's house. He'd been charged with the task of removing the debris that had spilled across the pavement and on to the road, stacking it up, ready for repair. Some men just seemed to know how to re-erect a dry-stone wall, in the same way they knew how to fit a new clutch or plait a horse's tail. Noel was not one of them. And because of this, Bruce was overseeing his work, the death of his only daughter seemingly not deterring him from issuing orders or pointing out Noel's general incompetence. After four days of mourning Bruce was ready to get active.

The rain was lashing down hard but Bruce was in shorts and cross-terrain shoes, a fluorescent cycling jacket covering his upper half and a wide-brimmed hat on his head. He'd told Noel that he, too, should wear shorts when out in the rain (saves having to dry out the wet clothes) but Noel thanked him for the advice, saying no, he would not be doing that.

This was what Bruce did in a crisis – took charge. Noel knew it was his way of handling things and not for one second would he try to talk him out of it, but even he was surprised when Bruce told him to 'Get dressed. There's a hazard outside that needs our attention,' thinking that, surely, for once, general household maintenance could take a breather.

'Best you keep yourself busy, Noel,' Bruce said, as Noel wrestled with an irregularly shaped rock, the tip of which had become lodged in the grid. He should have worn gloves. He had work gloves in the garage and, when he told Bruce he needed a minute to find them, Bruce looked at him like he was a giant sissy. Now his hands were red raw from the cold and he'd torn the skin from three of his knuckles.

'Busyness is probably key,' Noel muttered in agreement.

'Those kids are going to need to be kept in line,' Bruce said.

Noel nodded without looking up.

'Because they've lost their rock,' Bruce said.

Which Noel thought was an odd turn of phrase, considering he was actually *pulling on a rock*. But then he remembered Princess Diana saying the same thing about that creepy butler of hers, Paul Burrell. 'He's my rock,' she would say. Perhaps Bruce had heard it there.

'She was the glue that kept this family together,' Bruce said.

Noel booted the rock twice with his foot until it finally came loose. 'She was,' he said.

'She ran a tight ship. You'll need to do the same. Teenagers need a strict set of rules to live by. You can't give them free rein. They'll run amok.'

'I'll be sure to do that, Bruce.'

'And you'll need a housekeeper. To keep this place in some sort of order.'

Noel was thinking about what Karen had actually done around the house and, besides loading the washing machine, he was hard pressed to come up with anything. 'The kids can help out with the chores,' Noel said. 'And we have Rosa.'

Bruce looked unconvinced. 'Maybe I'll draw up a schedule.'

'Schedule?' asked Noel.

'For the chores,' Bruce explained.

'If you like,' Noel said, thinking he could bin it later.

Bruce had formally identified his daughter's body on Saturday. Noel had told him there was no need, that it was his place to do it and, not that it would be an easy task by any means, but he did have experience of the mortuary.

But Bruce had flared at him: 'You don't think I've seen *death*, man? You don't think I've witnessed death on a large scale during my army career?'

And it took Noel a full five minutes to pacify him, saying that no, he didn't mean to be insensitive, that's not what he meant at all. He was just trying to make things easier and—

'Easier? How the hell can you make this easier?'

Noel stacked the last of the stones and followed Bruce inside. Mary was handing out bacon sandwiches to the three children and Dale. Her expression was one of nervous bewilderment, the type of expression worn by people when they didn't know which way to head in airports and were frightened of being told off by Security.

Bruce began drying his legs with a piece of kitchen towel before lifting his head and fixing Dale with an unhappy stare. 'You're here,' he said. A statement.

'I am,' replied Dale, quite proudly, unsure if this was a trick question.

'You're here, *again*?' Bruce said.

'I'm here again.'

Bruce turned to Noel. 'I'm not sure this is really appropriate. What did Karen make of this boy practically living here all the time? I can't see her liking it one bit. It's not normal.' And he gave Noel a look as if to say, *He's not normal.*

But before Noel had a chance to answer, Verity spoke up. 'Karen liked having Dale around. Didn't she, Dad?'

'Hmm. Yes, I suppose,' agreed Noel hesitantly. What was she up to?

'She was very good like that,' Verity went on. 'You see, Dale's mum is not at home a lot, and she didn't like him to be on his own. So she would often ask him to stay . . . Plus, he keeps Ewan out of trouble. Doesn't he, Ewan?'

'He's a very stabilizing force in my life,' Ewan said, without any trace of irony.

Bruce surveyed them sceptically.

'Well, I suppose if Karen didn't have a problem with it . . .' and he told them he was off to buy fuel and to check the car's oil, water and tyres before their trip home later that day.

Noel couldn't wait to get rid of them.

Mary, he could cope with. She wasn't really with it, and her frequent wanderings from room to room had become kind of comforting. When she wasn't wandering around she would bake or else sit with Brontë, the two of them watching back-to-back Disney movies, Brontë nestled against Mary's bosom. Noel kept a watchful eye on his younger daughter. She had been his main worry in all of this. How would she cope without Karen? How does any child cope with the loss of a parent? It wasn't something you could really prepare for.

And, of course, he had to watch his own behaviour. He was aiming for sadness, without being completely bleak.

Had he got it right?

He wasn't sure. He'd catch Bruce watching him and he'd know he was moving towards recovery just a shade too fast. Then he'd have to revert to the eye-rubbing, grabbing-on-to-something-solid-while-he-regained-his-composure routine.

Karen had been stabbed, they said.

One wound to the neck, two to the chest.

Bruce had asked, 'But who on earth would want to hurt my beautiful girl?'

And Noel had to shake his head, saying, 'I'm so sorry, Bruce. I'm at a complete loss.'

39

THE THING STILL needling at Joanne was what had happened to Karen's ex? As in, the guy who fathered Ewan. Over the past couple of days, while waiting for news from Forensics, Joanne had spent her time tracing, interviewing and subsequently eliminating other boyfriends from Karen's past. None had been in a relationship with her in the months preceding Ewan's birth.

She had asked Noel Bloom, and he had claimed to know nothing. She had asked Karen's acquaintances from school, the gym and so forth, and each was adamant that there had never been talk of an ex-boyfriend or a husband from the past. Ewan Rigby had Karen's maiden name, did not know who his biological father was and, when Joanne had raised the strangeness of the situation with Noel, he'd merely shrugged, saying, 'Karen didn't like to talk about the past,' which was hardly an explanation.

But Joanne still didn't have a suspect. And she needed to know everything there was to know about Karen. They'd taken swabs from just about everyone they could think of related to the case, even collecting samples from as far away as South Wales, from a family with which Karen was having a particularly nasty interaction on Facebook. But until the results of the blood smear from the tree came back from the lab, really, she had nothing.

And, of course, there was always the possibility of the blood not belonging to the suspect. But Joanne tried not to dwell for too long on that.

Sad fact but true: a woman is more likely to be murdered by her partner, or ex-partner, than by anyone else. Almost half of the women murdered in the UK last year were killed by their partners or their exes. Hence Joanne's interest in Ewan's father. Except, no one seemed to know anything about him.

'Well, somebody got Karen Bloom pregnant,' she said to Oliver Black. 'And if her husband and her own son don't know who that person is, then that leaves her parents. They *have* to know.'

'But we *don't* know,' Bruce Rigby replied. Joanne had found him packing up his car in preparation for the trip home to Macclesfield. 'She wouldn't tell us,' he said. 'Karen turned up pregnant, saying the father had walked out on her, and that yes, she knew being a single parent would be tough but she was better off without him.'

They went inside to the Blooms' kitchen.

'So as far as you know,' Oliver Black said, 'Karen has had no contact with the father for the past – what? – eighteen years?'

'I'm certain of it,' said Bruce.

'What was his name?'

'She wouldn't say.'

'And where was she living before she returned home?'

'Sussex. That's what she said. She went to Brighton to enjoy the summer and ended up staying. She had a casual job in a hotel. That's where she met the guy.'

'Do you remember the name of the hotel?' Oliver asked.

Bruce tried his best to think. 'I'm afraid I don't.'

'Did she ever talk about the people she worked with? Any names you can recall?'

'It was such a long time ago.'

'Nothing at all?' pressed Oliver.

And, all at once, Bruce's manner changed, and he became borderline hostile. 'I told you, I can't remember!'

Joanne did feel for Bruce Rigby. Trying to cast his mind back to what he'd always thought of as a regrettable episode in his daughter's life was physically paining him. His voice had become shrill, and his eyes had taken on a wild, terrified look. What if this was the missing link? What if only *he* could unlock the mystery of his daughter's killer?

'Mr Rigby,' Joanne said gently, 'this is only one line of inquiry we're pursuing. Try not to get upset. Something may come to you later today, or even next week. Memories tend to resurface at the strangest of times.'

'But I *want* to remember,' he said, panting a little, his brow beginning to sweat. 'I need to remember, for Karen's sake.'

During this exchange Mary Rigby stayed mute. Apart from, that is, offering tea, coffee and slices of a particularly good-looking Victoria sponge, which Joanne declined, somewhat reluctantly, on professional grounds. Murder inquiries and cake did not go together in Joanne's book.

'What was Karen's job description at the hotel?' Joanne asked. 'Was she a chambermaid? On reception? Did she work in the bar?'

Bruce looked blank.

He turned to Mary. 'Do you remember, Mary?' he asked, and she shook her head. Then she excused herself and began putting cups on the drainer.

'I'm sorry,' Bruce said. 'If I said she was waitressing or working in the bar, I'd be lying. I don't think she ever told us. Or, if she did, we can't remember.'

Joanne closed her notepad and handed Bruce her card. 'I know you probably have one of these, but here's another. Call me any time. Call me any time, with anything at all you remember. Even if you think it's unrelated.'

Bruce took the card and held her gaze. He had spittle welling at the corners of his mouth. 'You really have no idea who is responsible for this, do you?' he said.

*

Back in the car, Oliver Black was deep in thought.

'Penny for them?' Joanne asked.

'Aside from Karen Bloom's father, no one else in that family seems to be mourning her loss too deeply.'

'What about the mother?'

Oliver gave her a dismissive look. 'I'm not sure that woman knows what day it is at the best of times.'

'So you're thinking that it might have been Noel?'

'Or the daughter,' he said.

'Well, Verity's not Karen's daughter, so maybe that explains her behaviour. They don't exactly have a history of playing happy families.'

'Even so,' said Oliver, 'there's a strange atmosphere. I've covered enough murders in my time to know that what's going on in there is not exactly normal.'

'Not normal in what way?' she asked.

Oliver paused. And then, after a moment's thought, he said, 'I'm just reading the body language, so I could be way off. But if I had to put my finger on it, then I'd say they look almost . . . relieved.'

Oliver went home early. He'd had a call from his wife to say the River Kent was running high and water was rapidly flooding into their kitchen. She couldn't stave it off on her own any longer. If it got through to the lounge they would lose the carpet. Oliver left armed with six sandbags and an extra mop and bucket from the cleaner's cupboard, which Joanne supposed wouldn't be greatly missed.

Joanne had the Blooms' phone records up on the screen in front of her. Karen's mobile had been analysed, and each call over the last few weeks accounted for. So Joanne turned back to the home phone line. A DC had been through the records when Karen's car was first found, but she was banking on him having missed something. She scanned the area codes, looking for incoming and outgoing calls from Brighton. This didn't take long, because, as with most families, the home line received very little usage, as people relied more and more on their mobiles. There were no calls from Brighton.

Of course, Karen's ex might *not* be living in the Brighton area any more. Joanne had visited Brighton only once and thought it was the type of place that attracted lost souls, people running away from their real lives – kind of like Marbella, but with shittier weather. It was unlikely that Karen's ex – being part of the transient hotel-worker population – had put down permanent roots there. Most likely, he'd moved on, further afield. Even so, short of any better ideas, checking the surrounding area was worth a shot. Joanne typed 'Brighton' into Google Maps, and when the image appeared she zoomed out. Nearby towns were Worthing, Eastbourne, Bognor, Crawley and Hastings.

She checked her watch. It would take no more than half an hour to check the area codes of these towns against the Blooms' phone records. Then she could put aside the niggling ex-boyfriend issue and move on to something else. Really, she ought to have questioned Noel about his wife's infidelity by now. Did he know about her brief affair with Roger Nicholls? Had she done it before? Had another affair ended particularly badly? Was there a string of disgruntled, vengeful wives waiting in the wings ready to mount an attack on Karen?

She needed answers to these questions, but she had been reluctant to ask Noel in the hours immediately following the discovery of Karen's body. He might not *look* as if he was grieving too deeply, but that didn't mean he was ready to talk about his wife putting it out there all over town.

She would drop by and ask him in a round-about way, see what he knew about Karen's affair – or affairs.

She finished Bognor and moved on to Worthing. There was

bound to be an easier way to do this. A way to feed in the area code and cross-check the phone records automatically. But she couldn't be bothered to find a tech person to help her, and there was something quite enjoyable in the tedious nature of the task. Joanne liked a bit of tedium now and again. She found it soothing. She could lose herself when peeling and preparing vegetables or polishing her shoes for work. Sometimes she yearned for simpler times and could imagine gaining a heady kind of pleasure from feeding wet sheets into a mangle, watching them air-dry in the wind. Or else spending dismal afternoons darning socks, or rubbing silver, or pickling jars of onions.

Joanne scanned the phone records, checking for Crawley and Eastbourne codes but again found nothing. And she had only half her attention on the task in front of her when something jumped out.

Hastings.

Two calls had been received from Hastings. One had lasted six minutes and forty-three seconds.

She copied down the number and was about to dial it when her mobile began ringing. It was Noel Bloom.

'Hello, Noel,' she said.

'Joanne.'

'How are things?' she asked.

'I was wondering if there had been any developments. If you could tell us anything more? Brontë's had a tricky afternoon and is finding it a bit hard to take in. She can't grasp the idea that someone has done this to Karen and not yet been caught – of course, she doesn't know the details. She doesn't know how Karen was killed. Anyway, I know it's probably pointless, but I said I'd give you a call, find out if there was any news.'

'I'm afraid there isn't, Noel.'

'Okay, well, that's as expected, I suppose. I'll—'

'There is one thing, actually.'

'Oh?'

'I was going to drop by later today. I could do with chatting to you about something.'

'Something to do with the case?' he asked.

And Joanne replied, 'Yes,' thinking, *What else would it be about?*

'Oh, right,' said Noel, brightening somewhat. 'Do you want to come to the house?' he asked.

'That was the plan.'

'It's just that . . . I . . . well, it's just—'

'It's just what, Noel?'

Noel cleared his throat. 'I don't suppose you fancy meeting up for a drink, do you? The kids are off to the cinema to cheer Brontë up. I know you probably don't. I mean, there are probably rules about this sort of thing. But, well, the truth is, I've been housebound since Thursday, and I could really do with some adult company. A change of scenery, so to speak. And to be honest, I could do with talking to someone who isn't actively *grieving*.'

'A drink,' said Joanne, deadpan.

'That's what I was thinking.'

'It's not really ethical.'

Noel paused. Considered her statement. After a moment he said, 'Am I a suspect?'

'At the moment, no.'

'So . . .'

'So, that doesn't mean you won't *become* a suspect.'

And Noel laughed as if she'd said something quite hilarious.

'I'd say that's rather unlikely, Joanne . . . wouldn't you?'

40

'YOU'RE DOING *WHAT*?' Jackie put down her mug. (Hot water with a slice of lemon in it. She was detoxing after all that meat.) 'Are you out of your mind?' she said.

'It's just a drink. In a pub,' Joanne replied.

'A drink with a murdering husband.'

'You mean "murderous". And there's nothing to say he did it.'

'I *meant* "murdering",' Jackie said crossly. 'And it's *always* the husband what did it. You should know that. You're supposed to be a detective. Maybe slitting your throat is next on his list. Maybe seducing you first is part of the plan.'

'Maybe. And her throat wasn't slit. She was stabbed . . . And how do you know about her throat?'

'Someone at work told me.'

'Anyway, I thought you liked Dr Bloom,' Joanne said.

'I did . . . but that was before he murdered his wife.'

'Okay, let's say he *did* murder his wife. Why'd he do it?'

'Oh, the usual, I expect,' Jackie said. 'Money . . . love.'

'I don't think he stands to gain financially from Karen's death.'

'Love, then.'

'Who does he love?' Joanne asked

And Jackie tutted loudly. 'Well, not *her*, obviously.'

Joanne had her own reasons for accepting the invitation to go out for a drink. First of all, she wanted to know what it was that made Noel Bloom brazen enough to ask her. It wasn't exactly typical widower behaviour. So if he'd somehow managed to suppress his latent psychopathic traits up until this point, Joanne wanted to pick at him. Pick at him until he dropped his cover.

Joanne had only met what she considered to be one true psychopath in her life so far and Noel was nothing like him.

But Noel *was* a doctor. So he was far from being an idiot. And from what she understood, psychopaths were often very high-functioning, with the capability of fooling even the most discerning of people. But Noel seemed warm and genuine. Sometimes tender. *And* he didn't dye his hair. (Joanne wasn't sure if colouring one's hair was on the official list of psychopathic traits, but if it wasn't, it should be.) It could be argued, though, that Noel was sexually promiscuous. And that definitely *was* on the list.

Of course, it went without saying that Noel didn't need to be a psychopath to murder his wife. As Jackie had stated, lots of men murdered their wives and few were deemed to be mentally ill. But to plan a murder such as Karen's and then to behave as if it hadn't really happened? That did pique Joanne's interest.

And so she *had* to accept Noel's invitation, because she'd be a fool not to.

'If it was me, I'd have a Stanley knife in my handbag,' Jackie said. 'Just to be sure.'

'What, so I can stab him before he stabs me?'

'You're making light of this, but that's how people end up dead. By being too complacent.'

'I'm not making light of it. And anyway, I'm not planning on going anywhere secluded. As I said. This is a drink. In a pub.'

'What pub?'

'I don't know.'

'Why not?'

'He didn't tell me. He just said he'd pick me up at eight.'

Jackie gave Joanne a look of vindication as if to say, *And that was your first mistake.* 'So ask him, then,' she said. 'Tell him your worried aunt likes to keep track of you.'

'I'm forty years old, Jackie.'

'So?'

'So, I'm not telling him that.'

'Who else knows you're going?'

'No one.'

'Joanne,' Jackie said wearily, 'drinking with a suspect is hardly the most sensible thing to do if you're—'

'He's not a suspect.'

'So, you've told your fellow officers all about this drink, then?'

'No.'

'And that's because . . .?'

'Because,' Joanne admitted, 'the meeting doesn't exactly follow protocol.'

Jackie sucked in her breath before letting it out as a long, low whistle.

'Rather you than me,' she said.

Noel drove like a nonagenarian. Slowly and carefully, as if the road might throw up some random obstacle that wasn't there the day before. There were plenty of ninety-year-old drivers in the South Lakes and, generally, Joanne didn't have a problem with them. They were, statistically speaking, one of the safest age groups on the road. If Joanne could have her way, she'd make it illegal for all newly qualified seventeen-year-old boys to drive after dark, and she would ban them from carrying adolescent passengers until they'd held their licence for at least two years. That would cut down on the road deaths. And everyone's insurance premiums. Every year they would lose a few teenagers in either a Renault Clio or a Peugeot 107. Always a young lad driving. Always taking a bend too fast. Joanne took bends too fast.

But she was a member of the Institute of Advanced Motorists, so she was allowed to (sort of).

'Shall we speed up a little?' she asked Noel.

'I'd like to get you there safely, if that's okay.'

'But you're doing twenty-two. In a thirty zone. It's embarrassing.'

'There are some shades in the glove compartment. Put them on if you want to ride incognito.'

Joanne wondered what she might find inside the glove box. A long-bladed knife perhaps.

She flicked it open. Sunglasses, screen wipes, satnav. No knife.

They were heading towards the ferry. Noel had suggested going across the lake to have a drink and a bite to eat. He didn't cover Sawrey or Hawkshead in his job, he said, so he was largely unknown in the pubs over there. And not that they were hiding or anything, he added, but it might be nice to talk without prying eyes.

'What are your kids watching this evening?' Joanne said.

'Something from Pixar. They've all gone – Ewan, Verity, Brontë and Dale.'

'And Dale?'

'He seems to be a permanent fixture since Karen's death. It's an odd thing, but I think he's keeping them all together somehow. Brontë seems to respond particularly well to him. Her hand even seems to improve when he's around. The cinema was his idea.'

'How is Brontë in herself?'

'Bewildered. She's old enough to understand what death means, and yet I sense she hasn't fully grasped that Karen isn't coming home. She was going to go back with Bruce and Mary for a few days but at the last moment decided she wanted to stay put.'

'What about *your* parents?' she asked. 'Do they live around here?'

'Dead,' he said. 'Yours?'

'My mum's in Tenerife.'

'Nice.'

Not really, thought Joanne. Her mother lived the typical life of an expat in Spain: drinking cheap wine from 3 p.m. onwards to stave off the boredom, rubbing anti-ageing cream into the ptero-dactyl skin between her breasts, and all the while declaring to anyone who'd listen that she could *never go back to England. Not ever.*

'You miss them?' Joanne asked.

'Every day. My mum would have been wonderful with the girls. They would have adored her. Verity, in particular, because she missed out altogether on the grandparent thing. Jennifer's parents, like mine, died young, from ill health. And Bruce and Mary . . . well, let's just say it's not the same as with their own flesh and blood.'

They boarded the ferry. It had been closed for the past two days on account of the high winds but had reopened this morn-ing. There was only a handful of cars. The attendant was in full waterproofs and wore a peaked cap to keep the rain from his face. Noel seemed to know him. And if the guy was surprised to see another woman in the passenger seat while Noel's wife wasn't yet in the ground, he didn't show it.

The ferry shuddered away from the shore and Noel cut the engine and turned off the headlights. The rain pelted the screen. Joanne had not turned out particularly well prepared for the weather. She wore jeans, high-heeled boots and a short, belted, woollen coat that, although warm, smelled like a stray dog when it was wet.

The coat had been an impulse buy after the breast reduction, when, suddenly, short, belted coats (nipped in nicely at the waist) would now fit and she didn't have to buy something four sizes too big just to get the thing to close. Everyone thought she'd lost weight. 'You look wonderful. How much weight've you lost?' they'd say, and even though she'd lost a few pounds recently, after the operation itself, she'd actually gained some on account of all the sitting around. She gave up saying 'none', though, as it was too confusing for people. Instead she would reply: 'Almost two stone. Never felt better. I've got so much more energy with the weight off.' Which was true.

Before the surgery, Joanne would only undress for a man in the pitch dark, which Jackie thought was utterly ridiculous. 'Do you know how much they'd be prepared to *pay* to bury their faces in those?' she'd ask, and Joanne said she didn't want to know. Once, she'd been waiting to cross the road in Windermere when a car passed: windows down, music blaring, and a boy of approximately fifteen had yelled out, 'Tits!'

Not 'Big tits.'

Or 'Nice tits.'

Or even 'Can I have a feel of your . . .?'

Just 'Tits.'

That was the deciding factor for Joanne. That's when she made the appointment.

Apart from anything else, she was sick of attracting the wrong kind of bloke. She would stand at the bar waiting to be served and, invariably, she'd catch the attention of some pissed-up nuisance who wouldn't leave her alone for the night. The kind of persistent dickhead that didn't understand a gentle *'No' actually means 'no'*, and she'd have to resort to telling him to fuck off or she'd arrest him.

Joanne wondered idly if Noel was a boob man or a leg man. Or if he had no preference after being exposed to all that naked female flesh over the years. Perhaps naked women didn't excite him any longer. Perhaps overexposure to the female form had dulled his senses.

Joanne's senses had certainly become dulled to dead bodies.

She found them neither thrilling nor repulsive. They were just dead. Though she did wonder, if she came across one outside of work, whether she would have the same response.

They pulled into the pub car park. It was not a place Joanne had been to before. It was what her old partner, Ron Quigley, would have called a 'proper boozer' – the kind of place that would have once had a snug filled with men smoking pipe tobacco and from which women were banned.

They would not be getting any gastro-pub fare here.

The barmaid was sixty, with dyed magenta hair and white roots that ran like a zip down the middle of her head. She was friendly and totally unwelcoming at the same time, and told them if they wanted food, there was steak-and-onion pie and battered haddock.

They ordered a round of drinks. Joanne asked what the pie came with, and the barmaid frowned before saying, 'Mash,' as though Joanne had asked something blindingly obvious.

'Nice place,' Joanne said, and they took their seats in the corner, away from the bar.

'It does have a certain charm,' Noel replied. 'I come here to escape the tourists,' he said. 'Particularly during half-term.'

October half-term saw an influx of a different type of tourist. Gone were the summer folk who ate cream teas and walked sedately around the chocolate-box villages, looking to spend money on something – *anything*. October half-term attracted families who *did* stuff. Joanne would feel sorry for the teenagers trudging around in full waterproofs and walking boots, looking entirely miserable, wishing more than anything else that they could exchange their parents for a less energetic set.

'There's always some idiot wanting to tell me how he ran up Helvellyn with his six-year-old son in record time,' Noel said. 'So I come in here. They never come in here.'

Noel advised going for the pie, saying it was nicer than it

sounded, so they ordered two (no mash) and another round of drinks. Joanne had that loose, lazy feeling that came from a second shot of alcohol, and it occurred to her that they could very well end up in bed together that night if she wasn't careful. Though where, she couldn't imagine. She couldn't go back to his, obviously. And the sudden thought of trying to sneak him in past Jackie made her put her drink down.

The hot stirring in her belly dissipated fast. Good. Because, really, what was she *thinking*?

'What are you thinking?' Noel asked.

Joanne muttered something vague to do with station politics, which Noel received with an amused 'Really?'

'Yes, really,' she said.

'Thought you might be thinking about me.'

'Well, I wasn't.'

'That's a shame.'

'If you really want to know, I was thinking about your wife, but it didn't seem appropriate to bring her up just yet.'

'You want to ask something. Go ahead,' and he spread his hands wide as though to suggest he was an open book. 'Ask away. Anything you like.'

'Did you know she'd had an affair with Roger Nicholls?'

And Noel laughed. 'No,' he said. Then he sat back in his chair, highly amused. Still chuckling, he said, 'Really? She was sleeping with Roger?'

'You had no idea?'

'None.'

Then he looked past Joanne towards the bar. He was smiling openly as, Joanne assumed, he thought about the two of them together. 'That old goat, Roger.' Then he said, 'Good for Karen. Good for her.'

'You're not put out about it?'

Noel shook his head. 'Not at all. I think she thought I was a shitty husband. I'm not sure she felt much for me over the past few years. If she found a bit of pleasure on the side, I'm glad for her.'

'I only brought it up because it could be relevant.'

Noel puffed out his cheeks, shaking his head at the same time. 'Well, I can tell you right now, Roger didn't murder Karen. I'm surprised he had it in him to have an affair, to be honest.'

Joanne had visited Roger Nicholls at the solicitor's office where he worked. When asked if he would mind providing a DNA sample, 'Just so we can rule you out of our inquiries . . .' he'd come over all cold and clammy, with shortness of breath, and Joanne had to fetch him a glass of water. He ended up crying into a tissue, explaining afterwards how he'd made such a terrible mess of everything. Joanne had managed to calm him down, and he was ever so grateful. So grateful for her discretion, he said. Then he went on to tell her that his son had applied to Oxford.

Joanne *had* hoped that Noel Bloom would be able to acquaint her with Karen's other extramarital affairs but, judging by his reaction to her relationship with Roger, she suspected not. He was still smiling and shaking his head when their food arrived, saying, 'Karen and Roger, eh? Pia can't know, or she'd have his head.'

'Oh, she knows. She opted to keep it quiet, though, so maybe best not to bring it up if you come across either of them.'

Noel tapped the side of his nose conspiratorially before telling Joanne she was very adept at finding out all sorts of hidden information.

'Wonder what you'll discover about me,' he said.

'I wonder,' she replied flatly.

Joanne also wondered about Russell Wallbank.

Was he, as she suspected, Karen Bloom's long-lost boyfriend and father of Ewan?

After agreeing to meet with Noel Bloom for a drink, Joanne had called the number in Hastings which had flagged up on the Blooms' phone records.

'Beachcomber Guest House?' a voice had said. She sounded young, maybe early twenties, and she spoke the words as though posing a question, as though she wasn't entirely sure where she was and was seeking verification from the caller.

'This is Detective Sergeant Joanne Aspinall, and I'm after some information. I wonder if you can help.'

Deathly silence.

'Are you still there?' Joanne asked.

'Hmm-mm.'

'A call was placed from your number, from . . . what did you say the establishment was called again?'

'Beachcomber Guest House.'

'Yes. Two calls were placed from the Beachcomber around ten – no, make that twelve – days ago to an address in Windermere.'

'Windermere?'

'That's right.'

'That's north, isn't it?'

'It is.'

'The lake, right?'

'You've got it,' Joanne said. 'I'm trying to find out who made that call. I don't suppose you have any idea?'

'None at all.'

'Okay,' Joanne said, thinking this was going to be harder than she had anticipated. 'Are you a receptionist at the Beachcomber?'

The girl laughed. 'I do a bit of everything.'

'Do the guests have access to the hotel phone?'

'Not usually. They all have mobiles.'

'So it would have been a member of staff?'

'I suppose. Why do you need to know anyway?'

'We're conducting an investigation.' She didn't say into what. 'Do you have a member of staff working there, a male, between the ages of, say, forty-five and fifty-five?'

'Nah,' she said. 'Not here.'

'Anyone who used to work there?'

'Don't think so . . .' She paused, and Joanne could almost hear the cogs turning in her brain. 'Hang on. Yes, actually, thinking about it now, we did have a kitchen porter around that age, but he took off.'

'When?'

'Maybe the week before last. I can't be exact because I was in Ibiza—'

'What's his name?'

'Russell Wallbank.'

'Do you have a number for him? An address?'

'I can get them. Might take me a few minutes.'

'I can wait. As a matter of interest, what did you make of him? What kind of guy was Russell?'

'Jealous fucker,' she said. ''Scuse my language.'

'That's okay. Jealous about who?'

'He had a girlfriend. I don't know her . . . Siobhan, Sinéad, Sian . . . one of those. He'd slam the pots around all day if she looked at anyone else. I've been out with a guy like that, so I know the type. They're trouble.'

Joanne agreed with her. Jealous fuckers *were* trouble.

They did, however, make excellent suspects.

Joanne looked at Noel now and said, 'Does the name Russell Wallbank mean anything to you?'

Noel looked blank.

'He called your house and had a conversation with someone for over five minutes. You're sure Karen never mentioned it? Never mentioned his name?'

'I'm not sure. Maybe. We had a lot of nonsense callers for a while.'

'I think there's a chance Russell Wallbank may be Ewan's father,' Joanne said carefully. 'At the moment, it's still a long shot, but I'm trying to track him down, nonetheless. I think it's a line of inquiry worth pursuing.'

Before she'd left work, Joanne fed Wallbank's name into the Police National Database and had found two Russell Wallbanks with a history of criminal activity in the Sussex area. One interested her particularly, since his crimes fell into the categories of domestic violence and aggravated assault (under the influence of alcohol) against a woman. The last known address for this particular Wallbank was a staff house for a large hotel at Bexhill-on-Sea, but when Joanne inquired she was told he'd left there the previous year.

'So you think he saw Karen on the news and called her?' Noel asked.

Joanne nodded. 'She clearly wanted to keep Ewan's father out of her life for good. She didn't discuss him with anyone. She must have had good reason for that. When Brontë disappeared, perhaps he saw Karen make that statement and tracked her down. It wouldn't be hard to do.'

'And he came here and killed her? Why?'

'Nursing old wounds, perhaps. She did disappear with his child, after all.'

'Perhaps,' he replied, but Joanne could see he didn't buy it.

'Someone killed her, Noel,' she said. 'And if that person wasn't you—'

'I know it wasn't me.'

'Then who was it?'

Noel shrugged non-committally.

Joanne put down her drink.

After a moment she said, 'Noel, do you even *want* to know who did this to your wife?'

41

All things considered, Karen's murder had been timed pretty well. Brontë and Verity were off school for the half-term break and, if Karen had died a few weeks, or even a few days, later, Noel would have had the problem of childcare. As it turned out, it was expected he'd take some time away from the surgery to be with the family after Karen died. The problem was what to do with them. This was normally Karen's domain. He didn't often schedule time off from work to coincide with the girls' holidays, except during the summer, so he wasn't sure how to fill the days. And it was starting to dawn on him that future childcare was something he'd not given enough thought to. Granted, Verity could watch her sister for the odd hour here and there, but he couldn't expect her to do it full-time. She was sixteen. She had a life of her own. And was it even legal to leave a sixteen-year-old in charge of a minor for extended periods?

He'd told the girls they could go anywhere they liked. Do anything they wanted. He was about to say the same to Ewan but, in a peculiar turnaround, Ewan surprised him by returning home with a job interview lined up.

'Really?' Noel said, stunned.

'Really,' replied Ewan. 'At Dale's place. Thought I might try gardening, to see if I like it.'

'I think that's a splendid idea.'

Noel suppressed the urge to take things any further, stopping himself from doing that typical parent thing: talking about Ewan's potential and might he think of training to become a landscape architect further down the line? For now, a job – *any job* – was welcome. He did quietly wonder if Ewan's sudden interest in horticulture stemmed from a desire to cultivate his own weed but, again, he didn't let it cloud the moment.

'Splendid,' Noel said again. 'Anything I can do to help, just ask.'

And so it was that he found himself on the M6, heading south in thick traffic, en route to the Trafford Centre. Ewan was in the passenger seat; the two girls were in the back (Dale was working). Noel had never been to the Trafford Centre before. He'd never been forced into a day's shopping in Manchester, and he'd certainly never had the desire to suggest it himself. But now that they'd made the decision that this was what they ought to do with the day, he was quietly looking forward to the experience. To them all being out and about together. Ewan wanted to buy a pair of steel-toe-capped boots; Verity wanted new jeans, new tops, new underwear, new anything he was prepared to buy her; and Brontë said she would like to visit the Build-a-Bear shop. Ewan was oddly charmed by the teddy-bear idea, and offered to chaperone Brontë while Noel escorted Verity around with his credit card. It was to be an expensive day, but Noel had never thrown money at his children in an attempt to cheer them up and thought it was high time he started. Everyone else seemed to be doing it.

They arrived at eleven and the place was already heaving. They were forced to leave the car just about as far away as it was possible to get from the entrance. Noel mumbled that it was probably wise to park near the exit to allow a swift getaway. Once inside, though, he realized why he'd never been before. It was as if all the slow-witted, lumpen people on earth had been rounded up and deposited in one place and instructed to get under Noel's feet.

It was dreadful. And as Noel understood it, shopping was now the nation's favourite pastime. Britain was most certainly on the decline, he thought. And it wasn't as if Noel *never* went out, but living in Windermere tended to give you a distorted perspective of society. Elderly men were fit and wiry and wore suits on a weekday. Teenagers were polite, on the whole. Pedestrians said hello to strangers in the street. Motorists were considerate to their fellow road users: *You go. No, you go first, dear.* The only time Noel came into contact with the general population was at airports. And so the Trafford Centre came as quite a shock: great swathes of people moving so slowly they were almost in reverse, each one a picture of ill health, with the athletic capability of a professional darts player. Noel couldn't bear it. He handed Verity his credit card and told her he'd meet her outside Zara in forty-five minutes. He would browse the selection of plasma TVs at Currys, along with all the other dads who had lost the will.

Which was exactly where he should have stayed.

But there was a family of undesirables crowded around the particular model he was interested in and so he made his way to the ground floor. Before he knew it, he was in Calvin Klein, buying underwear. Karen had always bought his underwear, and he'd happily worn whatever turned up inside his top drawer without being overly interested in the garments. And yet, now, suddenly, he was. He bought six pairs of Superior trunks in neutral shades: *Err on the side of safety,* he thought. He was too embarrassed to ask about the difference between those and Bold or Air and decided Superior sounded, well, superior.

He was vaguely aware of a fellow shopper lurking a little too close for comfort, but he didn't think anything of it and had quite a nice conversation with a cheerful young sales assistant from Utah. She told him she was living with her extended family for a year, as she wanted to be a writer and needed to 'see life'.

'I can't imagine you see much life in here,' Noel commented, and she said, 'Oh, you'd be surprised.'

Noel left the shop feeling strangely buoyed by his purchases. So much so that he thought about adding a few other things to his wardrobe (a new winter coat? skinny jeans?), when his attention was caught by the shop opposite. Ann Summers.

Not really thinking, he moved towards the entrance, almost in a trance. In the window stood a mannequin wearing a red basque and – here was the thing that amused him – a blindfold. It was all very *Fifty Shades*.

Would Joanne Aspinall wear a blindfold? he wondered.

He gazed at the mannequin. She wore a dark wig. He thought of Joanne's hair. She had good hair.

With the exception of Karen, Noel had always gone for brunettes. Sometimes, a redhead. He left the blondes to his friends. He'd be in a bar and a busty, made-up blonde would walk in and every man in the room would make a beeline for her, and Noel would think, *Go for it, fools.* Then he'd sit back, in the smug knowledge that he'd have the pick of the brunettes, now that the competition had its attention firmly elsewhere.

Joanne had thick, shiny, dark hair, the kind he liked to smooth away from a woman's face, the kind he liked to feel against his own skin.

He tried to imagine what a life with Joanne Aspinall would look like. Would she want to give up work and play house, as both Jennifer and Karen had? He suspected not. He couldn't envisage her parting with her warrant card. He reckoned she'd had the thing spot-welded to her wrist.

He also liked that about her – the fact that she didn't just have a job but a *vocation*. As it was with Noel, the job was more than just a job. You signed up for life. Well, you used to do, anyway. GPs were scarpering off to Australia at an alarming rate for better pay, better hours, better weather.

Lost in pleasant contemplation, Noel didn't realize at first that he was being spoken to.

'Dr Bloom,' he heard vaguely. Then, more insistent: 'Dr Bloom, over here!'

The voice was coming from over his right shoulder.

He turned around, smiling a little. 'Just a couple more, if you don't mind, doctor,' the man said.

It was the same guy who'd been skulking around the Calvin Klein shop, and it was only now that Noel realized he was holding a camera. He was holding a camera, and he was pointing it straight at Noel.

'Why do you want to photograph me?' Noel asked, bewildered.

'You're Karen Bloom's husband?' the photographer asked, not making eye contact, still snapping away.

'Yes, but—'

Then the photographer raised his hand to bid Noel goodbye.

'Very much obliged, Dr Bloom.'

And he was gone.

42

JOANNE SPENT THE morning trying to track down Russell Wallbank, without success, and now the lab was on the phone wanting to talk to her.

'Good news,' the voice said. 'The blood sample was viable. We have a DNA profile. Now, do you want the bad news?'

'Go ahead.'

'It matches none of the samples that were collected from the potential suspects. And I've run it through the DNA database, and . . . the donor's not on there. Which means—'

'Which means I have nothing,' Joanne said.

Because most crimes are committed by repeat offenders, Joanne had felt certain that the killer's DNA would already be on the database. Everyone convicted of a crime in the UK has their DNA profile stored indefinitely. So if Karen's killer wasn't on there, it meant he was a first-time offender. And she had absolutely no idea who he was.

She had not expected this. She had really not expected this. It was almost unheard of for a person to go from law abider to murderer without any steps in between.

Joanne rang off and rubbed her face with her hands. Back to the drawing board.

From the angle of the stab wound on Karen's neck, it was thought the killer was right-handed. She'd been stabbed from behind, the forensic pathologist thought, which placed the killer in the back seat of the car. Nine out of ten people are right-handed. So now Joanne had narrowed down her search to ninety per cent of the population. Great.

Noel Bloom was right-handed. Had he had the means, motive and opportunity to kill his wife? Theoretically, Joanne supposed he did. But she could do sod all about it, because she didn't have one scrap of physical evidence, not one eye-witness statement to place Noel at the scene. Joanne wasn't exactly sure whether she was relieved about this or not.

'Fuck,' she said out loud, and she turned to Oliver Black.

'Don't look at me,' he said. 'I'm all out of ideas as well.'

Short of anything better to do, Joanne grabbed her bag from beneath the desk, telling Oliver to 'Sit tight.'

She told him she'd be back within the hour.

DCI McAleese had his chemo at the same time each fortnight at Helme Chase Hospital in Kendal. Joanne had accompanied him twice before to lend moral support because, apart from his daughter, he didn't have any family in the area. Not that he wanted any support, but sometimes she missed him and it seemed as good a place as any to pay him a visit. Pete was on a low dose, he said. It wasn't wreaking havoc on his body, he said. But today he looked shrunken and ashen, and Joanne wished he would let her do more. He was still insistent, though, that he wanted to go this alone, so when she walked in he greeted her with 'I told you I don't need you here, Joanne.'

And so she said, 'Relax.' She told him she could do with some help with the case. 'I don't know what I'm missing.'

'You're probably missing nothing,' he replied. 'How's Pat Gilmore doing anyway? She a better DI than me?'

'She's more cheerful. That makes for a nice change.'

'What about your new partner? DS Black?'

'Oliver? Oh, he's working out pretty well. I like him.'

'You *like* him like him?'

'He's married, Pete. And no, I don't like him that way. Tell me, how's the treatment going?' and Pete waved away her concern with his free hand, as if to say, *Fine, fine.*

'You look a little tired.'

'I look a little fucked, you mean.'

'A bit,' she admitted.

'Well, I'm not, apparently.' He rested his eyes on Joanne and said, 'We are very pleased with your response to the treatment, Mr McAleese,' mimicking his oncologist, Joanne assumed.

'How many more of these?' she asked, meaning the chemo.

'Three.'

'And then?'

'And then you get me back as your boss, DS Aspinall. But enough about me. You're looking really quite radiant. What's going on? You found a replacement lover for me already?'

'No.'

'You're sure? Because you can tell me. I'm a big boy. I can cope.'

'There's no one,' she said firmly, but she did wonder privately if her feelings towards Noel Bloom were somehow clouding her ability to conduct this investigation effectively.

She took out her notes and gave Pete a quick overview of Karen Bloom's murder. When she'd finished, he said, 'Same as always, Joanne. Go back to the beginning.'

'But I have. I've been back to the crime scene and nothing is speaking to me.'

Pete McAleese looked at her straight. 'I mean the very start, Joanne. You want to go back to the girl going missing. Begin there. That's where you'll find your answer.'

43

Wednesday, 28 October

The calls started coming just after seven. They were relentless.

'Would you like to comment, Dr Bloom?' 'How do you feel about your wife's death now, Dr Bloom?'

He'd fucked up. That much was obvious. Lessons had been learned.

Pictures of him appeared in the *Daily Express* under the head-line: DOCTOR SHOPS FOR UNDERWEAR DAYS AFTER WIFE MURDERED.

He had been photographed at the till in the Calvin Klein shop, laughing with the sales assistant, handing her his Superior trunks. And then, once more, outside Ann Summers. That was the money ball. He had his head turned, and he was smiling in the direction of the photographer, with the blindfolded manne-quin in the background. Noel had to agree it was an excellent shot – if you were trying to create a narrative for some poor bastard you wanted to nail. He wondered how much the photo-grapher had been paid. An easy day's work, he should think.

Noel made the front page (though, it had to be said, it was a slow news day) and his thoughts immediately turned to Amanda Knox. Escorted by her boyfriend, Miss Knox had bought new underwear after her housemate had been found murdered in Italy, and the press had crucified her for it. Amanda's excuse had been that she'd shopped for underwear because she wasn't allowed at the crime scene, her home, but she also bought a host of other essentials that day. Which had always seemed a pretty plausible explanation to Noel. But he didn't have that excuse. He'd bought new underwear because he wanted to spruce himself up a bit for DS Joanne Aspinall, should they have the opportunity to get together again. But he could hardly say that, could he?

So instead he said, 'No comment . . . no comment . . . no comment,' and then he unplugged the phone, before nipping out to pick up a paper to survey the full extent of the damage. He'd read it online first, of course, but he wanted to see the hard copy in all its glory. And it was worse than he thought. The only other story on the front page was one of more bad weather on the way, so Noel was the main feature. The story continued on page two, where a photograph of Karen had been included. Except that it looked nothing like Karen. At this blunder, Noel's heart leapt, as he thought of the possibility of suing the *Daily Express* for getting their facts wrong. But then he realized they'd copied Karen's Facebook profile picture. The one of her lying on the bedroom floor. The one she'd taken from above in an attempt to make her appear younger. The wind-tunnel picture, as he'd come to think of it.

At nine thirty, his mobile rang.

'Noel,' she said.

'Joanne,' he replied.

'You're famous, I see.'

'It's looking that way, yes.'

'Not a great move,' she said. 'Have you spoken to the press?'

'I'm avoiding their calls. The kids don't know yet either. They were with me yesterday, incidentally. The story doesn't mention that. We were having a day out, the four of us, in an attempt to take Brontë's mind off things, and I don't know if you've been to the Trafford Centre, but it's quite ghastly. Anyway, I took myself off to a quieter section in an attempt to keep sane. Sadly, my plan backfired.'

'You should probably warn the kids to stay inside,' Joanne said. 'The press may turn up,' and Noel detected something in her voice. Was it weariness? Or was she just plain pissed off with him?

'Joanne?' he said.

'What?'

'Will this affect the investigation?'

'Hard to say,' she said.

44

JOANNE WAS GOING back through her case notes from the time of Brontë Bloom's disappearance when she received a piece of interesting news.

She hadn't told Noel or the rest of the Bloom family about her plan to re-interview the girls. She wanted to catch them unawares. Brontë had been a stubborn little urchin the first time Joanne had spoken to her, revealing nothing – which was harder to do in practice than you might think. Brontë had not been brought up as the type of kid who loathed the police. She was a nice girl who respected authority. So Joanne reckoned she'd been primed.

Perhaps without any forewarning, and if Joanne could apply the right amount of pressure, Brontë Bloom might crack.

She was eager to get going when she got a call from a bobby at Windermere station.

The day before, Joanne had put in a request for information on Russell Wallbank. She'd expected nothing back. The guy had dropped off the radar in Sussex and, as much as she hoped he'd headed north and put a knife to Karen Bloom's carotid artery, she knew it was unlikely. Russell Wallbank was fast turning into one of those lines of inquiry that Joanne pursued for no reason other than she couldn't let it go until she had a satisfactory answer. The kind of loose end that would be needling her at four in the morning unless she did something about it.

'You're looking for Russell Wallbank?' the bobby had asked.

'I am,' she'd replied.

'Well, you're in luck, detective. He's been staying at our hotel since last night.'

By 'our hotel', he meant the cells.

'We picked him up for drunk-and-disorderly conduct at the Wheelhouse,' he said. 'Broke the leg off a table and went for a bouncer, but the club's not pressing charges.'

'I'll be there in twenty minutes.'

It wasn't against the law to be weird, but it did stir Joanne's interest all the same. Russell Wallbank was like a kid with ADHD. He sat in his chair, tapping his fingers, twitching and writhing like a snared rabbit. He weighed no more than eight stone.

On paper, this Russell Wallbank fell into the right age bracket – forty-five to fifty-five – though he appeared much older. His skin drooped from his face, as if pulled down by invisible hands, and strings of dark, ratty hair haloed a white, perfectly circular bald patch on the top of his head.

Despite this, if Joanne had to pick out one man in the county who could be Ewan Rigby's father, her money would be on this guy. He had Ewan's dark, dark, shadowed eyes, his elfin ears and, when he wasn't twitching and jerking, he held his head over to the right slightly, in much the same manner as Ewan.

Life had not been kind to our Mr Wallbank. He was typical of the type of transient worker Joanne often saw passing through the Lakes: broke, shitty social life, drink problem.

'Can you tell me what brings you to Windermere, Mr Wallbank?'

He gave a sardonic laugh. 'The great weather.'

'Believe you got yourself in a spot of bother last night. Care to tell me what happened?'

'Not really. Who are you anyway?'

'I'm Detective Sergeant Joanne Aspinall. I told you that a moment ago.'

'But what do you want?'

'Just to ask a few questions, that's all.'

Russell Wallbank rolled his eyes and then fixed her with a glare that said: *Drop dead.* Russell Wallbank had had plenty of run-ins with the police, and it was a look a seasoned criminal like him had perfected.

'I haven't done anything,' he said.

'Then you have nothing to worry about. The quicker you answer my questions, the quicker I'll be out of your hair.' At this, Russell touched his bald patch, and Joanne winced. 'So to speak,' she added quickly.

'The guy hit me first,' he said.

'Which guy?'

'In the club.'

'Oh,' said Joanne. 'Right. I'll make sure that's noted. How about you tell me what brought you north in the first place? Your accent tells me you're not from around here.'

'Just passing through. No crime in that, as far as I'm aware.'

'Where are you staying?'

Russell shrugged. 'Here and there.'

'Do you have accommodation?'

'Not really.'

'Where do you plan on staying tonight?'

'I've got a number. A guy I met said he had a free settee.'

'And then you're heading back to Hastings?'

At this, Russell Wallbank stopped moving in his seat and sat deadly still.

'How do you know where I'm from?' he asked.

'Lucky guess,' she said. 'How about you tell me why you're really here, Mr Wallbank? Like I said, the sooner you answer my questions, the sooner they can get you processed and get you out of here.'

'I came to find someone,' he said.

'Who?'

'Just someone.'

'And did you find them?'

Russell Wallbank dropped his head. 'No,' he said.

'When did you arrive in the Lakes?'

He hesitated. Then he said, 'Day before yesterday.'

'And you got here by . . .?'

'Train.'

'So if I were to check the CCTV at Oxenholme station I would find you disembarking?'

'Yes?' he said, sounding unsure.

'See, I have a slight problem with that, Mr Wallbank. When I spoke to a member of staff at the Beachcomber Guest House, they told me you'd done a bunk from there around two weeks ago. You haven't been seen in the area since.' That last sentence was not strictly true. Joanne had not been told that at all. But she could see Russell was freaking out a little at the mention of the Beachcomber, so she decided to run with it.

She waited. And Russell was suddenly having trouble answering her questions.

'Do you know what I think, Mr Wallbank? I think you left your job and headed north to find someone in particular. That's what I think. And that person is now dead. So why don't you start trying to convince me that I'm wrong about that because, right now, you're the only person I have earmarked for this crime. You should also be aware that I know all about the history you have with the victim . . . and I know about the phone calls you made to her.'

'I want a lawyer. I should have a lawyer.'

'You're not under arrest. And if you want a solicitor present, I can arrange that. But I have to tell you, you'll be waiting some time.'

'How long?'

'I can't give you an exact time. It varies. It depends on availability and how far they have to travel. Though it shouldn't be more than three hours or so.'

Russell Wallbank began rapidly tapping his fingers on his thighs.

Again, Joanne waited.

Eventually, she said, 'You know, you really look like you could do with a drink.'

And he nodded.

'Faster you tell me what I need to know, faster you can be on your way. All I'm looking for is the truth, Russell. Mind if I call you Russell?'

He shook his head.

'How do I know you're not fucking with me?' he asked.

'Because I'm a detective. If I fuck with you, I get into trouble. Tell me something logical, Russell. That's what I'm after. I know you didn't arrive here two days ago. The duty sergeant himself says you were in an altercation in the Stag's Head last week, so I know you're lying.'

Russell sat on his hands.

'I came to see Karen,' he said.

'Great,' replied Joanne. 'Now we're getting somewhere.'

'She has my kid.'

'How did you know where to find her?'

'Saw her on the news shouting her mouth off, and I recognized her. I found her number and I told her I wanted to know about my kid, but she wouldn't tell me. She always was a bitch.'

'Did you threaten her?'

'No.'

'What did you tell her?'

'I told her I knew where she lived and if she wouldn't tell me about the kid then I'd come looking.'

'And what did Karen say?'

'She didn't say anything.'

'So, you're obviously aware that Karen was murdered, Russell. What do you make of that?'

'I'd say someone had it in for her. But it wasn't me. I'd say she probably had it coming. She got pregnant on purpose, you know? She told me she was on the pill. She thought I had money. Thought my folks were minted. When she found out they weren't, she bailed. Bitch.'

'We have some DNA,' Joanne said, watching Russell's face carefully, 'something found at the scene belonging to the killer. What we'd like is for you to provide a sample, Russell. That would eliminate you from the crime scene. Would you do that for us?'

Of course, a sample from Russell wouldn't really eliminate him, as they didn't know whether the blood on the tree was the killer's or not. But Russell didn't need to know that. And Joanne had to work with what she had. If he refused to offer a sample, then he had something to hide. She'd haul him into Kendal and interview him under caution.

'I'll give you my DNA,' Russell Wallbank said quickly. 'Because I never fucking touched her.'

As it turned out, Joanne didn't need the swab. She submitted it anyway, for the sake of dotting the 'i's and crossing the 't's, but once she told Russell Wallbank she would not be keeping him for further questioning, he handed over his train ticket. 'There,' he said defiantly. And on checking the date, Joanne immediately saw that he'd travelled to Oxenholme from London Euston the day *after* Karen's car was found. Unless he was working with someone else, Russell Wallbank was in the clear.

'Just out of interest,' she asked him, 'what had you intended to do when you met Karen?' and he told her he hadn't really had a plan.

'Frighten her a bit, I suppose,' he said. 'She deserved it. Taking off the way she did and leaving me with no idea what happened to her.'

'Do you still want to see your child?'

'I don't even know if she had a girl or a boy.'

Joanne gave an empathetic smile. 'Can't really help you there, I'm afraid. I think social services are your next stop.'

She wondered what Noel would make of this tragic-looking deadbeat turning up on his doorstep claiming parental rights over Ewan. Ewan was almost an adult. He could make his own decisions about whether he wanted to meet his father. Joanne couldn't help thinking Russell might be better off getting back on the train and forgetting all about it. But it wasn't her call.

'Good luck,' she told Russell. 'I'll be in touch if anything comes back with the sample.'

'It won't,' he said.

Driving back to Kendal, Joanne thought back to the murder cases she'd been involved in. There hadn't been many. Cumbria had one of the lowest murder rates in the country. Surprisingly, both South Yorkshire and Bedfordshire had higher rates than London – something Joanne had learned while studying for her sergeant's exams. In Cumbria, you were more likely to die from falling out of bed or banging your head on an open kitchen cupboard. Random, unmotivated murders were practically non-existent. People in Cumbria tended to kill their drinking partners after a stupid argument, or kill their mother as a result of simmering, decades-long tensions. Which made Joanne think about

Russell Wallbank's comment about Karen Bloom deserving her fate. Perhaps the key to this wasn't the forensics or trying to find and interview all the skeletons marching out of Karen's closet. Perhaps the only thing Joanne needed to do was find the one person, other than Russell Wallbank, who thought Karen deserved to die.

45

'I THOUGHT THE press would be here,' Joanne said to Noel.
'Been and gone. There were two reporters here for most of
the morning, but I think they're taking a lunch break.'

They were in Noel's kitchen. He'd made her a sausage-and-egg
sandwich, which was really rather good, and they both stood at
the kitchen island, eating. Joanne often stood to eat, so she didn't
think it was unusual. When you spent most of your day behind
a desk or behind the wheel, it made for a pleasant change.

Noel didn't ask the reason for her dropping in on him
unannounced, and Joanne didn't offer one. He seemed to assume
this was a social call, and took it upon himself to feed her while
she was there: lightly toasting the bread as though he were making her a club sandwich. He appeared to take pleasure in
providing her with a meal and, as she watched him work, whist-
ling a little, she thought the kids should do okay with him. 'I
would have thought you doctors were against all this cholesterol,'
she remarked as she chewed.

'Whatever gave you that idea?'

Joanne bit into the second half of her sandwich and felt the
welcome sensation of yolk bursting inside her mouth. 'This is
good,' she said.

Noel nodded in agreement. 'I was going to call you today.'

'Oh?'

'See if you fancied going out for dinner.'

'Again?' She smiled.

'Or if not dinner,' he said, 'something else maybe? Whatever you want to do.'

'So, another date, then?'

'Yes,' he said. 'That's what I was thinking. Of course, I can't be out all night . . .' And he gestured towards the hallway, where Joanne could hear the sound of the TV piping through from the living room.

'You're needed here,' she said.

'Exactly.'

'You were right about Karen's ex, by the way. He wasn't involved in the murder.'

'You found him?' Noel said, surprised. 'What was he like?'

Joanne shrugged non-committally. 'I told him if he wanted to make contact with Ewan he needed to go through social services.'

'That seems sensible. I don't really like the idea of him just turning up here.'

'I don't think he will,' she said. 'He'd got himself into a bit of bother, and I warned him that it wouldn't look good if he didn't go via the proper channels. So . . .'

'So, now you don't have a suspect,' Noel said.

'No.' She paused. Thought about how to word what she wanted to say next. 'To be honest, Noel,' she said, 'that's pretty much why I called in today. I wondered if I might have a quick word with Brontë?'

Noel put down his sandwich. 'Brontë?'

'That's if you think her state of mind is okay. I wouldn't want to upset her, but it would be really helpful if—'

'Why would you need to talk to Brontë?'

'Just tying up loose ends. I'm going back over the whole investigation, checking I've not missed anything. It's normal procedure. And of course, when you think about it . . . all of this did actually start with her.'

'Surely you don't think the two incidents are related?' Noel said.

He was jittery, she noticed.

'I don't see how they could be,' he added.

Joanne's expression remained impassive. 'Well, that's my job, Noel. To figure out what *is* related to what. To find connections where there are none. My job,' she said, locking her eyes on his, 'is to see the things other people *don't* see.'

Brontë was already in the office, seated on Noel's large leather chair, when Joanne returned from her car, carrying the box. Brontë's hair was escaping from her French plait, she had a wet, pink lower lip and a furtive look in her eyes. Joanne suspected that Noel had done the plait himself.

'Don't look so worried, Brontë,' Joanne said mildly. 'This will only take a minute. I've got something I want to show you.'

Brontë looked to Noel for reassurance. But he, too, was anxious, as if Joanne might produce the murder weapon directly from her secret box: *voilà!* – his prints all over it.

'Here,' Joanne said, laying out the pieces of paper in front of Brontë. 'You remember these?'

Brontë stared straight ahead, unwilling, it seemed, to engage.

'Brontë?' Joanne urged. 'These are yours, aren't they, honey?'

Joanne moved the cards a little closer, the cards that were covered in love hearts, the ones she'd removed from Brontë's desk when she had gone missing, the cards with the messages of love written in Brontë's hand.

'Joanne,' Noel said quickly. 'I think Brontë may be a little embarrassed. These are personal items of hers, after all. They're not really meant for public viewing.'

Joanne looked at Brontë. The girl remained expressionless.

'How about this one?' Joanne said, opening it. 'It says here "Thank you for being kind." Did you write that?'

Again, nothing.

Joanne moved on to the second one.

'How about this one? This one says—'

'I don't remember,' Brontë said, barely audible. A mouse's voice.

And Joanne said, 'You don't?' Her tone was more cajoling than disbelieving. 'It's just that your teacher, Miss Gilbert, told me that you made these. You made them. It's your handwriting inside. Miss Gilbert is a lovely teacher, isn't she?'

Brontë nodded.

'She seems ever so nice,' Joanne said. 'I don't think Miss Gilbert would lie about a thing like that, do you?'

Brontë looked over to the far wall and, suddenly, her eyes started to fill.

Joanne waited.

On seeing his daughter's discomfort, Noel whispered, '*Joanne,*' urgently.

She ignored him.

'How about this one, Brontë?' she continued. 'Do you remember making this? It's a beautiful card. It says here, "You are the best person I know." That's a really nice thing to say to someone. I would love to get a card like that.'

Brontë wiped at her eyes.

'Who did you make this card for, Brontë?'

'Joanne, stop,' said Noel.

'Who is the best person you know, Brontë?' Joanne said.

'Joanne!' he repeated.

'It's really important you tell me,' Joanne said, unabated. 'You understand that I'm a police officer. I won't tell any of your friends, if that's what you're worried about. I'm not allowed to. It will be between us.'

Silence.

And just when Joanne was thinking she should really brush up on her interrogation technique, Brontë whispered, 'I can't.'

Joanne moved from her seat and squatted on her haunches beside her. '*Why* can't you?'

A beat.

Brontë started to cry. 'Because I promised I wouldn't tell,' she said.

'Oh, for Christ's sake, Joanne, stop!' Noel shouted. 'She doesn't want to tell you. What the hell does this have to do with anything anyway? Look at her. You're upsetting her.'

Joanne ignored him and kept her eyes on Brontë. 'Sometimes, keeping a promise is not the right thing to do,' she said. 'Sometimes, it's really important that people know the truth so they can protect you. That's my job, Brontë, to find out the truth so I can help people. You're not being a bad person if you don't keep this promise. No one will think badly of you.'

Brontë still didn't seem convinced.

'You could whisper it if you like,' Joanne said. 'Or perhaps you might want to write it down?'

Brontë went to speak, then hesitated.

'*Who* did you promise?' Joanne pressed. 'Who was it, Brontë?'

46

ASTONISHINGLY, NOEL THREW her out.

He actually threw her out of his house.

He grabbed the cards, put them in the box and told Brontë not to utter another word, before carrying the box to the front door and dropping it on the step.

Joanne stood there, her mouth hanging open as he handed over her keys, telling her that if she wanted to question his daughter again she would have to do it with a lawyer present.

Joanne sped out of the Blooms' driveway, gravel flying.

When she was a safe distance away, she pulled over. What the hell was Noel playing at? Why wouldn't he let Brontë speak? Why was he covering for her?

She'd parked outside Applemead, directly opposite the recreation ground. Back where this had all started. Joanne gave a bark of laughter. Had she done that intentionally? She didn't know. She felt like she didn't know anything.

When Joanne had interviewed the child before, she had known she was protecting someone. Knew she was not revealing something crucial.

Had Karen stumbled on this, perhaps? Joanne couldn't make sense of it. She could do with a drink to steady her nerves.

A car pulled alongside and began the process of parallel parking. Joanne watched in her wing mirror. The woman pulled her steering wheel down to the left, keeping it there just a shade too long. A common problem with older drivers, Joanne reflected, her thoughts momentarily rerouted. They would forget to straighten the wheel and the car would end up sticking out of the space, the nose of the vehicle still in the road. Once it was like that, there was just no righting it and it was necessary to start over. Which is what the woman was doing. Going through the whole process but making exactly the same mistake again.

By now, there were a few cars queued behind her. But if the woman felt compelled to hurry, she didn't show it. She pulled out for a third attempt. It was painful to watch, and Joanne thought about offering to do it for her. But just at that moment the woman cracked it, releasing her wheel at exactly the right second and whipping into the space like a pro.

Joanne caught the woman's eye in the rear-view mirror and the woman gave a small bow in her seat.

Joanne smiled. She recognized her. She saw her around the village – always well dressed, often carrying flowers. She was attractive. Had a look of Helen Mirren about her; Joanne hoped she might be lucky enough to age so elegantly. Then she brushed away the thought, knowing that was unlikely to happen.

Helen Mirren.

What film did she win the Oscar for again?

Oh, that's right, she remembered, *The Queen.*

And then Joanne jolted in her seat as though she'd been bitten.

The witness with dementia had said the woman who had abducted Brontë Bloom was the Queen.

She had said she was the Queen of England.

47

J ACKIE WAGSTAFF ANSWERED the door to Applemead.
'Eh up,' she said. 'What brings you?'

Joanne had her warrant card ready, but closed her fingers around it on seeing Jackie.

'I need to speak to someone,' Joanne said. 'A woman.'

'Can you narrow it down? Any distinguishing features? Tattoos? Missing limbs?'

Joanne's face remained stony. 'She just came in. I think she's a volunteer. Looks like Helen Mirren.'

'Ah,' said Jackie. 'You want Madeleine Kramer. She's making tea in the kitchen. What do you want her for?'

'Can't say. What does she do here?'

'Bit of everything,' replied Jackie. 'Reads to those who want it, bakes scones, arranges flowers. Doesn't like to get her hands dirty . . . but who does?'

'You ever see her with Verity Bloom?'

Jackie shrugged. 'Sometimes.'

'Are they friends?'

'I couldn't say. I just let the visitors in and get back to work. I don't go eavesdropping.'

Joanne arched an eyebrow.

'Okay,' admitted Jackie, 'I don't go eavesdropping on *them*. Doesn't seem right, listening in on a teenager. She's very close to Verity's mum, if that's any use. They spend a lot of time together. She's Jennifer's favourite helper. What do you want with her?'

'Like I said, I can't say.'

Jackie dropped her voice. 'You don't think she murdered that woman, do you?' And when Joanne wouldn't answer, Jackie huffed, saying, 'Suit yourself,' somewhat affronted that Joanne wasn't playing ball. 'Well, if you're coming in, you'll need to sign that,' she said. 'Case there's a fire or something.'

She handed Joanne a pen and slid the leather-bound book along the table towards her. 'Have a humbug,' she said. 'I'll go and find your *Mrs Kramer*.'

Jackie stressed the name as if mocking Joanne for playing her cards close to her chest, and flounced off, her leather clogs making a soft thwacking sound. Jackie couldn't bear secrets. She couldn't keep one to save her life, but if she thought Joanne was withholding information she'd sulk and pick at her niece until Joanne lost her temper. She could be quite the baby.

Joanne could hear the metallic crunching sound of a walking frame approaching and lifted her head to see an elderly woman with a pronounced dowager's hump making slow progress along the hallway. She was bent over to such an extent that she needed to tilt her head to a forty-five-degree angle just to see where she was going. Old age could be such a bastard, thought Joanne, offering the woman a sympathetic smile. Whether the smile was registered or not, she couldn't tell, as before the woman came any closer, Madeleine Kramer emerged from the rear of the building, wearing a wipeable apron and a pair of yellow rubber gloves. She pulled off the gloves as she grew closer to Joanne. 'Do excuse my attire,' she said, holding out her right hand. 'I'm sorry, but I don't think we've met . . . Madeleine Kramer.'

Joanne shook her hand and pulled her warrant card from her pocket. 'Detective Sergeant Joanne Aspinall. Is there anywhere we could go for a minute?'

Madeleine Kramer's expression of mild curiosity stayed fixed. She didn't even blink. 'Of course, dear,' she said. 'I'll check if the office is free.'

Joanne followed on behind. They passed the lady with the frame, and Madeleine Kramer wished her 'Good afternoon.' Madeleine had an air of calm efficiency; she was the type of woman you'd find managing a stately home in an episode of *Midsomer Murders*.

Madeleine Kramer knocked once on the office door, which had been left ajar. When there was no reply from within, she pushed it open, saying, 'We should be safe in here.'

They settled themselves among the general detritus of an office run in a slightly slipshod fashion – boxes on the floor, dusty Hewlett Packard printer by Joanne's elbow, four discarded coffee cups – and Madeleine Kramer looked at Joanne and nodded, as if permitting her to begin. Usually, a woman of Madeleine's years would be eager to talk to a detective, excited to impart what she knew in a way that made her appear both helpful and a valuable source of information to the police. Not so here. This woman wasn't about to offer anything unless Joanne prised it from her. She had her lips shut tight – evident by the small pockets of flesh that had formed at either side of her mouth. Madeleine Kramer was like a toddler refusing food.

Before entering Applemead, Joanne had retrieved the cardboard box with Brontë Bloom's case notes from the boot of her car. Flicking through them again, she made an interesting discovery: Madeleine Kramer listened to Brontë Bloom read at Reid's Grammar fairly frequently. She knew the child. She had been interviewed by telephone during Brontë's disappearance, by DC Hannah Gidley. But not face to face, Joanne noted. No one actually went to Madeleine Kramer's home and spoke to her, and the phone interview wasn't followed up on because Brontë returned home unharmed.

Joanne had Brontë's notes on her lap now.

'Mrs Kramer,' she began.

'Madeleine is fine.'

'You work here often?'

'I wouldn't exactly call it work. I volunteer.'

'Of course.' Joanne pulled out her notepad. 'Do you remember volunteering the day that Brontë Bloom disappeared?'

Madeleine Kramer didn't flinch, and Joanne was sure she'd been expecting the question. 'I'm very sorry,' she said, 'but I don't. I don't tend to keep to a set schedule. I come to Applemead whenever my other responsibilities will allow.'

'Try casting your mind back. It was around a month ago, a Sunday – the twenty-seventh of September. An event like that would usually stick in a person's mind, wouldn't you say?'

'I'm afraid, when you get to my age, dear, the days become a bit of a blur. How is it I can remember practically everything that happened to me as a child, but I can't remember what I had for breakfast? Terrible, really. I should start doing – what is it they call it? – suzuki?'

'Sudoku.'

'Quite. Or they say learning a foreign language can be useful.'

'They do,' agreed Joanne. Though she did wonder, not for the first time, just who exactly *they* were, the people who kept saying these things.

'It was a hot day, if that helps,' said Joanne, and Madeleine Kramer made a great show of closing her eyes, tilting her head back to reveal her slim neck, as if Rolodexing through all the hot days they'd had leading up to this point.

Finally, she opened her eyes. 'Sorry,' she said, shaking her head decisively. 'Nothing.'

'One of the residents here reported seeing a woman matching your description talking to Brontë Bloom outside Applemead. On the day she went missing.'

'Well, I don't see how that's possible. It must have been someone who looked like me.'

'She was adamant it was you,' Joanne pressed. Not exactly true, but Joanne was improvising.

'I assure you, if I *had* seen Brontë Bloom the day she went missing, I would have gone straight to the police. Why wouldn't I have?'

'I don't know, Madeleine. Why wouldn't you?'

Madeleine Kramer gave Joanne a look as if to say she was testing her patience. She took a long breath in and then exhaled, smoothing her silver, bobbed hair behind her ears. She was still an attractive woman. Must have been quite a beauty when she was younger. Joanne admired women who held on to the haircuts from their youth. It was refreshing to see a woman in her seventies with a fringe, a ponytail, long hair past her shoulders. As far as Joanne could tell, most women emerged from the salon with exactly the same haircut as everyone else, once they got to sixty-five. Maybe wigs were the way to go, she thought. Like Joan Collins and Raquel Welch.

'Brontë reads to you, doesn't she?' Joanne said. 'At Reid's Grammar.'

'That's right. I listen to the pupils read there, two, sometimes three, mornings each week.'

'Is Brontë a particular favourite?'

'No more than any of the other children. I like to think I don't have favourites.'

'I'd say we all have favourites,' Joanne said. 'Impossible not to, in my opinion. Maybe you're a better person than me.'

'Maybe.'

'Did Brontë ever confide to you that she was unhappy at home?'

'Brontë is a very quiet child, detective, as I'm sure you're aware. She is not the type to communicate problems easily.'

'But you knew Karen was – how can I put it? – very invested in her daughter?'

'I did.'

'How so?'

'The teachers would talk about it. And on a number of occasions Karen Bloom became quite heated with both the teachers and the support staff, accusing them of neglecting Brontë's education.'

'Did she ever get quite heated with you in particular?' Joanne asked.

'She did. Once. But I must say, in her defence, that all parents have very high expectations of their offspring nowadays. Especially when they're paying for such an education.'

'Do you think Karen was wrong in the way she pushed Brontë to achieve?'

Madeleine took a moment to consider the question. 'I think,' she said carefully, 'that, for the most part, Karen had Brontë's best interests at heart.'

'Let me rephrase. Did *you* personally have a problem with the way she was bringing up Brontë?'

'It's not my place to comment on something like that.'

Joanne nodded. The woman was a closed book.

'What does Verity's mother have to say about it?' Joanne asked. 'Jennifer, isn't it? You read to her, too, I believe.'

'I can't say it ever comes up.'

'Really? I hear you two are pretty close.'

'If you met Jennifer, you would understand why. She has great trouble speaking, now that her multiple sclerosis has advanced. She enjoys being read to, but if you think we sit around gossiping about her husband's other family, then I can assure you you're greatly mistaken.'

For the first time since the start of their exchange Madeleine Kramer's tone had become slightly shrill.

She was either genuinely offended by Joanne's accusation or else she was acting as if she was. Joanne couldn't tell which.

'My apologies,' Joanne said. 'I didn't mean to upset you.'

'You did *not* upset me. You are simply incorrect in your assumptions.'

'All the same, I apologize. Let me ask you this: Brontë Bloom made a number of home-made cards at school.' As she spoke, Joanne opened Brontë's case notes and retrieved the plastic envelope containing them. She placed each one in front of Madeleine and watched her reaction. 'You ever seen these before?'

'No.'

'Take your time. Open the first one and read what it says inside.'

Madeleine seemed reluctant.

'Go ahead,' Joanne prompted.

Gingerly, Madeleine fingered the card, lifting the flap before saying, 'No. I have never seen this.'

'Did you ever receive such a card from Brontë?'

And her eyes wouldn't meet Joanne's. 'No, detective,' she said, shakily now. 'I did not.'

Joanne didn't believe her.

'I don't believe you, Madeleine,' she said.

And Madeleine Kramer flinched.

Joanne took her moment.

'Look, I just chatted with Brontë Bloom,' Joanne said casually, 'and she got rather emotional when I mentioned you. Said how much she thinks of you, and talked of the special bond the two of you have together. If I didn't know better, I'd say that some might misconstrue this relationship, maybe they might think there was something odd going on between the two of—'

'She wanted me to take her!' Madeleine Kramer said out of nowhere.

'I'm sorry – what?'

Suddenly, Madeleine's breath was hard and ragged. 'She wanted me to take her,' she repeated, more quietly this time.

'I'm not sure I understand,' Joanne said. 'We're talking about Brontë, yes? She wanted you to take her where, exactly?'

'Away from Karen.'

'And why would she want you to do that?'

'Because she was miserable. Because she was exhausted. Because Karen was a deluded tyrant who didn't know how to love her own daughter properly. So yes, you're right, those cards *were* meant for me. Brontë made many more. She gave them to me because I was nice to her. Because I liked being with her. Because I didn't require anything from her other than to be herself.'

For a second, Joanne wondered if Madeleine Kramer had a proper screw loose. Perhaps she was one of those women who steals someone else's child because she lost a child herself years before. Or else can't stand to see another woman with something she can't have.

But as she surveyed the slightly frayed but generally poised, self-possessed woman in front of her, Joanne really didn't get that feeling.

'She was just supposed to stay for a couple of hours,' Madeleine explained. 'We only meant—'

'We?' asked Joanne, frowning.

'I meant *I*,' she replied quickly. 'It was a terrible lapse of judgement . . . and *I* meant Brontë to stay for only a short while, but—'

'But you thought you'd keep her overnight to teach Karen a *real* lesson?'

Madeleine Kramer closed her eyes.

'I kept her overnight,' she said steadily, 'because she begged me. Brontë begged me over and over not to take her back to her mother.'

48

WHEN SHE ARRIVED at her desk, Joanne found Oliver Black, eyes focused on his computer screen. She put the cardboard box down and said, 'So now we have Brontë Bloom's abductor. Madeleine Kramer. She knows the kid from school but she also works at Applemead.'

Oliver Black looked up. 'You're not bringing her in?'

'Long story. Turns out the child *asked* to go with her, and so of course went willingly.' Joanne rolled her eyes, thinking back to the wasted hours they had spent trying to find Brontë. 'Apparently, she wanted to escape her mother for a while. Anyway, I'm not sure where we stand, legally speaking, so I'll need to run it by the CPS before I think about charging her.'

'I have something for you,' Oliver said, and he pushed a piece of paper her way. Then he leaned back in his chair with his fingers laced together behind his head. He looked smug, which could only mean one thing.

'What is it?' she asked.

'You know about familial DNA?'

'Of course,' she replied.

And Joanne had the sudden urge to smack her forehead.

'You checked it,' she whispered. 'Why didn't I check it? Why didn't I think to put in a request for familial DNA?'

'You're impressed, right?' Oliver said. 'It's okay, you can say it. I get it a lot. I'm used to the compliments.'

Joanne sat down heavily in her chair and let this breakthrough settle upon her.

Oliver said, 'So even though the blood you found on the tree didn't match to a criminal on the DNA database, when they compared it to other DNA profiles they found it shared the DNA of someone else who *is* on the list. There was a fifty per cent match – which means the two people are closely related. It means they're family.'

Joanne felt giddy. 'A fifty per cent match means the person on the database is either the parent of Karen Bloom's killer, or else their child is the killer.'

'Yes, exactly. And the match is to a forty-nine-year-old male,' Oliver said. 'So let's assume for now that Karen Bloom's killer is the match's son, rather than his aged father . . .'

'Low odds that the killer is seventy-plus,' said Joanne.

'The match's name is Dominic O'Riordan,' he said. 'He's from Windermere.'

Joanne immediately thought of Sonny O'Riordan, her hard-to-trace drug dealer and wearer of offensive T-shirts. Were they related?

'Dominic was imprisoned for a series of robberies back in 2003,' Oliver said. Joanne hadn't worked CID then.

'Nothing major,' Oliver went on, 'just houses, small businesses, and so on. Problem is, he doesn't have just one son.'

'How many does he have?'

'Three,' he said. 'Two daughters as well but, as we know, the DNA's from a male.'

'Tell me you know where this Dominic O'Riordan lives?' she said, and Oliver smiled.

'I've got a pretty good idea.'

Joanne drove. She had a good feeling. 'We'll do a spot of house-to-house first,' she said to Oliver.

'If you like.'

Whenever Joanne had a lead like this, she liked to ask around first. Granted, she had Dominic O'Riordan's record, but she wanted to find out more about him and his sons before she tried to locate them. And there was no better place to start than with the neighbours.

You generally got the truth out of neighbours. If they had an axe to grind, they came right out with it; you heard about it in the first sentence. And unless folk had particular reasons to hate the police (that is, were criminals themselves), they were generally happy to offer up anything incriminating about a person who, say, repeatedly took their parking space, or kept unsociable hours, or became abusive to their wife in the front garden after a few cans. In Joanne's experience, with perhaps the odd exception, most people who resided outside of the law would display one or more of these tendencies.

Joanne drove over Bannerigg, some twit in front braking too hard in the dip, forcing her to drop down to third gear. She could feel her guts starting to respond in their usual way, loosening up, giving her the feeling of anticipation she'd come to know and love when she was close to solving a case. That extra feeling of nervousness she was experiencing right now came from not wanting to screw up.

She had to keep reminding herself that she had *only* a blood sample. That was it. Something that could put one of Dominic O'Riordan's sons in the general area of Karen's murder. Right now, it was circumstantial evidence, not enough to secure a conviction, by a long shot. But if Dominic O'Riordan's son was your typical criminal (so particularly stupid, as well as having a skewed sense of his own invincibility), then she had a shot at tripping him up.

She had a chance of getting him to say *just* the right amount of stupid to warrant an arrest.

Of course, what she really hoped for was a confession. Then she could put this case to bed and not worry about spending the next Christ knows how long substantiating her reasons to the Crown Prosecution Service, persuading them to let her charge him for the murder of Karen Bloom.

'What are the names of Dominic's sons?' she asked Oliver.

Oliver reviewed his notes. 'Kyle, Shane and . . . Michael. Kyle and Shane are listed as still living at home with the parents. Michael's proving harder to pin down. He's been arrested but never charged. Suspicion of supplying—'

'Michael O'Riordan,' Joanne said flatly.

'Aye.'

'Michael O'Riordan as in *Sonny* O'Riordan.'

Oliver flicked a page. 'Yes. That's his nickname. You know him?'

So it was him. 'Not personally,' she said. 'But I've spent plenty of time trying to find him. He moves various class As around the area, but we've never been able to collar him. I had a DC watching his parents' house about a month ago, but he never turned up there. He's a nasty little shit. It'll be him who killed Karen, for sure. When we've swabbed and got a DNA match for him, I'm going to push for a confession. Okay?'

'Easiest way to go,' agreed Oliver.

Dominic O'Riordan rented an ex-council property not far from the recreation ground, along with his wife, Yvonne, who was claiming disability allowance for a syndrome Joanne had never heard of.

'What *is* a syndrome?' Joanne asked Oliver as they waited nose to tail in Windermere village. An articulated lorry full of Dutch flowers was making a delivery.

'I had to look it up,' admitted Oliver. 'It's a collection of symptoms rather than a straightforward disease. So if you've got, say, ten out of the twenty symptoms, they issue you with a diagnosis.'

'So we don't know what kind of state this woman's in? Is she wheelchair-bound? Bed-bound?'

'No idea.'

The lorry finally moved on and they made their way along Oak Street, past Joanne's house, in fact. She pointed out the small mid-terrace to Oliver, saying, 'My humble abode,' and he said, 'Humble, my eye. I know how much these places cost.'

'I rent,' she said.

Outside Dominic O'Riordan's house was a brand-new Honda 4x4 with a Motability sticker in the window. Joanne parked further along, in front of a row of garages set back from the road with Do Not Park Here notices displayed. She didn't park there by choice, though. She did it because there wasn't a scrap of road left on which to leave the Focus. 'Don't these people have jobs to go to?' she complained to Oliver.

They climbed out. 'You okay with the right side, and I'll take the houses on the left?' she asked, and Oliver said he was fine with that.

Joanne stood outside a house three along from the O'Riordans'. It was a run-down property. There was pebbledash render scabbing off in pieces, old aluminium window frames blackening in the corners and unlit Christmas lights strung around the door frame. The light cable disappeared through the letterbox and Joanne thought that the occupant was either very late in removing their decorations or else premature in putting them up.

She rang the bell and the door opened. There stood an elderly gentleman in a dirty cardigan. He had bloodshot eyes. A wiry tabby was weaving around his ankles.

Joanne showed her warrant card.

'Police?' he said accusingly.

'That's right.'

'About time,' he said gruffly. 'Follow me.'

He shuffled off inside, leaving Joanne perplexed on the

doorstep. She hadn't got the chance to say she only wanted to ask him a few questions.

She took a step forward and quickly drew back. There was a smell. Not nice.

'Sir?' she called out.

Nothing.

'Yoohoo! Excuse me,' she tried. No answer. 'Shit,' she muttered and crossed the threshold. She walked on her tiptoes, wary of planting her feet fully on the sticky carpet.

This was the thing she had hated most when she was back in uniform – people's homes. A lot of folk the police had to deal with lived in absolute squalor. But it was the animals that most upset Joanne: large dogs kept in cages in the corner of the room, turds in their beds. Cats with tumours on their faces. Birds that had pulled out all their feathers.

Joanne picked her way through the mess in the living room to where the man was standing by the kitchen window.

'I'd really like to ask you a few questions about your neighbours, the O'Riordans, if that's okay,' she said.

The man was frowning at her.

'It's out there,' he said. 'I rang your lot yesterday and no one came. I don't know why I bother paying tax.'

Joanne got this a lot. And she was pretty sure everyone who said it didn't actually pay any tax.

'I'm not certain what I'm looking at,' Joanne said.

What she was looking at was a small back garden. The grass was knee-high, with a broken, revolving washing maiden in the centre. The garden was enclosed by a low fence, also broken.

The man gestured to the row of garages to the left of the garden. 'There,' he said. 'You see them?'

'Do I see what?'

He looked at Joanne as though she was stupid. 'Flies,' he said.

'Flies,' she replied.

'Bluebottles. Lots of 'em. There's summat dead in there. You don't get flies this time of year.'

'Well, it has been particularly warm,' she reasoned. 'That's why we've had so much rain.'

Joanne couldn't see any flies. And she didn't have time for this. She had a murderer to apprehend.

'Listen,' she said, trying to get back to the point. 'What can you tell me about the O'Riordans?'

The guy tutted. '*He's* a first-class crook,' he said. 'An' his wife's no better, cheating the system. There's nothing wrong with her. I should film her. They've never done an honest day's work in their lives.'

'Do you ever see anyone else around there? Anyone visit on a regular basis?'

'There's a lot of O'Riordans,' he said. 'And they've all got a load o' kids. Catholics,' he said by way of explanation. 'They don't know when to stop.'

'Have you noticed any strange behaviour recently? Anything out the ordinary?'

He thought for a moment. Then he hawked up some phlegm and spat it into the sink. 'Pardon me,' he said, running the tap. 'What have they done this time?'

'Have you noticed anything at all?' Joanne said, ignoring the question.

And he looked at Joanne steadily for a good fifteen seconds.

Then he shook his head, a sad look in his eye. He seemed disappointed he had nothing at all to give.

Joanne joined up with Oliver. 'What have you got?' she asked.

'They're not exactly Windermere's most popular, are they? What about you?'

'Nothing as yet. And I feel quite soiled after being in number thirty-six.'

Oliver wrinkled his nose.

'Okay,' Joanne said, 'you carry on with the neighbours. I'll head over there.' She gestured to the house behind her. 'Let's see what the O'Riordans have to say about their lovely offspring.'

'Mrs Yvonne O'Riordan?'

The woman was the wrong side of fifty and had yellow hair hanging past her shoulders, frayed at the ends like a fancy-dress wig. She wore heavy, air-hostess make-up.

Her eyes seemed to take Joanne in but at the same time look entirely past her.

Hearing her full name, the woman snapped to attention, grabbing a crutch from a nearby umbrella stand and leaning her weight on it heavily. Wincing from, Joanne assumed, some imaginary pain.

'Who are you?' she asked.

'Detective Sergeant Joanne Aspinall. Mind if I come in and ask you a few questions?'

'About what?'

Joanne dropped her voice. 'Mrs O'Riordan, I need to discuss something of a rather sensitive nature. You might prefer it if the neighbours can't hear our conversation?'

Joanne wanted to get inside. There was always the chance of stumbling on something she wasn't supposed to.

Yvonne O'Riordan hesitated. 'I'm not sure,' she said.

'You're not sure about what?'

'I'm not sure it's a good idea.'

Yvonne O'Riordan's eyes were alive now, furtive. She looked from side to side. She was like a cat about to step on enemy territory.

'We could always do this at the station, if that's easier for you?' Joanne said pleasantly. 'Although that would be Kendal, Mrs

O'Riordan, not Windermere. That's where I'm based . . . Is your husband home today?'

'Who?'

'Dominic. Is he home?'

She dropped her gaze. 'He's out. I don't know where.'

It sounded like a rehearsed answer.

'What about your sons?' Joanne asked. 'They around?'

'They're out, too.'

Joanne waited. When Yvonne O'Riordan made no attempt to move, Joanne made a show of checking her watch.

When she *still* didn't move, Joanne said, 'What'll it be, then?' rubbing her hands together and flashing the woman a friendly smile. 'Here or the station?'

Yvonne O'Riordan grudgingly took a step backwards.

They went into the lounge.

This was a house-proud woman. The room was decorated in a sickly tone of peach, not at all to Joanne's taste, but it was clean and nicely furnished. Just about every available surface and wall space was covered with family photographs. There was also a sixty-inch TV, new sofas and a cream shag-pile carpet, freshly vacuumed.

'I won't offer you a drink,' Yvonne said.

Joanne told her she'd not long had a coffee. Untrue, but Yvonne O'Riordan was not a woman to whom small talk came easily, and Joanne wanted to get her to relax.

Joanne removed her coat and took out her notepad. When she raised her head she saw that Yvonne was eyeing her sceptically. 'So you say you're a policewoman?'

'Would you like to see my warrant card again?'

Yvonne nodded, so Joanne handed it over. She could only assume Yvonne O'Riordan thought she was an undercover DSS officer or something. 'No uniform?' Yvonne said, handing it back.

'CID,' explained Joanne.

'What do you want with me? I've done nothing wrong.'

Joanne dropped her eyes to the group of photographs on the coffee table. 'Lovely family,' she said.

Yvonne waited, unsure.

'How many grandchildren do you have?' Joanne asked.

'Eleven. No, twelve.'

'You must be very proud.'

'What's this about? You're making me nervous.'

'No need to be nervous, Mrs O'Riordan. Like you say, you've done nothing wrong.'

She let the weight of her words settle and watched as Yvonne scowled back at her, saying, 'That's what I said, wasn't it?'

'I'd like to ask you a few questions about your sons, if I may.'

'They're not here.'

'Yes, you said. I'm trying to find an address for Michael.'

Yvonne's jaw started working overtime. 'Listen,' she said. 'My husband'll be back in a bit. It's probably best you talk to him. He's my carer. I have a terrible memory and he'll be able to help you out better than me. He's a good man.'

'I don't doubt it.'

'He doesn't really like me talking to people without him being here.'

Joanne smiled as though she understood. 'Perhaps you have his address written down? Perhaps in an address book or something? It would save waiting for your husband,' she said innocently. 'Or do you mind if I just have a quick look around?'

'I don't think he'd like it.'

'Won't take a second,' said Joanne, thinking she'd be a fool not to have a quick poke about the place before they got wind of the fact they were all wanted for questioning. 'Then I can leave you in peace, Mrs O'Riordan.'

Joanne was on her feet. Yvonne O'Riordan's face had become moist and pallid.

'I'm not sure—'

Yvonne O'Riordan was the type of woman used to covering for her family, but she wasn't particularly good at it. Joanne could envision the neighbours hauling her boys to her door, back when they were kids, Yvonne meeting them with those blank, innocent eyes, as if she really couldn't imagine them doing any of the things they were accused of.

Joanne moved into the hallway and spotted the telephone table. She walked towards it. On it was a scented candle, an Audrey Hepburn calendar, a Penny Vincenzi paperback and a large Forever Friends address book. She studied October's Audrey momentarily before opening the address book and flicking through the pages until—

'Hey.'

A man's voice. Joanne turned around to find the source of the voice that had seemingly come out of nowhere.

She was met by a gloved fist to the face.

Joanne had never taken a proper punch. Like a lot of women, she dreaded the day when it would happen, knowing she would be woefully unprepared for the pain and the instant incapacitating effect.

She fell. The small of her back hit the telephone table.

No time to save herself, the full weight of Joanne's body smashed backwards into the wood and a white shock of pain travelled all the way up to her scalp. Slumped, all she could do was try to protect her face from further punches with her hands.

There was blood. Quite a lot of blood. Might she die?

She really hoped not.

For one thing, she had her least favourite suit on. The one from Dorothy Perkins that was a panic buy. She didn't want to be condemned to wear it for all eternity (her ghost outfit, as it were). She didn't want to spend for ever stuck in a shitty black suit that was beginning to sag at the knees.

Tentatively, Joanne touched her nose with the end of her ring finger and found all was not as it should be. It was as if her nose wasn't quite there any more.

'Please,' she pleaded. She could hear her assailant breathing heavily nearby. She tried to open her eyes, but her vision swam and swayed.

She went to speak again but at the same time felt a belt of cold air hit her. She turned her head to the right and could sense light coming from the doorway.

'Get out,' the voice said. 'Get out of here now.'

And so, pitiably, on her hands and knees, blood running down her chin, Joanne crawled away.

49

'DOES THAT HURT?' asked the nurse.

'Yes,' replied Joanne. But it came out sounding more like *yeth*. As though she was imitating that annoying ad from the eighties for Tunes lozenges . . . *A thecond-clath return to Dotting-ham, pleath.*

Oliver had found her kneeling on the pavement outside the O'Riordans', head cocked back, trying to stem the blood flow, and had insisted on bringing her to the health centre. He'd wanted to call an ambulance, but Joanne had said no. Yes, her nose was probably broken. And, yes, she'd lost some blood. But hospital was overkill. 'And it will take for ever to be seen by someone,' she reasoned, 'being half-term.' The place would be full of kids with broken arms, sprained ankles, bangs to the head.

Oliver had relented. But once he'd called for back-up, cuffing Joanne's assailant, arresting him for the assault of a police officer, he told Joanne they *would* be visiting her GP's surgery, regardless of what she had to say about it, so she may as well just agree.

Joanne wasn't trying to be brave. She didn't especially like brave women. They were usually nurturing a particular kind of martyrdom which Joanne didn't care for. No, she didn't want to see a hospital nurse for three reasons: one, she was embarrassed. Quite mortified, actually, that she'd been caught so unawares, rifling through the O'Riordans' address book. Two, she was in a lot of pain. And Joanne went feral when she was injured, taking herself off to a darkened room and curling up. She certainly did not want anyone touching her or poking at her. And three, and this was the really non-negotiable thing, it was *Sonny O'Riordan* who'd hit her. Sonny O'Riordan, all-round undesirable, whom Joanne had been trying to locate, but to no avail, before she had been switched to the Brontë Bloom case.

She'd found him.

Clever Joanne.

If she weren't in so much pain, she would have done a little jig.

Joanne now lay with her head angled backwards on a treatment couch while the nurse shone a light up each nostril, trying to determine if Joanne's septum had been damaged by the impact of Sonny O'Riordan's fist. They didn't straighten broken noses like they used to. Gone were the days when they manually pulled the thing back in line before it had time to set. 'Not any more!' sang the nurse when she first examined her, to Joanne's considerable relief. 'We get rid of the swelling and, if it *is* deemed to be broken, we make an appointment with the plastic surgeon in around two weeks' time.'

'Wonderful,' sniffled Joanne.

'I'm just not sure whether to refer you or not,' she said, cleaning the end of her torch with an alcohol wipe. 'Sit tight,' she said, 'while I get a second opinion.'

When she left, Oliver rose and came to stand at Joanne's side.

'How are you holding up?' he asked.

'Not bad. How do I look?'

Oliver grimaced. 'You've looked better. You've got a couple of black eyes forming. And this one's pretty bloodshot,' he said, gesturing to her right.

'I want to question him.'

Oliver sighed. 'I know.'

'No, seriously, Oliver. You can't just go taking over because I'm injured. I've been after this kid for so long, and if it turns out to be his blood . . . you'll have to lay off questioning until—'

'Joanne,' he said. 'I won't question him, okay? But you know it's going to be Pat Gilmore who has the final say. And I really can't see her letting you near him, not like this.'

Joanne closed her eyes. She felt like she had acid beneath her lids. She could feel the swelling glueing up her eyelashes.

What a fuck-up.

Sonny O'Riordan said he thought she was a burglar. That was his excuse. Not that he really needed one. He had come across a stranger inside his parents' house, flicking through a book on the telephone table. 'I thought me mam was in danger,' he said innocently to Oliver. 'You would have done the same, mate.'

'What were you thinking, going through their stuff?' Oliver asked her.

And she replied, 'Please, don't.'

Joanne had once had a boyfriend who would ask similarly annoying questions. If she should smash a glass: 'What did you do that for?' If she should burn her finger: 'Why weren't you being more careful?' Joanne had put up with him for a short while before coming back with 'Because I thought injuring myself would be exactly the right thing to do in this instance.'

They didn't last long together after that.

The nurse returned, apologizing for the wait, saying the doctor had his hands full with another patient, and Joanne was about to say something in return when Noel Bloom appeared at her feet.

'Bloody hell,' he said to her. 'What happened to the other guy?'

'On his way to Kendal station,' she said simply.

Noel's eyes went wide. 'Actually, I was joking. I assumed you'd fallen over. You really got hit in the face?'

Joanne nodded. 'I really did.' Then she winced as a needle of pain shot from her neck to the middle of her back.

Oliver stepped away, giving them some space, as Noel moved quickly to her.

'Are you all right?'

His face was a worried mask of concern.

'I didn't think you'd be back at work yet,' she said coldly. She was still annoyed at him for turfing her out of his house, calling a halt to the interview with Brontë. Now that Joanne knew it was Madeleine Kramer who'd taken the child, she wondered what had motivated Noel to do such a thing. Who was he trying to protect?

'We were short-staffed,' Noel explained. 'We've been putting rather a lot on the locum recently, and she couldn't make it in today. But I asked if *you* were all right, Joanne. *Are* you?'

'I'll be fine.'

'You don't look fine. Are you injured anywhere else? I should really take a proper look at you.'

'I'd rather you didn't,' she said stiffly.

Oliver cleared his throat. 'I'll just be outside, Joanne,' and he was out the door with discreet haste.

'*Joanne*,' Noel said, insistently.

'Noel,' she replied, flatly.

Joanne stole a look across to the nurse. She was busying herself among the boxes of Tubigrip, pretending not to listen.

'It's not what you think, you know . . . with Brontë.'

'What do I think, Noel?'

'I can't . . .' He bit down on his lower lip. 'I'm just not able to tell you because . . .' Noel dropped his voice to just above a whisper. 'None of this is my fault. I swear to you, Joanne. It's not.'

'None of *what* is your fault?' she asked, and Noel looked at her kind of helplessly. She looked away. 'What is it you want from me, Noel?'

He went to speak but paused instead. 'Cathy,' he said to the nurse, 'would you mind giving us a minute?'

The nurse turned slowly on the spot. 'Of course,' she said brightly. 'Although,' she said to Joanne, 'you are entitled to a chaperone if you're undressing, Miss Aspinall. It's up to you. I can stay if you need me to.'

'I won't be undressing.'

The nurse gave something between a nod and a small bow: *As you wish*. Then she left them to it, closing the door behind her.

'I didn't think I'd get to see you again,' Noel said.

'Well, as you can see, I totally planned this.'

Noel smiled.

'And there's still the small matter of finding your wife's killer, Noel.'

'Yes, yes, I know. Here, let me look at you.'

'You are looking at me.'

'You know what I mean,' he said. 'Let me examine you. There's a lot of soft-tissue damage below your eye. It may need X-raying. Let me, Joanne. Please.'

Noel switched on an Anglepoise lamp above Joanne's head. 'Too bright?' he asked.

'It's okay.'

He pulled on a pair of green surgical gloves. 'This might hurt a bit . . . I'll write you a prescription for some heavy-duty pain-killers, and you'll want to ice-pack your nose every few hours, for twenty minutes or so. Okay,' he said, moving in, 'here we go.'

Joanne closed her eyes at the sight of Noel's face looming. She should really have asked to see another doctor. That would have been the sensible thing to do.

She could feel his touch, butterfly wings against her skin again, then a little deeper as he felt around her eye socket.

Noel stroked down the line of her nose, then ran his finger

332

and thumb along, pinching a little as he went. Her eyes watered slightly but she didn't move.

Be brave, she said to herself.

Then she sensed his touch on her lips. It was the oddest sensation, because her top lip had become partially numbed. It actually felt like . . . *oh*.

She realized he was kissing her.

'Hello,' she whispered softly.

'Hello again,' he whispered back.

50

IT WASN'T BROKEN. Neither was her anterior maxillary wall, nor her orbital rim. These were the things Noel wanted checked, asking the radiography department if they could push Joanne to the top of their list, as she had a suspect in custody who needed interviewing. 'Of course, Dr Bloom,' the reception-ist had said. Noel had her on speakerphone. 'Lovely to talk to you again, Dr Bloom,' she giggled, and Joanne put two fingers in her mouth and pretended to gag.

By the time she got to the station, it was after six. She'd not eaten since lunch and so Oliver pushed a bruised banana her way and a cup of sweet tea to see her through the next couple of hours. She had to cut the banana up with a knife and fork and eat it in miniature pieces the size a doll would eat as opening her mouth wider than a small 'o' made her cheek throb like hell. And the painkillers weren't helping. What she needed was whisky.

Sonny O'Riordan was still small and wiry. But he'd developed a neat musculature to his upper body that was absent in those Facebook photos she'd viewed of him. He'd been working out. His own nose was pushed over to one side, and Joanne assumed he boxed. That would also account for his good aim and well-timed punch.

'Sorry about your face,' he said, as she sat down opposite him.

Noel had fitted a dressing which ran across the bridge of her nose and underneath her right eye, 'So you don't frighten the children,' he said. But the radiographer had difficulty reapplying it after her X-ray, so Joanne had discarded it.

'But I've still not found out what you were doing inside me mam's house,' Sonny O'Riordan added.

Joanne opened up her notes. 'We'll come to that. How about you begin by telling me where you were on the afternoon of Tuesday, 20 October.'

'No idea,' he said, rather pleased with himself.

'Karen Bloom went missing on that day and was later found murdered.'

He pantomimed shock. 'And this affects me how?'

'We have reason to believe that you were in the area of Karen's murder at around the same time.'

'What reason?'

'I'll come to that,' Joanne said again. '*Were* you in the area?'

'Of course I wasn't.'

'How well did you know Karen Bloom?'

'I don't.'

'Not at all?' she asked doubtfully. 'Windermere's a small place, Mr O'Riordan. You must have stumbled across her once or twice in your lifetime.'

'If I did I can't remember. I expect we move in different circles.'

'Even so.'

'Even so,' he repeated, smiling at her, his tone now mocking.

This was how your average, seasoned criminal behaved when being interviewed. They knew nothing, saw nothing, couldn't give a shit what the police had to say. They knew their rights and liked to take the piss as much as possible. Something to relay to their buddies over a pint later. It was like dealing with a recalcitrant child.

'Mind showing me your hands?' Joanne asked.

'I don't mind,' he said, but he didn't offer them.

'You right- or left-handed?' she asked.

'Right.'

Joanne got up. She moved around to Sonny O'Riordan's side of the desk. 'Can I take a look?'

He held out his right hand. Joanne turned it over, palm side up. She glanced at Oliver Black and gave a small nod. There, just shy of his heart line, was a raised pink line of flesh. The skin around it was white and flaking: damaged cells in the process of sloughing off.

'You had yourself an injury here, Mr O'Riordan?' she asked, releasing his hand.

And he shrugged as though he really couldn't remember.

'Looks like a fairly nasty knife wound.'

'If you say so.'

'See, when a person gets stabbed, as was the case with Mrs Bloom, sometimes the person doing the stabbing gets injured, too.'

Joanne acted out a stabbing motion.

O'Riordan's face was impassive. Bored, even.

'After the first cut to the victim,' she explained, 'when the knife is covered in blood, the attacker's hand can slip down on to the blade.' Joanne winced as the imaginary knife she was holding cut into her flesh. 'They can sustain a nasty cut to the palm, Mr O'Riordan. Which in turn would give rise to a scar. A scar quite similar in fact to the one on your hand right now.'

'Really,' he said.

'Yes. Really . . . Add to that the presence of your blood at the crime scene—'

'*My* blood?' he said.

'*Your* blood,' she said. 'Put those two things together, and I'd say you find yourself in a bit of a pickle, Mr O'Riordan.'

He requested a lawyer. They always did nowadays.

Joanne *had* been hoping to avoid it. Hoping she could spook him with the forensics, spook him into blabbing out a confession. No deal. And she didn't have enough to charge him: no weapon, no motive, and the small amount of physical evidence she did have would be viewed as circumstantial. But she *knew* he'd done it. She could smell it on him. For all his swagger, his conceit, his sweat still stank of fear.

The thing that she didn't know yet was: why?

In the presence of his lawyer, Sonny O'Riordan was interviewed again under caution.

Katie Fellows, a young, drippy solicitor from Ulverston, blanched visibly on seeing Joanne's battered face.

'It's not as bad as it looks,' Joanne said vaguely, and Katie eyed her as if she weren't sure whether it was Joanne beneath those black eyes or an imposter.

'I thought she was a burglar,' O'Riordan explained, his tone both joking and cajoling, but Katie showed no response. A moment later, she whispered to her client, and from then on Joanne was met by a succession of 'No comment's every time she posed a question.

'Where were you on the afternoon of 20 October?'

'No comment.'

'How did you get that scar on your hand?'

'No comment.'

'Can you explain how your blood was found at the murder scene?'

'No comment.'

Oddly, O'Riordan never asked how they knew it was *his* blood they found there. Perhaps he assumed, wrongly, that the police held a DNA profile of every single person ever arrested in the UK. Instead of only the ones who had actually been convicted of a crime.

'Why did you target Karen Bloom?'

'No comment.'

'What had she done to you?'

'No comment.'

'What did you do with your bloodied clothing once you'd disposed of her body?'

A hesitation.

Joanne met Sonny O'Riordan's eyes. A flicker of panic.

'The clothes, Mr O'Riordan?' she repeated. 'What did you do with them?'

Another hesitation.

Finally: 'No comment.'

They broke for coffee. Not that Joanne wanted one – she hated to halt questioning a suspect mid-session – but she needed to regroup. She was running out of ideas. She had nothing to hold him on and if she didn't do something soon, Katie Fellows would be pushing for a release.

'So he's hidden the clothes, then,' Oliver stated.

'You saw that, too?'

'His face said everything,' Oliver said. 'So, where would *you* put the clothes if you were of less than average intelligence?'

'Somewhere they could be found easily,' she replied dryly. 'Somewhere close to home, where I didn't think anyone would look.'

'If we find them . . . and they *do* have Karen Bloom's blood on them, along with O'Riordan's DNA, we have enough to charge him, don't we?'

Joanne nodded. 'We do.' Then she sipped her coffee in silence.

Oliver got himself another drink. Sugar had been spilled next to the kettle, and no one had bothered to clean it up. Joanne thought about getting a cloth but something stopped her. A lone bluebottle was moving among the grains.

Joanne stared at the fly.

'Oliver,' she said, 'I need you to go and check out a garage for me.'

The fly rubbed its front legs together.

51

Tuesday, 3 November

Noel searched Ewan's flat.

It took him an unconscionably long time to find what he was looking for. Far longer than he'd anticipated. It turned out Ewan was more adept at subterfuge than he'd given him credit for. Although, when he did finally find it, Noel had to admit that it was so gloriously simple he couldn't understand why he hadn't looked there in the first place.

Armed, he made his way down the hill. He chose to walk. It was a dry day. One of those strange November days when the sky could be almost black, the clouds hanging on to their rain until it was past funny, when you'd expect a raw edge to the air. But striding along, a definite spring in his step, Noel decided it was positively balmy. Actually, he could have done without his coat. Which was just as well really, with what he had in mind.

He pressed the doorbell twice. Sometimes, they were busy and didn't hear. Sometimes, he could be left standing outside for an age and he would have to try to mask his irritation; he was a busy man, after all. Today was different, though. Today was a social call. He was without his tie, his scripts, without his bearing of *eager to get on.*

The door opened. 'Hello, Dr Bloom,' the care assistant said.

'Afternoon.'

'You're here to see—?'

'Jennifer,' he replied, and he was asked to sign in. 'I wonder if I might take her to the garden?' he said. 'It's very mild out, and you know how she likes to be outdoors.'

The care assistant agreed that yes, Jennifer always benefited from some air, and went to find a blanket. 'Save trying to get a coat on to her,' she explained.

Jennifer weighed less than seven stone now, but attempting to manoeuvre her could require brute strength. Noel could still lift her well enough. That wasn't a problem. But he'd given up trying to guide her spastic limbs into the arms and legs of clothing. It made him feel pathetically incompetent and he hated to imagine the effect that all that public pulling and manipulating had on his ex-wife.

The care assistant wheeled her outside. She'd placed a multi-coloured beanie on Jennifer's head but had pulled it a little low. The wool rested on Jennifer's eyelashes. When they were alone, Noel adjusted the hat. He lifted it slightly but in doing so he set off a succession of quaking spasms that rocked Jennifer's small frame.

'Sorry,' he muttered, annoyed with himself. 'Sorry.'

Jennifer didn't reply. If he were someone else, she would try to speak. Try to convey with a look that it was okay, that this is what *happens* with MS. But they both waited it out, unspeaking, Noel wanting to reach out and steady her but knowing, if he did so, that he risked setting her off again.

Noel wheeled Jennifer to the end of the garden. It still destroyed him how helpless she was. If she didn't want to go outside or to the end of the garden, or anywhere else for that matter, she couldn't resist. She went where she was taken.

Once there, he parked the chair before asking if she was warm enough. Silly, really, because she couldn't speak today. And he knew she couldn't speak because, if she could, she would've already said something. He did this more than he meant to, asked her questions she had no hope of answering.

He touched her face. Then he sat down. They were facing one another.

He took out the joint. He'd not smoked weed in – goodness, how long was it? He couldn't remember.

He inhaled long and hard, waited to feel the familiar warmth move through his chest, spread up the back of his neck, and then he put the joint to Jennifer's lips.

Four drags, and she was back.

'You have something to say,' she said. A statement. Her mouth was a little droopy but her words were clear enough.

'They've arrested Sonny,' he said. 'And your brother Dominic. They've arrested Dominic as an accomplice, I think.'

She closed her eyes briefly. *Yeah, I heard.*

Noel took another drag. 'They also found clothes in Dominic's garage – a T-shirt, apparently, with Sonny's blood on it. Karen's blood is on it, too.'

'Stupid,' she said quietly.

'It doesn't look good, Jen.'

'Give me some more of that.'

Noel held the joint to her lips. Then he touched her hand. He was able to handle her now without having her dissolve into spasms, and so he wrapped his fingers around hers.

She motioned to the polo shirt he was wearing. It was a striped, unbranded thing that Karen had bought and he wore it now with the top button fastened, just as he'd seen young men on TV do. Noel assumed it was fashionable.

'You look like you're on the autistic spectrum,' Jennifer said, attempting a smile.

Noel undid the top button.

'Can they charge them?' she asked.

'I think so.' He sighed. 'They took Yvonne's phone and

341

analysed it. They found she'd been googling things like "stabbing" and "Windermere", together with "body" and "lake". This was on the day that Karen disappeared. I don't see how they can get themselves out of it, to be honest.'

Jennifer frowned at their ineptitude. 'Yvonne,' she said, 'she was never the brightest.'

Noel gave her hand a squeeze.

'Why'd you get them to do it, Jen?' he asked after a moment.

And she held his gaze.

'I had to,' she said.

'Did you? Your nephew's going to do twenty years for this, at least.'

'I don't feel bad about Sonny,' she said. 'He's been ruining lives for long enough with what he's been supplying. Dom's another story. He wasn't supposed to get caught. He wasn't supposed to be involved in getting rid of Karen.'

'But, Jen,' said Noel, leaning towards her, 'we were doing okay. Me and the kids, we were doing well. We were doing the best we could. You didn't need to—'

'No, you weren't. You weren't living, Noel. I did you a favour.'

Her words were starting to slur a little, and she had to concentrate hard to get them out.

'But—'

'Now you can salvage what's left of your life,' she said. 'Try to find some happiness.'

Noel hung his head.

'Look, Noel,' she said, 'my life's over. I'm dying. And I actually don't mind. I'm kind of done here. But Verity? I couldn't sit in this chair, doing nothing, while that bitch was under the same roof as my daughter, screwing up her lovely mind. And she wanted to send her away to school in Inverness. I did what I had to do, Noel. I did it for *her*. For Verity.'

Noel nodded.

'When did you realize it was me?' Jennifer asked after a moment.

'Brontë wouldn't tell anyone where she'd been when she went missing. She said she'd been in her friend's shed. I didn't believe her and when I pushed her for answers a few weeks later she admitted she'd been with Madeleine Kramer. You two have been very close over the years and it got me thinking that you might have had something to do with Karen's disappearance as well. It was a hunch. I couldn't know for sure, but I couldn't see who else it could be.'

'We really thought she'd stop, you know? We thought, if we gave her a scare, she'd realize how much she loved her child. We thought she'd lay off you all and let you be . . . She didn't.'

'No,' agreed Noel. 'She didn't.'

'Sorry it came to this,' she said.

Noel shrugged.

'What if they realize you're involved, too?' he asked, and Jennifer laughed.

'What are they going to do? Put me in an institution? Oh, wait, I'm already in one. Noel, go and be a family. That's what I want. Be happy. See if you can make a go of this. I've given you another chance.'

Noel smiled ruefully at his ex-wife. 'I'm not sure I really deserve another chance at happiness.'

And she said, 'No. You probably don't. But the kids do, so take it. Go and make yourself a life, Noel.'

Epilogue

SUFFICE TO SAY, the day they said their final goodbyes to Karen was one of mixed emotions.

They'd already had the funeral. And though Verity had nothing to compare it to, it being her first, she understood that it had gone smoothly, under the circumstances.

At the church, Verity had been placed in charge of Brontë – double-checking she had everything she needed, making sure she felt secure under the heavy gaze of the local community – and Verity was glad of it. She felt better knowing she had a responsibility, something to do.

So that just left the matter of Karen's ashes.

What to do with them?

Bruce and Mary had already taken a portion of Karen back to Macclesfield.

'*Which* portion?' Brontë had asked, brow furrowed, when she overheard them discussing it, as though they'd made off with Karen's right leg or something.

Bruce and Mary thought the remainder of Karen should be scattered in the garden. Among the azaleas, to the right of the patio, as this was where Mary and Karen shared mother-and-daughter time when the sun was out, and where Bruce remembered his daughter being at her happiest.

But Noel didn't like the idea. He didn't come right out and *say* he didn't like the idea, but Verity could see by the look of aversion on his face that he didn't want Karen in the azaleas. Or anywhere else in the garden for that matter.

'We'll have a ceremony of our own,' he had announced.

'Where?' asked Bruce.

But her father didn't have an answer.

Brontë was all for hiring a boat, rowing out into the centre of the lake and releasing Karen to the wind. But Verity had to explain, very gently, that though this was a lovely, thoughtful idea, it might not be the best resting place for Karen. She neglected to say this was because Brontë's mother's dead body had been found in the lake. Instead she had concocted a story about the place needing to hold special relevance for Karen.

The problem was they couldn't think of anywhere that *did* hold special relevance for Karen. She didn't like the fells, so that was out. And, apparently, you now had to get a special permit, as there'd been a spate of people leaving their urns behind. Karen didn't do water. Nor did she like to garden, walk or cycle.

In the end, Verity's dad had decided they would walk to the top of Orrest Head and they would let her go there. The spot didn't hold any particular significance for Karen, but the rest of them had been up there often enough as a family, so it would have to do. And the wind would blow Karen's ashes over Windermere, her home, the village she loved. Verity knew this wasn't *strictly* true, as the prevailing winds tended to be of a south-westerly persuasion and would carry Karen's ashes *away* from Windermere, more in the direction of Kentmere. But she desisted from airing this, as she had a feeling her dad had invented this bit of romance merely for Brontë's benefit.

So, on the next clear day, they went. And it was okay. Brontë had a little cry when Ewan spoke to Karen directly. 'Mum,' he said, 'I'm sorry you're not with us. It's nice up here, I think you'd like it. You can see the mountains and the lake and the sky . . . it's actually pretty cool. Brontë's here, too. She misses you. We all do. We all hope you're not alone wherever you are, and maybe, maybe you can check in with us from time to time? Make sure we're all doing okay? That'd be good . . . oh yeah,' he said, 'I forgot to tell you, I have a job. It's good. I like my boss . . . I love you, Mum. Goodbye.'

Verity found she was unexpectedly moved by his efforts.

Her dad also went on to do a good, solid job of making Karen appear loved and grieved for (although he did speak to the mountains opposite rather than address Karen straight, as Ewan had).

'Eulogies are so hard to give,' he began. 'Forgive me as I stumble through this as I'm unable to sum up all that was Karen, Karen, my wife, in just a few short lines. How can I express the kind of woman she was, what she did for us every day, her mighty presence? I simply can't. All I can say is that she's left a huge hole. I will miss her terribly. This family will never be the same, but we must stick together. And we must honour Karen's memory by being kind to one another. I think – no, I'm certain – I'm certain that we can do that.'

He said, 'Amen', quietly, as though he wasn't sure if it was appropriate or not. And the whole thing took less than an hour (including ascent and descent).

After their makeshift ceremony, the sombreness of the preceding days seemed to lift somewhat, and Verity could feel a kind of normality begin to return to the house. Karen's murder was rarely talked about. And never in front of Brontë. Her mother had been killed, but she didn't know how, or by whom. Sonny was pleading not guilty to the crime, which Verity's father said was 'utterly ridiculous: anyone with half a brain can see he's guilty. And now, because of his lack of consideration we have to endure weeks of a bloody trial.' But though Sonny's plea was ridiculous, it was not totally unexpected.

Her dad said Jennifer's nephew had made a career out of

making life as difficult as possible for all concerned and why should this be any different?

It was the one and only time Ewan came right out and asked why he thought Sonny had murdered his mother. And Noel replied, 'I'm not sure we'll ever really know what happened on that day, son,' after which he cast Verity a shifty, sidelong glance which convinced her that he *did* have a fair inkling of what had happened on that day.

She had a fair inkling of her own. But she never raised the subject with her mother, firstly, for fear of being overheard, and secondly, for fear of it being true.

That was four months ago now. Sonny O'Riordan was on remand and, as yet, a date for the trial had not been set. Brontë was doing well – her hand had recovered fully – though she'd not returned to the piano or the harp, as, with their dad working evenings at the surgery, there was no one to take her to her music lessons. Ewan was learning to drive and had promised to run Brontë around as soon as he passed his test (though, so far, he'd failed his theory three times). But Brontë didn't seem to mind. The novelty of coming home from school, lying on the sofa, watching TV for two hours, with absolutely nothing to do, had not yet worn off.

Verity's dad, meanwhile, was officially dating. He'd been doing it in an *unofficial* capacity for a couple of months, but there was a kind of unspoken agreement between Ewan, Verity and Brontë – Dale, too – whereby they didn't mention Joanne Aspinall's name outside of the house. People might get the wrong idea. Joanne came for dinner twice a week. She didn't have a key. Never stayed over. And never kissed her dad in front of any of them.

Verity was pretty sure they were having sex. But she appreciated the fact that they were being discreet about it all the same.

Verity wondered if Joanne would move in eventually. She

wouldn't mind if she did. Joanne had a calmness about her that Verity appreciated after the tumultuous years she'd spent living with Karen.

Perhaps Verity would mention it to her dad. Tell him it was okay by her.

Yes, she decided. When he returned home later that evening, that's exactly what she would do.

Acknowledgements

Huge thanks to the fantastic editors who worked so hard on this book: Frankie Gray and Sarah Day at Transworld, Corinna Barsan at Grove Atlantic, Zoe Maslow at Doubleday Canada and Stephanie Glencross at Gregory and Company.

Thanks to my early readers: Debbie Leatherbarrow, James Long, Zoe Lea, Lucy Hay. To Katharine Hamel for tea and chats about horrible mothers. And to my marvellous agent, Jane Gregory, as well as the lovely team at Gregory and Co.

Lastly, the following books were immensely helpful when writing *The Trophy Child*: *Forensics* by Val McDermid, *Battle Hymn of the Tiger Mother* by Amy Chua and *Beyond the Tiger Mom* by Maya Thiagarajan.

Paula Daly lives in Cumbria with her husband, three children and whippet Skippy. Before becoming a writer she was a freelance physiotherapist.